DATE DUE

EMPIRE OF LIES

Also by Andrew Klavan

Damnation Street

Shotgun Alley

Dynamite Road

Man and Wife

Hunting Down Amanda

The Uncanny

True Crime

Corruption

The Animal Hour

Don't Say a Word

ANDREW KLAVAN

EMPIRE OF LIES

An Otto Penzler Book
Harcourt, Inc.
Orlando   Austin   New York   San Diego   London

www.HarcourtBooks.com

Library of Congress Cataloging-in-Publication Data
Klavan, Andrew.
Empire of lies/Andrew Klavan.—1st ed.
p.   cm.
"An Otto Penzler book."
1. Missing children—Fiction.   2. Terrorists—Fiction.
3. New York (N.Y.)—Fiction.   I. Title.
PS3561.L334E47   2008
813'.54—dc22   2007033052
ISBN 978-0-15-101223-7

Text set in Bodoni Std Book
Designed by Linda Lockowitz

Printed in the United States of America

First edition
K J I H G F E D C B A

This book is for Otto Penzler.

At issue . . . was the question whether this sick society, which we call Western civilization, could in its extremity still cast up a man whose faith in it was so great that he would voluntarily abandon those things which men hold good, including life, to defend it.

—Whittaker Chambers

EMPIRE OF LIES

My name is Jason Harrow. I live on the Hill. It's an exclusive neighborhood in a small city about 800 miles west of New York. I won't say where exactly because I still get death threats from time to time.

You've probably heard of me in connection with the End of Civilization as We Know It. Unfortunately, if you get your news from the mainstream media—the television networks and the *Times* and so on—much of what you've heard has been distorted or is downright untrue. You know how that goes. If I had been some left-leaning crackpot who blamed America for being under attack, no doubt they'd have portrayed me as a hero, likely given me some neo-superman nickname like "Peace Dad" or "Heartland Patriot," as in "Heartland Patriot Assails American Foreign Policy." Even if I'd been an Islamo-fascist madman plotting to slaughter the innocent in their thousands, they'd have at least made me out to be a victim of some sort, a hapless product of Western imperialism, something like that, whatever.

But because I'm a political conservative and, even worse, a believing Christian, the networks and the *Times* and all the rest have consistently depicted me as small-minded and pinch-hearted, a bigot and an ill-educated fool. My motives have been impugned, my past raked over for scandal, and my religious convictions ridiculed and dismissed. Before I attempted to speak my mind during a television interview—when, because of my past associations, the media assumed I was a liberal, one of them—I was described in news reports mostly as "a Midwestern developer." After the truth became known, all that changed. The *Times,* for instance, has never once written about me since that day without referring to me as "conservative Christian asshole Jason Harrow." Of course, for *Times* readers, the "asshole" is understood.

So I've decided to tell my story myself, all of it, as honestly as I can. I won't try to pretty myself up or argue my case or win your good opinion. I won't leave out the things I've done that I'm ashamed of, even the thoughts I've thought that I wish I hadn't, and there are plenty of them. I know that God has forgiven me, but God is funny that way; I won't expect the same from you. I ask only that you hear me out and save your final judgment until the end.

SATURDAY

1 · Out of the Past

The day it began was an autumn day, a Saturday afternoon in October.

I was sitting in a cushioned chair on the brick patio at the edge of my backyard. The air was clear and warm with a hint of chill in it. There was a wind off the lake across the way—thunderstorms coming, though they weren't yet visible over the water.

I was looking down half an acre of grassy slope to where my two boys, Chad, ten, and Nathan, seven, were organizing some kind of Frisbee game around the swing set with some of their friends from the neighborhood. The boys were letting their three-year-old sister, Terry, tag along with them. I found this very heartwarming.

I was forty-five years old. The reedy figure of my youth was growing thicker at the chest and waist, but I was still trim enough. My once-sandy hair was thinner and darker, with a sprinkling of gray. My once-boyish face was not so boyish anymore, though I think it was what they used to call an honest face, smooth, clean, and open, the blue eyes bright.

My wife was in the kitchen making us some lemonade. My wife was named Cathy and I can't say how much I loved her, not without sounding like a sentimental idiot, anyway. We had been together twelve years then, and I still sat up sometimes at night and watched her sleeping. Sometimes I woke her because I felt so grateful for her and so passionate I couldn't help but trace her features with my fingertips. If this bugged the hell out of her, she never let on. But then, she was a cheerful and generous creature who would melt into lovemaking at a look or a touch.

We had a deal between us, Cathy and I. Our deal was simple. It was agreed to at the start in no uncertain terms.

When I first came to this town from New York seventeen years ago, I edited the local paper. I started out as city editor and was promoted to managing editor pretty quickly. The city had an insanely left-wing government at the time, and so, of course, it was spiraling into bankruptcy and chaos. There were high taxes supporting lavish payoffs to the unions, high crime because of lenient judges and tight restrictions on the police, and strangulation by regulation for any businessman stupid enough to hang around. It was a government like a garrulous fat man moralizing over a dinner for which he would never pick up the bill. I helped run them out of town. My paper printed story after story showing why every one of their policies would fail and proving it by showing where they had failed in the past. Plus we exposed the corrupt political machine churning away as usual under all the welfare. Within three years, the voters threw the bums out. The unions were crushed in the next round of contract negotiations. Taxes and useless programs were cut. Bad guys started going to prison. New businesses started popping up, people started making money again, and—surprise, surprise!—the government's share of the profits brought it back from the brink despite the lower taxes. In short, the streets grew clean and the city grew rich, and my newspaper and I had a hand in it. For this, I can proudly say, I was roundly despised by some of the best-educated and wealthiest people in town. Something about my uncaring, insensitive editorial policy. Elites hate to be proved wrong by the common man.

My boss, however, liked me. The man who owned the paper was a billionaire land developer named Lawrence Tyner. He convinced me to leave the paper and come into his real-estate business. He taught me the ropes and helped me to invest in the city itself and the surrounding countryside. Ultimately, I made my fortune with him. And I met Cathy, who was one of his lawyers.

I didn't think much of Cathy at first. I didn't think she was all that pretty, for one thing. "Efficient-looking," I would've called her. She was short and full-figured, bordering on pudgy. She had medium-length brown hair and a sweet, friendly face. She always seemed harried, hurried, on the edge of panic, was always running off to some zoning-board hearing or other with her giant purse and a stack of folders under her arm. It made me nervous just to look at her.

Then one day around Christmas, her boyfriend broke up with her. I didn't know this at the time. He lived in another city halfway across the state. He'd been stringing her along for years. He was one of those horrible mild guys. You know? Really earnest and caring all the time. Narrowed his eyes a lot and nodded without lowering his chin, his lips all pursed and serious. For about five years, he used this New Man sensitivity to manipulate Cathy into hanging around. Then he met someone he liked more, and Cathy was out.

Anyway, our office Christmas party came along. Everyone was drinking and singing and getting up to mischief and so forth. I wasn't much of a drinker anymore, so after a while I took a stroll through the back offices to get some quiet. There was Cathy. She was sitting at her desk in the dark with a paper cup full of bourbon. She wasn't drunk or anything. She was just sitting there, staring into space. I peeked my head in her door.

"Everything all right?" I asked.

"I hate my life," she told me. This was a woman I'd said maybe twenty sentences to in the year since I'd been working for Tyner. "I did everything right, everything my mother said. She was a feminist, my mother, very fierce. She said I could have it all. She

told me what to do, and I did it. I got good grades, the best grades.
I went to law school. I got a big job. I never depended on anyone.
I even played softball when I was in high school. I hate softball."

This sounded like the start of a long evening. I went into her
office and sat down across the desk from her.

"I have a sister," she said, gazing not at me but into the shadows. "She dropped out of college and got married. My parents
went nuts, screamed and yelled. It was awful. My sister went to
work as a secretary until she got pregnant. A secretary! Pregnant
at twenty-two! And then she quit and stayed home and kept house!
My mother nearly died. Now she has four children. Her husband
owns a small construction company. He's a great guy. Treats her
well. Loves the kids. And my sister is the single happiest person
I've ever met." She was silent a moment. Her eyes seemed to
grope for something in the darkness. Then she said, "I want her
life. My sister has the life I want. I know I'm supposed to want my
life, but I don't. I hate my life. I want hers."

It was a funny thing. Sitting still like that, staring into space
like that, talking so quietly, she didn't seem as frantic and efficient
as usual. She seemed softer, more vulnerable and much prettier
than I thought she was at first.

We dated for three months after that, but I think I knew I loved
her that night. We started talking about getting married. I was living in a quaint old two-story shingle on River Street back then.
We were downstairs in the kitchen there, sitting over sandwiches.
I said to her, "Listen, this thing, this modern thing where, you
know, marriage is a partnership and we're equals, and we share
housework and child care and all that—I'm not that guy. I'm, like,
the because-I-said-so guy, the head-of-the-household guy, that's
me. Marry me and I call the shots. I'll break my butt to make
you happy, and I'll try to give you the life you said you wanted.

I don't cheat, I don't leave, and I am what I say I am. In return, I expect—I don't know—sex, dinner, some peace and quiet now and then; maybe some affection, if you've got any. That's the best I can do. What do you think?"

Without cracking a smile, she stuck her hand out to me across the table. "Deal," she said.

We shook on it. Then I chased her around the table, tossed her over my shoulder, and carried her upstairs.

So that was our deal. And I was thinking about our deal that very day—the day it all began. I was sitting on the patio, watching my children play and thinking about our deal and also thinking about a girl named Tanya. Now, Tanya was a college girl who worked in my office over the summer, an energetic, cheerful blonde with a bright, pretty face and a tight, electrifying figure. And I was thinking about her because I had spent a certain amount of late July and part of August fighting the urge to fuck her senseless.

She had given me a number of indications that fucked senseless was exactly what she wanted to be. She was an expert flirt. Her gaze was admiring whenever I spoke. Her smile was warm, her perfume intoxicating. She encouraged me to play the mentor with her. I often found myself lecturing her on local zoning policy or whatever, just to get a taste of that gaze, that smile. At first, she flattered me a little. After a while, she flattered me a lot, calibrating her praise to my increasing credulity. And then there was her touch. . . . As the weeks wore on, she would sometimes lay a hand on my forearm when we spoke, or straighten my collar or brush an imaginary piece of lint from my chest. Once she even came up behind me and massaged my shoulders briefly as I was working at my keyboard. And yet . . . yet she never took that last step. She never propositioned me. She never tried to kiss me, never so much as stood on tiptoe. That last step, with all its risk of rejection and with all its moral responsibility—that she left up to me.

So it gave me a lot to think about. On the one hand, I thought about breaking the heart and losing the trust of the woman I loved; about shattering the idol of my two sons who looked to me for their image of manly strength and integrity; and about disintegrating the emotional universe of my daughter which rested primly, like a ruby on a turtle's shell, atop her parents' affection for each other. On the other hand, I thought about twenty golden minutes with Tanya, with the youth and heat of her flesh against my flesh. Twenty yahoo-screaming minutes with those glossed lips parting to gasp at the force of my urgent entry, until our mutual climax which, who knows, might never end, might never dump me from its height into the black tar pit of shame and remorse. My family or Tanya. It was a tough choice to make.

Maybe women will call me shallow for saying that, but that's women for you. Men wrestle with these matters at a deeper level than women know. In the end, though, a deal is a deal. Cathy had lived up to her part of it. She'd been a full-time mother, a dedicated homemaker, a wife of endless tenderness and surrender. I adored her. And—yes—a deal's a deal.

So bye-bye, what's-your-name—Tanya—bye-bye. I avoided her for the rest of the summer. No more of her quick, gentle touches. No more imaginary lint on my chest, no more massages. And hold the flattery, thanks, just go type up the application forms and get me a cup of coffee while you're at it.

She ended up sleeping with Stan Halsey instead. He was one of our environmental-impact experts, a thirty-five-year-old idealist with a social-worker wife and a brand-new baby girl. By the time Tanya went back to college, Stan was living in a motel, trying to grovel his way out of a separation. All the same, he was a lucky schmuck for those twenty minutes, I had to admit.

Well, it's a world of choices, that's the thing. I'd always have my fantasies. Plus I still had my wife.

And that's what I was musing about when the whole thing started. Sitting on the cushioned chair, on the brick patio, watching my kids play in the backyard.

At some point then, the wife in question brought me a glass of lemonade and kissed me.

"What the hell is this game anyway?" I asked her, tilting the glass toward the kids on the lawn. "I mean, they never actually seem to play it. They've just been making up the rules for the past half hour."

"I think that *is* the game," Cathy said. She sat down in the chair next to me, one leg tucked up under her.

I sipped my lemonade. "Strange creatures."

"Our children?"

"You think if we put them in cages out front, people'd pay a dollar a pop to see them?"

"If we include the Cavanaughs' kids, they'd probably pay us a dollar just for putting them in cages."

I laughed. "The get-rich-quick scheme we've been looking for."

"Has anyone ever told you that you have the nicest laugh in the world?" Cathy said. "I love that about you. The way you laugh all the time."

"Ah, you're just saying that to get me to have sex with you."

"Speaking of which, the kids are all going over to the Matthews house later for pizza and a video. We should have a couple of hours to ourselves."

"I'm going to run you to ground like a cheetah running down a deer."

"Ooh," she said.

"Like a panther. I may even wear my panther costume."

"You know your panther costume drives me wild."

We held hands and drank lemonade and watched our children for a while in companionable silence.

That, in brief, was my life before the End of Civilization as We Know It. And I loved it. I loved her, Cathy, and to hell with all the Tanyas of the world, let them go. I loved our children. I loved our neighborhood, Horizon Hill, the Hill for short. Big yards, Craftsman houses, lake views. Friendly, mostly like-minded people, hardworking dads, housewife moms, not too many divorces, lots of kids. Most of us were white and Christian, I guess, but we had a good number of Jews mixed in and a few blacks as well. In fact, I think we were a little overfond of them—our Jews and blacks—a little overfriendly to them sometimes because we wanted them to know they were part of the gang, that it was our values that made us what we were, not the other stuff. It was a place of goodwill— that's what I'm saying. I was very happy on the Hill.

Now, after a few moments, Cathy spoke again. It was the last thing she said to me before the phone rang, before the lies and the violence and all the craziness started.

She said, "Have you decided yet what you're going to do about the house?"

It was my mother's house she was talking about. My mother— my poor old crazy mother—had finally died about eight months before. Her will had just cleared probate, and now her house had to be sold so my brother and I could split the money. Someone had to go back east and clean the place out and arrange to put it on the market. Cathy's question: Was I going to go now, or wait for my brother to turn up so he could help me?

We'll never know what I would've answered. Even I don't know. Just then, the phone rang inside the house.

"I'll get it," I said.

My children's voices, the sough and birdsong of the world outside, were muffled as the sliding glass patio door whisked and thudded shut behind me. I walked two steps across our back room, our family room, to where the phone sat beside the stereo. I picked up the handset before the third ring.

"Hello?"

"Is this Jason Harrow?" It was a woman, a voice I didn't recognize.

"Yes?"

I heard her give a quick breath, a sort of bitter laugh. "It's funny to hear you talk after all this time."

"I'm sorry. Who is this?" I still didn't know. My mind was racing, trying to figure it out.

"This is Lauren Wilmont," she said. "Formerly Lauren Goldberg. Formerly your girlfriend, if that's what I was."

It was a strange feeling. Standing there with the phone in my hand, with the family room around me and that voice I barely remembered speaking in my ear. My eyes flitted over the sofa and the stuffed chair; over the rug that was a blended tweed so it would hide juice stains and pizza and soda stains. There was a 36-inch flat-screen Sony TV in one corner. Shelves with board games stacked on them; Monopoly, Pictionary, Clue. Some of Nathan's cars and a couple of Terry's dolls were lying around. Outside, through the glass doors, I could see the tops of the kids' heads moving at the bottom of the slope of the backyard. I saw Cathy, in the foreground, turning in her chair, pointing a finger at her chest and raising her eyebrows to ask: *Is the call for me?* I smiled thinly. I shook my head no.

And all the while that voice on the phone was talking on:

"You have to come back east, Jason. You have to help me. Please. Come back. I need you."

I had been honest with my wife about Lauren. I hadn't told her all the details, but I'd told her as much as she wanted to hear. She knew about The Scene and That Night in Bedford. Sometimes in church she saw me make a fist, and she knew I was holding fast to Christ's hand, and she knew why. I had been honest with her about all that.

I didn't really start lying to her until after I'd hung up the phone, until I'd settled back into the patio chair beside her.

And she said, "Who was it?"

And I said, "Just someone from the office with a question."

"You'd think they could give you your weekend, at least."

"It was nothing. What were we talking about?"

"About your mother's house . . ."

"About the house—right," I said. I gazed down the slope of grass to the children playing around the swings. They were laughing loudly, chasing each other around in circles. The Frisbee was lying in the grass, and as far as I could tell, the elaborate structure of their game had already collapsed into hilarious confusion.

I sat and gazed at them as if I were considering my answer, but my mind was blank.

And then I said, "I think I'll go back east. I might as well. I might as well just go and get the whole thing over with."

SUNDAY

2 · Another Life

The jet dropped out of low clouds and there was Manhattan, the dense skyline thrusting toward the mist. I gazed out the porthole, watching the spires sail past. I thought of Lauren down there somewhere. What could she want? I wondered—wondered for the umpteenth time. What could she want and why call me about it? She wouldn't tell me over the phone, and I couldn't stop trying to figure it out. Was it money? That was the only thing I could think of, the only thing that made sense. She must need money. She must've heard I'd done well and figured I could help her. It had to be that—or why call me?

After all these years, why call me?

My gaze focused on the Empire State Building—and then went beyond it over the undulating fall of stone to the island's southern tip, to the place where I had seen her last. My mind went back to that day and to all the days before it until, as the plane descended, I was lost in another life—a life that used to be my life.

I said I would tell you everything, so here it is:

When I was twenty-eight, I went a little mad. There were good enough reasons for it, I guess. My mother's illness, my father's suicide, my own guilt about both because of my discovery of the Spiral Notebooks. My brother's cruelty had twisted me. The company I kept had led me astray. There were plenty of reasons.

Still, in the end, it was me, my thoughts, my actions, my choices that sent me down the road into darkness until I became sick—morally sick; lost and mad and desperately unhappy.

It was seventeen years before all this began, before that autumn afternoon on the patio and the End of Civilization as We Know It. Picture me handsome, edgy, dripping with urban sophistication. I smoked in a curt, defiant way. I was quick-witted and funny. I had a good line in irony and sneering left-wing cant.

All in all, I would say I was deceptively presentable back then, considering what a mess I was inwardly. I dressed conservatively, in a pressed, preppy style. I thought it made a piquant contrast with my opinions and my job. I was an investigative reporter for the *Soho Star*, a radical weekly with an office on lower Broadway. I spent my working hours hunting down obnoxious landlords, highlighting cultural offenses against blacks and homosexuals, and seeking out corruption in any official who did not believe in the state as a sort of Nanny Robin Hood, stealing from the rich to fund its infantilizing care for the poor. I liked to claim that my creased khakis and my button-down shirt, my navy blue jacket and school tie were a sort of clever disguise to help me mingle with the ruling class and get the goods on them. But I'm afraid the ugly truth was: I liked the way I looked in that outfit. And the upshot was I appeared in those days as every inch the solid pillar of society I would one day come to be.

But oh, my soul.

I was miserable. I was miserable and I was proud of it, the way intelligent young people often are. I wore my inner pain like a badge of honor. It showed I was too sensitive for the harsh world, too honest for its corruption, too independent for its iron chains of conformity. Oh, I had all sorts of ego-polishing notions about my unhappy self. And I had theories, too. What, after all, is a depressed intellectual without his theories? I can't reconstruct the details of them now. It would be too boring to try. But there was a lot of Nietzsche involved and Freud, too—oh, and Marx. That was it, my trinity: Nietzsche, Freud, and Marx. Which is to say I believed that power, sex, and money explained all human interactions, all history, and all the world. To pretend anything else, I thought, was rank hypocrisy, the worst of intellectual sins. Faith was a scam, Hope was a lie, Love was an illusion. Power, sex, and money—these three—were the real, the only stuff of life.

And the greatest of these, of course, was sex.

I don't remember how I worked all this out philosophically. But for some reason, the other two persons of my trinity—power and money—were things to be disdained. They were motive forces for *them,* you know, for society's evil masters, the greedy, the corrupt, the makers of orthodoxy.

Sex, though—sex was for *us.* It was the expressive medium of the liberated, the unconventional, the unbowed, the Natural Man. When it came to sex, there was nothing—nothing consensual— that could repel or alienate such enlightened folk as we. Anyone who questioned that doctrine or looked askance at some sexual practice, anyone who even wondered aloud if perhaps, like any other appetite—for food, say, or alcohol or material goods—our sexual desire might occasionally require discipline or restraint, was painfully irrelevant, grossly out of the loop, unhip in the extreme. No, no. A free man, a natural man, a new man—so my theories went—threw off hypocrisy and explored his sexuality to its depths.

My depths, unfortunately, had been forged in the fire of a very unhappy youth. Rage at my mother's fate, confusion at my father's, a wellspring of pent violence opened by my brother's bullying brutality all played a part. And when I really delved into the nature of my desires—and how, given my theories, could I do otherwise?—I discovered I had a simmering penchant for cruelty. This had to be developed—so I decreed in the name of liberation and integrity—not to mention the fact that it turned me on.

Which brings me to Lauren Goldberg.

Lauren was the child of a teacher-slash-filmmaker and the paralegal-slash-wannabe-artist whom he divorced. The years of their marriage, of course, were Lauren's golden era. Till the age of eight, she could trust and believe in family and love and the gentle guidance of the teachers at her private school. After that, her world was all recriminations and disillusionment and shifting sand—plus the cold chaos of public education when the parental breakup sent the family budget to hell. The contrast between these two periods was the source of—or at least the excuse for—all Lauren's bitterness and all her yearning.

She had long black hair, a small, thin, nicely proportioned body, a harshly attractive face with her father's aquiline Jewish features and her mother's white German-Irish skin. She was young, like me. Smoked, like me. Saw sneeringly, like me, into the grimy heart of the pseudo-immaculate American dream or whatever it was we were sneeringly seeing into the heart of. She worked as a photographer's assistant. Her ambition was to become a photographer herself.

We met at a poetry reading held in a church. We drank wine out of plastic cups and talked, standing close to each other in the corner under a station of the cross. She agreed with me—or at least nodded eagerly—when I expounded on what a con job, what a lie it all was. Society, I mean, Western culture: all just a disguise for the will to power and money and sex. She nodded and said in a scintillating tone of admiration, "That is incredibly true."

And so to bed.

Now, the media have portrayed me as such a withered puritanical moralist that I suppose I ought to say right up front: I have no qualms whatsoever about the games lovers play, and may God bless you all in your variety. But this is my story, so I can only tell you about the things I did and how they affected me.

Anyway, Lauren and I didn't get up to anything too grotesque or dangerous, not at first. We just tied each other up with belts and bathrobe ties and slapped each other's butts and pretended to choke each other, snarling nasty words and so on. All in good fun, you know. And I mean, I liked Lauren well enough. I liked the fragility and the longing I sensed under her sullen, cynical hide. We had, I guess, a relationship of sorts. Pasta and philosophy in the wine cellars of Alphabet City. Wrist-bound, red-bottomed nights in her apartment—because her apartment was nicer than mine, a sparkly brick-walled wood-floored studio in Chelsea her father helped her rent.

Then, of course, after a while, I grew bored with her. Nothing surprising there. The urge to sexual variety in men is just as strong as the urge to bear young in women. And since our relationship was based mostly on sex, I saw no reason to draw things out. No hypocrisy, remember. I simply broke the news to her: I wanted to see other people. To my surprise, she eagerly agreed: Yes, yes, we should. In fact, through her photography contacts, she knew some other couples who were into what she called The Scene. Maybe we should get together with them. Well, yeah! I said.

I didn't understand, you see, that Lauren likely would've done anything to stop me from going, to win my love, to be the girl she thought I wanted her to be. To my idiot mind, we were just a couple of free spirits exploring the dangerous boundaries of our desires. It never occurred to me until it was too late that I was the natural leader of us, that I was in charge of her and therefore responsible for her welfare.

So we entered The Scene, becoming part of a loose company of people who enjoyed rough sex and other shenanigans. We would get together, two or sometimes three couples at a time, play out roles and scenarios, expose our most secret, most violent hungers and proceed to satisfy them on each other.

If you are wondering what that feels like—what it feels like to hurt other people for your sexual pleasure—I mean, to really bind them hard and hurt them cruelly—I will tell you: It feels good. At least it did to me. There was a dull-minded, feverish heat to having sex that way. No, it was not like lovemaking exactly. There were no deep draughts of pleasure from someone else's pleasure, no long, slow immersion in another's face, another's body, beautiful because they were *her* face and body, exciting because they were hers. Acting out the universal male fantasies of rape and conquest and domination had instead a childishly gluttonous quality. It was like sitting cross-legged on the floor and stuffing chocolate cake into your mouth until the whole cake was gone. It was just like that, in fact: delicious—then compulsive—and finally sickening.

Sickening, yes. Because when it was over—never mind the morning after, I mean the second it was over—I felt my spirit— that spirit I did not believe existed—flooded with moral revulsion as if a bubbling tarlike substance was rising into my throat and choking me. But here was the funny thing—the strange thing. I somehow managed to hide this feeling from myself. It's odd, I know. I meant to be so honest about everything, to expose my deepest nature, to act upon my most primal instincts without restraint—no hypocrisy. And yet about this—this most basic fact of the experience—I lied shamelessly. I told myself I felt deliciously wicked. I told myself I felt a free man who had broken the bonds of moral conformity. Oh God—my God, my God—the things I told myself. Anything to hide the truth of my moral revulsion.

Finally, when the lies were not enough, I used drugs. Well, we all used drugs, all of us in The Scene. They were to heighten the sensation, we said—without considering that the sensation needed heightening only so that the urges of our desire would continue to outstrip the commandments of our self-disgust. We started with cocaine and later added Ecstasy, which was just beginning to make the rounds in a big way. Before long, I was using something almost daily.

And yet I still had my theories—and according to my theories, everything was going great! I had the joys of honest sensuality to set against the lies that mask society's emptiness and corruption. I had the bulwark of philosophical truth to protect me against the oppressive meaninglessness of existence. I had the satisfaction of answering ever-present Death with Physical Pleasure, the only thing that was both good and real.

That was how it was, according to my theories.

In practice, my personality was disintegrating and I was plunging into a dull fog of depression, illuminated by sharp flashes of suicidal despair. Go figure.

It happened slowly at first, then it happened fast, like a child going down a playground slide, push, push, then picking up speed, then falling finally plump into the sandpit below. That was how I fell—plump—into That Night in Bedford.

That's what we always called it, Lauren and I: That Night in Bedford. As in "I can't stop thinking about That Night in Bedford." Or: "After That Night in Bedford, nothing was the same."

That Night in Bedford, we rented a car and drove up to Westchester to meet a new couple involved in The Scene. He was some kind of Wall Street guy, maybe forty, hopped-up, snappy. She was his wife, a Realtor, a little younger but not much. She was brimming with forced sophistication, broad, limp-wristed gestures, loud laughter. She actually said, *That's just delightful, darling.* She said it several times, in fact, during the course of the evening.

They had a spectacular sprawling farmhouse off a wooded lane. She called it that when she gave us the directions: "It's a sprawling farmhouse off a wooded lane." They invited Lauren and me to stay with them for the weekend.

I won't pretend I don't remember what happened. That would be nice, but I remember only too well, in spite of the chemical fog that was curling through the twisted byways of my brain at the time. The blow-by-blow of it doesn't matter much anymore. The point is: It ended with the woman sobbing. The wife, the Realtor. All her pretense at sophistication gone. Curled naked on the floor in a corner of the master bedroom, weirdly small-looking under the ceiling's enormous, exposed wooden beams. Her hand was wedged between her legs, and she was sobbing so convulsively, I thought she might rupture something. Lauren was in the master bathroom puking up pills. And me, I was holding my head in one hand and trying to find my clothes with the other.

The husband, the Wall Street guy—he was worse even than the rest of us. If there were some sort of award for this kind of thing he would've won it: Most Disgraceful Behavior in a Disgraceful Situation or something like that. The clown was actually scream-ing at his wife. Standing over her in his ridiculous bikini briefs, his bland face scarlet, his pearly hands flying every which way. Screaming at her: "You always do this! You always goddamn find a way to pull this fucking shit on me!" With the poor woman curled up at his feet, convulsing, sobbing so that a stone would've pitied her: "I didn't want to. I told you I didn't want to."

After that, after That Night in Bedford—that's when I cracked. It was the disgust, you know, the moral disgust. And yet, I had worked so hard at hiding it from myself that it could only reveal itself to me in other forms and symptoms.

So I would wake up in the predawn dark or just go still, staring at my desk in daylight. My skin would suddenly turn clammy, my heart suddenly flutter and race. I would think about the sobbing Bedford woman. And outlandish fears would swim into my mind:

What if she accuses me of rape? Or: *What if she dies of internal injuries and I'm arrested for murder?* I laughed these worries off at first. They were nonsense. She'd agreed to everything and I knew she hadn't been hurt in any serious way. And yet the fears kept coming back. And then other fears came, too, small emberlike worries that had been smoldering in me a long time but now suddenly burst into larger flame. What if I got sick? Having sex with so many strangers, careless because of the drugs. What if I had syphilis and didn't know it? What if I had AIDS? What if I got cancer of some kind? Cancer of the penis? Cancer of the balls?

I grew sick with fear. I grew small and hunched and sallow, worrying. There were days when I thought about it every hour, hours when I thought about it every minute. What if she accuses me of rape? What if she dies? What if I get a venereal disease? What if I get cancer? I went to the library and pored over legal books. I pored over medical articles, looking for symptoms. I checked my body constantly and panicked at every pimple and rash. I turned my face away whenever police cars went by. I was in an agony of terror: the symptom of my buried revulsion.

Lauren tried to help, but she only made things worse. She would lay her fingertips gently on my chest in the darkness and whisper to me with impatient tenderness: "Look, you didn't mean it. She said she wanted to. She did."

She didn't understand. How could she? She was part of my guilt. I saw that finally. I could tell myself that she had brought me into The Scene, that she'd suggested it and made the introductions. But I knew the truth. She had followed my lead. She had admired me, had wanted to please and impress me. She had shaped herself to my desires.

And now here she lay, whispering comforts into my sleepless ear, while another voice—my own voice—was whispering: "Look at you! Sniveling, fearful, sweating in the dark. Where're your

theories now, Philosophy Boy? Where's the great enlightenment,
the freedom and liberation you promised? You scuzzy shithead.
Look at what you are."

So much for sex as a path to the good life. So much for power,
too, when you came to think of it. So much for Freud and Nietzsche
as guides to happiness. And as for Marx? Well, Marx, it turned
out, was done for, too. It was not so very long before that I had
watched the Berlin Wall come tumbling down, watched that signature monstrosity of a monstrous century die its miniature death
on the piece-of-paper–sized TV on Lauren's kitchenette counter.
I had seen Marx's children come blinking out of the pit of tyranny
into the bright, gaudy light of the big, beautiful market-driven
world, seen them lift their grateful hands to that glad radiance
where it reflected blindingly off the teeth of movie stars and the
fenders of Corvettes and the bare skin of Western women, hot
and spoiled and blessedly free. The hard-hearted, war-mongering,
greed-is-good troglodytes of conservatism had prophesied it would
be so, those suit-and-tie defenders of old truths and old religions
and the silly, old, outmoded American way. They had predicted
it would be like this and we—we the fine, sophisticated, enlightened, chattering self-certain of the left—we had called them every
name we could think of, anything we could think of that might
intimidate them into silence. And now look. Look. It was no good
denying it, though all my radical friends made haste to: They had
been right, those conservatives—they had been right and we had
been wrong. The truths we'd held to be self-evident were nothing
more than a comfortable climate of opinion, self-congratulatory
certainties that made us feel righteous and progressive and bold
and yet had nothing to do with facts. This, too, I understood now.
We had been wrong. I had been wrong.

I had been wrong about everything.

What an awful thing to discover. My whole sense of myself was shattered. I felt as if I were falling apart. I had to do something.

I don't know why I went to the Church of the Incarnation. I had been raised without religion, mostly. I had certainly never been baptized or anything like that. My father, the child of a sometimes-radical academic, always swatted away my metaphysical questions as if they were mosquitoes. My mother, who'd been brought up Catholic, retained some vague notion of a gentle infant deity as long as her mind held out, but for the most part the Christ she knew was a figment of her later madness. For myself, I was an atheist, tolerant of faith only in the form of that vague Western version of Eastern mysticism so popular among my colleagues and friends.

Still, one afternoon, I was walking along Madison Avenue, and there was the church and I stopped in front of it. It was a beautiful old place, an old Gothic Revival brownstone sitting on the banks of the avenue almost defiantly serene as the flood of nervy pedestrians and deafening traffic went rushing past. Dwarfed by the towering modern apartment buildings all around it, it seemed to me a thing of more human dimensions than they somehow, aspiring skyward in this sort of small, hopeful way, peak to peak, pediment to gable to steepled tower, each crowned with a finial cross. I seized on it as if it were a piece of driftwood in the boiling sea. I went inside.

The traffic noise died away as the big wooden door swung shut behind me. I stepped across the tiled vestibule to the head of the nave. The light in here seemed white and golden, the effect of its play on the marble altar and its gilded cross. Lancets and quatrefoils of vivid stained glass ran along the walls to either side of me. Christ enthroned, Lazarus risen, Virgin with child all flamed into relief or drew back into shadow as the sun shone through them or moved past.

There was no service going on, but a few people were bowed prayerfully in the pews here and there. I didn't want them to see me, so I retreated into the vestibule and stepped into an empty side chapel.

I took a seat at the front before a small altar, also of marble. There was a wooden crucifix on it, framed against a multicolored triptych on the wall behind. Jesus hung wracked and mournful on the cross, his dying eyes turned up to heaven, the thorns carved into his head, the blood carved onto his brow.

I didn't know what I was supposed to say to him. "Hi," I said finally, in a barely audible whisper. "I hate to bother you, but I'm really feeling like shit here." Embarrassed, I screwed my palms together in my lap. "Frankly," I added with a laugh, "you're not looking so good yourself." Then I buried my face in my hands and started weeping. I said to him: "Help me! Forgive me! Forgive me, help me, help me!"

The storm passed. I waited there, just like that. I'm not sure what for, exactly. Maybe I thought I would peek through my fingers and see the celestial cavalry charging over the altar to my rescue. More likely, I was hoping for an enlightening interior blast of some kind. Some hallelujah conversion maybe. But there was nothing. Nothing at all. I stayed a while longer, trying to force it, trying to get a little uplift and inspiration going by sheer willpower. But no. Nothing.

Well, what did I expect? This whole God thing was bullshit. Everyone knew that. Everyone I knew knew that anyway. I got up and got the hell out of that place in a hurry. If you're going to get past things like this, I told myself bitterly, you have to get past them on your own. I was a man, wasn't I? Well, I was going to act like one. To hell with my damn theories. I knew what was right. I just had to do it, that's all—and I would. I was going to call up the Bedford woman and apologize for being a brute and a blind fool. I was going to dump the ugly sex that made me feel good in the moment and lousy ever afterward. I was going to stop using these awful drugs and clear my head and try to be kinder to people, try to be more honest about what I thought and felt and saw, more honest and forthright and kind all around. I was going to change everything, damn it. I was going to start everything over from scratch.

And I did. With God's help, I did. Because, of course, over time I realized what should've been obvious to me right away: that my prayer in the chapel that afternoon had been answered, after all. The celestial cavalry had, in fact, charged over the hill at the first sound of my cry for help. I didn't see it at first because there was no magic to it. It was just real—as real as real. My prayer had been answered almost in the saying of it.

So I quit The Scene. I quit the drugs. I quit the *Soho Star*. I sent out résumés and got offered a new job at a small paper in the Midwest.

Which left me with only one other thing I had to do.

"I'm going away," I told Lauren. We were walking by the harbor path in Battery Park on a winter Sunday. She had her arm in mine. I was looking away over the unbroken line of benches, squinting through the brittle sunlight to watch the tiered ferries sputter through the water toward the Statue of Liberty. I heard Lauren beside me release a trembling sigh. "I've been offered a job in another city, and I'm going to take it."

She slipped her arm out of mine. She slipped her hands into the pockets of her dark woolen overcoat. "I'm assuming this isn't an invitation," she said.

I took a slow scan of the water back to the tip of the island, up to the twin towers of the World Trade Center standing massive against the afternoon sky. I was going to miss this city, I thought. "Lauren, look," I said. "I never lied to you about the way I felt."

"No. No, you didn't. God knows I tried to get you to, but you never did."

"I've just . . . changed too much. I can't make any more small adjustments. I'm going to be thirty soon. I need to start again somewhere else."

She stopped on the path and I stopped, and we faced each other. I don't know why it surprised me to see her wiping her nose with the woolen gloves on her hands. We'd been so glib and cynical and crazy with each other, it was hard for me to realize how much I meant to her.

"Well, listen," she said with a miserable laugh. "Fuck you and all that. If you don't mind, I'm not gonna go through the whole routine. Crying gives me a headache, and I'm sure you can fill in the blanks. Anyway, it won't change anything. Have a nice life, Jason, okay?"

She walked off quickly, looking small and sad in the long coat and the watch cap pulled down over her hair, the knit scarf trailing behind her. A hunched, unhappy figure against the sparkling harbor. I wanted to call her back but what for? I knew I'd only browbeat her into forgiving me so I'd feel better. I watched her go, watched her blend with the crowds around the ferry stand, meld with the scenery—people, plane trees, and those two stalwart towers.

Then I turned away and walked off in the opposite direction.

Now, Manhattan's skyline sank out of sight as the plane settled down toward the runway. I came out of myself and turned away from the porthole. I had an odd, heavy sensation inside me—an intimation of danger—a feeling that I was coming here for deeper and more perilous reasons than I knew. Because it was strange, wasn't it? That call from Lauren just as I had to decide what to do with my mother's house. The timing was strange, the coincidence of it. It gave me the feeling that I was returning not just to the East Coast but to the past itself, returning to confront the past itself, to face it as a new man and prove to its ghosts and shadows that I was a wholly different man than I had been.

The plane touched down with a jolt. I shook myself, trying to throw that feeling off, that odd, heavy intimation of danger.

It wouldn't go away.

3 · The Television Room

Night had long fallen by the time I left the airport to drive out to the island. There were spots of rain on the windshield of my rental car. It was a sleek, jolly little red Mustang, low to the ground. It dodged and wove sweetly through the expressway traffic.

I talked to Cathy most of the way out. Her voice was thin and tinny and faraway in my cell-phone earpiece. She told me about the kids, their day at school: a good grade on a spelling test, a part in a school play. It was still daylight where they were, she said. The sky, she said, was clear.

Man oh man, I wished I hadn't lied to her about Lauren. I wished I had told her I was going to see her while I was here. She wouldn't have minded. She would've trusted me. I wasn't sure why I had kept it to myself. Just an impulse really, a momentary whim. It wasn't that I was planning to sleep with Lauren again, or anything. I wasn't an idiot, after all. I think it's just that sometimes— sometimes when you live a good life, a stable life—you want to leave room for the possibility of something else, for the excitement of the possibility. It was like letting Tanya touch my arm . . . just for a moment sometimes, you feel compelled to leave life open to the thrill of disaster.

Anyway, I hadn't told Cathy the truth, and I found I couldn't tell her now. Feeling uncomfortable and guilty, I asked her to put the children on. They said hi to me one by one. I asked them how they were. Fine, they said. When they were done, I switched off the phone and kept driving.

I slid from the highway into my hometown. I came along the broad road past the car dealerships and gas stations at the town limits. Then it was up the hill into the residential areas, where streetlights shone down on the canopies of maples and elms above me. Yellow and red and green leaves glistened, slick with the light rain. Behind the trees, entry lights gleamed white by the doorways of tranquil clapboard-and-shingle houses. Inside, behind the curtains, room lights burned yellow and warm.

It was just another Long Island suburban town, but it was my town. I'd been back here often over the years, of course, to visit Mom and my brother. Every time, it struck me with an almost-mystical familiarity. I felt I could walk its streets blindfolded, and if its streets were gone, I could walk blindfolded on the paths where they had been. I felt as if the map of the place were branded on the longest-living part of me, as if I could die and trace its outline on the after-darkness.

The house where I grew up and where my mother went mad and died was on the corner at the bottom of a hill. It was a substantial two-story colonial with white clapboards and dark green shutters. It was set back on a broad, flat lawn and shaded by oaks and a tall cherry tree. I'd been paying a caretaker to keep the grounds neat and a housekeeper to dust and air out the rooms, but when I pulled into the driveway, I thought the place had a forlorn, abandoned look to it all the same.

Inside, when the door had shut behind me, it seemed very still. I don't suppose that houses get any quieter when people die in them. I don't suppose it was any quieter than if my mother had gone out for a while on one of the rambling walks she sometimes took before her heart got too bad. But she hadn't gone out for a walk, and when I turned on the foyer light, the rest of the house spread dark around me and, as I say, it seemed almost preternaturally still.

I stood at the bottom of the stairs with my suitcase in my hand. I looked up into the shadows of the second-floor landing. Her bedroom was up there, haunted by my imagination of her last hour. I imagined her lying in bed alone, feverishly explaining the signs, the omens and connections that were so obvious to her, but that no one else could see. The fall of the Republic. The Second Coming of Christ. The coming of savagery again to the scattered nations. Explaining and explaining to no one in a whisper. Reaching out in the dark as if to take hold of my wrist—me, because I was the only one who had the patience to listen to her . . .

But I wasn't there. No one was. I had begged Mom for years to come live with me. Cathy and I had both begged her. But I think she liked taking care of my brother. Paying his keep, making his bed, his lunch, doing his laundry. I think it gave her a sense of purpose. Of course, he was no good to her when the crisis came. Alan—that's my brother's name—Alan—had been living with her for over a decade by then. A ruined, useless man. A great pontificator on What's Wrong with the World, but incapable of holding down a job or starting a family or putting bread in his own mouth. When he sensed that the end was near, he decided it was time to take what he called a "vacation." He withdrew about forty thousand dollars from Mom's various accounts and went off to Bermuda. As far as I knew, he was still there.

So she died alone. The maid came in one morning and found her. I wondered—I still wonder—if her whisper had faded to nothing or if she stopped suddenly in the middle of a word. I wondered if she felt relief as the last hoarded breath rattled out of her— relief that it was finally over, that her guardianship of the secret patterns of history was finally done. Or did she die grieving that there was no one there to hear her, no one else to understand and to take up the sacred burden when she was gone?

I stood at the bottom of the stairs and looked up into the shadows for a long time. Then I looked away. Confronting the past was all well and good, but there was no chance I was going up there tonight, not with the babbling ghost of her lying there in the darkness. Tonight, I decided, I would sleep in the television room.

The television room was a strange feature of the place. It was not connected to any other room in the house. You had to get to it by going through the garage. I reached the garage through the door in the kitchen, then edged my way between my mother's old Volvo and the gardening tools hanging on pegboards along the walls. The door to the television room was at the back beside stacked boxes of moldering books. I went through. Turned the light on. Tossed my suitcase onto the floor.

The room was a long and narrow rectangle. Call it ten feet by twenty. The walls were painted a deep, rich blue. There was a couch on one end, to my right. And to my left, all the way on the other end, taking up almost the entire wall, there was what to these rapidly aging eyes seemed the largest flat-screen rear-projection television set that could ever be conceived by the mind of man. Really, it was a monster, just huge. Seventy inches, if I remember my brother's boast right. Alan had treated himself to the machine about two years earlier, when some of my mother's CDs had rolled over.

Everything else here—everything else besides the couch and the TV—was incidental. Windows covered with wooden shutters. An ancient shag rug on the floor. Shelves and drawers against the longer walls to hold Alan's collections of old movies, television shows, and video games. A long coffee table in front of the couch, pinewood with ring stains and coffee stains on it. An Xbox on the table. And, of course, an amazingly complex super-duper remote

control that for all I knew could make the sun rise in the morning
and part the waters from the dry land.

I'd always liked this room. I'd always found it peaceful and
comforting. All the high-tech stuff was new, of course, but there
had always been a TV out here. Nothing as big as this cyclopean
beast but some kind of TV or other. When we were kids, Alan
and I would carry our cereal bowls through the garage of a Saturday morning, set them on the shag rug—the same shag rug, in
fact—and lie belly down, eating our Cheerios and watching the
cartoons. I remember it as the only time he and I could be alone
together without him punching or kicking me or throwing me to
the floor or stealing or breaking my toys or calling me names in a
wild, high voice like a demon's. The TV seemed to hypnotize and
pacify him and he would just lie on the rug beside me, munching
his Cheerios, staring at the screen. As far as I could make out,
that was pretty much all he'd been doing ever since.

My long trip over, I plumped down onto the sofa with a sigh.
I picked up the remote gizmo. Studied it for a few seconds and
pressed the buttons. The big TV made a sizzling sound. A red
light flickered at the bottom of it, then went green. The set came
on. Pictures. Voices. Drowning out the babbling ghost inside the
house. What a relief.

A woman appeared on the screen, a perky little blonde thing,
glossed and powdered to a fare-thee-well. Sally Sterling, she
was—so said the caption across her breasts. Her gigantic face
took up the entire far wall, her features so huge they fairly forced
themselves on my consciousness. Ultra-kissable bee-stung lips.
Glistening blue eyes that managed to be ambitious and imbecilic
at once. She struck me as the kind of girl who in a bygone age
would have set her sights on an aging millionaire. Now here she
was, blown up to the size of a bus, bothering all the rest of us. She
was holding a penis-shaped microphone in front of her mouth—

well, I couldn't help but perceive it that way with it jumping out at me as large as that. Her great white smile flashed. She looked as if she could barely contain her glee.

"Is this the end of civilization as we know it?" she drawled ironically, a laugh stuck in her throat. "Three major Hollywood studios certainly hope so as they get ready for the premiere of the first film ever using Real 3-D Technology at the New Coliseum Theater just off Times Square—"

I pressed the remote, hunting through the channels. An ad for car insurance went by, then an ad for soda, then a game show with lightbulbs flashing around a babe in a short skirt. I settled on the news. Enormous images tumbled past of American soldiers curling around the doorways of bomb-gutted houses, young men charging into bullet-riddled darkness with brave and fearful eyes. There were bodies in an Arab marketplace around an exploded car. There was an old woman in a black burqa weeping on her knees. In St. Petersburg, some Islamo-fascists had set off a bomb near the Church of Saints Peter and Anne. In Paris, a lone jihadi had gone apeshit at the Louvre, stabbing two tourists before he slashed a priceless painting, Ingres's *Odalisque.*

I stared at the images, but again, my mind drifted back to Lauren, wondering what she wanted, why she had called me. And suddenly, thinking of her, watching the images on the screen, a realization came to me. With all this business about confronting the past and so on, I realized I'd been imagining Lauren as if she would be the same, as if she would look the same as I remembered her. When she'd spoken to me on the phone, her voice was unchanged. It was still a low, throaty drawl, sardonic, mocking, secretly vulnerable. The image of her that came into my mind as I listened was the image of her as she once was: young, narrow, wired, with that braced, expectant air some women have as if they're waiting to be taken by storm. I remembered her mostly as

I saw her last, turning away from me, walking away, disappearing into the crowds by the harbor, Liberty in the distance to the left of her, the Twin Towers looming against the sky to her right.

But she will have changed, I reminded myself, as if talking to a simpleton. Of course she will have changed. I'd changed. Everyone had. The whole city was different, diminished, those towers themselves blown to rubble, the thousands in them dead. The whole world—that stunned, victorious West we lived in—our dumb, hilarious, in-the-money America with the slave colonies of the evil empire clacketing down like dominoes around our big clown feet: Seventeen years and it was all different, all gone. Look. Look at the TV: There was war after war in the Middle East now, war after war radiating like shock waves from the wound in the island where the towers had stood. Crazy jihadists taking over the failed kingdoms of Islam, fanatic hordes of fundamentalist warriors who seemed to have burst alive out of a mural of the Dark Ages, burst, complete with beards and turbans, frothing horses, scimitars upraised, to go galloping nutso through real life. They would brook no god but their god, their ferocious god, no law but their sharia law. They would kill anyone who might oppose or offend them, any Muslim who imagined a new future, any woman who wanted to be equal or free. And they dreamed of conquering all the infidel West, subjugating the whole mess of the modern world. They were murderers in Holland. Rioters in France. Bombers in England, Russia, Pakistan, and so on. They were armies fighting for entire nations in Africa. Here in America too, after the World Trade Center, they continued to pull off attacks now and then. Sometimes it was a terrorist cell, sometimes just a lone mad-for-Allah boy opening fire in a shopping mall or running down some nonbelievers with his SUV. But there were always bigger doings in the works, foiled plots and whispered conspiracies: to bring down more buildings, to bring down anything that stands—hell, to bring down the whole third dimension and make the world flat again.

Look at the TV, I told myself. Look at the news. The past wasn't there to be confronted anymore. This was the state of things now, the state of things since Lauren walked away from me with the Twin Towers looming over her.

No, I thought. It was unlikely she would look the same.

MONDAY

4 · Lauren as She Had Become

Nothing could have prepared me for her, though. No act, I mean, of my imagination. She was changed almost entirely from what she'd been.

She lived in Astoria, in Queens, a working-class neighborhood just across Hell Gate from Manhattan. She had the bottom floor of a two-story row house, one of a set of red-brick boxes standing side by side in a block-long line a stoop away from the sidewalk. It was eight o'clock when I got there. A lot of moms were rushing by me, towing their kids behind, hurrying to drop them off at school, I guess, so they could get themselves to work on time. There were other kids slouching off to school alone. Guys in windbreakers twisting their cars out of tight parking spaces. Guys in cheap suits marching to the train.

The clouds were breaking up over the low roofs. The sun was out, rising over the Island. The air was cool and fresh.

I climbed the stoop and knocked on Lauren's door. I heard her shout out, "Just a minute!" from inside.

I waited, squinting off toward the sun, nervous with anticipation. I heard the door open and turned to see her. The sight rocked me. I had to force a smile. Startlingly, she came into my arms. Her hair smelled the same, anyway: baby shampoo and cigarettes. She took my hand and drew me into the house.

We moved together into a small living room. It was cramped and depressing and stank of divorce: the sudden loss of income, a life cobbled back together in a rush. The walls were a slapdash beige slung on by the landlord. The tan carpet also must have come with the place. There was an aging TV on a stand in one corner. There was an aging sofa facing a mantelpiece. The mantelpiece should have surrounded a fireplace, but there was no fireplace, just the beige wall below and a mirror above it. There were framed photographs on the mantel in front of the mirror: a little girl, then the little girl older, then the same girl as a teenager. My eye flashed over them and I thought: *So she has a daughter now.*

I faced Lauren again. She was standing back from me, appraising me as if I were a statue in a gallery.

"Wow!" she said. "I mean, you look . . . you look good, Jason. You look like . . . no, you look good. I mean it."

"So do you, Lauren. It's nice to see you."

"Yeah, you too, I mean—wow." She examined me from this angle and that. "You look like you're doing really well."

I knew she was right. I did. When I'd gotten dressed that morning, I'd gone out of my way to look prosperous. I mean, I was prosperous, sure, but I'd gone out of my way to look it. I put on the blue button-down shirt and the tan sports jacket Cathy'd gotten me for Christmas, and the khaki slacks I'd picked up at Brooks Brothers in Chicago. It was a kind of bragging, showing off for an old girlfriend. I wanted her to see how well I'd done since we'd broken up. Petty and stupid and vain of me, I know. I told myself not to do it, but I did it anyway.

"Thanks," I said. "You look pretty good yourself."

That, on the other hand, was a lie. She looked like crap. Complete crap. The long straight black hair I remembered was now cut short in unbecoming curls. The thin, harsh, sensual face had become bloated, the pale skin strangely dimpled and rough. She was dressed in a baggy black sweater and a cheap straight-cut cotton skirt, dark blue, too tight around her hips. The outfit made her body—that once-lean-and-ready body—seem as if it had gone doughy, sloppy, as if it had settled and bulged like clay.

She looked old. Not just old: old and hard and hard-worn. Her pale brown eyes had been clear and even a little soft when I knew her. They were rheumy and narrow and watchful now. Her smile was bitter, the anger fairly twitching at the corners of her mouth.

How did it make me feel to see her like that? Well, it made me feel sorry for one thing, sorry for whatever had happened to her to make her look this way and sorry that the attractive young Lauren I had known was gone forever. But there's no point in lying: I felt other things, too. I felt smug and triumphant—you know, glad that things had gone better for me than they had for her. I was rich and she wasn't. I lived on the Hill and she lived here. I looked okay and she looked blasted. I didn't want to feel good or smug about it. I really didn't. But I did feel like that a little, and I bet she knew I did.

There was a box of Kents on a lamp stand by an ashtray. She scooped it up, flipped back the top, and offered one to me. Oh, yeah, she knew what I was feeling, all right. I could see her watching me as she held out the cigarette, reading my thoughts, gauging my every expression. She knew exactly how shocked and sorry and self-satisfied I was at the sight of her. She knew, and it made her bitter smile more bitter still.

I waved off the Kent. "No, thanks. I don't do it anymore."

She jabbed one into her mouth, fired it with a plastic lighter. "What's the matter? A little cancer scare you?"

"I got kids now. I'm not allowed to die."

She tossed the cigarette box down on the lampstand again. I noticed a couple of business cards lying near the ashtray: LAUREN WILMONT, WATSON & MANTLE, PARALEGAL. She hadn't become a photographer, the way she'd wanted. She was a divorced paralegal-slash-wannabe-artist, just like her mother before her.

She blew out a cloud of smoke. There was something nasty about the way she did it. Even though she blew it off to the side and up over my head, it felt as if she were blowing it right at me. She crossed an arm under her breasts and propped the other elbow on it, holding the cigarette high, pinning me with a knowing and ironic look.

"I Googled you, y'know," she said. "When I was trying to find out where you lived. Actually, that's bullshit. I'm always Googling people from my past. I've Googled you a lot."

"Yeah, I tried to Google you a couple of times, too, but I didn't know about the name change. So you're married."

"Was. And you're, like—what?" She gave me a great big man-eating smile. "You're some kind of right-wing Christian asshole now, huh."

I laughed. "That's me."

"Kind of cuts down on your S&M action, doesn't it?"

"You kidding me? That's all we do."

She grabbed a drag and laughed out more smoke. It was an angry, unpleasant laugh. "Whipping the sin out of naked school-girls. Repent! Swish!"

"Exactly."

"And you got the wife."

"Got the wife," I said.

"She hot?"

"The mother of my children, you mean?"

"Oh, well, sorry."

"As the hinges of hell, yeah."

She'd already managed to set up a hovering cloud in front of herself with that Kent of hers. She nodded and smiled at me through the haze but, boy oh boy, I could feel the bubblings and eruptions of nastiness going off just beneath the thin surface of her, her temper threatening every moment to explode right through. I wasn't sure if it was just the sight of me that had her so pissed off, or if she resented having to ask me for help or—who knows?—maybe she was always like this, percolating with wrath.

"And two kids?" she asked.

"Three. Two boys and a girl."

"And what do you—all, like, go to church together?"

"Whenever we can rustle up a Jew for the human sacrifice, sure."

"Well, jeez, don't get all defensive, Jason. I'm just asking."

"Yes, we go to church together. Every Sunday."

I got more of that appraising look from her. Her lips quirked, her eyes mocking and furious. More smoke. She shook her head. "I'm sorry. It's just when I think back . . ."

I shrugged.

"I can't believe anyone I used to fuck is a Republican. Oh, but maybe I can't say 'fuck' to you now."

"You can say anything you want."

"You mean because I'm going to hell anyway."

"Right, Lauren. That's what I mean." Hoping to deflect the on-slaught, I pointed to the mantelpiece, to the framed photos. "What about you? You take these? You still doing photography?"

"Shit, no. I don't have time. One day . . ."

"That's your daughter, though."

"Serena, yeah."

"She's beautiful. Serena. Very pretty name. She go to school?"

"High school. She's a sophomore." Her answers were curt and grudging like that. She didn't want to be distracted from the business of attacking me. She stuck her tongue in her cheek, looked me up and down again, shook her head again. "Man, look at you. I can't get over it." There was a drooping tube of ash on her cigarette now. She flicked it violently into the tray. "If they only knew, right? Your wife and kids. The sort of evil shit you used to get up to. Does your priest know? Your reverend or whatever he's called. What the hell? You should tell him, Jason. Might put a little excitement in his day." She made a sound like a laugh. Not a laugh, really, but a sound like a laugh. "The Scene. Right? Don't you ever miss it?"

"No."

"Liar."

"Why? Do you?"

"Not really. But it didn't come as naturally to me."

I shrugged again and waved her off. I didn't want her to think she was getting under my skin.

There was a dining alcove off one end of the room. A little space by the kitchen with an oval table and four wooden chairs—the kind of furniture that comes in boxes and you slap it together. I wandered in there as if to take a look around. I was really just trying to put some distance between us, maybe slow her down. Behind the table, there was a glass door. You could see through it into a postage stamp of backyard and on through a diamond-link fence into the backyard of the house on the next street over. There was a woman in the far yard, a woman in her forties but too soon old. She was slumped in a flannel nightgown. Holding a plastic bag full of trash. I watched her carry it to a can standing against the side of the house. What a depressing place this was.

"You know, I've been trying and trying to figure out why you called me," I said. "I mean, why you need help so urgently and why I would be the one you'd call for it after all these years."

I glanced back over my shoulder at her. She was still standing there the same as before. In her little cloud, her cigarette upraised. Still appraising me with that combination of mockery and rage.

"Maybe I just decided I need Jesus," she said. "I mean, when the spirit hits you . . . Right? There's no time to lose."

"I figured it was money," I said, keeping my voice even. "That was the only thing I could come up with that made sense."

There was a long silence. Then finally, I sensed the assault was over. She chewed on her lip and I could see in her eyes that she'd grudgingly called cease-fire. "You want some coffee?" she said.

We sat at the table in the alcove. She gave me coffee in a mug with a slogan printed on it: "I'm having my coffee, so fuck off!" She brought one of the pictures to the table too, one of the framed photos from the mantelpiece. It looked like it was taken for a high-school yearbook. It was posed and glossy, gauzy and sentimental.

The girl—Serena—didn't look like Lauren much. She had lighter hair and softer, rounder features, sweeter features than Lauren had ever had. A small, pouting, uncertain mouth. Serious brown eyes—even in the photo, I could look into them and see that she was hurting and lost.

"Men suck," said Lauren. She had a mug of her own with a slogan of her own: "Party Girl." She had a fresh cigarette going. "They really do. I mean, when I got pregnant, Carl was all, like, 'Oh, you're so beautiful, you're having my baby, I'll never stop loving you.' It was like we were in some commercial-free hour of crap music on AM radio. Then he hangs around long enough for Serena to love him. You know, girls—they just love their daddies. And he's, like, a Wall Street guy, so we had money, and I got to stay home and take care of her, so she got used to that, too. And I got used to it."

"You married a Wall Street guy?" I said.

"I met him on his day off. He was cooler then."

"Ah."

"Anyway, it was right after you and I broke up, so I was on the rebound, I guess. But he was nice to me, too. I gotta say that for him, to be fair. Men suck, but at least Carl was nice for a while before he sucked."

I hid my corkscrew smile in my coffee. It was pretty easy to guess where this story was going. A successful young guy like Carl with a sharp-tongued harpy like Lauren. It was only a question of what he'd leave her for: young tail, freedom, peace and quiet, the right to hang on to his own money. Or maybe just some girl who knew how to string together ten minutes of tenderness and respect and admiration to take his mind off his itching dick.

As it happened, it was a little of everything. The young tail came first. A girl at the office. Then, another girl someplace else. And so on until Lauren caught him one too many times, and it ended with him slamming the door in her screaming face as he stormed out. After that, he had a few party years on his own, so that took care of the freedom. And now he had the peace and quiet off in Arizona somewhere, living with a Life Partner type, the two of them running a homegrown investment firm together: lots of money and no kids.

"Fucking son of a bitch!" Lauren tore smoke out of her cigarette with her teeth. "He set this mad-dog lawyer on me. They threatened to have me declared an unfit mother, take Serena away from me. I ended up, I hardly even got child support—which he hardly ever pays, anyway. Never comes to see her. Sends her fucking birthday cards. When she was little, she used to sleep with them under her pillow. How pitiful is that?" I had set the picture of the girl down on the table. Lauren picked it up now, looked into her daughter's face. "I thought she'd gotten over it," she said plaintively. "I thought she was doing great."

Yeah, yeah, yeah, I thought. Single moms. Divorcé dads. They always think the kids are doing great. Cathy and I hear it all the time, in church, in our children's schools. *How're the kids doing? They're doing great!* They're always doing great. Until they're not doing great, until suddenly they're in rehab or on medication or off at some special camp for suicidal teens or whatever. Divorce fucks kids up.

"What happened?" I asked her.

She laid the photo down again. "She's gone."

"Serena is gone? You mean she ran away?"

She waved the cigarette in circles. "Moved out."

"Moved out? She's a sophomore, you said. She's—what?—sixteen? Call the cops; make her come back."

"I did that. She just leaves again. What am I gonna do? Chain her to the radiator? After a while, you know, you keep calling the cops, they set Child Protective Services on you. I'm not gonna let them put her in some foster home . . ."

I sighed, rubbed the back of my neck. "Well, where is she?"

"I don't know. She stays with friends, one friend, then another. I don't even know most of them."

"Friends like other kids? Kids with parents? Is she staying with other families?"

"Sometimes. I don't know. No. No, I don't think so." She averted her eyes the way people do when you press them for details and they don't want to talk about the details because then they'll have to face them straight on themselves. Holding her cigarette between two fingers, she massaged her forehead with her pinkie and thumb. "She gets involved with these characters. They get their claws into her . . ."

Oh, wonderful, I thought. *These characters . . . with their claws in her . . .* I had to fight down a flash of irritation. People make such messes for themselves—for themselves and for their children, too. And yes, I knew I shouldn't've passed judgment on her. And yes, I did feel bad for her, too. Poor woman, the way she looked, her face all swollen and pocked as if every day since I'd seen her last had been a punch in the jaw. For all her smart mouth and her bravado, Lauren had always needed someone to take charge of her, someone to lead her to a better place. Guys took advantage of that—guys like Carl—guys like me, like I was back then. She wanted leading? We led her, all right. We led her where we wanted to go, and then dumped her when we wanted to go somewhere else. Him off in Arizona, me on the Hill. And her left behind, looking like this. So, aside from all the petty stuff— you know, my smugness at having a good life, my satisfaction at doing better than an old girlfriend—I really did feel bad for her and guilty, to some degree. All the same, she'd sure made a mess of things, a mess for herself and a mess for her daughter. And it irritated me, I have to confess.

"Have you told her father about this?" I asked her. "Have you told Carl?"

She answered with an exasperated *Pah!*

"Well, what do you want me to do?"

"Talk to her," she said. "Just go talk to her. Get her to come home."

"That's ridiculous, Lauren, I don't even know her."

"I know but . . . she needs someone like you, Jason. She needs a man, a father figure, someone who's not an asshole. That's always been the big thing about you. I always remembered that. I mean, with all the fucked-up stuff we did and everything, you were never an asshole, not like Carl. I mean, this Jesus shit you're into—I don't know what all that's about. I guess everyone has their drug of choice, so fine, whatever, but . . . You're the only guy I know who hasn't turned out to be a piece of shit. Serena's gonna hurt herself or get hurt or get pregnant or I don't know what and . . . I can't be Daddy for her. I can't reach her. Please. Go and talk to her. She might listen to you."

I had no idea what to say to that. Baffled, I shook my head. My eyes were turned down to Serena's photograph. That child-woman face, the pouting Little Girl Lost, was gazing up at me. It seemed to me now that she did have her mother's eyes, after all, those same hurt, defiant eyes, begging for someone to take charge of her.

"Look," I said. "I'm sorry. I mean, I want to help you, Lauren. I do. I'd like to help Serena, too, but . . . This doesn't make any sense to me. I don't even know what I'm doing here. You and me—it's a long time ago now. You don't just call a guy up after all these years. Not for something like this. She must have a teacher or guidance counselor or something . . ."

She made that exasperated noise again, the same noise: *Pah!*

"What would I even say to her? How would I even find her?"

"I don't know . . . They go to this club all the time, her friends and her. The Den . . ." Her cigarette had burned to the nub. She let it burn, holding it up beside her head. With her other hand, she pinched the bridge of her nose. She shut her eyes. A crystal tear shone on her lashes.

"Lauren . . ." I said. "Really . . ."

"Shit. Just do this, will you, Jason. For old times' sake. I'm scared, okay? Every day, I'm so scared . . . I can't sleep at night . . . Will you just do this? Please."

I'm not sure what I was about to tell her. Something, some excuse, to get me out of there. It all just seemed wrong to me somehow. Wrong, suspect, illogical, bizarre, maybe even danger-ous. I was an idiot to have come. I had let myself be tempted by—whatever had tempted me—the promise of schadenfreude or the sexual charge of an old flame or the vague, imaginary prospect of an emotional adventure. And I was tempted now, too—by her ridiculous faith in me and by the chance to play her knight in shining armor and the chance to play Big Daddy to some pretty teenaged girl.

But no. I was finished here. I was sorry I'd come. I was sorry I'd left my sweet house on the Hill for this shabby rental with its secondhand couch and its furniture that came in boxes. I wanted to get out of here and get the hell home as fast as I could.

I started to push back from the table. I started to say, "I'm sorry, Lauren—"

But she dropped her hand—the hand that was pinching the bridge of her nose. She dropped it to the photograph lying between us. She lifted the photograph by its frame. She waggled it in front of me, grimacing in her anger.

"Shit, Jason," she said. "Look at her, would you? You have to do this. I mean, come on. Look at her! Why do you think I called you? She's not Carl's kid. She's yours."

5 · Waiting for Dark

I waited for dark in the television room. I was supposed to be up-stairs. I was supposed to be cleaning out my mother's room so the Realtor could stage the house for potential buyers. But I couldn't bring myself to do it. I waited in the television room instead.

There was a talk show on the massive screen. Some hip young host, a fidgety young guy, was sitting behind a desk against a backdrop of the Manhattan skyline. He was interviewing a pudgy, dissolute older actor and frantically working his hands and flash-ing glances at the audience as if he feared they might be as bored as he was.

I didn't recognize the guest at first. Then—wait a minute—yes, I did. Just as I was about to change the channel, I thought: *Son of a gun, that's Patrick Piersall.*

So it was. *God, look at him,* I thought. Of course, I had no idea just then the part he would ultimately play in all this, but still, I was riveted. When I was a miserable twelve-year-old, he was the admiral of *The Universal* on the TV series of the same name. Augustus Kane, the wise, battle-hardened leader of an interna-tional crew of humans and androids sent into space to find a new home for the denizens of a dying Earth. He was sleek and muscu-lar then in his skintight spaceship unitard. He had coiffed, wavy red-brown hair. Smooth, classic matinee-idol features highlighted by a hot, steady gaze. Oh, and the famous, mellifluous voice, its signature syncopated rhythm. *Ram. The force field. Full speed! If those Borgons escape. The galaxy. Is done for!*

No wonder I hadn't recognized him at first. What a roly-poly little wreck of a man he'd become. The dark jacket he'd closed artfully over an orange V-necked pullover couldn't hide his bowling-ball belly. And the once-dashing features were puffy and distorted, with a complexion like veiny yogurt, the sign of a lifelong drinker. His toupee was awful and sat like a hat over his grizzled sideburns.

Only the voice was the same, the liquid tone and the clipped, charged phrasing. And the dramatic gestures of his hands, too, as they chopped the air.

"Television. I think. Is such a wonderful vehicle for. Reality," he said as the host sat quietly climbing out of his skin with boredom. "And that's what my new show is about. Real crimes. Real mysteries. Murders. Disappearances. In which the investigation is still open, and the guilty party has not. Yet. Been found."

In other words, I'm a fat, has-been boozehound who couldn't get arrested in show business, and one of these True Crime show rip-offs was the only job I could find.

I changed the channel. There was a building blowing up: an ad for a movie. I gazed at it, but I didn't watch it. I just stared, thinking about Lauren, about Serena.

Look at her, Jason. Look at her. Lauren had kept saying the same thing to me, kept waving the framed photograph of her daughter in front of my face. *Anyone can see she's yours. Look at her.*

Oh, come on, Lauren. I was so upset, I almost shouted at her. I pushed back from the table, stood up from my chair. *Don't pull that crap on me. Come on! How stupid do you think I am?*

But she kept holding out the photograph, kept saying, *Look at her.*

And I did look at her. And my breath caught and my stomach felt as if it were circling the drain.

Her story was plausible. It was very plausible, knowing Lauren, knowing me. She said she had sensed, those many years ago, that I was going to break up with her. It was plain enough to see with all the changes I was going through. So she stopped taking her birth-control pills. She wanted to get pregnant before I had the chance to tell her I was leaving. That way, it would seem like an accident; it wouldn't seem as if she had done it on purpose to hold us together. She wanted to fool herself in this as much as me.

But she waited too long to speak up. Even though her period was already one week late, even though the test she'd gotten at the drugstore was positive, she wanted to be completely certain before breaking the news. Then came that day out by the harbor when I told her it was over. That changed the whole scenario. Now, she couldn't tell me about the baby. Now it would be obvious even to herself what a desperate ploy it was. She was too proud for that—too proud to go through with it once she could no longer lie to herself about her own motives. So she walked away grandly without saying a word, taking her fetus with her.

She had planned to have an abortion, she said, but the affair with Carl started up so soon after our breakup and he was so enthusiastic about the idea of being a father that she didn't see anything wrong with telling him the baby was his.

It's not like I'm asking you for child support, she said to me. *Shit, Jason, I'm not asking you for anything. I just need you to go talk to her, that's all, before something bad happens. Come on, man. Please. There's no one else I can turn to.*

I didn't know whether to believe any of this or not. I didn't know whether the sick swirling certainty in my gut was an intuition that she was telling the truth or just guilt and fear. Because,

I mean, what if it was true? What if Serena was my daughter? How was I going to break it to Cathy?

And what was I going to do now?

I thought about it, sitting on the couch with the TV going. And then I stopped thinking about it. I stopped thinking about anything, stopped seeing anything. I stared into space as evening came on outside the shuttered windows.

Now, it always kind of worried me when I did that: zoned out and stared into space like that. My mother used to do the same thing. It was the first sign of her madness.

When I was small, she would sit with me in the grass in our backyard. She would hold me on her lap and we would look at things together. She had light red hair that fell around her face and teased her mouth when the wind pushed at it. Her skin was pale and freckled. She had clear green eyes. I don't remember thinking she was beautiful, though I know she was. What I do remember is feeling that she was part of the landscape: the grass, the dandelions, the whispering leaves, my mother. Anyway, we would look at things and she would talk about them in her low voice, in her gentle, wondering way. How do the ants know to run for their lives when you come near them? How do the bees tell each other when to swarm and when to fly off? How did anyone ever imagine they could make flour out of wheat or bread out of flour? Then sometimes, in the middle of all this wondering, she would drift away, drift like a leaf on the surface of a slow stream into a silent, distant dream state, gazing. I would climb up over the front of her and touch her cheeks and put my fingers to her lips and press my face up close to hers, but she'd be gone.

As it turned out, those little dazes of hers—they were a kind of seizure, a sort of low-grade epileptic fit. Every time she had one, they did damage to her brain, to a part of her brain called the amygdala. The way I understand it, the amygdala makes emotional connections for you. You see an angry face, and your amygdala tells you to be afraid. You see a chocolate bar, and it tells you to be happy. When your amygdala goes wonky, like my mother's did, you start making all kinds of connections you shouldn't. You start to see a lot of coincidences everywhere, and every coincidence seems amazing and meaningful. It's like one long "Aha!" A cartoon lightbulb over your head that can't be turned off.

The doctors said the condition wasn't usually genetic, but they couldn't be sure in her case. Usually, they said, it was brought on by a trauma of some kind, a concussion, a fever, something like that. But with my mother, no one could figure out where it had come from. So it might've been inherited and it might've been passed on, in turn, to my brother and me. The doctors just didn't know.

So I worried. Whenever I found myself gazing into space that way, the way I was doing that evening in the television room, I'd come back to myself and get worried that what happened to my mother was happening to me. Sometimes when I'd notice a coincidence, or when I'd feel a fact or an event was particularly significant or important, I wouldn't trust myself. I'd think: Is this the start of it? Is it happening to me, too?

I came out of it now. Sitting there on the couch, I blinked and looked around. I thought of my mother, and a small clutch of anxiety tightened my chest.

I forced myself to focus on the TV.

There was a beautiful woman on the screen now. The sight of her reached through my troubled thoughts and touched off a small soothing cloud of desire in my loins. It was a soft-focus montage of a movie actress I recognized: Juliette Lovesey. There was Juliette stepping out of a car, Juliette walking down a red carpet, Juliette adjusting her bathing suit at the beach, all in slow motion. She was small and slender but shapely with a wonderful cleavage she kept on display. She had a face of fabulous fragility and yearning framed in achingly limp brown hair.

Now there were images of another actress, Angelica Eden. I felt the stirring of lust again and again it comforted me. Angelica was gorgeous, too, but in a different way. She had sensuous, dark, animalistic features, night black hair, and blood red lips. She had breasts you could drown in, aggressive, engulfing. She was walking along a sidewalk somewhere next to the actor Todd Bingham, a skinny, pretty boy with a wispy little beard.

"As these three mega-stars prepare for the opening of their new film—the first ever in holographic Real 3-D—the question is being asked all over Hollywood: Is this the end of civilization as we know it for Juliette and Todd?" So said the narrator, a perky female—maybe that same Sally Sterling girl, I don't know. "Rumors of an on-set romance between Todd and Angelica have sparked speculation that Todd's fairy-tale engagement to Juliette may be over."

She droned on. The same old thing. The usual celebrity game of pegs and holes. Todd, Juliette, Angelica. A peg with a pretty-boy head attached, and two holes with pretty-girl heads and breasts. The peg slotted into one hole, then later slotted into another, and it was all supposed to matter in some way because the heads were so pretty. But they were still just pegs and holes; it was still just a game.

"To add to the feverish gossip," the perky female narrator went on feverishly, "some sources close to the actress are saying that Juliette may be carrying Todd's child!"

That shook me. Whatever calm my lust had given me was gone on the instant. Talk of love triangles and pregnancy and desertion brought my own situation flooding back in on me: Lauren, Carl, Serena. I seized hold of the remote. I snapped off the TV. I leaned forward on the sofa in the gathering dark, my elbows propped on my thighs, my hands clasping and twisting against my lips. I prayed silently. *What am I going to do, Lord? What should I do now?*

Then I sat in the silent television room, staring into space.

Then, when deep night came, I went out to look for the girl.

6 · The Den

The Den—the club where Lauren said Serena hung out—was in the old meatpacking district on Manhattan's Lower West Side. I was surprised to see how crowded the neighborhood was in the middle of the week like this. All the old butcher shops were dance clubs now. There were partygoers on every sidewalk, passing in the dark under the long awnings, in the lee of the grimy brick walls, or spilling over into the broad, cobbled streets. They moved in packs and pairs through the night from club to club, entryway to entryway, cordon to cordon, line to line. The guys all looked alike to me: gawky dopes with spiky hair and untucked shirts, the long tails dangling over slacks or jeans. Each girl, on the other hand, was a sight to behold: young, some of them teens, some wearing small, sleek dresses and some in frilly taffeta, some wobbling on high heels they hadn't mastered yet, all of them poignant and pretty to my middle-aged eyes.

I found The Den near the corner of Twelfth Avenue. The line there was maybe twenty couples long. I moved beside it to the entrance, catching the smell of perfume as I passed. The perfume smelled like candy or fruit, something little girls would wear playing dress-up. In front, the club was like the other clubs I'd seen, all but unmarked, a discreet sign on the brick wall, a cordon in front of a pair of massive doors.

The guy guarding the approach was a masterpiece of cliché-without-irony. Muscle-bound, block-headed. Wearing a tight black

T-shirt even in the brittle autumn night. I flashed him a hundred-dollar bill and told him I was doing a review of New York clubs for a magazine in the Midwest. He muttered darkly into a walkie-talkie, then thumbed me in, playing it a little extra cool, I thought, now that he figured someone might describe him in the press.

Inside, the place was done up to look like a cave, with lights flickering in alcoves like fire, throwing the shadows of the dancers up on the fake rock walls. The dancers packed the place; the floor was dense with them. They thrashed and coiled like snakes touched by a live wire. The girls' bare shoulders and bare legs caught the colored lights and gleamed. The boys with their untucked shirts were sunk in glimmering nothingness. All of them, judging by flashes of their sweat-shiny faces, seemed to be in a kind of narcissistic trance, eyes closed, lips parted, their attention wholly inward. The music hammered at them. It hammered at me. Ephemeral bursts of electronic Morse code in a spastic melody. A jungle sideman amped up under it with a migraine beat. And out of the midst of all that noise, a woman's voice, thin as a drifting specter and full of a specter's longing. She was singing about sex, but she made it sound like love.

I moved along the outskirts of the dance floor, pushing through clusters of young, light, almost insubstantial flesh. The smell—I remembered that smell—not the patches of perfume and cologne here and there, but the pervasive smell beneath that: cold, processed air and fresh, hot skin together, an atmosphere like a zombie's eyes, torpid yet weirdly alive, full of aching and emptiness. It did that thing to me, that thing smells do, wafting through my limbic system like a smoky key, unlocking images and memories. Suddenly in my mind, I saw a girl I'd known when I was very young, a girl I'd danced with at a club like this one. She was in my mind with startling clarity and my heart ached to have her, just as it had ached back then.

I shouldered my way through the crowd to the bar, a bar of silver metal and glass. It was sunk into an alcove of its own with the fake rock jutting out on either side of it. The close space deadened the thumping, jittery music, brought down the volume a little. Which was a relief to my relatively ancient ears.

One of the two lady bartenders emptied some kind of soapy goop out of a cocktail shaker into a glass and pushed the concoction toward a girl too young to drink it. Then she stepped over and asked me, "What can I get you, partner?"

Anne. That was her name. That was the first time I saw her—saw her and heard her voice and caught a whiff of the scent she wore, which was flowery and sweet and made me think of that girl again, that girl I'd danced with and longed for. Anne was almost as young as I had been back then, in her early twenties at most. Tall with broad shoulders, but not strong-looking or mannish, soft and ungainly in an endearing way. She had the awkward, slightly goofy air of a girl who didn't realize how beautiful, how sensual she was. Her skin was olive, her face oval and big-eyed and innocent, her hair black and lavish, tumbling to those broad shoulders, which were bare in her black tube top. Maybe it was because I'd been thinking about that girl I'd danced with, or maybe it was just Anne, but I suddenly wished with a wish like fire that I had my youth to do over again.

I ordered a bottle of Dos Equis. She clunked it in front of me with a bright, sweet smile. Her eyes—her doe brown eyes—lingered on me frankly, looked me over up and down as I laid my money on the glass in front of her. The frankness of her appraisal was exciting. I couldn't tell if she was being flirtatious or just friendly and curious, but I felt so old in that place—I was probably twice her age at least—that it was exciting to have her look at me at all.

I wondered if Dos Equis was still a cool beer to drink. I hoped so. It used to be, back in the day.

"What're you looking at?" I said with a smile.

"I don't know," she said with an adorably silly tilt of her head. "What am I?"

"You're not gonna card me, are you?"

Likewise adorably, she put one hand on her hip and dropped the other in front of me, demanding my ID. I still had my wallet out, so I slapped it into her palm. Still adorably, she examined my license.

"Jason Harrow. I guessed you were from out of town. You're much better looking than your picture," she said as she returned the wallet to me.

"Thank you. You're much better looking than my picture, too."

She laughed and tossed her hair back. She had a ladybug tattoo on her left shoulder. She had a warm, open laugh like a girl from the country and a sort of raspy voice with a lot of humor in it. I wished the music would pipe down so I could hear her better. Also, I wished I were younger and still single.

As if she heard the thought, I saw her glance down at my left hand, at the gold band on my finger. Then she raised her eyes and saw that I'd seen her glance down. She smiled mischievously and jogged her eyebrows. Adorably. I laughed.

"Now, don't be bad," she said.

She was called away to make a drink for another guy. I shook my head into my beer. I told myself to stop flirting with her. Then she came back and I went on flirting with her. It was as if I was being carried along on a current. Telling myself to stop didn't matter. It was beside the point. The current carried me along.

"I'm Anne," she said, drying her hand on a towel. "Anne Smith." She stuck the hand out and I shook it. Her palm was cool from handling the glasses, but I could feel the heat of her underneath.

"Good name," I said. Even here I had to raise my voice to be heard above the music. "Anne Smith. No-nonsense."

She wrinkled her nose. "I hate it. It's too plain. I gotta marry a guy named Zucabatoni or something."

"I like your ladybug."

"Oh, thanks. It speaks highly of you, too."

She hit me with another of those smiles. I had to force myself to change the direction of the conversation.

"Listen," I said. I leaned toward her so I wouldn't have to speak so loudly. "I'm looking for someone. The daughter of an old friend. She left home, and her mother's worried about her. Her mother says she comes in here a lot."

I had a photo Lauren had given me, a snapshot of three friends she had taken from Serena's room. I laid it on the bar.

"She's the one in the middle," I said. "Her name's Serena."

Anne leaned on the bar and bowed her head over the snapshot. I used the opportunity to smell her hair. It had a rich, earthy smell.

Her elbows still on the bar, she raised her face. Now it was close to mine. "Yeah, she comes in here all the time. Every night, almost." She glanced at the neon clock on the wall to her right. It was about ten thirty. "Usually around now. Another half an hour, maybe. I'll tell you when I see her."

"Great, Anne. I appreciate it."

"She'll be messed up, though, if you're gonna try and talk to her."

"Drunk, you mean?"

She lifted the soft, broad, bare shoulder with the ladybug on it. "Drunk. High. You know."

She was called away again to draw a couple of beers. I slid the snapshot off the bar and slipped it back into my jacket pocket. I tipped my own bottle back a time or two, stealing glimpses of Anne as she pointed at customers, took their orders, poured their drinks. Now and then, she glanced my way and caught me looking and sent me a corner of a smile. After a while, she wandered back.

"How's your beer? You ready for another?"

"No. I'm good. What do you do?" I asked her. I was curious but I was flirting with her, too, riding the current. "When you're not here, I mean."

"How do you know I do anything? Maybe bartending is my life."

"Yeah, I'll bet."

"I go to school. Up at the university."

"Figured. What're you taking?"

"Cultural Studies."

"Cultural Studies? What the hell is that?"

"Oh, just books. You know. Like writers."

"Oh, yeah. We used to call that English. I majored in it," I said. "What writers do you like?"

She named some writers, the sort they teach in universities now. You know, mediocre, unimportant types no one will read in a generation, but since one was a black woman and one was an Arab and one a Mexican, everyone was supposed to pretend they were better and more interesting than they were. Cultural Studies.

"How about Shakespeare?" I asked her dryly.

"We haven't done him yet." She brightened. "But I think one of my professors is gonna lecture about him this week." Then she said, "There she is."

I followed her gesture, looked behind me. Serena was just coming through the door. She was in the middle of a small cluster of boys and girls. The boys looked to be in their twenties, the girls in their teens. Serena looked younger than any of them.

Even from across the room, through the dark and the flickering lights and the dancing shadows on the walls, I could see how drunk she was. Drunk in that way people sometimes get where they feel hard done by and sullen and, damn it, they want to do what they want to do for once in their lives, so leave them alone. She moved peevishly out of her cluster of companions. Frowning, she stumbled sideways a step. One of the boys took hold of her elbow. She yanked free, shaking her head, slashing her hand in front of her as if to say, "No, no, no." Whatever was on the schedule, she didn't want any. The boy rolled his eyes, giving up on her.

"Wow," I shouted back at Anne over the music. "Is she always like that?"

"Lately, yeah," Anne said. "I don't blame her mom for being worried."

I set my beer bottle on the bar. "All right. Well . . ."

Adorably, Anne gave me a regretful little wave. I reached out and squeezed her hand. I wanted to feel the heat of her one last time. The future Mrs. Zucabatoni.

Then back I went across the cavelike club, through the firelike light, along the cluster of thrashing dancers and their thrashing shadows on the fake-rock walls. By the time I reached Serena, she was giving her buddies hell about something, yelling at them, bent forward, her little fists clutched at her sides, her face pinched and ugly with rage. The boy who'd tried to take her arm was calling something back at her, but moving away with his friends at the same time, pushing with them out onto the dance floor.

"That's not what you said, Ray!" I heard Serena yell as I drew near her.

She was small, I could see now, small and slender, without much in the way of a figure. She was wearing a sparkly pink minidress that left her shoulders bare and her legs bare to high on the thigh. The outfit would've looked cute and sexy on her if she hadn't been such a mess otherwise. But her mouth was hanging open and her eyes were filmy, her hair was slovenly, and there were mascara stains over the sparkles on her cheeks.

I touched her naked shoulder. She spun around to me, belligerent, loaded like a blunderbuss, ready to go off.

Then—very suddenly—everything about her changed. One look at me, and her face went pale, her eyes went clear with what I was sure was terror. Her mouth opened and closed as if she'd been caught red-handed at something and were trying to come up with an excuse. For a second, I thought she might start to cry or try to run away, screaming for help.

"Serena!" I shouted over the Morse code music and the thumping sideman and a new singer yearning like the last. "Your mother sent me to find you."

I saw her try to understand me—then she understood me. I saw the color come back into her face as her small body sagged with relief. Whatever she was afraid of, apparently I wasn't it. As suddenly as she'd become frightened, she turned pugnacious again. She yanked away from me violently as if I'd been trying to drag her off somewhere.

"Ah . . ." she mumbled drunkenly. ". . . the fuck . . . fuck . . ."

I felt angry. At Lauren mostly. For letting her daughter come to this. Ugly drunk, foulmouthed, here in a club with a bunch of guys. I felt angry and, right after that, I felt guilty. Because maybe she was my daughter, too; maybe I'd let her come to this, too.

Well, that's why I was here. To get her out, to take her home. To try to, anyway. I moved in close, towering over her.

"Listen," I said, "we're leaving now."

She pulled that insolent and somehow pathetic pose teenagers have, rearing up openmouthed as if to look down on me, daring me to try to follow through on my threats. At the same time I could see in her eyes as plain as day how desperate she was to have someone take control of her.

"I'm serious," I said. "You either come with me or I call the police."

"The fuck . . ." she said, but her eyes went fearful again. The cops—that's what she was afraid of. She had thought I was a cop at first—that's why she'd looked so scared.

I pressed my advantage. "You're underage and drunk. I'm going to give you to the count of three, and then I'm calling the cops."

She fumbled with a tiny pink purse hanging from her shoulder on a long golden chain. "I'm . . . not underage. I have a license—"

I moved in even closer, crowding her hard. "I'm your mother's friend, Serena. I know how old you are. Let's go."

"Serena."

I turned. It was the kid, the boy who'd come in with her, who'd tried to take her elbow and reason with her. A reedy dark-skinned kid, of Indian extraction, maybe, or Pakistani, his face already shiny with sweat from the dance.

"You all right?" he asked her. He glared at me.

I smiled. Good for him. He was young, but he had some man in him. I cocked my head at Serena. It was her call now. How was she going to play it?

She hesitated. I held up one finger. Then I held up two. At three, I would call the cops.

"Yeah," Serena said quickly. She spoke to the kid, but her eyes stayed on me. She really was afraid. "It's okay. He's a friend of my mom's."

The dark-skinned kid tarried another second, giving me another threatening once-over. But he'd done his bit. He was eager to get back out on the dance floor.

"All right," he said. He swaggered away. Good for him.

I took Serena by the arm. "Let's go."

"Just a minute!"

"No, now." I moved her toward the door.

"All right. All right." She snaked her arm free angrily. "The fuck!"

I was glad to get out of there, glad for the fresh air, but glad for the quiet more than anything else. That music is an idiot's delight: The best thing about it is when it stops.

Side by side, we walked to the corner. Serena could barely keep straight. She kept wobbling on her low heels, bumping into me. Her head seemed balanced precariously on her neck. Her eyelids were getting heavy. I guess the open air was making her even drunker.

When we crossed the street, I took her arm again. Now she was too woozy to pull away. We reached my Mustang parked at the curb. She leaned against it as I got the door open. She looked like she would've tumbled right down to the gutter cobblestones without the car's support.

I got her into the passenger seat. Went around to the driver's side. As I went, I pulled my cell phone from its holster. I dialed Lauren's number. Her phone rang and rang. No answer. I bit back a curse. It was eleven o'clock at night. Where the hell was she? Finally, her answering machine picked up.

There was no hello or anything, just Lauren's voice, curt and harsh. "Leave a message for Lauren or Serena after the beep."

After the beep, I said, "I've got her. Call me back." Then I snapped the phone to my belt again.

I got behind the Mustang's wheel. Started up the engine. Serena sat blinking and nodding next to me, her mouth gaping like a fish mouth.

"Put your seat belt on," I told her.

She blinked some more and turned to the shoulder belt, stared at it as if she wondered what it was. After a while, she pawed at it. To hell with that. I leaned across her, pulled it out and over her, stuck it into the latch by her seat. I could smell her perfume, close to her like that. One of those fruity little-girl perfumes I'd smelled before. Christ, she was just a child. She should've been home, in her room, finishing her homework or giggling on the phone about who liked whom. I shoved the car into gear, cursing Lauren in my mind. Where the hell was she?

As I pulled the Mustang away from the curb, Serena snapped straight, trying to focus.

"No . . . No . . . I can't . . . I don't wanna . . ."

"Yeah, well . . ."

"No. Can't. Back there. Mom's—"

"You have to, Serena."

". . . find me . . ."

"How'd I find you? It was easy."

"No . . . no . . ." Her chin sank toward her chest as she shook her head. "They'll . . . find me . . ."

"What?"

She started to fade again, tilting forward against the seat belt. Then I guess the world must've started spinning around on her because she sat up fast and jacked her eyes wide open.

"I just . . . I gotta . . ."

I sighed.

She went on muttering. "I . . . just get me some . . . some coffee, something . . ."

"You don't need any coffee. The night's over."

"No, really, listen . . ." She had to fight off unconsciousness again. "Just gotta get a little straight, okay, then . . . I'll give you head."

"You'll what?"

"You let me go, okay? I'll give you head if you let me go."

I laughed. You've got to laugh. The way people treat them-selves, the shenanigans they get up to. "You're not giving me head," I said, laughing.

Serena looked at me, confused. She tried to smile and keep her eyes open at the same time. It didn't look easy. "No. Really. Just need . . . some coffee."

"Yeah, just take it easy, sweetheart. I'm taking you home. Then you can work it out with your mother in the morning."

". . . mean it," she insisted, her head slowly tilting forward again. ". . . serious."

"I understand. But just forget it."

Slumped forward, she turned her face my way. Narrowed her eyes at me. "You're my mother's friend?"

She sounded surprised. Sure. Most of her mother's friends probably would've opted for the blow job. I laughed again, shak-ing my head. Poor little creature. God take pity on us all.

Mercifully, she passed out then, her head falling limp, her mouth hanging open. She started snoring. I drove crosstown to-ward the expressway.

I took her out to Astoria first, to Lauren's place. But the brick row-house was dark. Lauren wasn't home. Of course. I sat out front in the car and dialed her number again. The phone rang and rang, and then the machine picked up. I gave a curse and broke the connection. Damn her.

I glanced at the girl in the seat beside me. She sat slumped and limp and snoring, dead to life. From where I sat, I could still catch traces of her perfume. She probably had a house key in that pink purse of hers. But what then? I couldn't just leave her inside alone. And the thought of waiting around for Lauren to turn up—if she ever did—was more than I could stomach.

I took off again. Got the car back on the expressway and

headed toward my mother's house. The pitted expressway pavement thumped and rattled under my tires. The late traffic streaked by on either side of me, red taillights pulling away up ahead, white headlights coming toward me in the oncoming lanes. The billboards, the grimy factories, and the bright main streets of Queens gave way to malls and gas stations and twinkling houses out amid the rolling shadow-shapes of trees on midnight lanes.

I cursed Lauren the whole way. What had she gotten me into? Something was up with this kid; something was wrong. She was scared—scared of the cops—scared of something, that was for sure. Her muttered words came back to me. *Can't. Back there. Mom's. They'll find me.* She didn't want to go home because if she went home, someone would find her. Maybe the cops, maybe someone else. Someone.

She was still out cold when I pulled into the driveway of my mother's house. I sighed again as I killed the engine. It was going to be hell getting her inside.

Out here, away from the city, the bracing night was full of the tang of autumn leaves. I went around to the car's passenger side and pulled the door open. I ducked inside and reached over her to release the seat belt. As I took it off her, Serena fell forward. I caught hold of her. She began muttering.

"Come on," I said.

"Why do I . . . ?"

She protested dully as I turned her around and worked her body to the edge of the seat. Her eyelids fluttered a little and she made a confused gesture with her hand as I got hold of her. One of her shoes had already fallen off in the car. I took off the other one and tossed it in with the first. Then I got one arm under her knees and the other under her arms, hoisted her into the air, and kicked the door shut. Her head fell against my shoulder. I turned with her in my arms to survey the houses around me, dark, most of them, hunkered under their oaks and maples. I hoped that meant the neighbors were asleep. God knew what they would think if they saw me carrying this drunken teenaged girl into the house.

I carried Serena up the front steps. I had to set her on her feet there so I could unlock the door. She swayed and took hold of me. She began trying to open her eyes, trying to figure out what was happening. Her head fell forward.

"Sick," she said.

"All right. Hold on."

I managed to get her inside and hurried her down the hall to the bathroom. I got the lights on and threw the toilet seat up just in time. She fell on the bowl as if it were water in the desert. I could hear her retching violently as I went back to shut the front door.

When I returned to the bathroom, she was sprawled on her ass, her legs spread, her dress up, her pink underpants showing. She was gripping the toilet rim to keep from falling onto her back. She stared up at me with her mouth open, mascara raccooning her eyes. Then she hauled herself up to the bowl again and vomited some more. The noise was loud and unpleasantly liquid. The smell of the vomit filled the room. When she was done, she clung to the toilet with her face over the bowl, grunting. After a while, she started to cry.

The housekeeper I'd hired kept the place in good shape. There were washcloths on the wall rack and everything. I grabbed a cloth and ran some cold water on it.

Serena sat there, holding to the toilet rim. She cried like a baby—exactly the way a baby cries, with that same crumpled look of grieved incomprehension, the same wild appeal to the Great Powers: *How can this be? How can this be?* I got down on one knee beside her.

"All right, all right," I said.

I wiped the flecks of vomit from her lips and cheeks. There were lumps of it on the front of her sparkly pink dress, too. I scraped the washcloth over the thin fabric, feeling the motion of her little breasts underneath.

She sobbed and gasped.

"All right," I said. "Take it easy."

"I didn't . . ." she said and her face crumpled like a baby's face again. "I didn't know . . ."

"Take it easy, Serena. Shush."

When I was finished cleaning her, I tossed the washcloth up into the sink above me. I pushed her short hair back behind one ear. "Are you done?"

She shook her head. She cried. "I didn't, I swear—" Then she turned and put her head in the bowl and retched some more. It was just convulsions now. There wasn't anything left in her. I fetched the washcloth and wet it and wiped her face again. Her skin looked rougher than before and more flushed. Maybe I'd wiped off her makeup. I couldn't be sure. I don't know very much about makeup. All I know is that now she looked like a child who'd hurt herself while playing dress-up and was lying on the floor and bawling in her grown-up clothes.

"I need to pee," she said miserably.

I left her there, shutting the door behind me. I went to the front stairs and jogged up. It was the first time I'd been upstairs since I'd come back to the house. The linen closet was on the second-floor landing. I got a spare blanket and a pillow and a couple of towels out of it. As I was piling them up in my arms, I could feel the presence of my mother's room down at the end of the hall. I didn't look that way for fear I would see my mother's ghost, standing in the shadows down there, watching me.

I went downstairs again, back to the bathroom. Just as I arrived, the door opened. Serena stepped out weakly, holding on to the edge of the door for support. She looked at the blankets and the pillow under my arm.

"I really feel sick," she said pitifully.

"I know you do, sweetheart. It'll be all right."

"I mean, I can't . . . I don't think I can do anything tonight. Anyway, I don't have any condoms or anything, y'know?"

It took a second before I understood her. Then I laughed. "You don't need condoms, you screwball. You're going to bed."

She massaged her forehead with one hand, confused. "I don't . . . I'm sorry. Who are you?"

"I'm a friend of your mother's, remember? Come on. Let's find you a place to sleep."

She sniffled once, then started to cry again.

I put my arm around her, guided her through the kitchen and out into the garage. I let her walk ahead of me along the narrow corridor between the wall and my mother's Volvo. She was crying and sniffling the whole way. I got her into the television room. I figured that was the best place for her. I'd be able to look after her in there.

I put the pillow on the end of the long sofa. Tossed the blanket on the coffee table. Laid the towels on the floor in case she needed to puke again. Serena stood, meanwhile, swaying, nodding, her eyes falling shut and starting open and drifting shut again. She'd lapsed now into little moans and half-formed phrases. The vomiting had sobered her up for a while, but the drunk was coming back. I could see she was close to passing out again.

"I didn't . . . didn't know . . . I swear . . ."

I sat her down on the sofa. She gaped and gulped and whimpered in a small, self-pitying sort of way. I tipped her gently over until she lay with her head on the pillow. I covered her with the blanket. As I tucked the blanket under her chin, she worked her hand free and took hold of my hand.

"I swear . . ." she murmured. She licked her lips, fighting to keep her eyes open.

I perched on the edge of the couch and sat there, holding her hand. She brought my hand close to her face and nuzzled it like a child with a teddy bear or a security blanket. I looked down at her, studied her features carefully. In all truth, I couldn't tell whether she resembled me or not.

She was on the brink of unconsciousness now. She shuddered with crying.

"I didn't know, I didn't . . . swear . . ." she whimpered.

"Quiet now, Serena," I said. "Just lie quiet. It'll be all right."

"I didn't know they were going to kill him," she said.

Then she was asleep.

7 · The Universal

When I was sure Serena was unconscious, I left her there and went back through the garage into the kitchen. Now I needed a drink myself. I'd bought some groceries that afternoon, including a couple of bottles of chardonnay. I poured myself a glass of wine and downed a good-sized portion of it in a single swig. I came gasping out of it and set the glass on the counter, holding on to the base as if it would keep me steady.

I didn't know they were going to kill him.

I was going to have a long night, wondering what the hell she meant by that. In my heart, I was afraid I already knew. The terror in Serena's eyes when I first approached her. Her fear of the police. Her reluctance to go home where "they" might find her. It all made sense if she had witnessed a murder. If she had witnessed someone being killed or knew about it somehow. If she was running from someone or if, more likely, in her clumsy, drunken, stupid, teenaged way, she was wandering around the city waiting for whatever catastrophic thing was going to happen next, hiding sometimes and sometimes haunting the very places where the axe might fall, because she couldn't stand the waiting, the suspense.

Well, the suspense was mine now, too. Until morning, at least, when I could talk to her again and find out more. There was no point even thinking about it until then. Good luck trying not to.

I let the wineglass go and walked over to the security keypad by the door to the garage. I pressed in the code to arm the house alarm and watched the light over the pad go from green to red. That made me feel a little safer. It was all I could do for now.

I went back to the counter. I took another long gulp of the wine, then refilled the glass. I looked at the window, at my reflection there on the surface of the night. I could feel the dark house hunkering silently around me. I could feel my mother's ghost moving in the upstairs hall. I could hear her whispering up there, pathetic, lost: *What happened to me? Where did I go?* I could feel the graveyard chill of her breath on the back of my neck. *Where did I go?*

Her disease had progressed through stages so subtle no one knew. So many of the things I loved about her stayed the same. Her slow, soft, gentle manner, her wistful wondering at things, her seemingly bottomless fascination with my own childish concerns—these all remained as her amygdala began to misfire more and more often, as it began to sing its mad song of coincidence and meaning, continually unearthing some new connection between one idea and another, one event or fact and another, until she'd filled the Spiral Notebooks, working out her whole grand historical scheme.

How much of this deterioration was apparent to my father earlier on, I just don't know. He was always distant, internal, burdened, impossible to read. Even when the great tragic love of his life was playing itself out behind the scenes—a story, really, so swept by tidal emotions it could've been an opera—he went about the business of a suburban bankruptcy attorney with impenetrable blandness. The line of his thin lips never altered; the eyes behind his square glasses never betrayed more than an empty blink or stare. He comes back to me in his white shirt always, with his tie always knotted, his long face pasty, never a slick black hair out of place.

So I don't really know what he knew. But for the longest time,

I know I knew nothing. In fact, I always sort of liked those dreamy little trances of hers, her secret seizures. They seemed so typical of her somehow, so much of a piece with her sweet, wondering nature. If I had known, if anyone had known, what they really were, she could've gotten medicine for them. The damage to her brain could've been slowed, even stopped.

I refilled my glass, standing there, listening to my mother's ghost pottering around upstairs, her little sighing plaints: *What happened to me? I had a life, a husband, my children. How I loved my children. Where did I go? I went into a reverie and when I came back, I was gone.*

I knocked down another shot of wine, feeling the heat of it spreading through me now like a stain marking the paths and byways of my bloodstream.

I didn't know, I told her. *I was just a kid. I didn't know.*

I didn't know they were going to kill him.

I collared the wine bottle and lifted my glass and carried them both out to the television room.

She was just a little slip of a being, Serena was. Curled up under her blanket like that, she still left room for me to sit at the end of the sofa. I pushed at her feet and wedged myself between them and the sofa arm. I picked up the remote and turned on the enormous TV. I cranked the sound way down low, but there wasn't a chance in hell it would wake her.

"After my husband died, I was listless," said a cherubic old woman, blown up to the size of a Volkswagen on the wall-sized screen. "I couldn't eat. I'd lie awake worrying all night long. Finally, my best friend said to me, 'This just isn't like you. Why don't you talk to your doctor about Cruxor?'"

And I'll be damned if that woman wasn't transformed right before my wondering eyes into her old happy, gregarious self.

"Man, I gotta get me some of that shit," I said, knocking back another slug of wine.

I settled in, bouncing from channel to channel.

A schoolful of Buddhist teachers murdered by "rebels" in Thailand, facedown in the yellow dust, the backs of their white shirts savaged with red.

A Christian village in Nigeria destroyed by "militia," clay huts gutted, orange flames snickering against the pale blue sky.

Jews blown up by "Palestinians," in Israel. Muslims castrated and beheaded by "insurgents" in Iraq.

I snorted to myself. Who did they think they were fooling? I wondered . . . a little drunkenly now, I must confess. These high-born Lords of the News, spoon-feeding us their carefully selected diet of euphemisms. *Rebels, militia, Palestinians, insurgents, French youths.* Did they think we were sitting here, thinking, *Hm, I guess those dark-skinned, angry-looking killers named Muhammed all over the world aren't radical Muslims after all. Now I will not be prejudiced against their religion.* Didn't they understand that we were bouncing on the sofa, screaming all the louder for our frustration, *Hey, News-clowns! Tell the truth for once in your use-less lives! Say the word! Say some word. Islamo-fascists! Jihadis! Something. Ya dumb fucks. Ya dumb, useless, lying, elitist fucks.*

Ah, well. I suppose that's neither here nor there. I mean, it just makes me angry now, you know, because maybe it would've been a little easier for me to figure out what the truth was if the people who were supposed to be bringing me information hadn't felt duty-bound to guide me instead into right-thinking with their lies, lies, lies. But really—really—it's neither here nor there. The important thing—the jarring, weird, and, yes, ultimately relevant thing—was what happened next.

I changed the channel. And "Hey!" I murmured aloud in my surprise.

Because—what do you think?—there he was again! Patrick Piersall. Weird, no? Well, it seemed weird to me. I mean, I hadn't thought of the guy more than five times since I was twelve years old, and here he was suddenly appearing on my TV twice in one day.

It was a rerun of *The Universal.* Now he was Augustus Kane in his prime, standing sleek in his silvery unitard in front of one of those papier-mâché boulders they seemed to have on other planets back then. Beside him was his archenemy, Smoldar of the Borgons, aka some poor bastard who dreamed of being Brando and wound up wearing a grotesque full-face mask with stringy black hair sprouting all over it.

"You Mindlings command us to. Live in Peace lest we destroy ourselves," said the admiral with his signature delivery, looking up at the painted sky in which his invisible captors hid. "But we would rather be free—free to choose our paths without the interference of a controlling hand no matter how benevolent. For without freedom—without choice—there can be no virtue—even in doing good. Without freedom—without a chance to choose virtue for ourselves—we can never find our destiny."

Now here's the thing. There was some channel—the Sci-Fi Channel—that played these reruns every night. So stumbling on Piersall again like this wasn't really that much of a coincidence at all. But I didn't know that. To me, the synchronicity seemed startling. More than that, it seemed downright scary. It made me start to worry again about the whole family-madness idea, the old amygdala going haywire. That was the last thing I needed on my mind right now.

So I had this brainstorm: I called up the TiVo, the digital-recording system. I programmed it to record anything that Piersall was in. That way, there would be no more coincidences, you see? The next time Patrick Piersall showed up on my television, it would be because I had chosen to record him, not because I was turning into my mother, seeing some secret network of connections governing the unseen world.

What can I say? I'd had too much to drink, all right? It made sense to me at the time.

And, of course, in the end, it made all the difference in the world.

TUESDAY

8 · Breakfast with Serena

I was in the kitchen making coffee when Serena stumbled in. Gray, small, and uncertain, she stood wavering in the doorway to the garage. Her narrow shoulders were hunched. Her face was screwed up painfully against the morning light. Her party dress hung on her like a wrinkled pink rag.

"You remember where the bathroom is?" I asked her.

She nodded weakly and shuffled across the room and off down the hall.

I set the coffeemaker going. Got some eggs and bread, butter and milk out of the refrigerator. Set them on the counter by the sink. I could see the backyard out of the window as I worked. It was a beautiful blue autumn day, the oaks red, the elm trees yellow, the rolling grass pale green. I had the window cracked open a little, and the cool air came to me. The smell of the dying leaves made my heart ache for the past. I used to play tag with my friends on that stretch of grass beneath the trees. My mother would stand right where I was now, making lunch, washing dishes, watching me.

"I can't find my purse."

Serena was back from the bathroom, even more hunched, even more gray than before. Water glistened on her cheeks, dripping from the curlicues of brown hair around her ears.

"I brought it in from the car," I said. "Your shoes, too. They're over there."

I gestured at the breakfast nook, one corner of the kitchen where a small rectangular table sat surrounded by four white wooden chairs. Her purse was on the table. Her shoes—open-toed straps with pointy little heels—were on the floor.

"Sit down," I said. "I'll make us some breakfast."

"Can't eat," she said. But she plopped down on one of the chairs.

"Eggs'll make you feel better. Also, they're the only things I know how to cook."

"Need some fucking coffee."

"It's almost done."

Still at the counter, I cracked the eggs into a bowl and used a fork to stir them up with milk. Standing there like that, I could see her out of the corner of my eye. She was in the midst of pulling this whole big complicated sneak maneuver, sort of rubbing her face and massaging her forehead with one hand as a way of hiding the fact that at the same time she was opening her little pink purse on her lap with the other hand and sneaking a look down into it.

"I didn't steal anything, Serena," I said with a laugh. "I didn't even open it."

She made that fish-frown teenaged girls make when you catch them at something, chin pulled back, upper lip jutting defiantly. She snapped the purse shut and tossed it onto the chair next to her. She held her head in her hands, rubbed her temples. Then she noticed a sheet of paper lying on the table: it was a draft of a flyer my Realtor was preparing for the house. She picked it up and studied it sullenly.

"Is this where we are? Long Island?"

"Mm-hmm. It's a house I own. It belonged to my mother."

She tossed the page aside without interest. "I need to get back to the city."

"Have some eggs first."

"I don't want any. I don't feel well."

I managed not to say anything snarky.

"Look, you don't have to play out this whole big, like, break-fast scenario," she said. "I said I'd blow you, I'll blow you. Only let's just do it, all right? I have to get back."

I laughed, shaking my head. "Thanks, but no thanks."

"Why not?" she shot back nastily. "What, are you, gay?"

"Oh, now you've rattled my sense of manhood to its depths," I said. "Have some coffee."

The machine was gurgling out the last drops of water. I took the carafe and slopped a dollop of coffee into a mug, plunked the mug in front of her. She did a real job on it, dumping as much milk into it as there was coffee and even more sugar. She was just a little girl, see, pretending to enjoy a grown-up drink. It was kind of sad, when you thought about it. Even when she was finished doctoring it, she didn't actually drink any of it, not right away. She just wrapped herself around the mug and inhaled the healing fumes.

I went to the stove and got to work making toast and cooking eggs. Now my back was to her.

"You remember who I am?" I asked her.

Her voice came sullenly from behind me. "A friend of my mother's, or something. I don't know."

"My name is Jason Harrow."

I was using my fork to scramble the sizzling eggs in the pan when I heard her say: "Hey. Yeah. My mother told me about you."

I was glad she couldn't see my face. This wasn't going to be good. I reminded myself to stay cool and patient, just like I did with my own kids. "Oh, yeah?" I said. "What'd she tell you?"

"She said you and her were together for a while. I remember now! She said you were into this whole, like, BDSM scene to-gether. Only you got freaked out by it, so you moved to the middle of nowhere and went on this whole religion trip. She says you're, like, some right-wing Christian asshole now."

I laughed again—what could I do but laugh? I worked the eggs. "My life story in a nutshell."

"Man, that is so fucked up."

"That's true," I said with a sigh. "It was."

But I had misunderstood her. "I mean, you're, like, a Christian?"

I was scraping the eggs onto a couple of plates now. Shaking my head, smiling. "Oh. That. Yes. I am."

"That's some really fucked-up shit."

I grabbed the toast from the toaster, slapped butter on it.

"I had this teacher once? Mr. Benson?" said Serena—as if she were asking questions instead of trying to start an argument. "He says if people didn't call Christianity a religion, it would be classified as a mental illness."

That got another laugh out of me, louder this time.

"I mean, like, you believe people, like, rise from the dead and go to Heaven and do miracles and all this shit."

"It's not for sissies, that's for sure."

"And, like, no one can have sex with anyone else or whatever."

"Right. No sex. That's how we get our magical powers."

I set a plate in front of her and one for myself. I poured myself a mug of coffee and sat down with her. I said a silent grace.

"All that stick-up-your-ass shit, it just makes everyone, like, crazy, you know?" Serena said. "I think anyone should be able to, like, fuck anybody they want to—it's no one's business."

"Uh-huh. And how's that philosophy working out for you?"

She had lifted her coffee mug to her lips with both hands and was just taking her first actual sip from it when I asked her that.

The question caught her off guard. She laughed. The coffee went up into her nose. She set the cup down, coughing.

That was the first time I liked her, liked anything about her. I liked her for laughing at that, for realizing how miserable she was making herself and being savvy enough to laugh. It was the first I'd felt anything for her besides pity and guilt and maybe disgust. I laughed, too.

But that made her angry—angry, you know, at having given so much of herself away. So she did that wonderful thing children do when they've unintentionally revealed their feelings: She pretended it hadn't happened, as if she could simply talk me out of having seen it.

"Would you stop laughing at me all the time?" she snapped. She yanked at her nose where the coffee had come out. "I mean it. It's so fucking rude. You laugh at, like, everything I say."

"You say funny things. I can't help it. They make me laugh."

"It's like you don't take anything I say seriously. It's really fucking rude. How would you like it?"

I was eating now, and I went on eating.

"Well? How would you?"

"You can laugh at me all you like, Serena. Then we'll be even. How's that?"

She withdrew to the sidelines, grumpy and dissatisfied. So far, I was ahead on points, see. But, to tell the truth, it was easy to beat her at this game. I had a big advantage. I was a dad, and she'd never had a dad, not really. I understood the rules, and she didn't have a clue. In order to win, you had to be clear about what you wanted. I wanted information, enough information to figure out what was going on in her life, what my responsibilities were, what I should do next. She thought she knew what she wanted, but in fact she didn't. She thought she wanted to outsmart me and make me look foolish and then get away from me and go brag about it to her friends. What she really wanted, of course, was for a grown-up to take charge of her and help her out of whatever jam she was in. She was working against herself and never had a chance.

I went on eating, but I watched her, too. I could see her thinking, scheming—looking for a new line of attack because she hadn't been able to get a rise out of me yet. That's what teenagers do, you know, they probe for weaknesses. They're smart enough to see the world is not what it seems, smart enough to see that we adults are all liars and hypocrites and so on, but they're not wise enough to know what to do with the information. All they can figure is to use their new insight as a weapon, a way of short-circuiting the power of the big people: You lied so I don't have to listen to what you say; you've done wrong so you have no authority. It's an idiot's game but they're young and it's all they know. Hell, some people never learn anything else.

Serena picked up a piece of toast. She examined it suspiciously as she thought things through. She nibbled at it, very delicate, very girly. There was another thing I could like about her. I approve of girly—especially in girls. Maybe she had enough woman inside her to make a lady out of, if anyone ever took the trouble. You never knew.

The next minute, though, I saw a wicked look come into her eyes, a sly smile to her lips. I could tell she'd come up with a new way to get at me.

"I remember something else my mother told me about you," she said.

"Oh, yeah?" I said around a mouthful of eggs. "What's that?"

"She said you might be my father."

I raised an eyebrow. That was interesting: might be—only might be. It'd be a hell of a relief if she turned out to be Carl's kid, after all. I tried not to sound too eager. "What else did she say?"

"She said she started fucking Carl right after you left, and she wasn't sure whose I was. She was gonna get me tested, but I wouldn't let her."

"Why not?"

"I thought she just said it 'cause she didn't like that I, you know, didn't hate Carl as much as she did."

I nodded. Smart girl.

"So do you think you're my father?" she asked, naughty and wheedling, looking for that weakness.

"I honestly don't know, Serena."

"Is that why you don't want to do anything with me?"

"I'm having breakfast with you. Doesn't that count?"

"I mean sex stuff."

"Oh." I dabbed at my mouth with one of the paper towels we were using for napkins. "I guess. That and the fact that I'm married and you're a child."

"I'm sixteen."

I'm afraid I smirked a bit at that.

She returned to the attack. "Like, is that why you're here? You think you're my father and you're gonna, like, swoop down suddenly and save me from my life. You're gonna, like, bring me to Jesus."

"I, like, might." I laughed. "You better be careful. Before you know it, you'll be singing hallelujah, handling snakes, God knows what else."

"Yeah. Like fat fucking Chinese chance. Y'know?" She reached down for her shoes. Slipped them on her feet. "Look, I gotta get back to the city," she said. She stood up. She took hold of her purse. "Are you gonna drive me, or do I have to hitchhike?"

I give myself some credit here. It would've been a lot easier to just let her go. Let her go and forget about her. Then I could've finished up with the Realtor, cleaned out the house, put it on the market and gone home, back to the Hill. I could've walked away from this, from all of it, even from the End of Civilization as We Know It. I mean, what was that to me?

But the thing is, when you take charge of someone, you take responsibility for her, too. If I've learned nothing else in life, I've learned that. So I took a sizable chomp out of a piece of toast. And chewing on the mouthful, I said, "Why don't you sit down, Serena."

"I gotta go," she insisted.

"Sit down," I insisted back.

She snorted with scorn. "Yeah, right. Like you're gonna make me? I didn't think so. 'Bye."

"Sit down. Right now."

"Oh? Or, like, what? You'll spank me? I know you're into all that sick shit."

I cracked up. I dropped my forehead into my hand, laughing. Kids. "For crying out loud, Serena. Would you sit down, please?"

"Stop laughing at me, God damn it! All right, that's it! I'll hitchhike."

She started to flounce off. I sighed. I reached out from my seat and grabbed hold of her arm. It was so thin, my thumb touched my knuckles.

"Let go of me!" She yanked away violently. I let her go and she stumbled back a step. "You fucking pervert."

I stood up, towered over her, blocked her way. "Sit. Down. Now. I'm not kidding."

Her eyes moved to the door. She thought of trying to rush past me. Then she thought better of it: She wouldn't have made it. She gave me her angry teenaged fish frown—she waggled it up at me.

"This is, like, kidnapping, you know. You could, like, go to jail for this."

"Call the police then."

She started, and her face went blank as if a little shock had gone through her. I seized the moment. I grabbed the purse out of her hand.

"Give that back!" she said, but weakly.

I snapped the purse open. I dug out her cell phone. I tossed the purse on the table. Held the phone out at her.

"Call them," I said. "Tell them you're being kidnapped. Call 911. Go ahead. I'll wait."

For once, she couldn't think of anything to say. No childish taunts, no naïve threats, no ignorant arguments. The whole teen arsenal was shot. Her pale face trembled; her eyes pleaded and grew damp.

"Now sit down, Serena," I said. "I'm not going to tell you again."

She sank slowly, resentfully, back into her chair. I stood above her, looking down at the top of her head. I could see her white scalp through the part in her dark hair. It made her seem very vulnerable somehow. I felt for her.

"Now who got killed?" I asked.

She looked up suddenly, shocked and terrified.

"Last night," I said. "You said you didn't know they would kill him. Who were you talking about?"

She lied in answer without any hope that I'd believe her. She let her head sink again, her gaze on the table. She didn't even bother to meet my eyes. "I didn't say . . . I don't remember saying anything like that."

I opened her phone. I laid it down open on the table in front of her, right under her nose. I pressed the numbers. As I pressed them, they showed up on the readout screen, large and bright. 9.1.1. I held my finger over the CALL button.

"Let me explain how this works," I said. "I'm the grown-up. You're the child. When I tell you to do something, you do it. All right? Now let's give it a try. Answer my question, Serena. Who got killed?"

She didn't answer. I heard her swallow.

I pressed the CALL button.

Her two hands fluttered out together. They seized the phone and snapped it shut. Her head sunk down, she clutched the phone close to her belly as if she were afraid I'd snatch it away again.

"If you call the police, they'll know," she said softly. "They'll know it was me."

"Who'll know?"

"The people. The people who . . . did it. They have guys who listen. To the radios. They can get into the computers, too. They'll know if the police find out. They'll know it was me who told them. There's no one else it could be."

She lifted her face to me then, her little-girl face, helpless and sick and pleading. I looked down at her and my heart just sank—it felt like a stone inside me dropping into a well of fathomless darkness.

I could see it now. I couldn't see it last night, but now in the morning light it was obvious. I could see the resemblance between us. I was certain she was mine.

"If you call the police," she said very quietly, "these people—they'll know. They'll know and they'll kill me, too."

Then, crying, she told me her story.

9 · The Great Swamp

It happened about a month ago. Serena was still living at home then. She was out on the town one night, the way she was almost every night, doing the clubs just as she was last night when I found her. She was wild and muddy-minded on Ecstasy and booze—same as last night. And same as last night, she ended up dancing in The Den with the fake flames throwing her shadow up among the other dancing shadows on the fake-rock walls.

She was out on the dance floor with a couple of girlfriends. Soon a guy broke in on them and separated her from the pack. She and the boy convulsed in unison to the Morse-code music and the stampede beat. Their hands waved in the air above their heads; their hips pulsed toward each other across an ever-smaller gap of darkness stroked by whirling colored lights. After a while, the music changed. It got sparkly and slow. Serena ended up hanging off the boy's neck like a pendant, her face against his chest. It was cozy dancing that way. She liked how he smelled. She decided she would spend the night with him.

She never found out his name. He told it to her, but she couldn't hear it over the music. He was a white guy, though; she remembered that. Most of the guys she hung out with were some shade of brown or yellow, some mix of bloodlines. But this guy was as white as she was—which was so white, it sometimes seemed to her a kind of racial nakedness. Sometimes she was vaguely embarrassed by her own whiteness. And she looked down on most of

the white boys she met. But tonight, for some reason, the white of
the boy against her whiteness struck her as exotic and attractive.
She liked it.

The boy was unusual in other ways, too. Tall and narrowly
built, he was disheveled and soft. He wasn't gym-rat ripped like
a lot of guys she knew with their heroic pecs and washboard abs.
He wasn't all skin and bones, either, like some guys who did more
meth than food. There was soft extra flesh on him, all of it pale.
She could imagine him in his college dorm room drinking non-
diet Coke and eating baloney on buttered white bread while he
studied. The image made her smile against him as they danced.

What else did she remember about him? He had short blond
hair; slow-blinking hazel eyes behind wireless glasses. His shirt
didn't hang loose in the going guy fashion, though half the tail had
worked free from where he'd tucked it into his khaki slacks. Up
top, his shirt was unbuttoned to show a wedge of chest, white and
shiny with sweat and as hairless, Serena said, as an Asian guy's.
Oh, yeah—and he was wearing something around his neck. She
felt it when she put her cheek against him. She reached into his
open shirt and took the thing out and looked it over in a drunken,
flirtatious way. She might even have asked him what it was, but
she couldn't remember what he told her. It looked to her like some
kind of nail or a little spike or something hanging on a leather
lanyard. It was weird, she said; sort of gothic, sort of violent like
a gang symbol or a cult sign or something. (Listening to her, I was
pretty sure I knew what it was. I was pretty sure it was one of those
"passion nails" some Christians took to wearing after that movie,
The Passion of the Christ, came out.)

Anyway, Serena and the boy left The Den together. It was
around one or two A.M., she thought; she wasn't sure. She was
wired from the Ecstasy, but the booze made everything go out

of focus. The boy was drunk, too, and they were both staggering along the sidewalk, his arm around her shoulders.

As they went, a big car pulled up on the cobbled street. It was an old green Cadillac. There were some boys inside. Their arms snaked out of the open windows and their hands slapped the flanks of the car as they shouted and whistled to get her attention. She looked and recognized the boy behind the wheel: Jamal. She hooked up with Jamal sometimes. The other boys were part of his posse. She didn't know any of their last names. They were just guys she knew, guys who hung around with Jamal.

They laughed and banged on the side of the car and invited Serena and her date to get in. They said a friend of theirs was throwing a party at his house upstate. It wasn't just a house, it was a mansion. Their friend was crazy rich, they said. They said there'd be all the drugs in creation there, plus celebrities and caviar and champagne and all that other rich-guy shit. It sounded good to Serena and her drunken white boy, so they crowded into the car with the others.

They drove out of the city on the western parkways. They drove a long, winding way. It was crowded in the car. It was stuffy. There were a lot of guys all scrunched in together—six guys total—and the car was filled with the dense musk of them. After a while, crushed between her white boy and some fidgety, gassed-up brown guy, Serena began to fade. She leaned against her white boy's shoulder and closed her eyes. She felt the rhythmic bumping of the car. The deep, laughing male voices all around her grew distant and intermittent. She remembered only certain moments after that, certain words that broke through to her. For instance, at one point, she remembered one boy saying, "twenty-two, twenty-two, twenty-two," three times like that, urgently. Right afterward, she felt the speed and rhythm of the car changing. She remembered

someone else saying, "The Great Swamp—grea-a-a-at!" dragging
out the word until they all started laughing.

She woke up stretched out on the backseat. She was alone in
the car. She thought she'd been awakened by the Caddy stopping,
but she didn't know how long ago it had stopped.

Slowly, working her dry mouth—rubbing her eyes in the crook
of one arm—rubbing her whole face with her two hands—she sat
up. With a groan and a sniffle, she looked out the window, blinking
heavily.

Where the fuck was she? It looked as if the car was parked
on a dirt road in the middle of nowhere, in the middle of endless
night. Was it the middle of a swamp, maybe? Or did she just think
that because she remembered someone saying the word *swamp*?
No. No: She could see a little now. There were trees on every side
of her, branchless trunks of trees standing like guardian phantoms
at every window. And there was water, too—she could see water
glinting in the light of a quarter moon. She could make out tall,
weirdly shaped reeds and thick, tangled grasses. And she could
hear frogs, about a million frogs all around her. Some of the frogs
were incredibly loud. In fact, at first, because she was still half
asleep, she thought maybe it was the boys. Maybe the boys had
gotten into one of those boy things, like a belching contest or
something, and maybe the competition had driven them to the
level of Belching Gods. Then, as her mind got clearer, she realized, oh, wait, she'd heard that sound before. Her mother had once
dragged her on some overnight to the country at some house one of
her boyfriends had and she couldn't sleep all night because of that
noise, that same noise, and in the morning her mother's boyfriend
told her: That was frogs.

She pressed her forehead to the window, trying to get a better
view, trying to see where the guys had gotten to. She looked out
past the tall, eerie guardian trees and over the glint of the quarter

moon on the water and the reeds and the high grasses. But where were the boys? She couldn't see them anywhere. She couldn't see anybody or any sign of a house or anything like that. She started to get scared. It wasn't that she thought the guys would just abandon her forever, or anything. She knew they wouldn't do that because eventually they'd have to come back for the car. But what if they'd tried to wake her up and they couldn't? Or what if they saw she was fast asleep and figured, fuck her, they'd just leave her there? They might've parked out here, somewhere near the mansion, and gone on to their rich friend's party without her. And now what if she couldn't find the place? She didn't see any lights anywhere. What if she couldn't find the place, and the party went on all night, and they didn't come back for her until morning or even afternoon? What was she supposed to do until then? Wander around in this swamp looking for them? There could be alligators out there. Or snakes. Or some crazy guy who lived in the forest and took women back to his cabin and tortured them to death. And she couldn't just stay locked up in the car either. She'd have to get out and pee eventually. In fact, she needed to pee already. Where the hell were they? What would she do if those assholes had left her to stay out in this swamp all night alone?

She began to feel the first flutterings of panic—and she really did need to pee, too. So she pushed the door of the car open. The Caddy's toplight came on. That calmed her down a little. It cut through the dark, gave her a view of a couple of feet's worth of dirt road just by the tire. No snakes there that she could see, although she knew there could be one under the car, just coiled there, waiting, licking its fangs with its forked tongue, drooling for the first sight of her heel.

Gingerly, she stepped out. She edged quickly away from the car and whatever snake might be hiding under it. Not too far, though. She kept within arm's length of the open door. She made

sure she could stretch her hand out and brush the side of the door
with her fingertips. She wanted the door open for the light, but she
was shy about peeing in the light in case the boys came back. But
she was even more shy about the darkness where the snakes might
be, not to mention the horrible frogs which were even louder now
that she was outside, so loud she thought the slimy things must
be huge. She couldn't stand the idea of one of those huge slimy
things leaping onto her or walking across her foot while she was
peeing. Somehow, though, she managed to find a clean, dry slice of
shadow between the car and the night. She rearranged her clothes
and squatted down and relieved herself.

While she was at it, she kept watch on the darkness with
darting eyes. It was warm and still here. The air was unpleasantly
thick and damp. Her glance leapt from one moonlit tree-specter to
another, then lifted at a sudden noise to scan the branches above.
The branches silhouetted against the purple sky looked like
grasping hands poised over her. In fact, the whole scene seemed
to her so much like something in a horror movie that she became
more certain with every moment that a killer with a butcher knife
was sneaking up behind her as she squatted there helpless. Her
panic started growing. It felt like a big bird inside her—an eagle,
maybe—opening and closing its wings, getting ready to take off.
She made a little whimpering noise and bit her lip. She felt like
crying.

But just then, just as she finished her pee, she caught a glimpse
of light up ahead. She felt a burst of hope.

She straightened, pulling up her underpants quickly, smooth-
ing down her party dress. She peered hard into the horror-show
tangle of the forest, thinking *please-please-please*, trying to catch
sight of that light again. She even pushed the car door back. She
didn't shut it because she wanted to be able to jump inside if any-

thing attacked her, but she pushed it toward the car until the light in the Caddy went out so she could see better into the darkness.

There it was again—that light. She got a longer look at it this time. It was the beam of a flashlight. It traced an erratic arc up out of the earth, then over some branches, then across a stretch of dirt road until, for a moment, it was a bright disc shining right at her from—she didn't know—not far, maybe twenty yards away.

Serena lifted her hand and almost shouted out. But quickly, she thought, *Oh, that's real bright, Serena,* because what if this was, in fact, the guy with the butcher knife who tortured women in his cabin? What if, in fact, just like in the horror movies, he'd already killed the boys one by one as they tried to scramble over the ground and get away from him? She knew it probably wasn't really the horror-movie guy—she wasn't stupid—she was just afraid it *might* be him or something else bad. Anyway, why would the regular guys—her guys—be wandering around this swamp with a flashlight? That didn't make any sense either.

She thought of turning on the car's headlights so she could see the road, but then that struck her as stupid, too. If there was some kind of bad guy out there, the headlights would lead him right to her. She had gotten a glimpse of the road when the flashlight swung over it. She had seen that it was a broad path, more than wide enough for a car. She thought if she went forward carefully, she could keep to it, keep away from the water and the snakes and frogs, and get to a place where she could make sure the flashlight belonged to her friends or to someone else who was all right.

Serena nerved herself with a big breath. She inched forward along the side of the car, keeping her fingertips on it the whole time. When she got to the front of the car and had to leave it behind, it was terrible, a terrible moment. She could barely take her hand off the hood, could barely force her feet to keep moving. It wouldn't have been so bad, she thought, if it wasn't for the frogs. They were so loud and slimy-sounding. And it sounded as if there weren't just frogs out there, either. It sounded as if there were animals growling, too, and other things she didn't even know the names of, or want to know. Also, she thought, it wouldn't have been so bad if it weren't for the shapes of the trees like phantoms watching her, and the silhouettes of the branches like grasping fingers. And it wouldn't have been so bad if it hadn't been so dark, too dark to see even two steps ahead of her, even by the light of the pale quarter moon.

But somehow she managed to keep going, to keep sliding her feet forward ever so carefully over the packed dirt, farther and farther away from the car, deeper and deeper into the darkness until—there it was!—the flashlight again, and not that far away now, not far at all. In fact, now, she could keep it in sight as she moved toward it. That gave her more courage. Another few sliding, cautious steps, and she heard voices—male voices. She was almost sure it was her friends. That gave her even more courage. She took another few steps. And now she heard the words:

"Just forget it."

It was Jamal's voice. What a relief! The tension flooded out of her with a sigh. She put her hand to her chest and her small shoulders sagged and her eyes fluttered upward: *Whew!* Now she felt much better, much more confident. As she came forward another step or two, she even started rehearsing the shit she was going to give the boys for abandoning her in the car like that, scaring her crazy like that. You don't just do that to someone, she was going to say. You don't just leave them out in the middle of a fucking swamp like that, assholes.

But then she saw them.

She saw the white boy first, the boy she'd been dancing with. The flashlight was right on him, right on his face. He was kneeling in the shallow swampwater with his head hanging down and his hands clasped together in front of him. Serena didn't understand what she was looking at for a second, but then she did. Because then she saw Jamal. The flashlight touched him, too. He was standing right behind the white boy. His arm was lifted straight out. He was pointing a gun at the back of the white boy's head.

The other four boys were all around, shadows hulking on every side of the kneeling boy—like forest ogres, Serena thought—with the quarter moon looking down on them through the silhouetted branches. The water came up over the boys' shins. Serena could hear them slosh as they moved. And she could see that one of them—she didn't know which one—had a knife. A big, horrible hunting knife. He kept jabbing it at the white boy's clasped hands and his face. The silvery blade would flick into the light, gleaming, and then dart back into the darkness.

Serena gasped—and then she clapped her hands over her mouth to keep the sound in so they wouldn't hear her. The frogs were so loud—there were so many millions of frogs and their belches were so constant, so incredibly loud—that she hoped they covered any noise she might make. But she could hear the voices of the boys, their low, murmuring voices and the sloshing sounds they made when they moved. They seemed almost to be part of the swamp noises, like the million frogs.

"You think you did something? You think you gave us trouble? We didn't even lose a wink of sleep," Jamal said. He was trying to sound high and sneering, Serena thought, but she could hear him choking back his rage. "You didn't do anything, and now look at you."

The white boy didn't answer. He kept his hands clasped in front of him. His eyes were closed and his lips were moving. He was praying, Serena thought. She could see his hands twisting together fretfully. His whole body was shivering.

"Fuck you—tell me!" Jamal yelled suddenly. The rage was suddenly thick and ragged in his voice.

The kneeling boy went on praying silently. Jamal growled and whacked him with the gun. He whipped the barrel across the kneeling boy's head. It made a ripe, hollow sound. The boy grunted and tilted over, splashing as he reached down into the water to brace himself against a fall.

Serena wanted to cry out. She wanted to scream at them, *Stop it! Stop it! What are you doing to him?* But she was so scared, it felt as if the fear had dissolved all the energy inside her, all the will. She couldn't scream. She couldn't do anything but stand there and stare with her hands pressed to her mouth.

And then Jamal said, "Do it," and they killed him—they killed the white boy as he leaned over with his hand in the swampwater. The boy with the knife grabbed the white boy's short blond hair, yanked his head up, and drove the hunting knife into his throat with terrible force. He ripped the blade to the side, dragging it free. Serena saw pieces of the white boy fly out into the air through the flashlight's glow. She saw black blood gout from him and splatter in the water. The white boy made a sick, gurgling sound. The boy with the knife flung the white boy aside, and the white boy pitched face-first into the water with a splash. The million frogs went silent. Everything was silent all around them. There was only the sound of the white boy convulsing and thrashing in the water. The water flew up, drops winking silver in the moonlit night. Then the boy subsided and sank down so that only the ballooning back of his shirt showed at the surface. The other boys hulked over the sunken body like forest ogres. The million frogs began to belch and croak and mutter again. The quarter moon went on watching through the branches. The phantom trees stood guard.

A moment before, Serena couldn't scream. Now the scream was forced out of her. She shuddered and bent forward with the thrust of it rising from her belly. She hugged her belly and the scream came retching out. Only at the last second did she cut the sound off, fight it down, but still, a high syllable of it broke out of her, out of her open mouth.

The boys heard it. They froze where they were standing shin-deep in the swamp. They cocked their heads, listening.

"Shit!" said the boy with the knife. "What was that?"

The boy with the flashlight jabbed it in the direction of the road. The beam cut through the trees and landed about ten feet to Serena's left. The boy started panning the light toward her. Serena could only stand there rigid and bent, clutching her middle, holding in her scream.

Run! she thought. And she *did* run. She broke out of her stance and tore up the dirt road with her arms flailing. She didn't know if the flashlight reached her. She didn't know if the boys saw her. She just ran with the breath hot and harsh in her throat and the hot, harsh tears streaming down her cheeks—ran until she reached the Caddy and grabbed the door, which was not quite shut, and yanked it open and hurled herself inside.

She pulled the door closed quick as she could to kill the top-light. She pulled it shut as quietly as she could. She sat in the backseat staring wildly through the windshield. She could feel her tears. She could hear her hitching, high-pitched sobs.

A second passed—and then she saw the flashlight beam. It was coming out of the swamp, moving toward the road. All the boys were coming up out of the water.

Serena dropped down onto the backseat. Quickly, she swiped the tears from her eyes. She curled up into the position she'd been in when she first came awake. She clutched her hands in front of her mouth. She couldn't stop trembling. She couldn't stop whimpering.

A twig snapped. She could hear the boys approaching the car. She could hear their voices.

She heard one of them say, "If she saw us, dude, we gotta do her. I mean, that's all."

Then they were at the window. She could hear their voices right above her. She knew they were looking down at her through the glass.

"She's still out." That was Jamal.

"I don't know. I heard something."

"So did I."

"Fucking kidding me?" Jamal said. "There's, like, a million fucking creatures and fuck-knows-what out here. It could've been anything. Probably, like, a bird or something."

"Could've been a bird. Kinda sounded like a bird, I thought."

"Listen to this shit," Jamal said. "It was probably just some fucking thing got freaked."

"I don't know. I mean, if she saw something . . ."

Serena lay curled on her side, listening to them. She was so scared, it seemed impossible she wouldn't tremble or cry and give herself away. With all her will, she made her body another thing from herself, a dead thing. She huddled deep inside her body as if she were hiding in it, as if she were some sort of worm hiding inside a big body-shaped shell. Inside the shell, she was trembling and whimpering and crying, but outside, her body was another thing from her, and lay so still it could've been a corpse. Even her tears had stopped falling.

"Look at her. She's dead to the world," said Jamal. "You saw her. She was so fucking drunk. She'll be passed out for hours."

"I always thought we should just fucking do her, just to be sure."

"Shut the fuck up!" Jamal hissed. "You want her to hear you?"

The other guy's voice dropped to a whisper. "I thought you said she was dead to the world."

"Come here, asshole."

Serena heard footsteps on pebbles and dirt as the boys moved away from the car. They went on speaking in lowered voices. She had to strain to hear them, but she could still make out most of what they were saying.

"We have a plan," said Jamal. "The plan's the plan."

"Yeah, but we were supposed to lose her before we did anything. That was the plan."

"It's *still* the plan. Only she passed out, that's all. It's the same thing. The plan was only him. He's taken care of. There's a whole story about him so no one will . . . you know: come around, come looking. People would look for her. The cops would look for her. That's a whole different thing. That's not the plan."

Another boy spoke. "What if the cops, y'know, like, interrogate her—whatever?"

And another boy: "Right. What if she goes to the cops? I mean, if she saw something on TV about this or something . . ."

There was a pause—as if Jamal was thinking it over, deciding whether the other boys were right or not, whether he should kill her or not. Serena, lying curled on the seat of the car, was startled by a small squeaking noise. After a second, she realized it was coming out of her own mouth. She forced herself back down, deeper away from the surface of her body. She lay in darkness there, waiting for Jamal to decide.

"Nah," Jamal said finally. "It's the same as before. It's the same plan. If she goes to the police, we'll know. She can't go to them without us knowing. We'll take care of her then, if we have to. For now, it's the same as before."

"Except she was here. That's not the same."

"She's dead to the world," said Jamal.

"Not dead enough for me," muttered another boy.

Another boy laughed.

"Fucking clowns!" said Jamal, and he laughed, too. "Get in the car. Let's get the fuck outta here."

There were footsteps again. The doors of the green Cadillac opened, and the boys piled in. Three got in front, and two got in back with Serena. They shoved her legs roughly off the seat to make room.

"Drunken skank. Get out of the way," one of them said.

She groaned as if she'd been asleep and sat up reluctantly.

"Where are we?" she murmured sleepily.

"Nowhere," said the boy next to her. "You're crunked. Just keep sleeping it off."

Serena stole a peek at him through half-closed eyes. It was the boy with the knife, the boy who had cut the white boy's throat. She could feel his haunch against her haunch, his arm against her arm. She could smell the musty boy-smell of him, a sweat smell now, and the dank smell of jeans wet with swampwater.

She laid her head against the window and pretended to go to sleep.

The engine started. The car backed over the dirt road. Serena laid against the door in a misery of fear, smelling the smell of them, feeling the touch of the boy who had cut the white boy's throat.

Somebody turned on the radio. There were drums like the footsteps of a giant running after her and a street-black voice like a machine gun threatening machine-gun violence in rhyme.

They drove with the music blaring all the long way back to the city.

10 · The Road to Disaster

For a long time after Serena finished talking, I couldn't answer a word. I sat at the kitchen table and looked at her—that's all. I tried to appear calm. I kept my hands folded on the tabletop. I kept my expression more or less impassive, maybe a little fatherly, a little stern. I showed her nothing of what was inside me: the smothering awareness of catastrophe, my sense that the walls of catastrophe were closing in on me while my mind scrabbled like a rat looking for the exit.

I kept picturing that boy, the white boy, his throat cut, his blood spewing into the moonlight, his body flopping in the swampwater. This was bad stuff. Big trouble. For her and for me, too. This was going to mean cops and courtrooms and killers with a grudge and maybe even jail time for Serena somewhere down the line. There'd be media, investigations, people digging into my past, people talking about my past in newspapers, on television. Cathy would wonder why I hadn't told her I was coming to see Lauren. The kids would hear that Serena was their half sister. The kids would hear all kinds of things, and my neighbors would hear. I could feel the walls of it closing in, and my mind was scrabbling for a way out. But I sat there, trying to look calm.

"All right," I said after a while. I spoke slowly, carefully, thinking it through. "The first thing we have to do is go talk to your mother."

Serena's eyes went wide, her mouth went wide. An enormous whine broke from her: "Why?"

"Because she's your mother, Serena."

"So what? It's not like she cares about me."

"She cares about you, and the two of you are going to have to decide what to do about this. Now come on. Get your stuff and let's go."

"But they'll know," she whined—as if I were forcing her to go to school with a bad haircut. "Jamal and the rest. They'll know where I am."

"Sweetheart," I said. "You've been wandering around the same clubs as always, drunk out of your mind—"

"I'll stop. I won't drink anymore. I promise."

"Well, that would be a good idea. But the fact remains: I found you. *They* can find you. So we're gonna go home and talk to your mother and figure out what to do. Now get your stuff."

All this I pronounced with fatherly calm and fatherly demeanor and authority, but my heart was sour with anxiety and I felt the walls closing in.

Dragging her heels and making that peculiarly ugly grimace teens reserve to express the illimitable vastness of their disgust with an unfair, hypocritical, and cruel adult world, Serena slouched back to the bathroom to prepare herself for the journey home.

Meanwhile, I phoned Lauren. Finally she answered. She sounded harried. "What?"

"Where the hell were you last night?" I said.

"I was out, Jason. All right? People go out sometimes."

"Well, I have Serena."

"I know. I got your message. That's great. I really, really appreciate it. Can you keep her till I'm finished working? I'll come pick her up on the way home."

"No," I said. "I'm bringing her over now."

"There won't be anyone here now, Jason. I have to go to work. Guess what: Not everyone's rich. Y'know?"

I remembered how she begged me to help her. *I'm scared. I can't sleep at night.* All that. I was glad she was on the phone just then, that she wasn't in the room with me. I'm an old-fashioned man in a lot of ways. I don't believe in hitting women. But frankly, I find the only way to avoid hitting women is to avoid women who need to be hit. Right then, Lauren needed a smack in the face, maybe a couple of them. I was itching to give them to her, so I was glad she wasn't in the room.

I spoke through a throat tight with anger. "I'm bringing her over. If you're not there, I'm bringing her to your office."

"You don't even know where my office is." Taunting me, she sounded just like her daughter.

So I treated her like her daughter. "You're a paralegal at Watson and Mantle. I'll bring her there."

That shut her up. It felt good to shut her up. Not as good as hitting her would've felt, but good.

"So you want me to get fired?" she said finally. "I need this job, Jason."

"Your daughter's in trouble, Lauren," I said. "I mean, real trouble—as in, you're gonna need to call the cops and get the lawyers you work for to help you. So look, I'm bringing her to your house or I'm bringing her to your office. Which is it gonna be?"

There was another pause on her end of the line. Then she said, "Shit. Shit! You are such a self-righteous asshole!"

"Yes, I am. And I'll be there in half an hour." I ended the call.

Serena took a long time in the bathroom. When she was done, I ushered her out to the red Mustang. I drove for the expressway.

We didn't try to make conversation. Serena huddled in her bucket seat, in her rumpled pink party dress. She pouted and stewed, sneering out the window. I sneered out the windshield, working the wheel. I was well pissed off by now. Pissed off at Lauren, pissed off at myself. I was furious at that helpless feeling of catastrophe closing in—cops and courts and killers—and my mind scrabbling like a rat, looking for a way out.

Ruefully, I remembered evenings sitting on my patio, on the patio of my house on the Hill. I remembered sitting with my wife whom I loved, watching my children, whom I likewise loved, playing in the grass. Everything was pretty much A-OK back then. What was it? Three days ago? I had money in the bank and a cheerful spouse who brought me lemonade and happy kids who got good grades in school and were eager to do well in the world. And when I thought back to those bygone times, I could remember how once or twice, my wife and I, gossiping together the way couples do, would sit on the patio and talk about some friends or neighbors who had gone down the Road to Disaster. We couldn't help but notice, at those times, that their turn onto the Road to Disaster was always very clearly marked. It was always very obvious what they had done wrong. Maybe they'd spent too much money or neglected their children or cheated on their spouses or become addicted to drugs or alcohol. Whatever it was, it was never anything subtle; it was always very plain what had led them down the Road to Disaster. Sometimes it even happened that these friends or neighbors would come to Cathy and me at some point and ask us for our advice. "We are heading down the Road to Disaster," they would say. "What can we do to avoid the Disaster at the end?" And Cathy and I would answer, "Stop. Stop going down that road. Stop cheating on your wife or spending too much money or neglecting your children or drinking. Turn around and go back and go down another road instead." And every time—every single time—they would say to us, "Oh, no. Oh, no, we can't do that. We can do anything else, but we can't go down another road. We have many good and sound and necessary reasons why we must go down the Road to Disaster. Therefore give us some other advice. Give us some advice that will make the Road to Disaster end somewhere other than in the Disaster to which it inevitably leads." It was the strangest thing, but that's what they would say. Then, when they reached the Disaster at the end of the road, when it loomed like a brick wall in front of them, and they struck it with a devastating crash that left everything they cherished in ruins, my wife and I would sit on the patio together and shake our heads and say to each other, "Why didn't they stop? Why didn't they turn around and go down another road?" We would talk like that, you know, in that way you do, as if you're sorry for your friends, and maybe you are sorry, but you can't help blaming them a little, too, and you're even secretly satisfied that it happened to them and not to you, that you are the sort of person who doesn't go down the Road to Disaster, who goes down a different road instead.

These conversations with my wife on the patio came back to me now and it was a bitter business. Because here I was, sure enough, hurtling along the Road to Disaster myself, and I had many good and sound and necessary reasons why I couldn't stop, why I couldn't turn around—Serena might be my daughter, Serena needed my help, Lauren had neither the money nor the common sense to do what was necessary—and at the same time it was as obvious as it could possibly be that I was a raging fool to be here, that I'd been a fool every stupid step of the way. Why had I agreed to go see Lauren in the first place? Why had I let her talk me into finding Serena? Why hadn't I told my wife what I was doing so we could discuss it, so I'd have someone on my side when things went wrong? What was your problem? I asked myself angrily. Was the good life too boring for you? Was it the idea of adventure that drew you away from your patio on the Hill or the fantasy that you might have sex with an old girlfriend or the need to show her what a big, solid, responsible man you'd become by rescuing her from her fucked-up existence, by fixing everything for her? Jesus in his Heaven, boy, are there ever going to be ten solid seconds between the cradle and the fucking grave when you aren't governed by vanity or greed or your heat-seeking dick?

So I drove on, past the car dealerships and gas stations. Turning onto the expressway service road away from the sun and into the bright blue sky. It was late morning. The rush was over. The traffic was breaking up, moving fast. I hit the entry ramp and gunned the engine just to blow some of the frustration out of my system. The Mustang sliced into the stream of cars, and melded with it. We headed toward Queens.

I stole a glance at Serena as I settled in at speed. The sight of her small and sullen there against the window made me hurt inside. God, I hoped to hell she wasn't mine. In my heart, I knew she was, but I hoped to hell she wasn't. I hated to think I had fathered a child and left her alone to this: this life, this trouble. It was more trouble than she knew, I think. I think she probably expected she could cajole and stomp her feet and whine, and it would all go away. But I knew it wouldn't, and I hurt for her.

She sat up suddenly.

"Shit, there they are!" she said. Flashing her face at me, then back at the window, pressing against the glass, looking into the sideview mirror. "They're following us."

I lifted my eyes to the rearview and saw the green Cadillac on my tail.

It was in the center lane, about three cars back. A 1970s Coupe de Ville, that old galumphing monster they called The Tank. Long and sleek from the side and broad across, with a great big angry grille up front like a shark coming at you. The sight of it got to me—as if the thing had leaped alive out of Serena's story, out of the scene at the swamp with the darkness and the frogs croaking and the boy thrashing and dying in the water. I had pictured it all in my mind as she was telling it, and now here it was, real as life on the highway behind me. It made the thing seem inevitable somehow, connected to my own imagination, impossible to shake.

"What are you gonna do?" said Serena. "Don't lead them back to my house, okay? Go somewhere else."

I stepped down on the gas. I pulled into the left lane, passed a car or two, and drew back over to the right. I watched the Caddy in the rearview to see how it would respond. The driver stayed cool, stayed back. He waited for the Toyota in front of him to slide out of his way. Then he moved up naturally, closing the gap between us. As if he was just rolling along the highway, not bothering anyone.

"Are you sure it's them?" I said.

"Yes! Yes! Definitely! I know the car."

Another car, a Volks Passat, cleared out of the Caddy's way. The green monster pressed ahead again, getting closer. Three cars back, same as before.

"Damn it," I said.

I watched it in the rearview. As far as I could tell, there was only one man in the wide front seat, only the driver. If there were others in the back, I couldn't make them out. I couldn't make out the license plate, either. It was too far away and—maybe intentionally, maybe not—it was dark with dirt so the numbers were obscure.

I looked up ahead and around. Where the hell were we? I saw a golf course, a couple of weathered white apartment buildings, a mall at the edge of the highway, a flat gray wasteland of a town petering out in the distance beyond.

"I'm gonna pull off," I said. "If he follows me, then I'll be sure. Then I'll have to call the cops."

I expected Serena to object, but she didn't. I shot a look at her. She was staring eagerly straight ahead. I knew the cops scared her, but it seemed these guys scared her even more. Well, they scared me, too. I didn't want to go to the police yet, either—not without Lauren, and not before Serena had herself a lawyer. But assuming these were our friends from the swamp, I wasn't going to tangle with them alone.

I saw an exit up ahead. I glided out of the stream of traffic, slowing on the ramp. My eyes flicked to the rearview as I pulled to the stop sign at the corner. I couldn't see much of the freeway from there. I couldn't see whether the Caddy kept going or not. But it must have—I figured it must have. I waited at the sign for several seconds. No one came off the expressway after me.

I breathed a sigh of relief. "I think they're gone," I said.

"Maybe we should pull over and wait, you know," she said. "Wait and see if they show up again."

I turned the corner and went down the street. It was a street of small houses, clapboard-and-shingle two-stories with peaked roofs and porches out front. It was one of those sad streets that must've been all right in the old days, before the highway came, before the traffic got to be what it was. People must've scrimped and saved to live in these homes back then. But now the paint was chipped on the clapboards and on the porch columns and some of the shingles had fallen and the lawns were shaggy and pocked with patches of brown. The only person in sight was a shapeless old lady in a shapeless blue dress. She shuffled along the sidewalk, bent over her cane, not going much of anywhere, I thought, just going, just about gone.

There were scraggly plane trees on either side of me. The sun came through their branches on my right. I rolled over the dead yellow leaves on the street beneath them. I heard them crunching under my tires.

There was another stop sign up ahead, and I saw what looked to be a broad boulevard about three blocks beyond that. I figured

I'd head up there, put some gas in the car, make sure there was no one after me before continuing on. I slowed to a stop at the sign.

Then—without warning, without a word—Serena leapt out of the car.

It took me completely by surprise. A foolish-sounding half-syllable of protest came up my throat. The next second, the Mustang's door slammed. She took off running.

"Damn it!" I said.

I glanced in the rearview mirror. I saw her racing like hell up the middle of the street, her arms flailing on either side of her. She was gripping her purse in her left hand and her shoes, too. She couldn't run in those pointy little heels, so she'd slipped them off in advance. Son of a bitch! She'd been planning her getaway the whole time!

I pushed my door open. She wasn't going very fast. I was pretty sure I could run her down if I had to. I stepped out into the street.

I remember, for some reason, that when I felt the autumn air and smelled the leaves and got a long view of the road with its porched houses and its lawns and saw the dead leaves blowing over the pavement in a light breeze and heard the rattle of them rising under the whoosh and rumble of the traffic—I remember a pang of loneliness and nostalgia hit me, as if I could feel the dreamless lives of the people who lived here, their loss and disappointment.

I shouted, "Serena!"

She didn't stop. She just kept running down the middle of the street, her pink dress sparkling, then growing dim as she passed through patches of sun and patches of shadow.

I was about to go after her. But just at that moment, the green Coupe de Ville came tearing around the corner.

I heard a screech of tires, and there it was. It came from the right as if it had continued on the highway to the next exit, then doubled back. It came at speed, swerving into the glare of sunlight and bursting ahead on a straight course at the running Serena.

I shouted again. "Watch out!" But there was no time to move, no time to think. I just stood there as Serena ran flailing toward the gleaming teeth of the monster's grille, as the grille plowed at her with a grinding roar. I just stood and watched and waited for the moment of impact.

There was no impact. Suddenly the car stopped with a jolt. Serena never slowed. She kept on running, ran right around the big tank's headlight. The Cadillac's passenger door flew open. Serena clambered into the wide front seat. The car started moving again, was moving even as she pulled the door shut behind her.

It was a rendezvous. She had known they would come for her. She had been waiting for them to rescue her from me.

Now, already, as the car started toward me again, my astonishment and fear were beginning to morph into something else. I felt a poisoned emptiness inside me. I realized I had been betrayed. I realized I had been lied to. It was humiliating. Even as I stood there gaping, I wondered: Was anything she'd told me true? Had I been fooled completely?

In the next second, the big green car rushed past me. I saw Serena inside as it went by. Her face was pressed to the window, twisted in a vulgar sneer. Her hand was held up beside her cheek. Her middle finger was stuck up in the air, stuck up at me.

Then the car streaked away under the yellowing plane trees, through the slanting beams of sunlight and past the faded houses and their scraggly lawns. With another scream of rubber and road, its great, sleek body careened around the corner, blasting across the path of the shapeless old lady in her shapeless blue dress.

And she—she just kept shuffling forward along the sidewalk, slowly, slowly approaching the whirlwind of dust and yellow leaves that lingered in the autumn air after the Cadillac was gone.

11 · The Real World

"So where is she?" said Lauren.

I was standing on the stoop of her row house. She was in the doorway, peering around me, looking for Serena.

"She ran away," I said, and brusquely stepped past her into the house.

I caught a glimpse of myself in the mirror above the mantelpiece in the living room. I looked angry. I was. At this point, it felt good to be angry. It felt better, anyway, than my other feeling—my feeling that Serena had made a jackass out of me.

I sat on the sofa. I told Lauren what had happened. She sat in a wooden chair beside the fireplace, smoking one Kent after another from the box on the lamp stand while she listened. A couple of times as I talked, she laughed out of the side of her mouth or shook her head. A couple of times, she made that exasperated, disdainful sound of hers—*Pah!*—with the smoke blowing out on the breath of it.

She was wearing the same kind of get-up as before, the sweater and skirt that made her look fleshy and ungainly. Her coarsened, bloated face and those damp, fierce, cynical eyes—so different from the way she looked when I first knew her—still came as a shock to me every time I looked at her.

"I guess she must've called these punks while she was in the bathroom," I said. "She must've gotten the address off the realty flyer and told them where we were. She was just waiting for me to pull over and stop somewhere, so she could jump out and run off with them. I probably should've just stuck to the expressway and called the cops from the car."

Lauren snorted, her elbow on the chair arm, the cigarette held straight up beside her ear. "That's my baby girl."

"Do you think it was bullshit top to bottom?" I asked her. "The whole story? The murder in the swamp, and so on. You figure it was all lies?"

Pah! "A true word out of that kid's mouth would die of loneliness. She's a born liar. I was there. I know." When I shrugged glumly, she gave me a shrewd once-over. "She really got you, didn't she?"

I hesitated. My instinct was to stop talking. There were all these doubts and suspicions still swirling around in my brain, but my instinct was: Leave them alone. See, to be honest, as humiliated as I felt, this wasn't really a bad situation for me. The way things were, I could just tell myself that Serena's story was a pack of lies, and I'd be finished here. No cops, no courts, no killers. Nothing more for me to do. Just head back to Long Island, put my mother's house on the market, then fly home to hearth and family and never see these people ever again.

But somehow that didn't work for me. Somehow I felt compelled to go on.

"It just bothers me," I said. "Her story was so detailed, there were so many specifics. The way it looked, the way it sounded. Not the kind of things a girl like Serena could just make up. It's hard for me to believe it was all just an out-and-out lie."

"Yeah, I know, she's good at that." Lauren waved the whole incident away with a casual gesture of her cigarette—a gesture so blithe and self-assured and unconcerned it made me want to knock her out of her chair ass over teakettle. "Kids. They're always fucking with your head one way or another. What can you do?"

I could hear my voice begin to take that ultracalm patriarchal tone it gets when I begin to become enraged. "Maybe you're right. But, just as a suggestion, it might not be a bad idea to look into it a little further, make sure she's not in any real danger."

"What do you want me to do, Jason? Call the FBI?"

"No, but . . . Does she have a computer? Does she go on any of those friend sites? MySpace or something?"

"I don't know. How the hell would I know? God, I hope not. I hear all kinds of shit goes down on those things."

"Well, you might want to check, Lauren. Find out if this guy Jamal is on her friends list—find out who she's hanging out with in general, you know."

Pah! "Are you kidding? Go into her computer? Come on, Jason. She's sixteen years old. That's practically a grown woman. I hate to even think about the kind of shit *I* was into when I was sixteen. I'm not gonna go snooping around in her computer. It's like reading her diary or something."

"Okay," I said—and my voice grew even more calm, even more patriarchal as I grew more enraged. "If that's the way you feel. But when you called me originally, you sounded kind of concerned about her."

"I *am* concerned about her."

"You told me you were so scared for her, you couldn't sleep."

She made that blithe gesture with her cigarette again, that gesture that made me want to knock her down. "Sure, 'cause at that point, I thought she could be dead or something. I mean, she just vanished on me. She could've been in the hospital for all I knew. I mean, look, I'm sorry she took you on this whole wild-goose chase and everything, hurt your pride or whatever, but at least now I know she's safe. You did a good thing. I appreciate it, Jason, really."

I had to draw a deep breath to keep that voice going, that calm fatherly voice that disguised my fury. "You feel pretty sure she's safe, then."

"Oh, yeah," said Lauren. "Yeah, look—she's with a guy. She found some guy she wants to be with, and she's having that experience. That's all. I did the same thing when I was her age. He'll tell her she's special while he bangs her for a while, then, about three months or whatever, it'll suddenly occur to him that other girls have exactly the same thing between their legs that she's got between hers, and she'll be all, 'I thought I was special,' and he'll be all, 'Yeah, no, what I meant was you were a convenient warm, fuzzy hole for me to stick my dick in,' and she'll be all, like, 'Boo hoo hoo,' and she'll come home and sleep with her teddy bear in her own little bed and everything'll be back to normal."

The gospels tell us to withhold judgment on other people's sins. I believe in that. But I'm not very good at doing it. I am pretty good at pretending to do it, though, so I sat there listening to this irresponsible horseshit Lauren was spewing with what I hoped was a more-or-less uncritical expression pasted on my face. Here, meanwhile, is the speech I was not making, the speech that I was making in my head and that I would go on making, revising and refining furiously for an hour or so after I left her:

Listen, you bitch, you coarse, ugly, reckless excuse for a bitch, I don't know whose husband you were out fucking last night while I was watching your daughter vomit pills and liquor into my toilet bowl, but maybe you ought to start paying attention to her because, one way or another, this child is in trouble, and it's your fault—yours. She needed a father and she needed a family and she needed a mother with half a mustard seed of moral sense and you gave her none of those things and now she's miserable and lost and poisoning herself and dressing and acting like a common whore and maybe she's even in danger and it's not just 'kids today' and it's not just 'boys and girls together' and it's not just the way things

*are—it's you, your fault, your responsibility, you bitch, bitch, ugly,
vulgar, irresponsible bitch.*

"All right," I said quietly in that ultracalm voice of mine, that
voice of the All-Father of the Fallen World. I stood up. "All right,
then I guess there's nothing else for me to do."

Lauren threw herself back against her chair and laughed.

"Oh ho ho! Oh! Jason! Jason! I mean, fuh-uk you!"

She had heard the whole thing, of course: the speech I hadn't
made, the thoughts I hadn't spoken; she had heard all of it.

"Why don't you just hit me?" she said, laughing. "Huh? Go
on, sweetheart, you want to, don't you? Go ahead. Like you used
to. I dug it. Give me a good one, right here."

She pointed her cigarette hand to a spot on her jaw. I won't say
I wasn't tempted.

"I'll see you around, Lauren," the calm All-Father said. "Have
a nice life."

"Oh, you fucking hypocrite." She jabbed her cigarette into the
ashtray, one time. It lay there bent and smoking. She stood up,
walking ahead of me, blocking my path to the door, not laughing
now. "Don't give me that You're-a-Bad-Girl face, that judgmental
shit. Mr. Big Daddy. 'Ooh, where were you last night? Ooh, you
were out having sex! You're a sinner, you'll burn in hell.' Don't
give me that shit, all right? Because I've seen you bare-assed doing shit you could get arrested for. So don't give me that."

I didn't answer. I had no answer. I settled for an imperturbable
All-Fatherly stare.

"You think this is all my fault?" Lauren went on—went on as
if I had answered, as if I didn't need to answer, as if she could read
my mind. "You're the one who left me with her, Jason, remember?
She's your daughter, too."

"Is she? She said you weren't sure."

"Yeah, because she lies, dickhead, as we learned in our last episode. Anyway, you know she's yours, you bastard. You're off in happy land with your nice home and your money and your family, and what do you give a shit? It's all my fault? Well, this is what you left behind, Jason. This is what life is like for the rest of us."

That neutral, cool, Good Father voice kept coming out of me: "That's why you really called me, isn't it?"

"Yes!"

"So I could see what's happened to you?"

"Damn right!"

"So you could blame me for it and drag me into it."

She pointed a long, witchy finger at me. "You know what you are, Jason? You're a coward. You live in some make-believe place where nothing bad ever happens and everyone's rich and married and happy like you so you can pretend that God's in Heaven watching over everyone. And anyone who's in trouble, well, it must be their own fault, right? 'Because look at me,' you think, 'I have so much money and I'm so happy, why aren't they?' You're a coward. You're just running away from reality. This is reality, Jason. This is the way things are. People get divorced and their children have problems, and you can't just go dancing around singing hymns of praise because you're so fucking rich that you don't have to deal with how fucked up everything is."

The gospels further tell us that we are liable for our hearts, not just for our actions but for the anger and lust and dishonesty hidden in our hearts. I don't think that's supposed to be some kind of moral equation or anything, as if being annoyed with someone were the same as killing him. No. I think it's an insight instead into the nature of our imaginations, into the connection between what we imagine and what we end up doing, the way our ideas and our imagination become the matrix of who we are.

Right then, for instance, for a second, for a flash, I was so furious, I imagined grabbing Lauren by the neck, forcing her over the back of her chair and sodomizing her with violent force while simultaneously whipping my open hand back and forth across the back of her head. *Go ahead. Like you used to. I dug it.* That was what was in my imagination, and it made my chest feel tight with excitement.

"Well, gee, thanks for those insights, Lauren," said the ultra-calm All-Father of the Fallen World, standing there face to face with her, my expression lofty while I imagined raping her, my gaze detached and calm. "But you know what? This"—and I gestured at her, at her apartment, at her life. "This isn't just 'the way things are.' This is the way you made them. This is the result of your choices, your actions. Yours. You don't live in 'the real world,' Lauren. You live in the world you made for yourself. I made different choices, so I live in a different world—that's all—but it's just as real. Instead of worrying about me and screaming at me and blaming me for everything and trying to bring me down to your level, it might be a good idea if you took care of yourself and your daughter. She needs you. She needs something, anyway and, the sad truth is, you're all she's got."

She tried to stand in front of me but I shouldered past her and she staggered back. She screamed at me—really screamed at the top of her lungs as I headed for the door: "She's your daughter, too! You coward! Hypocrite! She's your daughter, too, Jason! Fuck you! Go back to your wife! Maybe get her to get your freak on for a change, stop you from being such a tight-assed asshole! You shit!"

This—and more like it—was still going on when I left the house and shut the door behind me.

12 · The Spiral Notebooks

So. We find me next in the driveway of my mother's house. Yes, that's me there in the red Mustang, my forehead pressed against the steering wheel. I was still going over that speech in my mind. *You bitch, bitch, ugly, vulgar, irresponsible bitch* and so on. Fine-tuning it, adding a few choice sentiments here and there, polishing its style—and using it to feed my rage, to nurse my self-righteousness and my rage which, like drugs to an addict, no longer felt even good but merely desperately necessary. Without them, without my anger at Lauren, my feeling of moral superiority to her, what was there? There was just the girl, just Serena, lost out in the world. Okay, maybe there hadn't been any execution-style murder in the swamp. Maybe all that was lies—probably it was. Probably she got the whole story off some TV show or something. Still, the simple truth was bad enough without that. A sixteen-year-old child, a fatherless child with a feckless mother, was in the process of poisoning herself with drugs and booze and sex as if her body and soul were two different things. And she was my daughter—my daughter, whom I'd left behind and whom—let's face it—I was going to leave behind now again when I went home to the Hill. *You bitch, bitch, ugly, vulgar, irresponsible bitch.*

I got out of the car. I slammed the door. I walked up the path to the house, shaking my head, muttering under my breath.

Inside, I went to the kitchen. The phone was there, and an answering machine. There was a message on the machine from the

Realtor, a woman named Mitzi. She wanted to know if the house had been cleaned out yet, if she could have the stagers come over to get it ready for showing. While the message played, I stood at the kitchen window. I looked through the glass at the bright day nearing noon. I breathed the fresh autumn air with the smell of leaves in it. That ache of nostalgia came back to me and so did the image of my mother as she once had been: sitting in the backyard, gently wondering at things; sitting cross-legged in the grass with me climbing over her as if she were a feature of the landscape . . .

Oh, stop, I thought. The self-pity and the rage. As if I were a child again. As if the act of coming home had turned me back into a child.

I needed to get out of here—that's what. I needed to finish my business and go back to my wife and kids. I would tell Cathy what had happened, and she would help me figure out what to do next. Maybe we could send Serena some money or start a college fund for her or something. In the meantime, I had my own family to care for and my own life to think about. I needed to finish up my business here and go.

I returned to the front hall. I looked up the stairs. The stairs rose into the haunted shadows on the second floor. I climbed the stairs into the shadows.

My mother's bedroom had been dusted and aired by my cleaning lady once a week every week of the eight months since Mom had died. At this point, the scent of her, the scent of my mother, could have been nothing but a visceral memory. Still, there it was as I stepped into the unlit room. There it was—and it made me half afraid that I would see her in the half dark, see the shape of her on the bed before I turned the lights on. I turned the lights on quickly, my fingers fumbling at the double switch.

The room was large and simple, sparsely furnished. The carpet was an indistinct tan and the walls a muted yellow with white trim around the windows and wainscoting. My mother's bed—my parents' double bed with its elegantly curving headboard—was against the wall to my left. On the wall across from it, there was a dresser with a mirror. The windows were on the wall opposite me. They looked out on the backyard, but all I could see through them from where I stood were tangles of gray branches and a few yellow leaves shuddering in the wind.

That scent of her, the smell of the room, the smell, I mean, that I must've remembered, was the smell of her sickness and her later age. Closed up, dried up; the musty aroma of slack flesh without the juice of life in it, plus a faint trace of perfume, a faint, poignant dab of it. Lost and baffled in her loony inner world, she clung desperately to what habits of womanhood she could.

I smelled all that, or thought I did. And even with the lights on, I could almost see her lying there. I could almost feel her dry fingers urgent on my wrist and hear her urgent whisper. *Soon. You have to be ready. You have to see and prepare the way. Language . . . that hides it, hides the spiral, the spiraling cycle. Do you see? Watch the Jews. They have the book. The faces of God in the spiral, in the rise and fall. It's always the Jews; that's where God comes into history, where he'll come again. To relive the pattern. You see? To take the spiral into himself. We'll have to protect the Jews. Watch for that. Prepare the way.*

The breeze went through the branches at the window. The branches chattered against the glass. I could almost swear I heard her trying, trying, trying to explain.

The trapdoor was in the clothes closet. It was a long closet with several sets of folding doors that nearly took up the length of one wall. For the longest time, I never even knew the trapdoor was there. Then one day, when I was in fifth grade, I think, I came home from school excited. I'd gotten a good grade on a story I'd written. I wanted to tell my mother. I went through the house calling her. Finally I ran upstairs. I found the bedroom empty and was turning around to go, when I heard a noise—the clack of the folding door. I turned back and suddenly she was there—standing there, paper pale, with her eyes liquid and dazy, but still very tender to me, very beautiful to me in her tenderness. She was closing the door with one white hand, so I deduced she'd come from inside the closet. When I asked her about it, she murmured something vague and changed the subject. I became curious.

One day, not long after, while my father was at work and Mom was in the basement doing laundry, I snuck back into the bedroom. I went into the closet and pushed Mom's dresses aside, thinking—I don't know what—that I would find some secret stash of something hidden behind them or some secret passage, maybe. There was nothing—just shelves of shoes and sweaters—nothing special. I was about to give up and leave. Then my fingertips brushed a muslin blouse hanging from the clothes rod. Such intimate contact with so feminine a thing sent a zippy little frisson through my little-boy brain. My eyes rose up to look at it—and I spied the outline of the trapdoor in the ceiling above.

But it was another long time—months—before I went up into the attic. Partly this was because I hadn't found the pole yet and had no idea how I would get the damn trapdoor open. But partly, too, I was already beginning to suspect what I'd find, something anyway of what I'd find, and I didn't want to find it.

Now, today, the closet was empty. My wife had packed up my mother's clothes shortly after the funeral and sent them to Goodwill. There were just the naked yellow walls in there and the pole leaning in one corner. I hoisted the pole to the trapdoor, fitted its hook to the small eyebolt barely visible in the ceiling. I drew the door down. A metal ladder came rattling down with it. I set the pole aside, scooped up my bags, and, clutching them in one fist, climbed up into my mother's writing room.

More than thirty years had passed since the first time I saw it, but it was much the same. A room as delicate and gentle as my mother's features, with her same gliding elegance, the gliding silent elegance of a swan. Lace curtains framed the single window. A floral rug softened the wooden floor. Pastel prints of ballerinas and meditative ladies hung on the wall beside framed photographs of my brother and me when we were little boys. The pitch of the roof brought the ceiling low, which made the space and everything in it seem somehow miniature, as if it were a room in a dollhouse. Of nothing was this more true than the writing desk that stood against one wall: a little Regency-style thing that I've learned is called a *bonheur du jour*. It had slender legs and a small surface with a raised cabinet in back, all of it dark, shiny rosewood with brass inlays. Here my mother sat in a flower-backed chair and wrote with a fountain pen, filling notebook after notebook with her ladylike hand. Even now, it was easy to place her there in my imagination. The room, as I say, was so much like her. With her gone, it was like a symbol of her, or maybe her monument. The space and the décor represented the woman I saw for so long. The notebooks—the notebooks piled up high against every wall— stood for her mad, frantic, secretly failing mind.

I picked up one of the notebooks from the top of a stack as high as my knee. There were stacks like that all around me, just as high, against every wall. I laid the book on the writing table. I opened the cardboard cover and turned the pages, glancing over them. This was one of the later books, I guess. You couldn't tell by the look of it. They all looked just the same, the neat schoolgirl hand, the delicate sketches. But her thoughts became more fragmentary over time and the first great shocks of recognition, recorded in the beginning with hurried wonder as if she was in a rush to pin them to the page before they flew away, were now repeated wearily and almost hopelessly, the prophecies of a seer grown tired and hoarse with the effort to make someone, anyone, listen.

It's all true, it's all real, it's all happening . . . The Great Culture is passing . . . The marching armies have come to spread the remnants . . . Now the eastern rival has fallen, just as I predicted . . . Just as I predicted, the barbarians are on the move . . . The wars will make strong men great . . . The need for global governance will bring down the republic . . . Empire is a phase in the life of great nations . . . the pattern that spreads the revelation of the pattern . . . When it takes the Jews under its protection—that's when He will come again . . . The man in the spiral, the spiral in the man . . . I have to make them ready. I have to prepare the way.

All this, you have to understand, was squeezed into the narrow spaces between complex charts and graphs and elaborate illustrations: Plutarchian comparisons of American personalities with personalities from Greece and Rome, Spenglerian diagrams of imperial rises and falls, biblical predictions connected by arrows to recent headlines, and delicately executed drawings of anthills and beehives and the migration patterns of birds.

Nowadays they say it's all right for men to cry, but they're liars. The world is a better place when men behave like men. All the same, if you can get through life without shedding a couple of tears here and there, you're probably not paying attention. I cried that first time I came up here certainly, the first time I read these books and understood what she'd become. I plunked myself down on the floor cross-legged and put my chin on my chest and shuddered and cried for nearly half an hour.

But I was only a boy then, barely twelve years old. I was a child and she was my mother and I'd always loved her very much.

Now, though I felt my throat tighten, though I felt pity rising in me like floodwater—pity for her and for myself and for my father caught in his trap of passion and decency—I forced the feelings aside. I went about the business of cleaning the place out.

It didn't take long. I brought the pictures down the ladder, then the rug and the curtains, finally the writing table and chair. When the room was empty of everything else, I went at the notebooks. I gathered them in armloads and dropped them—whap and splatter—through the open trapdoor into the closet below.

At last, I climbed down the ladder myself. I pushed the trapdoor shut. Armload after armload, I carried the notebooks downstairs to the living room, to the fireplace. It was a gas fire, very steady. Still, there were so many pages covered in that precise and tidy schoolgirl script.

It took hours to burn them all.

13 · The Reality Show

What happened that night in the television room almost beggars belief, but I have to tell it because it's true.

When I finished cleaning out my mother's room, I was exhausted. Even my anger at Lauren was spent. Hollow-eyed, I watched the news on TV, sitting in the dark room, chomping my way through a tasteless store-bought turkey sandwich and polishing off another half bottle of white wine. After a while, I pressed the mute button on the remote. I picked my phone up off the coffee table and called my wife.

"I cleaned out my mother's attic," I told her.

"Good," she said. "I'm glad that's done." She was getting ready for bed. Her voice sounded sleepy and soft; warm, deep, cheerful, and content. I could almost taste her good-night kiss. I could almost feel her fingertips on my shoulder blades.

On the big TV screen across the room, the wars went on silently: smoking desert cities; women wailing on their knees; soldiers patrolling the burned-out shells of houses; tangled bodies of men; the body of a child.

I watched them. I chewed my lip. I wanted to tell Cathy what was happening here, about Lauren and Serena and everything. I was trying to find the right words to start with.

"Those notebooks—my mother's notebooks," I said. "The way she saw patterns in everything, everything falling into place, everything making sense. It makes you doubt yourself, makes you doubt your own perceptions. I mean, how do you know what's logical, what fits together? It's all just a bell ringing in your brain, isn't it? If the bell gets broken, if it won't stop ringing—how do you know?"

"I guess it's all a kind of faith in the end," Cathy said sleepily. "I guess God planned it that way."

"That God. He gets up to some shenanigans, doesn't he?"

"I know I love you though," she said. "I love you more than anything, I know that."

The dark room flickered with the images on the screen: a fireball blowing out the windows of a grand hotel; a general giving a press conference; a mob in Paris burning cars.

"I love you too," I said. "Sleep well."

I laid down the phone. I picked up the remote. I turned the TV's audio on again.

I remember well the first thing I saw then. Well, sure I do. It's what got me into so much trouble later on. There was some imam on the news show now, some chubby-cheeked, baby-faced brown guy in a funny black hat, patiently explaining things to some commentator or other.

"When atheist Communism threatened to take over the world, we stood beside Christian America to defeat the atheists. Those atheists have been swallowed up by hell as they deserved." He said all this in a pleasant tone of voice, the voice of a cherubic man of wisdom making all things clear. "Now that atheism is no more, we must have a Holy War to decide the question: Which God will rule? The West's God of materialism and selfishness and licentiousness—or the true God, Allah, His name be praised?"

At the time, I just snorted and started changing channels apathetically. Buy this car. Eat this burger. Take this pill to give you an erection. Call your doctor if your erection lasts more than four hours. Blah, blah, blah.

I did pause a moment when I saw Angelica Eden. The actress, remember. The raven-haired siren who seemed to have stolen wispy Todd Bingham away from sweet-faced, and possibly pregnant, Juliette Lovesey. All of which seemed to be their way of publicizing their new movie, *The End of Civilization as We Know It*. The first film ever in holographic Real 3-D.

"I mean, look, I believe in love, you know," she was saying. "But not this idea that you're with one person till you die. I think anyone should be able to be with anyone they want to. It's really no one's business, after all."

She was wearing a black dress with a hemline that rose to the top of her thighs and a neckline that plunged nearly to the hem. She was sitting in a director's chair, smiling over at the smiling bee-stung lips of our old friend Sally Sterling. When she crossed her creamy white legs, I felt it flow through me like liquid electricity.

"Tell us about the new movie," Sally said.

"It's called *The End of Civilization as We Know It*," said Angelica large-breastedly. "Because the filmmakers really believe that it's civilization as we know it that's causing all these wars all over the place. And since we're the most so-called 'civilized' country in the world, obviously we're really the ones who are most to blame."

Man, I thought, *look at the tits on this woman!* And have I mentioned her lips? Wonderful lips, lush, scarlet. Never mind calling your doctor. Those lips looked like they could make a four-hour erection last about thirty seconds.

I drank more wine. I changed the channel and then changed the channel again, then again. Tipsy, lonely, horny, I caught myself searching for one of those late-night porno movies so I could really make a night of it.

As it turned out, I couldn't find anything quite that exciting. In fact, on all those millions of channels, I couldn't find anything worth watching at all. So I switched to the TiVo screen, to its list of prerecorded programs. And whoa!, for a second there, I felt a little amygdaloid jolt of coincidence and meaning—did I ever! Because what name was up there on the screen? That's right. Patrick Piersall! Then, oh yeah, I remembered—I'd programmed him into the machine myself.

I pressed the button to open his file. The TiVo had recorded another episode of *The Universal* and—oh, look!—there was that new reality crime show he'd been touting on the talk circuit the other evening. *Patrick Piersall's True Crime America!* I started it playing.

At first, there was just a lot of noise and graphics. Police sirens screaming, thumping music. Cop cars and grocery holdups and murder victims on stretchers flashing by in a strobic montage. Then, like a prison door slamming shut, the title card whomped down over the screen: *Patrick Piersall's True Crime America!* And then there was Piersall in the flesh—in a lot of flesh. The lithe unitarded Augustus Kane we remembered from last night was gone—way gone. In his place once again stood today's pudgy, haggard little man, his red-veined, swollen-nosed alcoholic's face capped with a toupee that made him look as if a flying squirrel had been shot out of the sky and landed dead on his scalp.

He came walking toward us portentously down a residential street in Your Town, My Town, Anytown USA. He looked at us straight in the kisser and quirked an Augustus Kane eyebrow at us. It was sad: an ironic gesture without the old irony, a meaningless habit now. Meaningless, too, was that old hesitant, syncopated speaking rhythm of his. It still made him sound as if he were plucking each word from the Tree of Wisdom, but he couldn't have been, because this is what he said:

"A quiet street. A row of houses on well-tended lawns. Happy families leading respectable lives. This is the America we like to believe in. But for the police—and for the victims of crime—the reality is very different."

"Blaaa-laaaa-laaaa-laaaaggh," I said, holding my wineglass upside down over my head and shaking it to make the last drop fall onto my tongue.

"Welcome to *Patrick Piersall's True Crime America* . . ." said Patrick Piersall.

"'The only job I could get,'" I muttered back.

". . . where we're going to explore the sudden violence, the agony, and the mystery that lurk behind these seemingly respectable facades. Tonight," he went on—and now a fresh batch of crime-related images flashed in epilepsy-inducing fashion across the huge screen—"we're going to delve into the heart of an unsolved mystery, as we examine . . . the disappearance of university student Casey Diggs."

Then—like the rolling pictures on a slot machine finally ringing up a jackpot—the flashing graphics ended with a photograph of Casey Diggs.

And I whispered, "Wha-a-at?"

My hand—the hand holding the wineglass—dropped limply into my lap. My mouth hung open in drunken surprise. Sitting slightly tilted over, I blinked one long time, then stretched my eyes wide to get a better look at the young man on the gigantic screen in front of me.

It was a family snapshot, probably. A color snapshot taken in the woods, most likely at his parents' cabin or on vacation somewhere. It showed this Casey Diggs from the hips up, standing next to the trunk of an old car. Smiling at the camera. Lifting a soda can in salute. Enlarged to that size, it was a bit unfocused, but just a bit. You could make out the details well enough.

He was tall. He had narrow shoulders, but a bit of flab pushing against his T-shirt at the beltline. He had short blond hair and hazel eyes behind rimless glasses. He had a pale, round, almost-featureless face. I mean, talk about a white man! He could've been the product of a night of love between a loaf of Wonder Bread and a bowl of Cream of Wheat. And there on his shirt—hanging around his neck and lying on his port-colored T-shirt above the raised crest of Sacred Heart High School—was a leather lanyard with one of those iron nails dangling from it, those passion nails that Christians took to wearing after they saw the film *The Passion of the Christ.*

"That's him!" I murmured.

And I admit now, I was a little drunk. Sitting slouched and woozy on the couch, my head in a fog. Still—still—it was—I was sure of it—it was him.

It was the boy Serena saw knifed to death in the Great Swamp.

He was exactly as she described him. It was as if I'd seen him myself, as if I'd been there in The Den the night that he and Serena met. It was like a bell of recognition ringing in my brain.

"Casey Diggs vanished from his apartment six weeks ago," said Patrick Piersall. "Was he a troubled youth who ran away to find himself? Or was he the victim of a terrorist conspiracy . . . and murder?"

"Good God," I whispered.

And the words of my mother's notebook came back to me and I thought: *It's all true. It's all real. It all happened.*

14 · What Happened to Casey Diggs

Danger music. Images flashed on the screen again like memories of a lifetime in the mind of a dying man. Faces screaming in protest, a domed building on a university campus, a seedy railroad flat with a soiled futon open on the floor. Then the music faded to the volume of footsteps creeping up behind you. And there—once more—was Patrick Piersall. Well, it was his True Crime America, after all.

"Casey Diggs came to Manhattan full of hope and promise, eager to begin his university career. With a 4.1 high-school GPA, he already seemed well on his way to realizing his dream of becoming a journalist."

Then there was a lot of ya-ya-ya about his childhood. Son of two Philadelphia lawyers. Educated at fine private schools. Spent a couple of summers building classrooms and houses with church groups in Kenya and Louisiana. Became a committed Christian and even wrestled with the idea of becoming a minister. In the end, he decided journalism was his vocation. He was delighted when he was accepted into a university known for one of the finest journalism departments in the country.

"But only three short months after school began," Patrick Piersall intoned, "Casey's dreams—and his life—began to unravel."

Cut to commercials. But hey, this was a recording—no need to watch that crap now. I pressed the FAST FORWARD button on the remote. Ads for laundry detergent, more of those erection pills, and an extremely fast automobile of some sort raced past in a single blur: Take-your-hard-on-for-a-drive-in-whites-that-are-really-white! Then the story of Casey Diggs continued.

Casey arrived at school in Manhattan. He applied for a position at the student newspaper, the *Clarion*. He was told that, because he was a freshman, he would have to prove himself as a stringer before being taken on staff. His first opportunity: a demonstration near the campus, students calling for the university to remove all its investments from Israel.

"What he saw at that demonstration," said Patrick Piersall, "changed his life."

Music. Angry faces. Signs with slogans. A banner: STUDENTS FOR JUSTICE.

They were a strange coalition, these Students for Justice: on the one hand, radical leftists who believed in atheistic socialism, multiculturalism, and gender neutrality; on the other, radical Muslims who believed in theocracy, sharia law, and bagging their women in burqas. You wouldn't think they could agree on anything, would you? Well, you'd be wrong. They were together in this at least: They hated the Jews. Oh, and they hated America, too. Oh, yeah, and they were absolutely certain the one secretly controlled the other.

Here was Students for Justice Vice President Ahmed Ali during the demonstration, standing at the podium, hammering his fist against the air. There was his recorded voice accompanying the photo, and the sound of the cheering crowd. "Israel is the source of all the violence in the Middle East. How could there be violence in Islam if it weren't for the Zionists? Islam means peace!"

And here, too, was assistant English Professor Willis Freedgood at the same podium. "Look at the names in the present U.S. administration. Look at the Weintraubs and the Weinbergs and the

Schwartzes. It's pretty clear who is forcing America to support the Zionist entity!" More cheering. Protest signs waving in air.

Cut to Casey's roommate, Brent Withers. Kind of a stick insect of a guy with an adenoidal voice. He spoke carefully. "As far as I know, as far as Casey told me, he didn't write his story with a political agenda or anything. At that point, I think he just wanted to make sure to get his facts straight, you know. He wanted to impress the editor so he could get a job on the newspaper."

So Casey wrote his story. He reported the speeches: Ali's and Freedgood's and several others by students and faculty both. And then he reported what happened to Vanessa Gerston.

Vanessa Gerston was a nineteen-year-old student passing by the demonstration on her way to class. She heard Freedgood's speech. She was shocked. She surprised herself by shouting at him, "But that's just bigotry! That's just anti-Semitism!"

Here was the girl herself on *True Crime America,* describing what happened next.

"As soon as I started shouting, I was suddenly surrounded by maybe five or six guys," she said. She was a plain, dark, fat-faced young woman with curly black hair. "They came in really close to me. They backed me up against this wall. And they started screaming right in my face. I was literally terrified."

"What did they scream at you?" asked Patrick Piersall, his flushed, desiccated features pressing in toward her.

"They called me a Jewish bitch. And they said—" Vanessa hesitated. Her lower lip trembled as her eyes filled. "They said I was a Jewish whore who should be raped so I could be taught a lesson." She fought down the tremor. She tried to laugh it off. "Which is almost funny, you know? Because I'm Episcopalian."

"Did you report this to the police?" Patrick Piersall asked her.

"There were two policemen standing right there!" Vanessa shot back. "I said to them, 'Aren't you going to do anything?' They told me, 'We don't want this to get out of hand.' That's what they said. Those were their exact words. But then they kind of looked at each other, and they sort of cleared a way for me. I just ran out of there as fast as I could."

Casey reported all this. He quoted the speeches word for word. He described the assault on the coed start to finish. The story ran on page three of the *Clarion* the next day. There was the issue now, flashed up on the screen with words circled in the text: MUSLIMS. SOCIALISTS. JEWS.

The reaction on campus was swift and violent. A montage:

Newspaper boxes smashed.

Newspapers burning in wastebaskets with angry students gathered around.

Protesters outside the *Clarion*'s office. Raised fists, bared teeth, angry signs:

RACISM!

ISLAMO-PHOBIA!

FASCIST PIGS!

WE WILL NOT BE SILENCED BY NAZI *CLARION*.

Professor Freedgood accused the *Clarion* of violating the university's code forbidding hate speech against minorities—Muslims, in this case. Multiculturalists throughout the various humanities departments accused the paper of misrepresenting the understandable rage of the oppressed Palestinian people. Leftists— who made up 85 percent of the faculty—simply called the story "reactionary."

So far, this was all contained within the university. It wasn't reported in the local media. There was nothing on TV about it. Nothing in the papers. But then . . .

Ah, then, Arthur Rashid issued a statement to the press.

Now Rashid, of course, was a star in the intellectual world. Among his fellow academics, he was considered a great man. A hugely popular professor of multicultural studies, he was credited with formulating the very concept of multiculturalism in his best-selling book, *Eastern Mind, Western Eyes.* He was also a frequent contributor to the *Times*'s op-ed page. The *Times Sunday Book Review* loved everything he wrote.

Here was his photo: a handsome, elegant-looking fellow with a Middle Easterner's olive skin and an Englishman's classic, chiseled features. His statement appeared over his face and Patrick Piersall read the words: "It is the nature of culture that it directs our words and actions even when we are not aware of its influence. I fully trust and believe that Mr. Diggs and the *Clarion* editors did not intend their story as an offshoot of the West's imperialist project. But equally, from my perspective, from the perspective of anyone with roots in the Middle East, how else can it be read? When any protest against Israeli actions is deemed anti-Semitic, when any attempt to give voice to the West's former colonies is cast in an ugly light, what is it but an attempt to reconquer intellectually what has been lost militarily, to crush the fragile identities of these reemergent peoples under the so-called 'civilizing' worldview of the West? I invite Mr. Diggs and his collaborators to a dialogue in the hopes of raising their awareness of the sources of their Islamo-phobic assumptions."

Well, that did it. Now the *Times* weighed in, too.

"A story in a school newspaper that was deemed offensive by some students of Middle Eastern descent has been denounced by one of the university's most famous professors."

It was typical *Times* stuff, as I now have reason to know. There were no quotes from Diggs's article. Nothing about the anti-Jewish tirades at the demonstration. Nothing about the nineteen-year-old girl terrorized and insulted and threatened with rape. They just described the *Clarion* piece as "controversial," and ran a lot of patient, conciliatory, reasonable-sounding quotes from their man Rashid. The overall effect was to make the reader assume that Casey Diggs must be some kind of hothead white supremacist.

It was only a small piece on page 3 of the Metro section, but it was enough to move the university to action.

Casey Diggs and his editor, Miriam Bach, were both called before the dean. Ms. Bach, a frog-faced woman with a Prince Valiant haircut, apologized at once. "I ran the story without reading it carefully enough," she told Patrick Piersall. "I didn't see how insensitive it was, and I have to take responsibility for that." She escaped punishment by printing a front-page apology. She also agreed to have the *Clarion* run a series of stories "celebrating the diverse cultures that make up our university." The articles included "Chador—A Source of Pride for Muslim Women" and "The Faithful Find Commercialism, Materialism Mar a Secular World."

Casey Diggs, however, did not get off so easily.

"Casey refused to apologize for telling the truth and so he was put on six months' academic probation," Piersall explained, standing before the university's bronze gates. "He was also barred from working on the paper ever again. From that point on, his life went into a downward spiral that would end . . . in mystery."

I zipped through the next batch of commercials: lower-your-cholesterol-while-eating-Cheese-Spray-on-your-crackers-and-watching-back-to-back-reruns-of-Truth-and-Justice-every-week-night. Back to the show.

Interviews. The stick-insect roommate again. Casey's disapproving older sister. His tearful mother. His square-jawed dad. All said the same: Casey changed after he was barred from the newspaper. He began drinking heavily. He frequently missed classes.

And he became obsessed with taking vengeance on Arthur Rashid.

Danger Music. A Tragic Chord. Rapid shots of the headlines on a Web site Casey founded, The Diggs Memo:

RASHID'S BOOK: INSIDIOUS ANTI-AMERICAN PROPAGANDA.

RASHID: FREEDOM, BEAUTY AND REASON A WESTERN PLOT AGAINST "THE OTHER"

RASHID: PALESTINIAN ATROCITIES "JUSTIFIED."

Casey received hate mail calling him a racist. Hackers brought the Web site down more than once. Students for Justice called for his expulsion.

"The university warned Casey that his Web site violated campus speech codes," Piersall told us, "but for a time they took no other action. Soon, however, the nature of Casey's accusations against Rashid changed dramatically."

More shots of the Web site:

RASHID HAS LINKS TO TERRORIST GROUP

GROUP CALLED "UNIVERSAL SHARIA LAW" PLANS ATTACK ON NEW YORK

SOURCES: RASHID CONTROLS USL KILLERS

"In calling Rashid a terrorist," Piersall intoned, "Casey had gone too far."

The university asked Casey to leave. There was the dean's letter to his parents: "We strongly suggest that this troubled young man be convinced to seek psychiatric care."

Now here was Piersall, back on camera, his tubby torso and dissolute features filling the wall across from me. "With his dreams in ashes, Casey's descent into alcoholism and paranoia continued. He became a shadow of his former self, drifting from place to place, relationship to relationship, bar to bar until one day . . . he just wasn't there at all."

Final commercial break: beer-will-get-you-laid-pills-will-help-you-sleep-and-you-can-wake-up-to-some-really-scrumptious-potato-chips.

During which, I was thinking: *This isn't right. I must be getting drunk and crazy here. This can't be the same guy—the guy Serena was talking about. It can't be. I mean, if he is—if he's the guy Serena danced with—if he really was murdered in the Great Swamp—then that might mean that all these paranoid things he said about Rashid might not've been paranoid at . . .*

But then the show started again.

The rest of the story was quickly told.

Here was Brad Faulkner, a law student and party guy. Casey stayed with him for a month after he was expelled. "Dude was seriously putting it away. I'm talking martinis before lunch. Clubbing every night. Dumping major E. Some days, three in the morning, he'd be sitting here on the sofa going on and on at me about how this Rashid guy was running some massive conspiracy to blow up New York. After a while I was, like, 'Dude, let him blow it up already, I gotta get some sleep.'"

FBI Special Agent Mark Sarkell: "We had several contacts from Mr. Diggs, and our investigators listened to his scenario very carefully. But after thoroughly checking the facts we were satisfied there was no credible substance to his accusations. We have no reason to believe that Mr. Rashid is a terrorist."

Casey's tearful mother: "He called me that last day. He said he didn't think he could take it anymore. He said no one believed him and the city was going to be blown up, and he couldn't stand to just sit by and watch it happen."

That was the last anyone ever heard of Casey Diggs. By then, he was living alone in a run-down railroad flat on the Lower East Side. No one saw him go out that last night. No one knew until almost a week later that he had not returned. In fact, it wasn't entirely certain what date he actually disappeared. When his mother finally called the landlord and asked him to check the apartment, there was nothing there but a fold-out futon, a table, a chair, and some milk gone bad. Even Casey's laptop computer was, like Casey himself, nowhere to be found.

More interviews. A glamour-puss private-detective lady hired by Casey's parents: "My own theory is that Casey was suffering from the beginnings of schizophrenia. He's probably living on the streets somewhere now. Worst case: Maybe he committed suicide and his body hasn't been found yet. But I still have hope."

That seemed to be the consensus. The cops, the feds, even Casey's parents seemed to believe their son had gone mad and was wandering homeless somewhere. There was only one dissenter from that point of view, in fact: the stick-insect roommate, Brent Withers.

"I think we can all agree that Casey was out of control," he told us. "He was abusing any number of substances. Acting in an erratic, irrational way. But it wasn't my impression he was delusional or anything like that. I'm not a doctor, but he didn't seem that way to me."

"You think he might've been telling the truth?" This was Patrick Piersall's voice coming from offscreen. "You think there might've actually been some kind of conspiracy?"

There was a long silence, and Withers's eyes closed and opened once in slow motion. Then he lifted his hands from his lap and let them slowly, slowly sink down again. "I wouldn't say that. I wouldn't want to say that."

Then there was Piersall for the finale, walking toward us again down that same street in Anytown True Crime USA. He came right up to the camera this time, right into our living rooms practically, his veiny nose practically protruding from the screen. His right eyebrow was jacked to the max. His syncopated delivery was amped to the point where every phrase was delivered like a punch to the head.

"Is. Casey Diggs. Still alive? Did he. Commit suicide? Run away? Or. Is there. A darker possibility? Is it possible that this troubled young man—uncovered—a conspiracy of terror? That the—threat—that everyone claimed he imagined—was, in fact, real? Is it possible—that Casey Diggs's—paranoia—wasn't—paranoia at all? And that his—attempts—to expose a—deadly—plot against the city of New York—finally—brought vengeance down—upon his own head?"

Good questions, I thought, stretching my eye sockets, trying to clear the wine out of my brain. They were damn good questions. I mean, weren't they? I mean, if Casey Diggs really was Serena's mystery man, wasn't it at least possible that her story was true? And if her story was true, wasn't it possible that Diggs was murdered out in the Great Swamp because of what he found out about this Professor Rashid?

A phone number came up on the screen.

"If you have any information concerning the whereabouts of Casey Diggs—call this toll-free number," said Patrick Piersall. "Police investigators are standing by. Your call is completely confidential."

Without thinking, I sat up straight and swept my phone off the coffee table. I called the number on the screen. Instantly, I heard a busy signal. *Boop boop boop.* It happened so fast, it sounded as if the line had been disconnected. I tried again. Got the busy signal again. Right away: *Boop boop boop.*

I ended the call. I set the phone back down on the table. I considered it there. Did I even want to do this? I wondered. Did I want to call these people? Set the police on Serena? Set the media on her? Just because Casey Diggs reminded me of the guy in a story she told me that probably wasn't even true in the first place?

I mean, sure, if there really was a terrorist plot . . . If there'd really been a murder . . . If Diggs really was the right person . . . But was that the truth? Or was I just drunk? Just tired and unfocused after a long, emotional day. Seeing connections where none existed. Like my mother before me.

I picked up the remote and turned the TV off. I dropped back against the couch with a weary sigh. I pinched the bridge of my nose and closed my eyes. I had to think about this, pray about it. What was real here? What wasn't? What the hell should I do? What the hell was the right thing to do?

I was asleep in seconds.

WEDNESDAY

15 · You Don't Say

Let me say here, as I've said at least a dozen times in at least a dozen places, that contrary to what you may have heard on CBS News and read in the *Times,* I never "decided to take matters into my own hands." I never set out to "investigate Diggs's allegations on my own." And I certainly never thought to make any kind of end run around the police or the FBI or Homeland Security or anyone. Trust me on this. I'm trying to portray myself as honestly as I can, all my flaws and failings on parade. But I'm not an idiot. If you're dealing with serious bad guys, the people you want to call are professional anti-bad-guy good guys—I know that. In real life, mysteries are not going to be solved by some small-city land developer, a former journalist who hadn't done any street reporting for over a decade and a half.

No. I went to the university the next morning because I simply didn't know what to think and, not knowing what to think, I didn't know what I should do. By the light of day, all my fears and suspicions of the night before seemed ridiculously implausible. What on earth made me believe that Casey Diggs was the man Serena met at The Den? What were the odds I had fresh information about a terrorist plot the FBI had already investigated and dismissed? And also, what kind of unbelievable coincidence would it be if I discovered all this because of Patrick Piersall, this ghost of a former actor who had been weirdly haunting my TV the last couple of days? The whole scenario was creepy and preposterous, like

something out of my mother's notebooks. In fact, it was scary how
much it was like that.

In the light of day, it seemed far more likely that Serena was
a liar, that the FBI was on the job protecting America from its enemies, thank you very much, and that Casey Diggs was some bitter
schizo who had nothing to do with anything and would eventually
turn up drunk in a motel somewhere ranting about the end of the
world. The best thing for me to do was forget about all of them and
go home to my wife and children, where I belonged.

Which is exactly what I wanted to do. But I couldn't. Not until
I was sure.

So, just after sunrise, I drove the red Mustang back into the
city. I headed up to the Heights, to the university. It was another
bright morning with the air cold and sad. The sun was falling in
moted beams on the brownstones and the shop awnings. I had the
radio playing light rock as I cruised the avenue and side streets
around the campus looking for a parking space. I finally found
a metered spot about three blocks from the school. I pulled up
alongside it, my turn signal clicking.

Just then, the music on the radio ended and an announcer
said: "And now, an entertainment minute with Sally Sterling."

I laughed out loud as I put the car into reverse. America must
be starved for what this broad was feeding them because she
seemed to be everywhere.

"Will baby make four?" she wondered aloud. I hadn't noticed
it before, but she had a richly feminine voice, low and hoarse and
with the consistency of syrup. "That's the question on the minds
of Hollywood star-watchers as rumors fly over whether the alleged
Juliette-Todd-Angelica triangle is, in fact, becoming . . . well, a
rectangle. Is Juliette pregnant? And if so, will that bring Todd
rushing back to her from Angelica's arms?"

I made a wry, rueful grimace as I backed the Mustang into

the spot. These people—these Hollywood stars—the way they behaved—what were they but trailer trash with pretty faces? Or maybe that wasn't being fair to trailer trash.

"All three stars are heading to New York for the premiere of the first three-dimensional movie ever: *The End of Civilization as We Know It.*"

Glamorizing their fucked-up relationships at a theater near you.

The 'Stang slid into the parking place easily. I straightened it out. Slapped it into parking gear. I was reaching for the keys to turn off the ignition when Sally Sterling went on, a suppressed laugh turning her voice more viscous still:

"And on the lighter side . . . this has to be some kind of record: Patrick Piersall's attempt to jump-start his flagging career with a return to TV ended last night before . . . well, before it even ended."

My hand hovered where it was, my fingers surrounding the car keys without touching them.

"*Patrick Piersall's True Crime America!* was canceled by cable-network executives while the final credits were still rolling," Sally continued. "The network was apparently flooded with complaints that the Most Wanted–style crime show was racist and offensive to Arab-Americans. Phone lines set up to receive crime-solving tips were shut down while calls were still coming in. The network says episodes already taped and in production will not be shown. I guess Patrick should've never left the deck of *The Universal.* And that's your entertainment minute. I'm—"

I turned the car off, killing the radio. I sat there behind the wheel, my hand still holding the keys, the keys still in the ignition. *Boop boop boop,* I thought. So much for *Patrick Piersall's True Crime America!* What did it all mean? I asked myself. And I answered myself: Nothing, probably. Just some TV executives' typical cave-in under political pressure.

I pulled the keys free. I pushed out of the car. I went to see Brent Withers.

Casey Diggs's former roommate lived in a dormitory off Broadway. It was a red brick high-rise with a white concrete entryway, the sort of functional monstrosity they used to slap up a lot in the fifties. It rose above the older, more stately buildings around it, a sliver of dingy red towering over the campus's noble white arches and columns and domes.

I hadn't told the kid I was coming. It was a trick I used to use back when I was a journalist. I found if I showed up early in the morning, I could usually catch the people I was looking for, and that I got more out of them when I took them by surprise like that and they didn't have time to prepare. I had the guard buzz him from the phone at the security desk in the lobby. Then I took the phone and spoke to him myself. The same adenoidal voice I'd heard on TV last night came over the line. I heard him hesitate when I said I was here to talk about Casey Diggs. He told me to hand the phone back to the security guard. The guard listened for a second, then nodded me through.

Withers was waiting for me on the third floor, peeking out the doorway of his dorm room. He lifted a chin by way of greeting as I stepped off the elevator. I came down an empty hall of closed doors and blank walls. I wasn't sure, but I thought the kid actually looked right and left as I stepped into his room—checked, I mean, to see if anyone was there to witness my arrival.

If anything, Withers looked more like a stick insect in real life than he had on TV. He had the long thin body and the weirdly long thin head and his arms, which were mostly elbows, kind of waved around a lot like a bug's antennae. He was still in the room he'd shared with Casey, I guess, because there were two beds and two desks; only one bed was stripped to the mattress and one desk was empty.

He sat on his bed, the one with the tangle of covers. I sat on the chair by his desk, the only chair there was. The room was oppressively small and cramped the way dorm rooms are, a jumble of laptop, stereo, books, unwashed shirts and slacks and underpants, plus a million photographs, the whole stick-insect family one by one and two by two and all together, plus a torn poster on the wall right behind him: three black gangsta rappas snarling as they showed off their leather and muscles and chains.

The poster made a strange contrast to the woefully pallid student on the bed. He had a solemn, almost funereal face, a lot of black hair piled on top. He waved his antenna arms around as he spoke, and blinked in slow motion as if he were fighting to stay awake till the end of the sentence. "So what's this about?" he asked me.

I told him I'd seen him on the Patrick Piersall show and wanted to ask him some questions.

"What's this for?" he asked. "Is this for a newspaper story or TV or . . . ?" He spoke as slowly as he blinked. He seemed to be pondering every word, turning it this way and that in the light before he laid it down in front of you.

"It's purely personal," I told him. "If there's any truth to what Diggs believed, I have a friend who might be in danger. You were the one guy who seemed to think Diggs might be on to something, that maybe his conspiracy theories weren't as crazy as they sounded."

"I didn't say that."

"No, I guess you didn't. But I got the feeling there was a lot you weren't saying."

"Well, that's the whole point around this place, actually," said Brent Withers. "It's all about what you don't say."

"What is?"

"Everything. School. Business. Life."

"You mean, you're afraid you'll be punished if you speak the truth?"

"I didn't say that."

"You have any reason to think you would be?"

His hand sort of wafted over toward the empty desk behind him. "That's Casey's desk over there. Do you notice Casey sitting at it?"

"No."

"Notice his computer? His Pacers jacket? His cheesecake picture of Angelica Eden?"

"Okay. He's gone."

"Yes, he is. He got expelled. I can't afford to get expelled. My parents aren't rich. They run a couple of franchise stores in St. Louis. They made a lot of sacrifices so I could come here and I still have to get my MBA after this. You need a good MBA to get a start in business without connections. For me, a happy and successful life depends on what I don't say, so I don't say it."

"Don't say what?"

"A lot of things."

"Like what?"

"You want a for-instance?"

"Yeah. For instance, what don't you say?"

"Well, I don't say, 'Women aren't as good at math and science as men are.'"

"You don't say that?"

"I never say it."

"But you're thinking it, you mean."

"I didn't say that."

"So there's another thing you don't say."

"That's right."

"What else?"

"I don't know. How about 'African art and literature are simplistic and primitive compared to European art and literature.'"

"Uh-huh. It's a long list, I gather."

"I need that MBA."

"All right, I get you," I said. "It's a university campus, all political correctness, no free speech, pretty typical. But look: Casey Diggs didn't get expelled for saying petty stuff like that. The guy accused a famous professor of planning a terrorist attack. That's a very serious thing to do."

"Well, it is. But that's not the way things work. Not exactly." The kid paused before going on in his slow-blinking, hand-waving way. Considering every word. Planning every sentence. It was sort of hypnotic to watch. "Plenty of people at this university—not just students but professors, too—have made accusations just as serious as Casey's. They accused the United States government of destroying the World Trade Center and shuffling the blame onto innocent Islamics. They accused the president of ordering the flooding of New Orleans in order to kill black people. There are students who gathered outside the classroom of Professor Leonard Stein—a seventy-year-old man—and shouted accusations that he was complicit in the murder of Palestinians until Stein was forced to retire. None of those people has been expelled like Casey was. None of them has been penalized in any way."

"Okay. So what are you saying?"

"I'm not saying anything," said Brent Withers. "That's what I'm trying to tell you."

I massaged my forehead with one hand. "Let me start again. Why *was* Casey Diggs expelled, do you think?"

"Boy, that's a good question. It's kind of hard to explain, isn't it? Seeing those other people weren't expelled or fired. Why was he?"

I laughed. He didn't. Now I found myself doing what he did—not the blinking and insectile arm-waving stuff, but raising my eyes to the ceiling and carefully constructing a sentence before I spoke. "Okay," I said finally. "Explain to me how someone *like* Casey might possibly get expelled from a university *like* this one."

"Theoretically? Well," said Withers very slowly. "Theoretically, let's stipulate, for argument's sake, that there are a lot of powerful people at a university like this who believe things that aren't, strictly speaking, true."

"Leftists, you mean."

"Let's just call them people. Powerful people."

"All right."

"These powerful people believe things like: One culture is as good as another. Or, there's no such thing as good and evil. Therefore, if America is at odds or at war with someone, it must be America's fault. You only have to think about those statements for two minutes to see that they can't possibly be true. But these people think they should be true and they think they'll seem to be true if no one is allowed to say that they're not true. So they attack anyone who says that they're not true. They call him names. Racist, sexist, phobic, offensive, whatever. They demand apologies from him. They make his life a misery, so no one wants to speak up."

"So it's like the emperor's new clothes."

"Right. Except instead of clothes, it's all the emperor's lies. And in an Empire of Lies, only a crazy man would speak the truth."

"Okay."

"And crazy people do crazy things, right? They do stupid things and wrong things. We all do, but crazy people do especially."

"I think I see what you're saying."

"I'm not saying anything."

"Well, I see what you're not saying, then. I know what you

mean. You mean they don't destroy someone for saying that their false ideas are false—"

"Right. They destroy him for doing something crazy. But you have to be crazy to tell them their ideas are false, because if you do, they'll find a way to destroy you."

"And you're saying that's what happened to Casey Diggs."

"No."

"You're not."

"No."

"But you mean Casey Diggs . . . Wait a minute. I'm really confused."

Withers sat on the edge of the unmade bed with his long arms still now, his big hands clasped between his legs. He blinked and swayed like a drunken man, but thinking, considering. Then he said, "What happened to Casey is that, purely by accident at first, he made it seem as if anti-American, relativisitic, multicultural-ists like Arthur Rashid are not only wrong, but have also created a breeding ground on campus for hate-filled, violent, terrorist-sympathizing, anti-Semitic Islamic radicals. Casey was warned not to do that anymore, but he was crazy enough to keep doing it. And when finally he got so crazy he took his accusations too far, he was expelled."

"Ah, yes, but that's my question right there: *Did* he take his accusations too far? Were his accusations untrue?"

This time, the shrug, the blink—they seemed to last for half an hour. "The police obviously think so. I mean, the FBI says Casey is wrong. The FBI wouldn't cover up a terrorist plot, would they?"

"No, of course not."

"Right."

"So what are you saying?"

"I'm not saying anything."

The conversation was beginning to make my head hurt. "Kid. Listen. I can't read minds. Give me something here."

He thought about it. He blinked slowly. He waved one arm. "Why don't you go see for yourself? Arthur Rashid lectures twice a week. He lectures today. Eleven A.M. Godwin Hall."

16 · Auditing Rashid

Godwin Hall was an elegant old theater, a Roman temple of a place. Under yellowing plane trees and scarlet maples, its stone stairs rose majestically to four fluted columns before a solemn brick facade. The columns shouldered a pediment and the pediment sheltered a carved relief rising and falling in its triangular frieze: *Art and Philosophy Bearing Fruit to the Spirit of Freedom.* All right, I'm guessing, but it was some sort of allegory like that. I squinted up at it through the late-morning sunshine as I approached. Then I lowered my eyes to the scene below: masses and masses of shaggy-haired students in torn jeans and sweatshirts pressing up the stairs under the weight of their backpacks, shuffling out of the sunlight, into the shadows of the colonnade. *Ignorance Bearing Credulity to Nonsense.* All right, I'm guessing.

I jostled into the throng, and was soon being carried along in the sludgy tide, up the stairs and under the columns and through a pair of anachronistic glass doors. We moved on in a crush across a small foyer, through another set of doors. Then we were in the hall itself.

The size of it startled me. It was a semicircular vastness, rows on rows on rows of seats descending toward a stage far below. I'm not much good at estimating these things, but there must've been close to three hundred students already there when I arrived. Maybe a hundred and fifty more were still pouring in.

I grabbed a spot near the back and watched as the rest of the seats filled up quickly. A shuffling silence followed: the snap of binders, muted conversation, sudden bursts of laughter.

Then there he was.

In memory, I can make him out clearly, but at the time, he was so far away, his face was something of a blur. I think my mind may have supplied the details from the pictures I'd seen on television the night before: the pleasing combination of dark, Middle Eastern skin on the handsome, chiseled features of an English gentleman. In any case, even at that distance, he was a powerful presence.

He was an impressive performer, too. He had a dynamic stride that carried him swiftly to the lectern. He had a bright smile that flashed out and beamed to a startling distance like the beacon of a lighthouse. Also, he had a great suit. I remember thinking that: *Great suit!* It was formal, tailored, gray black, set off by a port red tie that projected power and confidence, yea, like his smile, even unto the back rows.

He brought no notes with him, no books. He stood at the lectern only long enough to fasten a microphone to his lapel. "Good morning," he murmured meanwhile in a personable tone, glancing down sweetly at the students in the front row right beneath him. Then he was off, strolling about the stage, down to one end, back to the other, ambling around the center, gesturing to us in a friendly, informal manner all the while. He spoke in the quiet, confidential tone of a gentleman sharing insights, wing chair to wing chair at his private club. His accent was like his face: elegant, English, and precise with only enough hint of the Levantine in it to lend it an exotic charm.

I sat back and listened to him—and what followed was one of the strangest experiences of my life.

It's difficult to describe what happened or why. Something about the man or the setting or the lecture itself must've set it off, but I'm not sure what. It was a charged atmosphere, certainly. The charismatic professor reeling off his ideas. The hundreds of rapt young faces either turned up to him with openmouthed wonder or pressed down close to their notebooks while they scribbled feverishly as if to transcribe every word. It was an atmosphere almost of reverence, almost of awe. And yet, I don't think that's what caused my bizarre reaction. I still can't entirely explain it.

The lecture was about the King James Bible and the works of William Shakespeare.

"These two so-beautiful jewels in the crown of the English language," Rashid called them. "Not one of us here can think a thought or form a phrase or have an impression of each other or ourselves without their having been shaped in some way by the concepts, by the vision, and by the language of these magnificent works of art."

The guy was riveting, I have to say. Incredibly eloquent, incredibly learned. There seemed to be no facet of the subject he hadn't mastered. Without notes, seemingly without even a plan, he took us on a leisurely, discursive survey of the world that had created Shakespeare and the King James, facts and ideas leaping each to each with a speed and natural ease that was captivating. I can't reconstruct it all. I wouldn't think to try. His thoughts were much too brilliant, too complex and erudite for me. I just want to try to tell enough of what I remember to describe the strange thing that happened to me.

He began with England's break from the Catholic Church and the sometimes-violent suppression of English Catholicism, including, perhaps, the Catholicism of Shakespeare's own family. Then he talked about Luther's declaration that all religious authority came from the Bible rather than the Church.

"Thus, translating the biblical text into English became an act of enormous political significance," he said. "Whoever controlled the language controlled the ruling religion itself. An observer as keen as Shakespeare had to ask himself: If power corrupts, can translations made under such conditions be trusted? It's no wonder that when Hamlet looked into books, he saw nothing more than 'words, words, words' devoid of any inherent truth value."

Now up to this point, I remember, I was enjoying myself. I was always a lover of both Shakespeare and the King James Bible, and Rashid made it very clear he loved them, too. It was exciting just to watch him think about the subject. I was swept up in it, as if I could see the lines of inspiration connecting thought to thought like lines on a planetarium ceiling linking seemingly random stars into a constellation.

"Perhaps Shakespeare, forced to abandon the Catholicism of his father, felt some strange mixture of identification with and repulsion from the native peoples now being estranged from their own traditions by European imperialism and the 'words, words, words' of its religious missionaries. The moor Othello, for instance, lives as a Christian and only identifies with his Muslim origins when he kills himself. Perhaps this is a reflection of Shakespeare's own—and thus England's own—religious displacement and internal division."

As he went on like this, my reaction began to change. My eyes wandered away from him. His genteel figure continued pacing and turning and gesturing onstage, but I looked instead at the students. I panned my gaze over their upturned faces and the faces pressed down into notebooks. They were young people, I saw, of many colors, white and yellow and brown, girls and boys from all over the country, I would've guessed, and from other countries, too. I found myself wondering: How many of them had actually read Shakespeare, or the King James Bible, for that matter? Myself, as I say, I had always loved them both. I could remember suffering over Othello's mistake, wanting to reach out and stop Desdemona's murder with my own hand. I could remember suddenly seeing the Bible as a single chain of thought, a single idea developed in the collective mind of a people over centuries, from their earliest understanding of creation to the discovery of Christ's empty tomb. I suspected many of these students would never experience any of that, would never know more about Shakespeare or the Bible than they learned at this lecture today.

"When Othello says he 'threw a pearl away richer than all his tribe,' by murdering his white Christian wife Desdemona," Rashid was saying now, "how can we not think of Jesus' admonition to not 'cast your pearls before swine'—that is, don't bother sharing Jewish truth with the piglike gentiles? Christianity has been wasted on Othello, you see. In the end, he has resorted to the kind of vicious, murderous behavior the worst enemies of Islam would have predicted of him. Savages may be brought to Christ by English missionaries, but they can't be trusted. They will return to their savage nature, in the end."

This is when it began. It was subtle at first. My heart fluttered, making me breathless. A cold clammy feeling ran down the back of my neck. I felt light-headed. I thought: *Maybe I'm coming down with something.*

"This English terror of the stranger, the other, exemplified by Shakespeare and arising from a fear of their own suppressed Catholicism, can't help but find its way into the King James translation," Rashid went on. "Thus these masterpieces of European literature, these cornerstones of our attitudes and our feelings and our thoughts, are also the vehicles for a fearful, urgent, kill-or-be-killed approach to different cultures. They carry within them the seed and the rationalization for colonization, conversion, and imperialism."

Then it came over me—this bizarre moment I'm talking about. Suddenly, violently, it was there: a red upsurge of revulsion, a strangling sense of horror as if something gory and terrible were happening right in front of my face. Sitting there, in that civilized hall, that Roman temple beneath the plane trees and maples, I felt the helpless, wild, careening panic of a witness to disaster. My mouth opened and closed. My hand clutched at my chest. All around me, the students continued taking notes, the professor continued ambling and chatting easily. Nothing was going on but a morning class at an excellent urban university—and yet I had the almost-overwhelming urge to cry out, to cover my eyes, to run to someone's aid amidst the smoke and rubble and blood—smoke and rubble and blood that simply weren't there, weren't there at all. How can I describe this? What can I compare it to? It wasn't a hallucination or a delusion or a fantasy, or anything like that. It was just an emotional response completely at odds with the facts of the experience. I was attending a lecture, and yet my feelings were those of a man watching the slaughtering clash of armies, a field of smoking corpses amidst smoldering ruins. It was as if one thing transformed itself into another inside me, as if I saw one thing and my heart translated it into something else.

And then—as I sat there breathless and sweaty—then the thought came to me—as clear as if it were spoken aloud—spoken with absolute certainty, absolute conviction:

Of course he's a terrorist. Of course he is.

That suddenly, that completely, I was convinced—utterly convinced—that Casey Diggs was right: Arthur Rashid was engineering a murderous attack on the city of New York.

The very next moment, the irrational wave of feeling began to ebb. The terror subsided and with it, the clarity and the certainty faded away as well. I dropped back in my chair, trying to catch my breath. I was nauseous. A clammy line of sweat was running down the back of my neck. Blinking hard, I thought, *My God, my God—*

this is what must've happened to my mother. This is exactly what must've happened in the mind of my mother when she went insane.

My gaze was shooting around in an abrupt, disjointed way now, from the professor to the walls of the room and back over the faces of the students in their seats. And as I began to recover from that bizarre moment of panic and conviction, my attention lit on one girl sitting five or six rows in front of me. She was off to my left, in the last seat on the left near the wall. She was writing intently in her notebook, her head down, her lush black hair spilling forward. But just as my eyes fell on her, she looked up. She brushed her hair off her face with a graceful sweeping gesture of one hand. She turned to look at the professor and so presented her profile to me.

Startled, I recognized her at once. The sight of her knocked every other crazy thought right out of me. I was so surprised to find her there—so mystified by the coincidence—and so glad, too—so glad and excited to see her again.

It was Anne Smith. Remember her? The beautiful bartender from The Den.

17 · Anne

I wanted to ask her something. It was important. That's why I waited for her after class. Really—that's why. All the same, I admit it: I felt like a schoolboy with a crush, standing at the bottom of the hall's stone steps, my hands in my pockets, my casual posture as studied as the schoolboy's, my heart just as secret and eager.

"Anne!" I called when I saw her step out through the glass doors. She didn't hear. She started down the stairs amid the crowd, her head down, her black hair pouring forward. "Anne!"

I didn't think she'd remember me. How could she? So many people must come and go in that nightclub every night. But, in fact, she lifted her broad, oval face, spotted me with those big doe-eyes, and broke into a radiant smile. She freed one hand from the books she was holding against herself, waved it at me with that quick metronomic wave girls have when they're shy and happy to see you.

"Hi!" she said with outsized delight. She joined me in the dappled shadows under the plane trees. She shone on me like the warmth of morning. "What are you doing here?"

She was wearing jeans and a maroon jacket over an open-throated shirt, nothing half so revealing as the shoulderless outfit she'd had on in the club. Dressed like that and in the light of day, she looked more composed and womanly somehow and even more appealing. Faced with all the freshness and the warmth and the ripeness of her and the youth, I found myself feeling ridiculously self-conscious in front of her, ridiculously aware of my appearance and how I spoke and the impression I might be making on her.

"I didn't think you'd remember me," I said.

"Jason Harrow," she answered as if she were showing off her powers of recall. "The guy who's not as ugly as his driver's license."

"My claim to fame."

She was as I remembered her: as friendly, as straightforward as she'd been at The Den, and with that touch of insecurity so appealing in such a pretty girl. Her raspy voice was full of humor. "Which brings me back to my original question," she said. "What are you doing here?"

"I've heard about this guy Rashid. I wanted to hear his lecture."

She did that thing teenaged girls do when they're talking about some movie actor or rock star they love: Her hips went slack, her mouth went open, her eyes rolled heavenward. "Is that guy a super-genius or what? He must need, like, two heads to keep his brains in or something."

I felt a pang at that. Maybe I was still in the grips of that weird horror I'd experienced in the lecture hall. Or maybe I was just jealous and didn't want her to admire another man.

"I thought you told me you've never read Shakespeare," I said.

"No. I know. I really want to now. Rashid makes it sound so interesting."

"Mm. Yeah."

"Listen, I gotta get to my next class. You want to walk me?"

"Sure."

"There's only, like, twelve people, so I can't sneak in, and if you're late, Mr. Roth gives you, like, seven kinds of shit."

I managed only a faint smile. I've never gotten used to women cursing. The young ones almost all do it now, even the sweet country things like Anne. It's all fair and equal and so on, but

I don't like it. Still, a man will tolerate just about anything in a pretty girl, especially one he is trying to sleep with.

Which was the odd thing about Anne, by the way—the odd thing for me about walking beside her like that. It was a strangely doubled experience, as if I had two selves, one overlapping the other like images superimposed in a photograph. In one of those selves, I had no intention of trying to sleep with her—none. She was young enough to be my daughter. I felt toward her as a responsible middle-aged man feels toward any young adult: interested, solicitous, ready to be charmed. In this first self, I was there to ask her a question, and that was all. But in my other self, everything was seduction. Every move I made, every word I spoke, every smile and gesture was designed to win her over. It was as if there were some sort of filter system in my brain. Before I did or said anything, it asked automatically: *Will this make her like you enough to have sex with you? Will this?*

And because I was two selves at once, I saw two images of her as well. On the one hand, she simply seemed amiable to me. Open, sweet, maybe a little flirtatious but only in an innocent, teasing kind of way. A college girl talking to an older man. And at the same time—I wasn't sure. Maybe she wasn't innocent. Maybe her flirtation was dead serious.

And to make matters even more confusing, I was also aware of an intense and sentimental autumn yearning. I had been so unhappy when I was young, so insane that I had missed the whole college thing irretrievably, wandered through it in a depressive daze. And now here I was—with young people in their packs and pairs moving along the campus paths, over the grass and under the trees together—here I was with her, with Anne, as other boys were with their girls. Chatting with her, turning to smile at her, turning to catch the vital, smiling spark in her eyes. It made me ache, I must confess, and the ache seemed everywhere, not just in me. It seemed to breathe out of the beams of sunlight falling through the dying leaves. It seemed the secret substance of the chill New York weather.

I glanced at the books she held propped against her middle: two large textbooks and a binder.

"Those look heavy," I said. "You want some help?"

She laughed at me. "You're offering to carry my books to school? Are we twelve?"

My face went hot. She was right, of course. Not only was I acting like a twelve-year-old, I was acting like someone who was twelve more than thirty years ago.

"I guess I'm old-fashioned," I said, my cheeks burning.

"I guess so! I kind of like it, though. Sure—you wanna carry them?"

She gave the books to me. My God, they were as heavy as anvils! I pretended to fall over from the weight. "Holy smokes! Now you'll have to carry *me*."

She laughed that big laugh that seemed to belong out in an open field somewhere. She tossed her hair behind her.

"What do you, lift weights or something?" I asked.

She growled and flexed her arm, as if to show me her muscle. We walked along in smiling silence a few paces, me with her books under my arm and my heart aching.

"Listen," I said then, "I have to ask you something."

"Okay."

"Did you ever know a guy named Casey Diggs?"

Anne seemed surprised. "The guy from the posters?"

"What posters?"

She started to gesture at the path around us, the trees, the lampposts—but she let the gesture die. "Oh, I guess they took them down."

My gaze followed the incomplete motion of her hand. It was

the first time it occurred to me to wonder: Why were there no posters? There should've been. *Have you seen this man? Missing. If you have information, call* . . . But there were none.

"They were all over for a couple of weeks," Anne said. "Here, this is me." We stopped in front of one of several stately brick buildings, three stories tall with stone pilasters running up from the base to beneath the eaves of a bronze roof, patina-green. Scruffy students were filing in at the glass doors. Soon Anne would be joining them. I wished I would be joining Anne, going to class with her and young.

Anne went on: "Anyway, yeah, sure, I knew him. Why? I mean, I didn't know him well or anything. I just talked to him a couple of times. He talked to everyone. All the people who took classes from Rashid. He used to wait outside and ask us questions: *What did he say? What was he talking about?* I heard he was crazy, you know? Making all these accusations against Rashid, like he was a terrorist or something. I guess they finally expelled him and he just disappeared somewhere. I heard they even did a TV show about him. I didn't see it, though." Her eyes, which had shifted away as she remembered Casey, shifted back to me. "Is that really why you waited for me? To ask me that?"

It was. Anne knew Serena, Serena may have known Casey, Casey attacked Rashid, Rashid lectured to Anne. When I saw Anne there in the hall, I thought it might've been just a coincidence—or there might've been more of a link between them.

"Yeah," I said. "Why?"

"And you really did come here to hear Rashid lecture."

"Yeah. Like I said."

She made a sweet little pouting frown. "I'm disappointed. I thought you were stalking me."

I laughed, looked away, bashful with her. "You know, you oughta stop saying things like that, Anne."

"Why?"

"Because I might take them seriously."

"And that's bad because . . . ?"

I rolled my eyes. "Never mind. Here, take these back before I get a hernia." I piled her books back into her arms. "Thank God. That's the last time I offer to do that. I must've been out of my mind."

She smiled at my kidding, but she was thinking about something else—I could see it going on behind her eyes. Then she said, "Well, here, anyway." She wrestled her binder to the top of the book pile. Opened it. Took a girly purple pen out of an opaque plastic case inside. She scribbled something on a notebook page quickly, tore out the corner, and handed it to me. "Take this."

I took it. "What is it?"

"Duh, stupid. It's my phone number. And my address."

I laughed once, excited, unnerved. "Anne . . ."

"And, y'know, you're making me work much too hard at this, Mr. Jason-man. Most guys have to ask for those."

"I'm sure they do." I held up the wedge of paper as if to give it back to her. "And believe me, I would've. But what am I gonna do with it?"

She made a face at me, openmouthed, a mocking show of dumb surprise. I waggled my left hand, my ring finger in answer.

"Married. Remember?"

"Oh, right, I forgot," she said—and she wrinkled her nose, as if I'd reminded her of some mild impediment between us, like a cold I didn't want her to catch. "But I mean, you can't be faithful all the time, right?"

She said this with a little smile and a naughty jog of her eyebrows, so cute and fun about the whole thing. I felt like the oldest of old fuddy-duddies for even entertaining the hoary notion that the ideas of *faithful* and *all the time* might somehow go together. It was

like talking to a creature from another planet—the planet Youth.
Everything about her made me feel like my own grandfather.

I gave her a look—disapproving, ironic, complicit . . . Oh, I
don't know what kind of look it was. I let the subject drop. And I
let the hand holding the piece of paper drop. And the other hand,
too, the one with the wedding band on it.

"Listen, goofy girl, let me ask you one more thing."

"Okay"—pointing her thumb over her shoulder at the building behind her—"then I really gotta go."

"Did Casey ever come to The Den?"

"Yeah, sure. Everybody goes to The Den. It's kind of like the
unofficial school hangout."

"Right. And you remember the girl I came in there to find the
other night?"

"Sure. Oh—is that what this is about?"

"Yeah. Yeah, it is. Did you ever see that girl—Serena—did
you ever see her and Casey together?"

"Ummmmm," she said, screwing her lips up, squinting up into
the trees. Then she remembered: "Oh, yeah. One night. I remember. They danced together."

"How long ago?"

"A month. Six weeks. I don't know."

"About the time he disappeared?"

"Maybe. I can't remember. Like I said, I didn't know him all
that well. I just remember she came in looking for him. She asked
me to point him out to her, and then she went up to him and they
started dancing."

It took a moment for this to register, for the implications to
register. "I'm sorry. Say that again."

"She came in one night. . . . She came up to me at the bar.
You know, just like you did. She was, like, 'You know Casey Diggs,

right?' And I was, like, 'Yeah, sure.' And she was, like, 'When he comes in, point him out to me.' Just like you did with her."

"She was looking for him," I said, my voice dull and soft suddenly, a distant monotone. "She knew his name."

"Yeah. She'd been wanting to meet him."

"How do you know that?"

"I have this friend—Jamal. He told me she'd be coming in. He told me she wanted to meet Casey Diggs, and I should watch out for him for her."

"You know Jamal?"

"Yeah, we had, like, a one-night thing once, but we're still friends. He's the one who got me to take this class. Look, I really gotta go."

"Wait. Did you tell any of this to the police?"

Anne gave a kind of comical start of surprise. "That some girl was looking for some guy in The Den?"

"They never asked you about it?"

"It's not exactly a big whoop, Jason. She just went up to him when I pointed him out and, you know, they danced. It was, like: whatever."

"Did they leave together?"

"Beats me. I didn't notice."

I was quiet, lost in the thought of it, the idea of it, what it meant.

"I really gotta . . ." She pointed a thumb at the building again.

Then, completely unexpectedly, she darted forward and kissed me gently. It was startling—startling and intense. A moment with her soft lips on mine, her black hair tickling my skin, and that sweet, flower perfume she wore, like a teenage girl's.

"I like you," she whispered, her breath warm on my mouth. "Call me."

As she drew back, I caught a flash of something—something glittering in the opening at the neck of her blouse. A chain with a familiar sterling silver ring at the end of it about a quarter of an inch thick.

Then, dazed and stupid, I stood watching her as she walked away. My eyes were on her retreating figure, the seat of her jeans, the toss of her hair. My mind was racing, trying to sort out too many different things at once.

Anne joined the other students going through the door of the stately building, and she was gone. But I kept standing there, full of her. Thinking about that flashing ring on her necklace. About her whisper: *I like you. Call me.* About the touch of her lips.

Finally I turned away. I had to force myself to do it, pivoting around quickly. The movement must've taken the man across the lawn by surprise because I caught him there, watching me. He was young, dark-skinned. He had hooded eyes and a mouth that turned down on one side. He was staring at me balefully from the shadows of a broad oak tree on the grass about twenty yards away.

I barely had time to notice him before he wasn't there anymore. He was hurrying down a path—slipping between two buildings— out of sight—gone.

18 · Lies, Lies, Lies

It was night, I don't know how late. I'd been in the television room for hours. I'd been through one bottle of wine already and was halfway through another. I slumped nearly horizontal on the sofa, the remote control held loosely in my hand. I was somewhere into the deep cable numbers. There was a soft-core porno movie playing on the immense screen across the room. It told the stirring story of a woman who took her clothes off and straddled a naked man while moaning loudly. You just can't delve more deeply into the human condition than that.

I watched the action through half-lidded eyes. The naked woman bounced up and down on the naked man. Her head was thrown back. Her mouth was open. A sheen of sweat glowed on her face. "Oh, oh, oh, oh!" she said, her fine breasts jiggling.

I had paused here while channel surfing. I thought it would help me stop thinking, stop worrying about what I should do next. At first, it delivered a tranquilizing thrill. Now boredom, like an anesthetic, stunned me. My mind drifted. I thought about Serena again. About Casey Diggs. Rashid. *Words, words, words,* I thought, drunkenly. *Lies, lies, lies.*

What was I supposed to believe? Was anything Serena told me true? Had she known Casey Diggs? Had she gone into The Den looking for him that night? Was she working with the people who'd killed him? But if she was, why would she confess to me like that? Or if she was some unwilling dupe, why run away with them in

their green Cadillac? Should I call the police? Would that get Serena killed? Or was her whole story about the murder another lie?
Or maybe it was Anne who lied. Maybe it was Anne . . .

Oh, wait, look now. There was a new wrinkle to the plot of
the movie. The woman had climbed down off the man and was
positioning herself on the bed on all fours. The man knelt behind
her and began pumping his hips while she cried out, throwing her
head around so that her hair whipped about her face. Stirring stuff.
I straightened a little on the couch. When the man ran his hands
along her flanks to cup her breasts, I could almost feel the yielding
flesh against my own palms. I could almost feel what Anne's flesh
would be like.

Anne, I thought, yearningly. *Anne . . .*

I kept thinking about her. I kept thinking about that ring she
wore around her neck. I knew that sort of ring. It was called an
O-ring, after *The Story of O.* At least, that's what I'd always heard
it called. Back when I was with Lauren. Back when we were in
The Scene. A ring like that around a woman's neck—or on her
wrist, or dangling from her ear—was meant to signal that she enjoyed being submissive during rough sex. It meant she liked to be
dominated. She liked to be hurt.

How do they know? I almost whispered aloud. *How do they
pick you out like that? How do they always know?*

Uh-oh, hold on, what was this? The bedroom door had come
open—in the movie, I mean; on the television. The wife, the man's
wife, barged into the room and caught her husband doing the naked bang-bang with this other woman. Now here was drama for
you. Look how shocked and hurt she was. Well, sure. The faithful love that had sustained her life, repaired the injuries of her
childhood, become the medium of her joy and self-esteem was
now revealed to be a lie—a lie, I tell you! How could she ever
trust the naked man again? How could she ever trust anyone or

anything? And the children—what of the children? Their parents' marriage was their universe. Divorce would bring the very stars down around their heads!

Quickly, the husband unplugged himself from the naked woman's backside. As well he should! He went to his wife. He stroked her shoulders in a conciliatory fashion.

"We wanted you to join us, but we were afraid to ask," he said.

Ah, never be afraid to ask. That was the underlying theme of the movie. Never, never, never be afraid to ask. Because now see: The wife was taking her clothes off, too. She was kneeling naked on the bed while the husband and his girlfriend climbed up her flanks like ivy. What relief. What joy. What tits.

Oh God, oh God, how I wanted Anne just then, how I wanted her naked in my arms!

I snagged my glass of wine off the table. I knocked back another swallow. Husband and girlfriend now had the wife on her back, the girlfriend's mouth on her breasts, the husband's face buried between her legs.

And shouldn't life be like that? I asked the empty room silently. Instead of all this fuss about adultery and morality and whatnot. Shouldn't life be just like that?

Take my father, for instance. My father could serve as an object lesson here. My father killed himself while I was away at college. He sat in his Lexus in the garage just outside this television room, just on the other side of the door. He turned on the engine and let it run. My brother Alan had already graduated by then and had more or less moved back home to begin his career as a leech and wastrel. He was the one who found Dad's body slumped behind the wheel.

And why? Why did the old man do it? Well, there was no suicide note—Dad died as he lived, in pale and thin-lipped silence—

but let's face facts: It was because of Margaret—of course it was—little mousy Margaret who adored him and whom he loved.

She was a client of his, bankrupt after her husband left her. My father restructured her finances, helped her get a bookkeeping job. She relied on him and came to look up to him and finally idolized him in her careful, mousy way. I saw them together once, in his office. Quite a comical pair, really, the two of them. He dry as a stick and colorless as a tax code, and she with her limp brown hair and the face of a painfully serious squirrel, sniffing and nibbling around his every word as if it were the meat she lived on.

I only learned the whole story later, from her, from Margaret herself. She came to Dad's funeral. I was sitting in the front pew of the mortuary, sitting with my arm around my mother. Poor Mom barely understood what had happened. She was looking at the floor, shaking her head, whispering to herself, trying to fit Dad's suicide into the grand historical scheme of things. At some point, I glanced over my shoulder and spotted Margaret sitting modestly in the back, alone, a stranger to everyone else, unobtrusive but clearly grief-stricken. I remembered seeing her in Dad's office that one time and somehow now, I guessed the truth. As the service ended, I saw her slip out the back door quietly. On instinct, I went after her, caught her elbow as she crossed the parking lot to her car. I thanked her for coming. She seemed grateful that anyone spoke to her at all. We arranged to have coffee together in the city.

What a funny little creature she was. Small and slump-shouldered and flat-chested and with that plain, humorless, squirrelly face: You never would've thought there could be so much passion in her. We met at a Starbucks near NYU, a big glass box of a café filled with round wooden tables and straight-backed wooden chairs. She sat in her colorless skirt and jacket suit, nearly quivering with formality amidst the crowd of students slouched all around her in hoodies and jeans. She spoke carefully, primly, with the superserious air of a little girl laying out a tea set, trying to get everything exactly right. I listened, in my own student hoodie and jeans, slouched across the table from her. This is what she told me:

My father's life with my mother could hardly be called a marriage, not for the last few years, anyway. Mom had finally gone too crazy to relate or even speak sense to him. Sometimes she even seemed to believe he was an impostor, a stranger only pretending to be her husband. At times like that, she refused to have sex with him. Even in her clearer moments, she'd submit to it only as a wifely duty. She obviously found it an irritating distraction from the realizations and inspirations constantly flashing in her brain. At best, Dad felt he was an annoyance to her. At worst, he felt like a rapist. Finally he gave up. They continued living in the same house—even sleeping in the same bed—but each was living alone.

Now Dad and Margaret, meanwhile—they were a different story. A veritable riptide of erotic longing was dragging their scrawny bodies and their bloodless lips together. They fought it with all their honor, all their might, trying like mad to do what they thought was the right thing. But once Mom and Dad stopped having sex altogether—well, then, Dad and Margaret, pursuant to what I imagine was a rather dry, legalistic discussion of the finer moral points, decided they were justified in giving in to the flow. Occasionally, furtively, they began meeting at her apartment where, not to put too fine a point on it, they went about the serious business of fucking each other like a pair of rabid wildcats.

Of course, it only made matters worse. The sex was like seawater, quenching their thirst only to leave them thirstier still. Once they had a taste of each other, they wanted to be with each other every night. They wanted to sleep with each other and wake in each other's arms. Their conversations returned to the problem again and again until they rarely talked of anything else. Their joy in being together from time to time quickly soured into painful longing to have each other always.

But my father wouldn't leave my mother. He and Margaret both agreed it wouldn't be right. She was his wife of twenty-five years. They had loved each other when she was well. She had cheerfully kept his home, cooked his meals, raised his children. Now she was ill beyond recovery. What was he going to do? Put her in an institution somewhere? Abandon her to sit gaping beneath the television set in some sterile dayroom, drugged and drooling, confused and alone? Oh, you could rationalize it all you wanted, but abandonment was what it would be.

There were days when Dad weakened, when he wondered aloud if maybe professionals might take care of her better than he could, when he wondered whether he and Margaret didn't deserve a little happiness for themselves. But Margaret stayed strong. You don't walk away from your obligations for mere happiness, she said. She loved him because he was a better man, a more honorable man, than that.

Then one day—Margaret told me in Starbucks—one day, my father said a terrible thing. He was sitting on the edge of her bed, dressed to go home. He was staring at his shoes, thinking. She was lying naked under a single sheet, looking up at his profile.

And he murmured, "It would be better for everyone if she were dead."

It wasn't just the words, Margaret told me. They'd both said almost as much any number of times. But the tone of his voice, the awful, serious tone, and the awful, serious look he turned on her—she could tell he was saying one thing but that he meant something else, something much worse.

Their eyes met and they understood each other. For a long moment, they were together in that strange world of emotional logic where to escape the horrible prospect of wronging someone, you contemplate the thought of murdering her instead.

The moment passed—of course it did; they weren't monsters, obviously. But they couldn't deny it had happened and that it might happen again—and again, until the idea began to seem almost reasonable to them.

They held another of their precise, judicious discussions of the moral issues. They both agreed: They had to end their affair. It was making them miserable as things stood, and the only way to change the situation was to act cruelly or do what was wrong. They wouldn't. They would act kindly. They would do what was right. They would separate from one another forever.

So they did. They did the moral thing. The responsible thing. The honorable thing. They parted. And the meaning went out of my father's life, and he went into the garage and sat in the Lexus and gassed himself to death.

It's an object lesson, you see? Because it raises the question: What's the point of it all? All this morality, all this restraint. Doing right and depriving yourself of so many vital delights. We're here only a day or so—alive, I mean, a dawn, a hurried day, a remorseful twilight before the impenetrable dark. How can we deny ourselves even a single moment of passion or joy or pleasure? Why should we transform ourselves into dismal church ladies when look what we could be doing with each other, just look, right there, on the TV! The wife with her ass in the air now and her face between the girlfriend's legs and hubby going at her from behind and everyone's happy. I mean, if the hole is sweet, dude, stick the peg in, yes? Why all this fuss and feeling about it, all these rules and regulations? A peg in a hole. A life and a death. What difference does any of it make in the long run?

"Anne," I groaned quietly.

Then out of some combination of—I don't know—call it lethargy and self-disgust, I took another swig of wine and changed the channel . . .

To *The Justice Room*—where MacNamara was prosecuting a Christian minister who'd murdered a man to keep him from euthanizing his brain-dead wife.

Anne . . . I went on thinking about Anne. But without the porn to distract me, my thoughts slowly returned to what she'd said to me on campus. What if it was the truth? I wondered. What if Serena went into The Den that night looking for Casey Diggs?

I changed the channel . . .

To *Undercover*—where—*kerpow!*—petite, sexy Jillian Blaine punches the traitor Robert right in the kisser, knocking him ass over teakettle, yeah!

What if Serena had actually *delivered* Casey to Jamal and his friends? What if she had brought him to them so they could take him out to the Great Swamp and murder him?

I changed the channel . . .

To the news—where some Middle Eastern rabble-rouser with a name like Kaka al-Iraqi was screaming to a cheering crowd, "This is Holy War! We will not rest until we bring the foul disease of freedom and rationalism to an end!"

And what if Diggs was murdered because he was right? Because he knew Rashid was at the center of a planned terrorist attack on the city?

I changed the channel . . .

To *Missing:* "You see a Saudi national who might be a terrorist," spat the heroic Agent Magruder. "I just see another overambitious FBI agent profiling a man because of his race and religion."

If no one believed Diggs, why would anyone believe *me*? I wasn't even sure *I* believed me. I had no proof of anything.

I changed the channel . . .

To *The Inner Circle*—news commentary—where a pink, bald newspaper columnist who looked like a cartoon pig was saying: "I think Mr. Kaka is simply trying to communicate his frustration with American foreign policy . . ."

Lies, lies, lies, I thought. *It's all lies. It's all about what they don't say.*

My thoughts returned to Rashid pacing the platform in that lecture hall. I recalled my moment of fear and certainty. *Of course he's a terrorist. Of course he is.*

Who could I go to? What would I tell them? How could I stop this thing before people died?

I changed the channel . . .

And there—there, so help me, God—was Patrick Piersall!

"You gotta be kidding me!" I said aloud.

It was a local news program out of New York. The scene was somewhere near City Hall Park. There was a wild, pudgy figure on screen, stumbling around the middle of the street. It was a fuzzy amateur video, taken from some distance. You couldn't really make out the guy's face, but there was a helpful caption on the bottom of the screen: UNIVERSAL STAR PATRICK PIERSALL ARRESTED FOR DUI AND WEAPONS POSSESSION.

I watched, dumbstruck.

The pudgy little figure went on raving, leaping here and there beside a silver BMW he'd apparently run halfway up onto the sidewalk. He waved his hands insanely in the air. He threw back his head and howled at the sky.

Then four cops swarmed over him and wrestled him to the ground.

19 · Under the Influence

I went on staring openmouthed at the television as they showed the video again and again. And again. Not to mention again. As if urging us to drain the drama of the moment down to its dregs, a magic elixir of vicarious life to warm us in our lassitude. Even when the newswoman came back on, they split the screen and kept running and rerunning the video to the right of her. The newswoman—a smart-eyed street reporter with brown hair and white-coffee skin—talked for a few moments into her hand mike on one side of the screen while Piersall confronted the cops again and again on the other. Then the newswoman was replaced by a head shot of Piersall in his prime. It was a nice effect. There he was to the left as we knew him best, chisel-featured and coiffed, with the silver shoulders and sparkly collar of his space admiral's unitard just visible at the bottom of the picture. Meanwhile, on the right, where the video kept replaying, there he was as a fat crazy man screaming in the middle of the street until the four officers tackled him, shoved his face into the pavement, wrenched his arms behind his back, and slapped the cuffs on. The two sides of the screen formed a sort of living mug shot, only instead of showing the suspect full-face and profile, they showed him past and present. Handsome TV star here, drunken has-been nutcase under arrest over there. A nice effect, as I say. It's a very pleasant sensation to watch a successful person fall from grace.

Anyway, here's what had happened to the poor bastard—here's

what the newswoman told us, I mean, while, oh look! they ran the video of Piersall's violent arrest three more times.

The day after having his *True Crime America* show canceled during its first broadcast, Piersall, according to police and eyewitnesses, stormed into the cable network's Manhattan headquarters just north of Times Square. Witnesses described him as "drunk and irate." Barging into the office of network president Cole Hondler, he brandished a .38 caliber revolver.

"There were women screaming, people diving under desks. It was terrifying," said one young doofus whose clueless face was captioned CABLE NETWORK OFFICE WORKER.

"According to Hondler," the newswoman said, "Piersall demanded that the network give him airtime to tell what he called 'his side of the story.'"

When Hondler tried to calm Piersall down, the former Augustus Kane waved the pistol around some more, then staggered out of the room. Hondler had his assistant call 911.

Outside the network, on Broadway, Piersall's silver BMW Z4 was illegally parked in a loading zone. He stumbled to it and plunked himself behind the wheel. One witness claimed she heard him say he was headed for the FBI field office in Federal Plaza. In any case, he ripped away southward jig-time. Ram the force field full speed. If those Borgons escape, the galaxy is done for.

It was late afternoon, but still before the evening rush. Traffic is always jammed up tight on that little island, but there was some movement to be found at this hour on the Great White Way. Piersall screeched away from the curb with the hot 3.0-liter, 255-horsepower engine tanked and cranked. Police said he managed to work the Z4 up to 50 miles per hour, oozing through the narrow gaps between the vans and taxis funneling into Times Square. The police were after him almost at once. The chase was on.

Nowadays it seems even the most minor celebrity can't go to

the bathroom without video footage of the event getting beamed into our homes on TV or over the Internet, and yet, miraculous to relate, there was not one single frame of Patrick Piersall and his silver Z4 weaving and tacking through the pulsing core of Manhattan. It must've been a sight to see, too: the sports car jamming under the thirty-yard-high billboard of a woman in her bra and panties and screaming past the four-thousand-square-foot television screen showing some comedian or other laughing through his humongous white teeth. But the best our news crew could do was some stock footage of Times Square with its towering, spotlit nakedness and neon. We viewers had to desperately spur our atrophied imaginations in order to envision the rest.

Back to our story, though. Piersall never slowed. He raced through red lights and green alike, leaving a trail of chaotic intersections in his wake. Only the traffic congealing around Herald Square got the best of him. At one point, in fact, the traffic got so bad that a pair of pursuing officers actually got out of their cruisers and darted past the George M. Cohan statue shoulder to shoulder, trying to catch up to the Beamer on foot. At the last moment, though, the sea of yellow cabs in front of Macy's window parted, and Piersall and his Z4 darted out of reach of the law again.

But more and more cop cars were pouring into the pursuit with each passing moment. By the time our hero reached City Hall, he was hemmed in on every side. A wall of cruisers blocked his path south and east. The park stopped him to the west. And City Hall's concrete security bunkers sealed him off northward. Swerving to avoid a collision with any or all of them, Piersall ran the sports car up on the sidewalk as pedestrians hurled themselves over park benches to get out of the way. A moment later, the actor spilled out of the driver's door and started raving and waving his hands in the air, whereupon . . . well, let's cut to the videotape.

Which they did—again—concluding the story now with a

statement from a "cable-network spokesman." The newswoman read the words as they appeared in white letters on one side of the screen.

"All of us at the network are deeply saddened by today's events. Patrick Piersall is a fine actor and an important part of television history. His presence at our network will be missed. We wish him the very best as he attempts to rehabilitate himself."

To this, the newswoman added, "The network says Piersall's series *True Crime America* was canceled due to low ratings and content some viewers found offensive. I'm Amy Lopez—*City News.*"

With that—guess what—they played the video of Piersall's arrest again. Except this time, they had the audio turned up higher. They let it run on after the newswoman's sign-off so we could hear Piersall's drunken shouts more clearly, the curse words bleeped out:

"Let me through, you [bleeps]! You stinking [bleep]ing [bleeps]! Call the FBI! I demand to see the FBI! Listen to me! Let me the [bleep] through! It's an emergency! I'm a . . . [bleep]ing TV . . . personality! I have friends! I'm somebody. I've got to get to the FBI!"

But his words were nearly drowned out by the cops who were simultaneously screaming, "Where's the gun, [bleep]er? Give us the [bleeping] gun! Give us the [bleep]ing rod! Now! [Bleep]ing now!" and so on, until—seeing his empty hands waving in the air, I guess—one of them shouted, "[Bleep,] let's just [bleep]ing do it!" and they rushed him.

The report concluded with video of Piersall being frog-marched to a waiting cruiser. This was a portion of the arrest that hadn't been shown before, or perhaps had been shown before I tuned in.

The people who had scattered off the sidewalk at the sight of the oncoming BMW regrouped to gawk at this part of the show. Their faces ringed the scene as the cops led Piersall away, their features fixed in various expressions of amusement or fascination or apathy—just as if they were watching it as I was, at home, on their sofas, on TV.

And at the center of them was Piersall. The amateur camera-man had gotten in close to him now, very close. The cameraman's hands were obviously shaking in his excitement and the lens was sent wild a few times by the jostling crowd. All the same, what with his zoom and everything, he was taping so tightly that we could make out individual burst blood vessels in Piersall's nose and chart the course of the sweat along the furrows of his brow and cheeks.

The actor had that baffled, hectic look that seems to be a stan-dard fashion accessory for Drunks Being Led Away by the Police. His eyes shifted back and forth, the only active part of his other-wise passive body. And he was talking, still talking, in a strange murmuring tone that seemed at once automatic and urgent, as if he had repeated his warning so many times it had grown meaning-less to him, but he knew he had to repeat it yet again until some-one listened to him. It was a tone I knew, a tone I remembered, a tone I'd heard for years from my crazy mother.

"You'll find out," he said breathlessly. "You'll find out. Whether you listen or not. Doesn't matter. Hope it's not too late. Too late. You wouldn't listen. Wouldn't listen to Casey Diggs. Wouldn't lis-ten to me. But you'll see. Diggs was right. It's true. It's all true. All of it."

I sat up straight on the sofa, the remote control gripped tight in my hand. I leaned forward, staring at the screen, at the dazed, wild face of Patrick Piersall.

Now one cop put a hand on top of the actor's head and folded him into the backseat of the cruiser. For another moment, you could still hear Piersall muttering, "It's all true. It's all real. It's all happening."

Then the cruiser's door slammed shut. The story was over.

THURSDAY

20 · The Amoeba

They arraigned Piersall the next morning at Manhattan Criminal Court. I was there.

It was a hell of a strange feeling. It was as if I'd stepped right into the giant TV screen: got up off the sofa, put my foot through the screen's liquefying glass and whirlpooled into the reality beyond like some character in a kids' sci-fi movie. I had parked my red Mustang in a lot on Chambers Street and walked to the courthouse. The route took me right past the spot where Piersall had been arrested the night before. I say "right past it" with a sort of awestruck emphasis because I'd been shown the damned video of the scene so many times that the location was blazoned on my imagination like some famous site—the Alamo, say, or the White House, some site where history had happened. The sparse grass of City Hall Park, the grimy white of the security bunkers, even the very gray of the street pavement seemed charged with last night's events, as if a roly-poly has-been of a second-rate TV actor being carted off to the drunk tank where he belonged were the stuff of song and story.

Beyond, down the street, was the court building, 100 Centre Street, a bold, imposing ziggurat looming against the turbulent autumn sky. As I came near, I saw a mob of between fifty and a hundred cameramen and reporters already gathered out in front, waiting for the disgraced space admiral to arrive. It was cold and growing colder. There was a damp, chill wind coiling off the harbor, cramming through the concrete corridors of Wall Street and bursting in staggered gusts over the open plaza. The reporters' coats and jackets and skirts blew around them, and their hair blew. I saw a print guy with his hands shoved deep in his leather bomber jacket, his chin pressed into his necktie. I saw a radio guy, thick as an Irish thug, hunched and shivering, clutching his heavy mike like a hammer. The TV reporters stood out from the others, their faces all made up for the lights, shiny and plastic as kewpie dolls. They looked colder than the others, too, because they were dressed lighter for the cameras, the girls in skirts, the guys in sports jackets. As my eye picked them out, I spotted Amy Lopez, the very same smart-eyed newswoman who had shared the screen with the Piersall video last night. She stood rigid, gripping her microphone down by her side, bouncing on the toes of her high-heeled shoes to keep her blood moving. Stray brown hairs blew onto her forehead. She scraped them off with a couple of fingernails as her keen eyes scanned the streets to the north. Now and again, she touched a hand to her ear, and I knew someone was speaking to her through an earpiece, keeping her up to date on Piersall's progress downtown from the Tombs, the city jail where he'd been kept overnight.

I had an unaccustomed fluttery feeling in my belly. I felt out of my element, on the spot. It had been a long time since I'd been a reporter and there were probably twenty-five-year-old punks in this crowd who had covered more big stories in the last month than I had in my whole career. I wasn't sure I could compete with them. And I had to. I had to get through them and reach Piersall myself.

That was my plan. Well, I had to do something, and that was all I could think of. If Piersall had information about Casey Diggs's death, maybe he could help me. Maybe we could help each other. Maybe together we could get the police to believe us.

And yes, for the record, I'd tried to call his lawyers. I got through to a bored secretary who sounded as if she'd taken a hundred calls about Piersall in the last half hour and would take a hundred more in the next. "He'll get back to you," she told me. But I knew he never would.

I neared the crowd of milling reporters. The Lopez girl was at the edge of the group, standing off to herself. Since she'd been on my TV last night, alone with me in my television room, I felt I knew her somehow. I felt maybe she would help me negotiate my way to Piersall's side so I could hand him the note I held folded in my jacket pocket. I approached her.

"You guys waiting for Piersall?" I asked.

She turned and looked at me like a dead fish looking at another dead fish. Her glance took in my sneakers, my jeans, my red windbreaker over my black sweatshirt. "You press?" she asked suspiciously.

I nodded. "Out of town," I lied.

"What, like, some blog?" She said the word with a snort and a sneer of disdain.

"A newspaper."

"Ever cover a celebrity perp walk before?"

I tried to think if I ever had. I hadn't. "No."

The girl put her tongue in her cheek. She considered my face—my honest, open, still-boyish face. Disdain gave way to amusement and pity. "Well, put your cup on, farmboy. It's a 24/7 cycle around here, and we're feeding the beast."

I did my best not to look as humiliated as I felt. Man, I thought bitterly, this dame was a lot sweeter on TV—though come to think of it, she wasn't all that sweet on TV, either.

"I didn't realize Piersall was this big a celebrity," I said.

Amy shrugged. "He is now. It's a good story. It's a big beast." Then she shot her elbow into my solar plexus as hard as she could.

I'm not sure she meant to do that. I'm not sure she didn't mean it, either. But the cops had just shown up, and the paddy wagon was right behind them. The crowd of reporters had erupted into motion and she—elbows flying—went charging into the thick of it.

A double line of patrolmen pushed into the mob, forcing a corridor through the crush. The reporters reacted instantly, surging back against the line of cops. They all wanted the same thing: to get to the front. The cameramen wanted to take their pictures there. The radio guys wanted to record their sound. The TV personalities wanted to be seen on the video shouting their questions. And the print guys—well, they weren't just going to be pushed out of the way. They all shoved forward together, congealing into one living force, a great plasmic creature with a single mindless mind, a single mindless purpose: to get to the front, to get close to the disgraced celebrity.

That was my purpose, too. Amy's elbow to my breadbasket got me off to a slow start just as it propelled her into the heart of the seething mass and out of sight. Taken completely by surprise, I caught the blow full force on the soft spot. I bent forward, grunting the air out of my lungs. At the same time, I was pressed from behind by a phalanx of technos hoisting mikes on booms like lances. They shoved me to the edge of the boiling, amoebic soup, and I was sucked in. The next moment I was part of it, spun round and drawn forward and pushed back all at the same time.

I got hit again. Another elbow, in the side of the head this time, and this time from a radio guy with a lot more meat on him than Amy had. Angry, I shoved him back with both hands. It barely budged him—there was no place for him to go. He grunted a curse at me through gritted teeth. I shouted a curse back at him. A woman tried to snake her way under my arm, deeper into the churning plasma. Angry now, I grabbed her by the shoulder and dragged her out of my way. I began fighting, elbowing, shoving, driving, like everyone else, toward the front.

The corrections van pulled up fast. It stopped hard at the corridor's opening. Two corrections officers leapt out of the front seats. The back of the van opened and two more jumped out there.

The thrashing of the media amoeba became more crazed and urgent. Then Piersall appeared and the jellylike mob roiled and surged with a force and frenzy I could barely believe.

I was deep in the gelatinous flow, struggling against it even as I helped create it. Between heads and over shoulders, I caught tidal glimpses of the action at the front. Two COs helped Patrick Piersall down from the back of the van. His hands were cuffed behind him. His suntanned face, suddenly so shockingly present in the flesh, was set in that wry insouciant smile people wear when they're trying to rise above their shame. Two tidy men in suits, both carrying briefcases—his lawyers—stepped down gingerly after him. These five—Piersall, the COs at his elbows, the lawyers at his back—formed the core of the parade. Two more COs strode ahead of them, two fell in behind. They marched into the corridor between the cops, between the crush of journalists, and headed swiftly for the courthouse doors.

The mindless mind of the amoebic press had a mindless voice now too, a choral cry of male and female tones, of high and low. It shouted what were phrased as questions but uttered as commands, without that uptick at the end that questions have, with only the coughing bark of the imperative.

"Why was your show canceled." *Tell me.*

"What did you say to Cole Hondler." *Tell me now.*

"What are you going to plead." *Say something.*

"Do you think your TV career is over." *Fill my airtime. Fill my computer screen. Feed my gobby substance with your shame!*

The shouts were coming from all around me, mingled with grunts and curses in the swirling turmoil. Up front, the parade with Piersall at its center was passing swiftly up the corridor. A few seconds more and they would be at the courthouse, inside it, out of reach. Desperate to get to them before they were gone, I struggled toward the police line with fresh force. I set my hands against another man's shoulder. I shoved at him, trying to compress him into a smaller space so I could squeeze past. The man rounded on me with the face of a devil, contorted with anger, eyes afire.

"Get your hands off me or I'll kill you," he said.

I got past him, tumbling deeper into the mass.

Then—the next moment—I was jostled hard from the right. I stumbled. The plasma of the media creature began closing over me. I felt the bodies of men pressing in on me as I nearly lost my footing, felt the comfortless closeness of women as the hurly-burly nearly bore me down. I smelled their aftershave and their perfume. I saw their twisted features above me, their bared teeth, their eyes both bright and dead. Jutted microphones shot past my cheek like bullets. Elbows knocked and clocked me from every side.

Falling, panicking, I thought, *What am I doing here? What am I doing?* I no longer cared about Patrick Piersall or Casey Diggs or plots and conspiracies and shadowy threats of danger. I just wanted to get out. I just wanted to go home, away from the sight of these slavering, crazy-faced men, from the sound of these women buzzing like locusts, screaming like harpies. Only a rage for survival, a terror of being trampled into the pavement and smothered down there, made me corkscrew viciously, gripping and tearing at the bodies around me in order to stay on my feet. Only that rage made me battle forward with all the strength I had. Somehow I got my balance back. I rammed myself headlong through the congealed human mass, looking for a clearing, for open air.

And then there I was. I was at the police line. I was at the edge of the corridor. I had broken through the mob and was standing between two NYPD patrolmen, at the point where their hands met to form their barricade against the press. There was no one else in front of me. I could see right into the corridor itself.

There was Piersall and his entourage of lawyers and lawmen—and they had already passed me by. I'd missed them by a few steps. The trailing pair of COs was a pace to my right, then the attorneys, then Piersall and the officers who held him, then the COs in the lead—who were nearly at the building's stairs, nearly at the door.

The pressure of the amoeba behind me drove me hard against the cops' arms. The creature's voices were shouting loudly on every side of me. I stuck my hand into the pocket of my windbreaker. I felt it close on the note I had folded there. I brought the note out, crumpled in my fist. But there was no way to get it to the lawyers or to Piersall. I had missed my chance.

But wait. The next moment, just before he reached the steps, Piersall stopped. He turned—swung around so hard that he brought the two startled corrections officers at his elbows swinging around with him. The actor was glowering with rage. His cheeks were red. His eyes were white and rolling. He was like a chained beast goaded into a fury by captivity and the mob and the questions hurled at him like stones.

He shouted. His voice was a ragged growl. He sounded just as I remembered him, as we all remembered him, from those moments of highest melodrama on the besieged deck of the spaceship *Universal.*

"This!" he bellowed at us. "This is not the news!"

He tried to charge at us like a bull. The force of it pulled his corrections officers after him a step before they could restrain him. The lawyers—the tidy men in suits—stumbled back several paces, jumbling together with the COs in the rear, who fell back too. One of the lawyers stuck his hand out to recover his balance.

On the instant, I saw my chance. I lunged forward, reaching out between the policemen. I grabbed the lawyer's hand and forced my note into it.

My name is Jason Harrow, it said. *I have information about the disappearance of Casey Diggs. I will only speak to Patrick Piersall. Call this number.*

21 · A Prayerful Interlude

Afterward, I felt awful: stupid, ashamed. I had bruises on my arms, one on my side. I thought I had one on my forehead, too—it felt bruised though I couldn't see it. My jaw hurt, my ribs ached. And for what? Piersall's lawyers would simply throw my note away. Of course they would. What had I accomplished? Nothing.

Wearily, I limped back to the parking lot, to my Mustang. I settled stiffly behind the wheel. I sat there, staring through the windshield at the Mercedes parked across from me. I felt far away from the living surface of the world. Dazed, dissociated, dead to feeling, confused about what was real and what wasn't. Why the hell had I come here? What was I thinking? I remembered, as if it were long ago, feeling some sense of threat, of danger. A sense I had to do something, do something fast. But why? What was it all about? A story told to me by a lying teenager? The wild accusations of a crazy college dropout? A lecture on Shakespeare by a college professor? The maunderings of a drunken, washed-up actor trying to jump-start his career with sensationalistic self-destruction? Nothing. It was all about nothing. Lies, rumor, suspicion hyped to an intensity of desperation by those days in my mother's house, those nights, those drunken nights, in the craziness of the television room. It really was true: I'd fallen through the screen and landed here, a drowning fall into other people's delusions.

I drove out of the lot and began wending the complicated way toward the East Side and the FDR Drive. The traffic was thick and

I kept finding my path frustrated by one-way streets and security barricades. It took me the better part of an hour to reach the highway. There, the traffic grew lighter. I went quickly up along the East River, glancing out the window at the water running turbulent and dull beneath a sky darkening with running clouds. I was heading for the Midtown Tunnel, for the Island and my mother's house.

But I went another way. I don't know why. Maybe it was just my reluctance to return to that house, that room—I'm not sure. But when I got off at the 34th Street exit, I turned away from the tunnel without thinking. I headed west instead, across the city.

At first, I wasn't sure where I was going—then I was: the Church of the Incarnation, the brownstone church on Madison Avenue I had come to in the depths of my craziness so many years ago.

I remembered that day as I stepped through the church doors, that day I had prayed in the side chapel: *Forgive me, help me.* I thought of that now as the great axial moment of my life, the moment around which my soul had swung like a compass needle from misery to happiness. I yearned to feel the intensity of that day again, even the intensity of its despair, anything rather than this zombie malaise that had come over me. I tried to milk the stately place for some celestial emotions. I grasped at the sweetness of the quiet as I stepped from the vestibule into the nave. I savored the door swinging shut behind me, muffling the hectic street sounds that had followed me in. I drank in the otherworldly light that fell in beams through the stained-glass windows, crimson and indigo and gold. I tried to lift myself from this daze of unreality into the crystal solidity of the high, imagined spheres. But my mind remained muddy and faraway.

I slipped into a pew near the middle of the church. There were only two other people there with me: an old woman sitting on the far right side, and an even older woman sitting on the left. In my sullen distraction, they looked to me like refugees from the battle for the world, survivors who had stumbled into this ruin to die. All that was left of the broken body of Christ.

I sat and clasped my hands in my lap. I bowed my head and closed my eyes and tried to pray. But a moment later, I looked up again. I looked around. My eyes came to rest on the reredos up behind the altar. Herald angels flanking a trio of cherubs who were unrolling a scroll. AND THE WORD WAS MADE FLESH AND DWELT AMONG US, the scroll read. *What the hell was that supposed to mean?* I wondered. I mean, now that you have your spaceships and quantum physics and computers and television sets? The Word was made flesh. What the hell was that?

I shook my head, looking over the apse and the empty pews. This place—this place that had been so important to me once. Now it just seemed like a hiding place for frightened old women, somewhere restful they could go to die, away from the crap and holler of life.

I closed my eyes again. I closed my hand into a fist, hoping to feel Christ's hand in mine. I felt nothing. I forced out a prayer.

Show me the way, Lord. Something terrible is happening—or is going to happen—I don't know which—something terrible is happening to my brain or is going to happen to this city—I don't know, I don't know which—maybe there's some kind of attack in the works—or maybe it's all me, maybe what happened to my mother is happening to me now, maybe even you are just some flash in my brain, some electrochemical kind of . . . Ach! Show me the way. Show me the way.

He answered by cell phone. Hey, it's the modern world, what can I tell you? I'd forgotten to turn the phone off and just at that moment, it sang out with a sort of shrill, gleeful rudeness, the way a mischievous demon might fart in a place like this. The two old ladies swung around at me, their faces wrinkled and wrathful and dark. I made an apologetic smile and unwound from my pew. I hurried up the aisle and pushed out the doors, back into the city.

I answered the phone as I stepped onto the sidewalk. I could barely hear the voice on the other end above the grind and rumble of a bus passing on its way uptown. I stuck a finger in my free ear.

I said, "I'm sorry. I couldn't hear you. What'd you say?"

The voice was a man's voice. It was featureless, nondescript: "Mr. Piersall will meet you in an hour," it said, "in the Ale House downtown."

22 · Augustus Kane and the Ale House of Doom

The Ale House was one of the oldest pubs in the city. Sawdustt covered the floor. Old newspapers and photos of dead Irishmen covered the walls. Left of the door as you came in, there was a brass-and-mahogany bar that probably predated the Draft Riots. Dusty bottles crowded the ancient shelves behind it. Above the bottles, there were more photos and more headlines, plus a mounted fish that looked like it might've been caught by James, son of Zebedee. Come to think of it, the bartender—with a face that had collapsed into a mass of frowning wrinkles—looked like he might've been there with James at the time. He was swiping down the top of the bar with a rag. There was an old pile of clothes in front of him that turned out to be a man drinking beer.

When I walked in, the barkeep took one look at me and tilted his head toward an archway. I went through the archway into the tavern's main room.

There were no windows here. The ceiling lights were dim as candles and had the same yellowish glow. The wooden tables were crowded against the walls left and right. Between them was the open floor with the sawdust on it streaked by passing footsteps. The place could've looked the same a hundred years ago. Only the paper napkins and glass bottles of ketchup on every table served as a jarring reminder of the modern world.

It was still early—before lunchtime. At first glance, the room seemed empty. Then I looked again at a potbellied woodstove whispering and snickering in one far corner. A lone drinker sat hunched at the table just beyond the stove, his back to me. He seemed, in that setting, like a figure in an old painting or photograph, a thing of more meaning than substance, a representative, say, of the Urban Man who carries the nation's lonely vastness inside himself, a symbol of that peculiar American solitude one finds in midnight diners and daylight bars.

I walked across the sawdust until I was standing over him. He raised his face to me. It was Piersall.

I'd seen him in the hectic crush that morning, of course, but it was different now, quiet and close like this. He had the glamour of TV on him, that camera magic that made him seem embossed on the flat facade of life, raised up from it, more real than real. His face was like a living billboard of itself—and not just his face, but the face beneath his face, the dashing features of Admiral Augustus Kane, distorted by bloat and hidden under wrinkles, but still glowing within somehow, still there.

He had his hand wrapped around a mug of beer. There was a shot of whiskey by it. They weren't his first of the morning, I could tell. His fat cheeks were flushed, his blue eyes hectic. A blood vessel throbbed on his mottled nose. Not quite noon, and he was already half in the tank.

"You Harrow?" he said. There was that voice, too—the same as it always had been: terse, rhythmic, distinctive, the admiral's voice.

I nodded down at him, tight and quiet in his starry presence.

"Have a seat. Have a seat," he said. He gestured to the chair across from him. He looked back over his shoulder. Startled me by shouting out, "Charlie! Two more!" Then he jacked the shot and finished the beer in two quick motions, his right hand flashing back and forth between the glasses.

I sat down. "Thanks for seeing me," I said.

He didn't answer. He looked me over, studied me, openly, not trying to hide it, cocking one outgrown eyebrow and running a sharp, narrow gaze up and down me. It gave him the aspect of a keen observer of men, a man who could peer right into your heart. As the moment went on and uncomfortably on, I began to get the feeling he meant me to think that about him. I began to suspect it was a part he was playing: the Keen Observer of Men. *I'm a guy you can't put anything past,* he seemed to be telling me. *Don't even try.*

Charlie—the wrinkly Bartender from Ages Past—clapped mugs of beer and whiskey shots on the table in front of us. He swept Piersall's empties onto his tray and retreated to the front room.

I put my hand on the mug, grateful to have something to fiddle with while Piersall stared. Piersall went on staring, waiting until the barkeep was gone. Then he said, "You've been. Following the news. I take it," in that syncopated way of his.

I wasn't sure what he meant: news of his canceled show? His arrest? The arraignment this morning? "I saw the news last night," I said. "Not today though."

He gave a snort, a sort of man-of-the-world, seen-it-all snort. I got the feeling this was a performance, too, another part he was playing: the Man of the World Who Has Seen It All.

"The news," he said. "The media! It's like *Alice in Wonderland*—only without the Wonderland. They have this—story they want to tell. This nonsense story. 'Angry TV Star Goes Nuts.' That's the story and if you challenge that—if you're brave enough, if you're—*sane* enough—to challenge that—then—oh, then they go at you. Tooth and nail. Hammer and tongs. Off with his head. You must be a drunk, a madman, a . . ." He waved one pudgy hand about dramatically, as if to conjure the word he was looking for out of the air. And he did: "A has-been." He lifted his shot glass to his lips, and added before he drank, "Which is rich, coming from a bunch of never-weres."

Then he did drink. He downed the shot whole and followed it with a knock at his beer.

I could only watch him, bemused. This was not what I'd expected. He didn't seem to care about the note I'd given to his lawyer. He didn't question me about it or try to find out more about me or what I wanted. He didn't seem interested in that at all. He didn't even seem interested in himself, in his situation. I mean, after the night he'd had—and the morning he'd had—I would've thought he'd want to at least try to appear sober in public. But no. He just showed himself as he was: a bitter and blasted man, a sort of Ancient Mariner with nothing left of life but the story he had to tell. And yet . . . and yet, even as I thought that, I thought: That little speech he'd just made, the laconic drama of it, the staccato syncopation—tooth and nail, hammer and tongs, off with his head. It was classic Patrick Piersall stuff, wasn't it? It could have been written for him. It could've been written for Augustus Kane. Was it possible that this, too, was a role he was playing: The Bitter, Blasted Man Who Had Yet a Story to Tell?

I watched him gaze into his beer like a lost soul, or like a Lost Soul in a movie during the scene in which he gazes into his beer. He had changed his clothes since the arraignment. He was wearing a natty corduroy sports coat and one of those turtlenecks older guys wear when they start to get wattles on their throats. I could just picture him getting dressed, thinking: *Let's see. What's my wardrobe for the scene where I meet the informant in the bar?* Was everything about him—every word, every gesture, every expression on his face—part of a performance of some kind? Was he all actor and no man?

"Are you a hard man, Harrow?" he asked me suddenly with the air of a storyteller in a movie suddenly asking his listener

a piercing question. And when I opened my mouth without answering, he said: "Mentally, I mean." And added: "Forgive me,"
with that oily graciousness actors and drunks do so well. "Forgive
me, but we don't know each other. I have to ask. Are you a hard
man—mentally?"

"Yeah, sure, I guess," I said—it seemed the best way to get
on with it.

"Good. Good. It takes a hard man to see the truth when everyone is telling him the lies he wants to hear." He raised his beer
mug to me in a toast—a toast to that little piece of wisdom, perhaps, or maybe to my hardness, or maybe just a toast so he could
drink some more.

I toasted, drank. The beer was tart and cold. It had a zingy
little tang to it. I wasn't used to drinking this early in the day.
"What happened at the arraignment?" I asked him. I guessed now
that's what we were talking about. "I haven't seen the news about
that."

Another studied gesture—lowered eyelids, a casual movement
of the hand—as if I had missed the point somehow, as if my question was a matter of no importance and he was brushing it aside.
"Do you want the news—or do you want the truth?"

I nearly laughed out loud at this. I couldn't help it. If he was
going to behave as if he were in a movie, I couldn't help watching
him as if I were a critic. I was thinking: *Do you want the news
or do you want the truth?" What kind of crappy, overwritten, corny
dialogue is that?* "Well . . . I'd like to know what happened at the
arraignment," I said, dryly.

"I was released," he declared in orotund tones, "on five thousand dollars bail."

Now here, I felt the line was okay, but he delivered it with
way too much melodrama. The pause between *released* and *on,*
the pregnant turning of his hand in air, the rolling tone of the bail

amount—it was all meant to suggest there was a deeper meaning to the words than there seemed to be. But I mean, come on, what meaning? He was released on bail. What was the big deal?

"Was there anything else?" I asked him. "Did you get to make any kind of statement? In court? To the press?"

He held up a finger and half-smiled, as if, ah, now I were beginning to see into the heart of things. "Ah," he said, "now you're beginning to see into the heart of things. Now you're starting—to ask—the right—questions."

I managed not to roll my eyes. "So did you? Make a statement?"

Up went the beer. Down went the empty glass with a bang. "Charlie!" he shouted over his shoulder. He waved a questioning finger at my drinks as well, but I'd barely touched them. "One more!" Then turning back to me, he said, "No statement. Not in court. Not to the press. On the advice—of counsel: no statement."

"So you haven't told them—the court or the press—you haven't told them any more about Casey Diggs."

"You don't understand. You don't—understand. The story . . . Oh, thank you, thank you, my friend," he said with a gracious, actorly smile as Charlie set another round in front of him. The wrinkly barkeep exchanged a glance with me, that expressionless yet somehow sardonic glance that sober men exchange over a drunk. Then he was gone again. "This is what you don't understand. The story boxes you in. Trust me. I've been in this business a long, long time. That's how it works." Piersall lifted his shot glass but set it down without drinking. "The story—their story, their prewritten script—ties you up in its own logic. It refuses to tell anything but itself. 'Disgruntled has-been actor arrested for DUI after holding a gun on the executive who canceled his show.' That's the story. That's the plot people are following. And if you—if you say, 'Listen. You dumb shits. That's not the story.

The story is that just because a couple of—*camel-jockey*—*rag-headed*—*dune-coon* pressure groups—who probably have fucking terrorist connections of their own—turned the screws on the cable station, we are being silenced. Silenced! We are failing to investigate a possible terrorist plot against the city of New York.' If you try to tell that story, see, if you break in on their script with the truth, it's too sudden, too unexpected for people. It's as if a love scene were interrupted by a helicopter crash. The audience says, 'What? No. No. That—doesn't make sense. That—doesn't fit. That's not what we expected. It's not the story.'"

There was no helicopter crash, and Piersall continued in his staccato way, with many a graceful gesture, many a knowing smile.

"So the truth is swallowed by the story line. The media, the audience—they *incorporate* the interruption into the plot and it disappears without a trace. 'Drunken has-been actor who waved disgruntled gun at canceled show exec goes on foulmouthed rant, calls Muslims dune coons.' And while you—because you're so furious—because no one will listen—while you rant like a lunatic trying to get someone to hear the truth, they air an interview with the elegant, articulate Ahmed Muhammed Ahmed, you know, of the Camel Jockey Ragheads for Media Fairness Association." Here he slipped into what I'll politely call an *outrageous* Middle Eastern accent. "'It is quite unfor-choo-nate dat Meester Pierce-all would stoop to cheap racial stereotyping . . .' Blah-de-blah-de-blah . . . You see? So the story continues on its way: 'Angry Actor Goes Nuts.' The story's like—like a road—a road that carries you where it wants you to go, even if the truth lies in the opposite direction."

"Well, all right," I said, trying hard not to sound impatient with him. "I'm listening. What is the truth? What is this possible terrorist plot? What exactly did Casey Diggs think was going to happen?"

"You see," Piersall mused, suddenly changing his tone to that of a Man Who Looks Back Wisely on a Much-lived Life. "America is an imaginary country." This, as everything, in that patented rhythm. *America. Is an. Imaginary country.* "Other countries have bloodlines. History. The ancient earth. Bloodlines that run through history into the ancient earth."

Oh, for Christ's sweet sake! I was thinking.

"Americans," he went on. "All we have is"—he tapped the side of his head with his forefinger—"up here. Ideas. Images. Who we are. What we're like. What we believe. Stories. Movies. The Bible. The Constitution. TV. Characters. In our mind. Jesus Christ. Thomas Jefferson. Augustus Kane. Patrick Piersall . . ."

His voice meandered off like a river winding away into the distance. He made another gesture with his hand and bowed his head, as much as to say: I could go on, my friend, but these deep things are understood between us.

Which they weren't, of course. I had no idea what the hell he was talking about. I sat there, bewildered, looking at the top of his head. If you're interested, I can tell you that his hair was dyed to its old reddish hue with a distinguished touch of silver left showing at the edges. I had thought it was a toupee on TV but, from that angle, I could see the line of scars where the Hair Club boys had put the plugs in. Not entirely without some Christian pity, I found myself thinking: *This poor bastard. What a loser. What a clown.*

"Just getting back to the terrorist plot for a minute," I said. "What was Casey Diggs's theory, exactly? I mean, he thought Professor Rashid was up to something, right? What exactly did he think he was going to do?"

"Ah!" he said—and he looked up—and he knocked down another shot, guzzled some more beer by way of an exclamation point. He leaned toward me, a Man Imparting the Secret History of the World. Also a Man Breathing Whiskey All Over My Face. "He.

Diggs: He. Understood. America. The Country of the Imagination. He—saw: that—that would be Rashid's target. Not some . . . towers." He waved off the three thousand people who had died in the Islamo-fascists' destruction of the World Trade Center—waved them away as if they were nothing. *Only in Hollywood*, I thought. "That's just money. That's just the economy," he said. "The Pentagon, too. What's that? The military." Another wave-off. "The Capitol? The White House? The government? No. No. None of those is what really matters. Casey—he understood. The Country of the Imagination. That—is what Rashid has spent a—a *lifetime* attacking, undermining. With his—theories—ideas—propaganda. Not the economy, the military, the government, but . . ." And here, unbelievably, Piersall lifted his two hands and tapped his fingertips against himself three times, each hand against one breast, rat-tat-tat. "The American Imagination. The Bible. The Constitution. Jesus Christ. Thomas Jefferson. Movies. TV. Augustus Kane. Patrick Piersall. That's what he's out to destroy."

I hid a smile behind my hand. I couldn't suppress it. I suppose I was smiling at myself as much as him. I mean, what an idiot I'd been to come here, right? To think that this goofus might have some information that could help me decide what was true and what wasn't. Hell, look at him.

I looked at him. He was an ego acting the part of a human being. He wasn't obsessed with Casey Diggs's theories because they were true. How could they be true? The police and the FBI had already investigated them, already dismissed them. But that didn't matter to Patrick Piersall. To his pickled mind, Diggs's theories were valid because they recentered the news of the world around the only thing that really mattered to him, the only thing that even existed to him: himself.

Once again, I felt as if I had stepped from reality into Television Land. Only now, I had followed the land's Yellow Brick Road

to its conclusion and stood before the Great Citizen of its Emerald
City: the Wonderful Wizard of Me. *Pay no attention to that narcissist behind the curtain. Just talk to the Giant Transparent Head.*

Which is what I did. "Did Casey have anything more specific
to go on? I mean, other than the idea that Rashid was organizing
an attack on"—I gestured at Piersall himself. I couldn't resist
the comedy of it—"the American Imagination. Had he uncovered
some specific plan?"

"Oh, yes! Oh-ho, yes," said the onetime admiral of the spaceship *Universal.* Then he barked in those very tones of command
that once struck fear into Borgons throughout the galaxy, "Charlie!
Another!"

Then he explained it all.

I won't go over the whole thing here. Diggs's obsessive, paranoid writings are public record now. You can look them up online
and read them yourself and good luck to you. You'll find detailed
glosses on all of Arthur Rashid's writings, translations of interviews
Rashid gave to the Arab press, interviews with sources Diggs had
uncovered on his own, not to mention a complex mathematical
and what I guess you'd call *symbological* calculation based on
religious prophecies and—so help me—the phases of the moon.
It was Casey Diggs's version of my mother's Spiral Notebooks.

And what it all came down to was this: Rashid, according to
Diggs, believed that Americans had become so rich through their
financial institutions, so powerful through their military, and so
free through their system of government that they had forgotten
that the financial institutions, the military, and the government
were merely the visible structures that had been built on the foun-
dation of an ancient culture and its ideas. Rashid, Diggs said,
loved this culture intellectually for its genius, but hated it in his
heart because it made him feel inferior on his father's side, made
him feel his British mother was humiliating his Egyptian father

every day the West thrived. He wanted to destroy America, said Diggs, and he believed the country could be decoyed into pouring all its resources into protecting the visible structures of its success while it left the cultural foundations open to a devastating attack. This attack—and here's where all the mathematical and symbological hoo-ha came in—this attack, Diggs believed, was to take place on the highly symbolic eve of both Ramadan and Yom Kippur, which arrived this year on the same day: Saturday.

"So Diggs thought Rashid was planning an attack for Friday, then?" I asked Piersall.

"Friday," the actor muttered. His words were becoming slurred now.

"Tomorrow."

"Tomorrow . . . yeah."

"You're not talking about an intellectual attack here, right? A diatribe or—I don't know—a really sharp editorial or something? You mean an actual bombing or assassination?"

Piersall nodded heavily, as if all that alcohol had gone to his head now and made it weigh twice as much as normal. His torso had begun to tilt forward in his chair with the weight so that he was hovering horizontally over the table, staring down at his hands where they sat wrapped around his latest beer glass. All of which is to say: The guy was so shit-faced, he looked like he was about to sink right into the table. A drop of drool fell from his open mouth and ran down the liver-spotted back of one hand.

I sat and studied him a long, quiet moment. I thought of him as I'd seen him on TV. Augustus Kane delivering the camp sci-fi histrionics that had somehow intersected with a momentary zeitgeist. The man who had watched that zeitgeist slip away like a balloon through a child's fingers, his career earthbound while the culture vanished into the blue.

Now here he was before me in the flesh, an old drunk raving

about the fate of the world. Like Casey Diggs raved after he got
booted off the school newspaper. Or like I had been raving these
last two nights, after I'd forced myself to clean out my mother's
attic and burn the Spiral Notebooks. The world always seems like
it's going to hell when you're depressed. And, of course, it always
is going to hell in some way. That's what makes it so hard to tell
the difference between Armageddon and the blues.

Well, I guess I was a little better off now than when I'd walked
into the bar anyway. Now, at least, I was certain that the Diggs
Conspiracy Theory was a lot of crazy nonsense. You only had to
listen to Piersall explain it to understand why the authorities had
brushed it aside.

But I still wasn't sure what to do. Even if it had nothing to do
with Rashid, Diggs could still have been murdered. Serena's story
about the Great Swamp might still be true. And while I hated to
set the police on the girl, I didn't see how I was going to avoid
it, especially now that Anne had confirmed seeing her and Diggs
together about the time he disappeared and had linked Jamal to
their meeting.

But there was one thing I knew I wasn't going to do. I wasn't
going to tell any of this to Patrick Piersall. Really, he was nearly
unconscious now. What would be the point?

"Well . . ." I said aloud. I stood up out of my chair.

The movement seemed to reach Piersall even in his stupor. He
roused himself a little. With what seemed a great effort, he lifted
his head. He reached out a hand spasmodically and seized my
wrist.

"They killed him, you know," he said—and I couldn't tell
anymore whether he was a drunk speaking his deepest truth or a
drunk playing the part of a Drunk Speaking His Deepest Truth.
He blinked slowly, trying to focus on me. "Diggs. They killed
him."

"Did they?"

He gave a short laugh, as much as to say: *Of course, you fool.* Then a sly smile came over his face, that famous, englamoured, once-handsome face. He let go of me. He raised his chin in a gesture meant to bid me stay and watch him. Then he tried to reach inside his natty corduroy sports coat. It took several attempts for his unsteady hand to find the coat's opening. Finally, the hand slipped in under his arm. When it came out again—just halfway out, just peeking out—I could see he was holding a gun. I don't know what kind of gun it was. I could just see the grip. It was something blocky, powerful, and deadly, by the look of it.

"Oh, fuck!" I believe I remarked.

"They won't get me, though," Piersall said.

"Would you put that away, please?"

The gun vanished inside his coat again. "There's more where that came from," he murmured darkly.

I sighed. I nodded. Again, not entirely without pity, I laid a hand on his shoulder by way of farewell.

"Oh," he said, with a final glimmering of that actorly graciousness he'd shown before, "on your way out, would you ask Charlie if he could possibly bring me another?"

23 · An Unscheduled Detour

I left the bar. A faint rain had begun to fall, a drizzling autumn mist. People hurried past on the sidewalks, their shoulders hunched, their heads ducked down, their hands shoved in their pockets. The cabs and cars and buses on the street had their headlights on against the gloom, their windshield wipers working wearily away at the weather. I had the impression that the day had ended early somehow, that the day had been called off midway and the night had come down at noon.

I had no hat. I wore only a light windbreaker over my sweatshirt. I felt the cold damp in my hair and on my scalp. The chilly air came through my clothes and made me shiver. Still, it was good to be outdoors, good to be away from the smell of morning beer, away from Piersall's whiskeyed breath and from the claustrophobic closeness of his outsized ego.

I joined the pedestrians hurrying past, shoulders hunched and head ducked down and hands shoved into my pockets like them. As I walked back to the parking lot where I'd left my car, the heaviness of the abrupt darkness seemed to settle inside me. So did the dead day's graveyard chill.

I felt—what's the word for it?—*bereft*, I guess. Bereft. Depressed. Adrift. Deprived of—what?—*purpose*. The purpose of my coming here today. The—how can I say it?—*justification*—yes— for my meeting with Piersall. I was *appalled*—appalled at myself for having daydreamed my way into the heart of a global con-

spiracy that I now saw was nothing but the fantasies of a troubled
boy and the narcissistic melodrama of a washed-up actor. This
was what I had convinced myself to worry about rather than—
what?—rather than confront my own—what is the word? What
is the word I want?—*grief.* Yes, that's it. My own grief. For my
mother. My poor father. My angry, brutal, waste of a brother. Myself. My crappy past. My damaged heart.

That's all this was about. This urgency I'd been feeling, this
sense of fear. It was really all about the past, wasn't it? I'd come
back here to confront the past, and instead I'd been swallowed
up in it. In my mother's madness and my father's death, in my
brother's cruelty, and in the consequences of my own mistakes.
You tried to break free of these things. You lived on your hill in a
studied, earnest happiness, clinging to your wife, your kids, your
faith, telling yourself you had won through to a better life. But it
was always there, the past, within you and without you, governing
your mind, your vision, your little unconsidered choices, creating
a destiny out of its own broken logic, waiting for you to return to
it, for its time to rise again. It was there in the surge of lust I felt
when I saw the ring around Anne's neck. It was there in Lauren
and her hold over me, the way she played my emotions and roped
me in. It was there in Serena—in Serena most of all. She was the
problem I'd been avoiding. She was the living token of the fact
that nothing ever goes away—not one act, not one error. The world
is a machine for turning sin into history and history back into sin.
It's a closed system, and there's no way out of it.

I reached the lot. A baleful-eyed Balkan sat hunched in his
little booth, glowering out through the rain-streaked glass. I pushed
money in at him through a slot in the window. He pushed my car
keys back out at me.

It's all about the past. I was still repeating the phrase in my head
as I lowered myself behind the wheel of my car; still repeating it as

I drove out into the city, and the Mustang became just one more of the cars with their headlights on and their wipers working wearily back and forth. The traffic had congealed, as it always does in New York when it rains. I drove uptown on Park Avenue South in a slow, sludgy line of cars and cabs and groaning buses. For interminable minutes, we got nowhere. Lights turned red, then green. Horns bleated uselessly in frustration. Finally, for no apparent reason, we moved on again, trudging like bent-backed slaves. The eccentric towers lining the boulevard—the columned porticoes, the mansard roofs, the arched windows framed with brick or stone—were all broken and prismatic images through the raindrops that flecked the windows. The facade of the terminal ahead—winged Mercury surmounting the clock above the entrance—seemed blurred and far away, nearly lost in the foggy distance.

I sat and drove and sat, lost in my thoughts. After a while, the traffic quickened a little. I came back to myself. I noticed Grand Central was growing nearer, Mercury growing clearer behind the moving wipers. As if someone else were driving, I suddenly realized the car had not turned off toward the tunnel, that I was not heading back to the Island and my mother's house at all. I was still traveling uptown.

That was the first time I understood that I was going to see Anne.

Shall I say that I wanted to ask her more questions? To clear up this matter of Serena and Diggs at The Den so I knew what to tell the police? Shall I say it was all part of my heroic efforts to get at the truth? To find out what else she knew about Jamal? What else he had told her? I would like to say those things. I would like to answer the insinuations of the left-wing media, of the *Times* and the *New Yorker* and that loudmouth on CNN and all the conspiracy theorists online and all the rest of them. I would like to make myself out to be a better man than I am. But that's the whole point. I'm not a better man than I am. I'm just a better man than they are. Because unlike the *Times* and the *New Yorker* and the CNN loudmouth, at least I'm trying to tell the truth.

And the truth is: I wanted to see her. I wanted to touch her. I wanted to do the rough things with her I used to do. If my desire for her was part of the past, then it was the past I was after. It had sucked me back in. I was sinking in it. And I did not want it to let me go.

Her place was off campus, one of a row of renovated brick apartment buildings on Broadway, with storefronts and cafés on the ground floors. I didn't call ahead to tell her I was coming. In some part of my mind, I didn't really believe I'd go through with it. Right up until I reached her neighborhood, I felt sure I was going to turn back. Even once I got there, I thought I would just drive by her building like a kid too frightened to take a dare. Hell, even when I lucked into a parking space right on the street not twenty paces from her door, even as I was *walking* to her door in the rain, I didn't believe anything would come of it. I would just keep walking past or I would turn around, and I would drive home, shaking my head at myself.

Then, of course, there I was, in the entryway, shuddering from the wet and cold, my heart pounding with excitement and anticipation. There was a triple row of brass mailboxes. I felt that surge below my belly again at the simple sight of her name—Anne Smith—on a mailbox in the middle row. I pressed the white button above the box. I was thinking: *I just want to see her, that's all. It's not as if I'm actually going to* do *anything.* But at the same time I was telling myself to stop—stop being a child about it. The truth was—I was telling myself—it didn't make a damn bit of difference what I did, not in the big scheme of things, not in any scheme, not really. It was just what it was, that's all; a moment of life, that's all. People did this sort of thing and you only lived once and it was a messy business and this was the sort of thing that happened. Ridiculous to make some big puritanical deal out of it. What were you supposed to do anyway? Live out your life in some sort of straitjacket of repression? Be some kind of good little boy all the time, some sort of eunuch? It wasn't your fault things were like this. You were what your life had made you, what nature made you, and history and so forth. You couldn't get away from that. It was useless to think you could. Even worse, it was phony and hypocritical to pretend you had.

"Yes?" the woman's voice was tinny and mechanical over the intercom.

"It's Jason Harrow," I said.

The door buzzed. I pushed in. It wasn't much warmer in the foyer. I kept shuddering. Or maybe that was the excitement. I wasn't sure.

Anne's apartment was on the fourth floor. I moved to the stairs. My heart was really thumping now—bang bang bang against my ribs. I started up the first flight. I was thinking: *It's not as if we're actually going to do anything.* And anyway, it was no big deal if we did. A peg in a hole. You had to stop tormenting yourself about these things.

Then, as I reached the second-floor landing, a door opened. A woman stood just within, looking out through the gap. She was about the same age as Anne, but skinny and blonde, with a narrow, pleasant face.

"Hi," she said uncertainly. "Can I help you?"

It startled me—I was so immersed in my own inner drama, the heart beating, the thoughts doubling up on themselves. For a moment, I just stood there, gaping at her, feeling flushed and hollow with a sense of having been caught out, pinned by a spotlight as I crept guiltily through the dark.

"No, I—" was all I could manage to say, and I pointed at the next flight to show I was headed upstairs.

"Oh," said the woman, with a friendly smile. "You rang my bell by mistake."

"I did? Oh, I'm sorry, I—"

"No—no problem. It happens all the time. You have to hit the button under the box, not on top of it."

I got off a smile back at her. "Sorry. Sorry I bothered you."

"No problem," she said again. She closed the door.

I continued on up the next flight, but my steps grew slower and slower as I reached the top as if I were a toy that was winding down. As I stepped onto the third-floor landing, I came to a full stop. My frantic thoughts faded and my mind went quiet except for the thunder of my beating heart.

It came to me then that I might change my mind. It came to me that I had an unlooked-for chance to do that. When I thought about it, I mean, it came to me: I had rung the wrong bell, not Anne's bell. Anne had no idea I was here. No one had any idea I was here. I could simply turn around and go back down the stairs. I could simply leave. I could still get out before I did something stupid—which, let's face it, was what I had come here to do.

Without really reaching any sort of definite decision or anything, I found that I had turned around. I was heading back down the stairs. I started to go more quickly—then even more quickly—afraid that the blonde woman on the second floor might open her door again and see me hightailing it out of there, running as if for my life. I didn't slow down when I got outside, either. I was afraid I might bump into Anne, afraid I would have to explain to her what I was doing here. By the time I reached my car, I was practically sprinting through the drizzling mist. I leapt into the front seat. I was in such a hurry, I had to wrangle my key into the ignition.

I peeled away from the curb like a fugitive, racing to beat the light at the corner. I drove off through the sparser uptown traffic quickly. I did not slow down until I had reached the park, until I was heading across town through the park.

I had done the right thing. I knew that. This adultery business—I mean, it's all right on TV and in the movies and such, in history books and in novels and so on, where no one gets hurt. But again, what's the point of telling a story if you don't at least try to tell the truth? And the truth is: My wife's life and happiness were all in our marriage. My children's happiness depended on ours. I was the head of our household—the man in charge—I had authority over all their lives and was responsible for them. Plus I loved them. I loved them. I didn't want them to become like . . . well, like everyone else, you know: mere artifacts and relics of a feckless era. With those grim, cynical faces you see everywhere. With those hurt, bitter eyes. Saying: *Well, that's the way of things. As we all know, that's just the way.* I want my family to be able to say instead: *No. A man can live by his word. A man can do the decent thing. My husband did. My father did. So can I.*

So I did it: the decent thing, the only wise, the only honest, the only honorable thing.

And, of course, I drove home despising myself for it, thinking: *What a coward you are, Jason. What a miserable fucking coward.*

24 · Juliette's Tear

That was the night it began. The worst of it, the end of it. Most of the details you probably already know: the race against time, the bloodshed, the devastation, and the rest. A lot of it you've probably seen replayed endlessly on TV. If you were paying attention—if you gave a damn—you know some of my part in it, too. You've heard me called a hero and a monster—sometimes by the same people. You've heard me accused of lying, of racism, and, yes, of murder. But no one—no one until now—has told the whole awful, grisly truth about the things I did, the role I played.

There were riots in Paris that night, I remember. Angry mobs ranged through the city setting cars on fire and throwing Molotov cocktails at the police. The trouble had started just after sundown. Earlier in the day, an official at the Louvre had announced that Ingres's *Odalisque*, the painting that had been slashed recently by an Islamo-fascist vandal, would soon be restored to the permanent exhibit. Rabble-rousing radical imams spread the word among their followers that this was an offense against Islam. The fires began in the suburbs and quickly spread. The government—being the French government—immediately surrendered and recanted. But it didn't matter: The disturbances went on. At the height of the violence—this was the lead story, the real shocker—there had been a seemingly organized assault against the Louvre itself. The video showed the army of white-shirted, brown-skinned men breaking like a moonlit wave out of the shadows into the museum's illuminated courtyard. Their faces were bright and twisted in the joy of their outrage. The line of police, their suits blue black, their shields black, their helmets black, looked like a phalanx of myrmidons as they fearfully tried to hold the onslaught at bay. The rioters threatened and shouted. Their Molotovs flew in bright arcs against the Paris sky. Some of the flaming bottles sailed over the cops' heads and smashed against Pei's pyramid, the museum's modern entranceway. The pyramid's glass caught the sudden crowns and medallions of flame and threw the light of them against the Renaissance facade of the palace itself. The palace's verdigris roof, its spotlit arches, the statues arrayed in its niches and around its base leapt with the bursts of sudden fire and seemed to come alive. Other homemade bombs, meanwhile, burst with savage gaiety against the black police shields. The explosions reflected off the cops' helmet visors, revealing glimpses of the tough, frightened eyes behind. The silhouettes of the rioters danced and whirled out of the darkness and across the firelight then melded back into the surrounding darkness again. On my brother's gigantic TV, it all had a sort of hellish grace.

"These are not riots," one policeman said—speaking anonymously for fear of losing his job. "This is Holy War."

I sat on the sofa in the television room, looking up at all this from a turkey sandwich on a paper plate. Now and then, I sat back and tipped a plastic water bottle to my lips. No more wine. I was finished with that. I wanted my head clear so I could come to a final decision about what I was going to do about Serena.

After a while, I got tired of watching Europe die. I started changing channels.

On *Feel the Fear!* contestants were eating dung beetles for cash prizes.

On *Sparkle for the Prosecution,* a single mother-slash-DA was trying to convict a group of Christian child molesters.

On *Shoutdown,* an Egyptian feminist was crying out to an interviewer, "They're taking over our mosques, they stone and mutilate our women, they murder dissenters. If the West will not condemn them, who will save us?"

Oh, and look! Here was Sally Sterling on *Hollywood Tonight*— perky blond Sally with her kissable lips—saying, "Juliette Lovesey reveals the shocking truth in this exclusive emotional interview."

Listen, I wouldn't mention this, but it turned out to be important. No, really. What happened on this show during the next few minutes changed everything in the end. Hard as it may be to believe, Sally's interview with Juliette became a matter of life and death.

Juliette, you see, had cried on camera. Now this was a big deal. You could tell it was a big deal, because Sally wouldn't even show the whole interview right away. She just kept tantalizing us, showing us the moment when Juliette's lips trembled, when her eyes swam, showing it again and again, only to cut it off cruelly, saying, "We'll have more of that interview later in the program."

Then we—we whose tears fall piteously but off camera—we, the Great Unwatched—had to wait through the commercials for the full catharsis. Buy a pad that keeps your menstrual blood from staining your underwear. Get cheaper loans online, get a better credit card, watch a new TV series about a serial killer who works for the police. And don't forget to pick up a box of laundry detergent to get those really tough bloodstains out of your panties . . .

And then at last, at last, Sally delivered the goods. There was Juliette in the usual canvas chair, her tanned, shapely legs crossed, her hands resting ladylike on her skirted thigh.

"This is not something I ever wanted to talk about publicly," she was beginning to say, when . . . well, you remember that scene where the monster latched onto the guy's face in the movie *Alien*? That's how close the camera got to Juliette. It zoomed in so hard

and tight we could almost feed on the trembling of her lips, practically drink the single tear that glistened on the long underlashes
of one fabulously vulnerable eye. That crystal droplet hung there
for a moment of indescribable pathos and suspense and then, as
a grateful nation gasped with compassion and release, it spilled
down over one sweet, high, fragile cheekbone to leave a trail of
shine on the peach complexion by L'Oréal and . . .

"Yes," said Juliette, dabbing at the corner of her eye with a
fingertip. "Yes. I am going to have Todd's baby."

Well, you could have knocked me over with a feather.

"And you're going to keep it," said Sally. She had her Compas-
sionate Face on now. She was leaning forward in her own canvas
chair, her own legs in their elegant black slacks crossed ladylike
at the knee.

"Oh, yes," said Juliette, bravely flicking another tear from her
eyelashes with a slender knuckle. "I love children, and I just don't
think another abortion would be right for me right now."

"And Todd . . . ?" Sally asked, with that infinite gentleness
and sensitivity she did so well.

"Well, you know, in the end, he wasn't ready for the commit-
ment I was hoping he would make," Juliette replied nobly. "But
he really is a wonderful man, and I wish him every happiness."

"Even"—it was a hard question but, as a professional journalist, Sally had to ask it—"even if that happiness is with Angelica
Eden?"

"Yes. Yes. Of course." Juliette's tears were over now. You could
see in the set of her cleft chin that her native strength was flooding back into her. What a woman. "This is the way of things, you
know. Love doesn't always last. People move on. It happens. You
have to let them follow their hearts."

Now, gauging her moment, Sally began to alter the interview's
tone, to lighten it, to bring it back from its dark, confessional

depths. With a girlish, conspiratorial smile, she asked, "Do you know yet if it's a boy or a girl?"

And Juliette brightened instantly, pleased and shy as any young mother, only so much more beautiful. "It's a boy! I'm going to name him Portobello."

"Portobello." Sally giggled. "Like the mushroom?"

"Yes. I really—oh, I can't tell you how much I love them. And it's just always seemed to me such a beautiful word."

"Wonderful," said Sally. "So let's talk about your new film, *The End of Civilization as We Know It.*"

So it went on—as it would, in fact, go on, days and years and even decades, I suspect. Because the thing is, the audience— the Great Unwatched—they loved her from that moment forward. From then on, endlessly it seemed, the TV, the magazines, the Internet would leap upon her every little lust and rumbling, spreading her joys and twitches and discontents across our consciousness as if they were some ocean-sized puddle making up in area what it lacked in depth. The audience would tune in for all of it. The pregnancy, the birth, the difficult partings when Juliette tore herself away from her baby to go filming on location, her son's picture-perfect childhood, his own early movie roles, his wild nightclubbing, his first stint in rehab, and Juliette's selfless dedication to preventing teen depression and suicide through the Portobello Fund, named in his memory. Even in her twilight, when her looks were fading, she would still command the magazine covers with interviews asking why—why? why?—were there no good parts in Hollywood for older actresses? On this night—this last night before the worst of it—Juliette went from being a starlet to a star.

And that, as I say, changed everything.

25 · Cathy on the Phone

I turned the TV off after that. No Patrick Piersall tonight. I'd had enough of him that morning in the Ale House. And then, too, it was all Patrick Piersall somehow. On every show on every channel, he was the presiding spirit: The Wonderful Wizard of Me.

I phoned my wife.

"Hey you," she said. "When are you coming home? It's lonely in my bed at night."

"Tomorrow. The house is all cleaned out. Mitzi can stage it and put it on the market without me."

"Excellent. I can't wait to have you back."

"I have to tell you something," I said. "It's kind of nasty."

"All right." The warm, cheerful voice changed tone. It became flat and cautious. "What's the matter?"

"I went to see an old girlfriend the other day. . . ."

I heard her breathing stop hundreds of miles away. Then, with false and pitiable lightheartedness she said, "And did you set your marriage vows at naught and destroy my happiness, your children's, and your own?"

I laughed. "No. I'm crazy, but I'm not stupid." She breathed again and I loved her. It was the first time it occurred to me to feel glad that I hadn't gone through with my visit to Anne that day. "I should've told you before I went. I'm sorry."

"Never mind. What happened?" It was typical Cathy. Not a word of anger out of her. Just another shift in tone. Now she sounded a little less like the wife and mother she was and more like the lawyer she used to be, ready to figure it all out, whatever it was.

I sighed. I pinched my eyes closed, holding the phone to my ear. "She has a kid. A daughter. She claims she's mine from the old days."

I heard her give a little grunt, as if I'd struck her. "Oh, no, Jason. Oh, no," she said. "Do you think it's true?"

"I can't be sure. I don't think she's even sure. She married another guy and told him the kid was his, too."

"All right. All right." Now I could practically hear her gathering herself, gathering her resources to confront the thing. "So she's not really someone we can trust, in other words."

"No."

"And the girl. Have you seen her? Does she look like you?"

"I don't know. A little, I guess. Everybody looks pretty much like everybody when you come right down to it."

"All right," she said again. "All right. Well, we'll have to get a DNA test. What does the woman want from you? The mother? Does she want money?"

"I don't think so. She just . . ."

"Wants you back."

"Wants to draw me back into her life, yeah. Show me her life. Make me feel bad about it."

"Misery loves company."

"Pretty much, yeah. The thing is: It kind of worked. I mean, the kid's a mess."

"Well, I'm not surprised," said Cathy primly.

"Yeah, but I mean she's really gotten herself into a situation. She says—the girl—Serena—she says she witnessed a murder."

I told her about Casey Diggs, if it was Casey Diggs. I told her what I knew about the Great Swamp and Diggs's conspiracy theories and so on. When I was done, there was another pause:

Cathy considering, gathering her resources again. I sat in the silent television room, listening to her breathe.

"Are you asking for wifely counsel," she asked me then, "or
are you just keeping me informed while you handle this on your
own?"

"Wifely counsel."

"Go tell the police what you just told me, then come home."

I nodded as if she were there. "Yeah, that's pretty much what I
figured. That's pretty much my plan. I'm gonna go to the cops first
thing in the morning."

"Good. Then get out of there. Whatever we have to do for this
girl, whatever's the right thing, we can figure it out together at
home. You have no reason to stay there anymore. That's not your
life anymore. Your life is here."

I gave a bitter laugh. "But that's the whole point, isn't it? You
can never get away from any of it. Anything you've done. Anything
that's ever happened. It all just keeps being about that, again and
again."

"No," she said. "No. You wanted wifely counsel, right?"

"Yes."

"Well, then: No. That's not the whole point. In fact, that's not
the point at all. 'Forget the former things and do not dwell on the
past.' Right? 'Behold, I make all things new.'"

"Well, you do make all things new, Cathy . . ."

"Not me. I'm quoting God, stupid."

"Oh. I knew that."

"'I make all things new.' That includes you, Jason."

I couldn't answer her for a moment. I sat there with the phone
in one hand, pinching my eyes shut with the other. "Right," I
finally whispered hoarsely. "Right. It includes me. I forgot."

"I know. That's okay. You forgot because you're there and you
had to clean out your mom's room and everything, and it sent you

back. But it's all right. You did all right. You didn't do anything
horrible, and I'm still here and everything's fine. So now it's time
to remember that you've been made new, and forget the past and
come home."

I was quiet again. I went on pinching my eyes shut. I thought
of her sitting there in our house on the other end of the line,
listening to my story and telling me to come home and leave the
former things behind because God had made me new. I thought
about that, and then I thought about how I'd thought the past was
swallowing me and how I'd wanted it to swallow me and had gone
to see Anne. And I thought: *What are you, Jason, some kind of
fucking idiot?*

"God, I'm an idiot," I said.

"You're not an idiot. You're the king of my life and I love you,"
she said.

I nodded a long time. Finally I managed to say, "Thank you.
Thank you. I'll see you tomorrow."

And if I had—if I had gone home and seen her tomorrow—
then everything would've been easier—easier for me, at least. I
would've confronted the past and returned triumphant and never
have done the things I did or faced the parts of myself I finally
had to face.

But, of course, it didn't work out that way.

After I closed the phone, I sat for a while, staring into space.
I prayed. It wasn't like before, in the church, when I felt nothing, when I felt alone. The lines of communication were up again
somehow. I felt better—steadier, surer—when I was done.

I opened my laptop on the coffee table. I went online and
picked up my e-mail. There were only a few notes, a few from my
office, one each from my kids. I answered the ones that needed
answering. Then I fell into another staring spell, my eyes on the
computer screen.

The next time I became aware, the image on the monitor had changed. The e-mail file was gone and the screen saver had kicked in. The screen saver drew colorful fractals on the dark background: snowflakes and jellyfish and patterns like galaxies and patterns like DNA. My ten-year-old son Chad had installed the thing for me. Chad had explained fractals to me, too. Apparently, mathematicians had discovered that seemingly random forms in the universe could be reproduced by charting a few simple equations again and again. We couldn't know that in the old days because you needed a computer to chart them so many times, but now we saw that things that we thought were jumbly bits of chance—weather and bird migration and the tumbling of a woman's hair when it's undone—were actually elaborate designs based on mathematical instructions played out almost endlessly. The instructions, the equations, were like thoughts in the mind of God, pure ideas capable of taking physical shape. What made the resulting patterns unpredictable was that the repetitions of the underlying equations magnified the effects of small distorting events. That was what they called the Butterfly Effect, where something as small as a butterfly's fluttering wings changed the pattern of the wind, say, until it became a hurricane.

I gazed at the pictures and designs unfolding on the laptop screen. They were very beautiful and hypnotic. I wondered how many things in the world were like them, how many things that seemed arbitrary actually made a sense beyond our ability to know: evolution, maybe, with its seemingly random selection and love and the creation of worlds. Maybe even the stories people tell were all designs thrown up by the few simple equations of the human heart repeated and repeated. Maybe even history itself is a design like that, too large for us to comprehend.

The thought made me smile fondly to myself. I was thinking of my mother, of course, wondering if maybe her illness had opened up her mind somehow and allowed her to catch sight of some gigantic historical fractal beyond the vision of the rest of us.

And I was sitting like that, staring like that, smiling, thinking like that, when I slowly became aware of a noise that had been going on for some time, perhaps more than a minute. It was a clicking sound. At first I took it for the working of a mechanism: a clock or the cooling TV or some glitch in the computer. But as it drew me out of my fugue state, I realized that, no, it was coming from the window. It was the sound of something hard hitting tick-tick-tick against the glass. A tree blown by the wind, I thought, or an animal scratching.

I didn't have to get off the sofa to look. I simply leaned over and reached to the shutters. I pulled the bar to open the louvers.

I started back and a small noise of surprise escaped me: The face was there in front of me so suddenly, so close to the glass. I couldn't take it in right away. It was just eyes staring in at me, a hand reaching out at me. Then I saw the finger rapping a ring against the pane. Then the face came into focus and I recognized it.

It was Serena.

26 · Serena for Dinner

The alarm went off when I let her in. I was so shaken by the sight of her I had forgotten to disarm it before I opened the door. It gave a high-pitched warning whistle, a noise like a teakettle programmed to sound for sixty seconds before the system let fly with the real clanging blast. Even as Serena stepped into the foyer, I hurried away from her, back into the kitchen to key in the code to turn it off.

When I was done, I returned to the hall. There she was, standing at the other end of it. She was wearing cargo pants and a T-shirt and a hoodie sweatshirt. She had her hands stuffed in the sweatshirt pockets. She looked slumped and withdrawn and small. I couldn't really make out her face in the dim foyer light. It was only when I approached her that I got the full picture.

She had a black eye. She'd tried to cover it with makeup, but it was unmistakable. And she had scratches on one cheek and a red mark on her neck, too. Plus her lower lip was swollen.

One sympathetic glance from me and the tears came to her eyes. I took her chin in my fingers and gently turned her face so I could get a better look at the damage.

"I'm not going to the fucking police," she said.

"Ssh," I said, looking her over.

"All right?" she said.

"Just take it easy. You want something to eat?"

She shrugged sullenly.

I locked up the house again. Brought her into the kitchen. Turned the alarm back on. I sat her down in the breakfast nook, at the same table where we'd eaten before. Luckily, the refrigerator was still pretty well stocked.

"How about a turkey sandwich?"

"I'm a vegetarian."

I laughed. "No kidding? Is Ecstasy a vegetable?"

"Ha ha."

I slapped a few slices of cheese onto some rye bread. I poured her a 7UP on ice. She ate like what she was: a ravenous teenager. She ripped great chunks out of the sandwich and swallowed them in great gulps. I sat at the table across from her. Watched her till she was nearly done.

After a while, gaining strength, she glared at me, her cheeks bulging with food. "I only came here because I don't have anywhere else to go," she said. The words were muffled in her mouthful.

I didn't argue with her. I knew why she'd come. A good father is hard to find. "How'd you get here?" I asked.

"Took the train, then walked."

"All the way from the station?"

She shrugged. She picked slyly at the crust of her bread. "I'm a good walker," she said.

For some reason, this more than anything—more than the shiner, more than the fat lip—hurt my heart and made me feel for her. She wanted me to be proud of her, see. She wanted me to think well of her, and that was all she had, all she could think of to brag about: *I'm a good walker.*

"You must be. That's quite a way," I said.

"I walked all the way into Manhattan once."

"Wow."

"It's, like, five miles or something." She stuffed the rest of her sandwich into her mouth. Chomped on it like a cow on grass. "Can

I ask you something?" she said, offering me an excellent view of the chewed food.

"You can ask."

"Did you really do all that sick shit my mom said?"

I smiled. We were back to the teenager games. "That's not really any of your business, Serena," I said. "Now tell me about your black eye."

She got that look on her face that people get when they want you to take charge of them, but they don't want to admit it: that smile at the corner of the mouth they try to pretend is ironic but isn't. She buried herself in her 7UP glass to hide it. When she came up for air again, the smile was nearly gone.

"You'll just try to make me go to the police again. I'm not going. I mean it."

"Did your boyfriend do it? Jamal?"

Her mouth turned down in a frown and the tears welled in her eyes again. "He's such an asshole."

"Did it have to do with what happened to Casey Diggs in the swamp?" I asked her. "Did it have to do with what you told me about last time?"

She looked away. "No. No, that was just . . . Forget about that. All right? That was just me being stupid. Anyway, I don't want to talk about it anymore."

I felt something—a slight drop inside me—like a pebble falling into a pond. It was a hint, an intimation of what was coming. All afternoon, ever since I'd talked to Patrick Piersall in the Ale House, I'd been telling myself that Casey Diggs was crazy, that Piersall was a useless drunk, that their conspiracy theories were nonsense. There was no urgency to the situation, even if tomorrow was Friday, the day Casey said Rashid would attack. There wasn't going to be any attack. That's what I'd been telling myself.

But when I mentioned Casey Diggs's name to Serena, she didn't say *Casey who?* She knew exactly who I was talking about. She didn't even try to convince me the story about the Great Swamp was a lie. I felt that little pebble drop inside me and the ripples spread out from it like echoing whispers: *It's all true, it's all real, it's all happening* . . .

Serena must've sensed what I was thinking. She stole a glance at me and I saw an expression on her face, a look composed of guilt and fear, desperate appeal and naked longing. I knew that look. Every father does. She was hoping that just coming to me would make it all better somehow, that I would uncreate the disaster.

"I can't help you if you don't tell me the truth," I said.

"Can't we just go away somewhere?" Serena said. All at once, she was pleading with me, her voice trembling. "Mom says you're rich. Can't you just take me somewhere? They'll kill me if I tell."

"Jamal sent you into the club that night, didn't he?" I asked her.

She began to cry. "He got me so fucked up."

"He gave you drugs?"

She nodded, wiping her nose with her hands. "E. And all these White Russians."

"Then he sent you inside to get Casey."

"He said he just wanted to talk to him."

"You went in and asked Anne, the girl behind the bar, to point him out."

"He told me to. He said she was waiting for me, she was his friend. I just did what he said. I was so fucked up. I didn't know what they were gonna do to him. That's true. I swear. That's true."

"And the rest of the story you told me? Out at the swamp. That's how it happened."

She dug the heel of her palm in one eye then the other, trying to stanch the tears. The tears kept coming. "They just killed him. They just fucking, like, cut his throat. It was so horrible."

"But not you."

"What?"

"They didn't kill you."

"Jamal wouldn't let them."

"Because he thought you were sleeping . . ."

"Because he loves me. He says he loves me, anyway."

Right, right. Love. There's a word for you. It's the only action people think they can take without actually doing anything. All right, so he loved her—or wanted her, or whatever it was. And he figured he could control her, that she would keep quiet, do whatever he said. Which she did for the most part. But after she witnessed what happened to Casey, the guilt ate at her. She thought if she kept drinking, kept partying, she could make it stop. Then, when I took her out of The Den that night, when I took her home and she spent that morning with me, the truth came out of her—a version of the truth, anyway. She told it to Daddy to get it off her chest. But when I threatened to take her to the cops, she got scared, she bolted. She went back to her man.

"What happened tonight?" I asked her. "You got in an argument with him?"

"Yeah. I mean, he treats me like shit sometimes." She said this as if she were trying to explain herself, justify herself, as if I were going to blame her for getting beaten up. "And he's just always with his friends. Like they're this secret club. Whispering. Their big plans. Always closing the door on me. He doesn't tell me anything. And he sends me out of the room like I'm a child or something. It's, like, he snaps his fingers and I'm supposed to do whatever he says."

"But you knew they were planning something."

She went on rubbing at her eyes. I gently pulled her hands away from them. The sockets were starting to look as red as raw meat. "Big criminal masterminds," she said bitterly. "His friends are such assholes."

"So is that why he hit you tonight? Did you try to get him to tell you what they were going to do?"

"No-o," she whined, again as if I'd accused her—as if I might take Jamal's side. "I don't give a shit about their big . . . fucking thing, whatever it is. Their big ideas. Like they're some impor-tant . . . y'know, big thing. I just wanted him to spend some time with me, that's all. He can't just treat me like 'Do this, do that.' I'm a person, too. I fucking told him that, too." She drank her 7UP defiantly. "I did."

I bowed my head against my hand, rubbed my forehead. "Oh, Lord, Serena," I murmured.

"What?" she said.

Those whispers in me were spreading, echoing, louder now. I felt the urgency rising out of my belly into my throat. I had to call the cops—not tomorrow—tonight, now. But again—again—I hes-itated. I felt a sickening certainty they wouldn't believe me. They hadn't believed Casey. They hadn't believed Piersall. I needed more information to bring to them. I needed to hear everything Serena had to say, everything I could get out of her.

"Serena," I said slowly, lowering my hand, pressing my two hands together in front of me. "Serena, you must know something, you must've heard something. About what they're planning. When they sent you out of the room, you must've been curious—angry—you must've tried to listen in sometimes."

She made a sad little gesture: a wave, a shrug. "I just know it was supposed to be some big deal. Some 'major victory' or some-thing. Like it was so important."

"But you don't know what or where?"

She sniffled, shook her head. She'd managed to stop crying now. "I think it's tomorrow, though."

I forced down a curse. "What else?"

"Nothing."

"You're sure?"

"Yes!"

"All right," I said. I tried to bring her back to her story. "So tonight. You told him you wanted him to pay attention to you—"

"I just want him to be nice to me sometimes."

"And that made him angry. He yelled at you."

She made a childishly mocking face, a childishly taunting voice, imitating Jamal. "'You don't understand. You're just a stupid girl. It's so important! It's so important!' Blah-de-blah. I was, like: 'Fuck you, y'know? I don't care how important you are. I'm important, too.' And he was, like—" that taunting voice again— "'You're nothing. You're just a stupid female. I'm the master of the universe.' And I'm, like: 'Whatever.' I'm, like: 'You dumb fucking Arabs treat girls like shit, y'know that?' And so then he, like, just hits me, like, with his fist." She moved her fist as if it were a hammer. "I mean, he's such a little wimp, it's not like he's strong or anything. And I'm, like, 'Yeah, well, you and your big plans are all bullshit anyway because I told Jason and he's investigating everything now and he's gonna tell the whole story to the police.'"

It was a second before I registered what she was telling me, before I could bridge the gap between her childlike tone, her childlike inner world, and the terrible meaning of what she said.

"You told him about me? You told him you were coming here?"

She gave me a sort of sidelong glance, a sort of conspiratorial smirk. She was trying to please me, flatter me, enlist me to her side of the fight against her boyfriend. "I told him you were my real father. I said, like, you were this rich, important guy from, like, the Midwest or something, and you were, like, totally in with the police and you were really pissed off that he was bossing me around and giving me shit all the time. I was, like: 'I told Jason all about what happened in the swamp and now he has the police investigating the whole thing and if I get hurt he's gonna find out about it and come after you.' I was, like: 'You're not so important after all, are you?'"

"My God," I whispered.

She just went on, frowning again, near tears again. "And he was, like, choking me. Motherfucker. I fell down. He, like, threw me down. I think I hurt my back. I did! I think I, like, sprained it or something. And then he said, 'You're going to see how important I am.' And he starts calling his stupid friends."

I stood up quickly, my heart beating hard.

"He was, like, so into it, he never even saw me sneak out," she went on proudly. "Like I was just gonna lie there and do whatever he said. Like, bullshit. Where are you going?"

My cell phone was still in the television room. I went to the phone on the kitchen wall. I snapped up the headset. I started to dial 911.

But it was too late. The teakettle whistle of the alarm warning began again.

They were already in the house.

27 · The Battle for My Mother's House

There were four of them. One had a gun. Two broke through a back door, two broke through the front. They swarmed into the kitchen from both directions.

The second the alarm started singing, I knew they were on their way. I dropped the phone on the counter.

"Come on!" I shouted.

I lunged across the little room. I grabbed Serena by the wrist. I pulled her to her feet. She worked her way out from behind the table even as she protested.

"What's the—"

Then they were on us. Four dark-skinned young men in dark blue sweatsuits, the hoods pulled over their heads. Two out of the living room, two out of the front hall. Swarming us, shouting at the top of their lungs, the alarm whistling under them.

"Get on the ground! Get on the ground! Put up your hands or I'll kill you! Get down on the floor now! Now!"

They were all shouting at once, their angry faces closing in on us, their teeth bared, their eyes wild underneath their cowls. A chaos of rough noise swelled to the walls, to the ceiling of my mother's kitchen. I felt fear and confusion wash through the place like a flood. The gun was trained on my face. The bore of the barrel became the black focus of everything, like a drain down which the whole world swirled.

All this in an instant. Then Serena started shrieking, too, hoarse, ugly, tearful shouts.

"Jamal, you fucker, you fucker! Get out of here!"

She hit the young man with the gun. She pounded his shoulder with a small useless fist. Snarling and shouting with rage, he put his forearm into her face and shoved her away from him roughly. She stumbled against one of the others and the second man grabbed her arms. Then Jamal bore down on me, his gun stuck out in front of him, his hooded face blurred and enormous behind the black barrel. He was still shouting and they were all shouting and the alarm was whistling and Serena was screaming, struggling, in tears.

"Get on the ground!" Jamal roared, sticking the gun at me.

I punched him in the throat.

Strangely enough, through all this, I was thinking very clearly. The onslaught was so loud, so violent, so furious, that it swamped me in an instant. It was meant, I think, to throw me into confusion, to bear me down beneath the sheer weight and force of its initial blow. And yet my mind seemed to have gone into that crisis state of silence and slow motion. There seemed plenty of time to think and to react. I thought that in the next count of one–one thousand, everything would be decided. I thought: If I gave in to the power of their rush and to the noise and the shouting and the gun—if I lay down on the floor—if I surrendered to them—they would kill me. I thought: They would kill me and they would take Serena. I thought: *Do something, Jason. Fight back.*

So I ducked inside the gun barrel and pistoned an uppercut into Jamal's Adam's apple.

The bastard gagged and doubled over, crumpling backward into the table. I tried to grab the gun but it flew from his hand, spun through a little arc of air and skittered and twirled on the

fake bricks of the kitchen's linoleum floor. The other men were
still shouting, attacking. One had Serena by the elbows. She was
struggling against him, cursing and screaming. There was a moment—part of a moment—when none of them—no one but me—
fully realized what had happened to Jamal and to the gun. In that
moment, with a quick, panicky movement, I kicked the weapon
under the stove. You know that narrow space under the stove that's
impossible to get to when you want to clean? I kicked the gun
there. It was a slim, elegant automatic, and it slid right through
the gap.

Then two of the hooded men slammed into me. One punched
me in the head, twice, hard, quickly. The other one grabbed my
hair and kicked me in the calf. The next thing I knew I was on the
floor, the thugs carrying me down like an iron wave, hammering
at me with fists, kicking me as I fell. Those blows, those first two
blows to my head especially, sent me deep into a dangerous stillness, far from the tumult above. The men's shouts became muffled
and far away. The whistle of the alarm warning disappeared completely. I saw the screaming faces over me and the wild eyes, and
my arms went up to try to fend off the rain of blows but it was as
if the arms belonged to someone else, as if the falling blows were
a circumstance beyond my comprehension. Through the tumble
of bodies, I caught glimpses of my mother's kitchen: the breakfast nook, the yellow walls, the silver sink, the window above it
through which she used to gaze out at me dreamily as I played
in the backyard. I saw Jamal in the nook where my family would
eat our breakfast before we broke apart for work and school. My
father would read the *Journal* there and my brother and I would
bicker and complain and my mother would hummingbird from
place to place, cosseting and reproving us and bringing us bowls
of cereal or glasses of juice. Jamal was propped against the edge
of the table we ate around, his mouth open, his tongue out. He

was clutching his throat with one hand while the other reached out to his henchmen, trying to tell them something, trying to direct them.

And there was Serena in my mother's kitchen, too—there against the sink where my mother used to stand while she washed the dishes. I used to play on the floor by her feet when I was little, snapping together wooden men that were made to stand on each other's shoulders like acrobats so you could make pyramids and buildings out of them. They still made some toys out of good-quality wood back then. Later, they were made of plastic, and then they stopped making them altogether. Now, there was Serena, struggling wildly and helplessly in the grip of that shouting man in the cowled hood. I saw her face twisted and red and ugly in her rage and her mouth with flecks of spit on the corners of it, flecks of spit flying from it, the lips forming words that young ladies really, it occurred to me in my foggy state, shouldn't say.

The man on top of me was close and horrible, his stink in my nostrils as he tried to punch my face through my raised arm or snuck in punches to my sides and belly. Another man somewhere was trying to get a clean kick at me, kicking my rib cage hard, then trying to kick at my head. The teakettle whistle of the alarm seeped back into my consciousness, as if I had forgotten it and was just remembering it now. I thought in a sort of distant, disinterested way that time seemed to be passing very slowly, that the sixty seconds it would take before the alarm actually went off were going to last a long, long time. I thought by the time the thing really let loose and started ringing, by the time it alerted the security firm and the police, I would probably be unconscious, possibly dead. That deep fall into myself after the first blows to my head, all these impressions that had gone through my mind—all of it had taken no more than maybe a second, maybe two or three. And it was all getting slower and quieter and farther away.

I struggled up toward the world. I knew they would kill me if I didn't. They would kill me and take Serena, so I struggled up and, all at once, I burst to the surface. The shouting and confusion and the pain of the blows became loud and immediate as time sped up in a great sudden rush. A frenzied strength of panic went through me.

With a grunt, I lifted up on one side, spilling the man on top of me onto the floor. I got a weak punch in on him before the other son of a bitch stopped kicking me in the back and jumped on me and grabbed my arm. I reached back around with my other arm and grabbed his hair, pulled his face to me, and sank my teeth into his cheek. He screamed and pushed off my chest and tore himself away, leaving blood and flesh in my mouth. The other guy tried to get back on top of me, clawing at my face, but I elbowed him in the ear, knocking him away.

Jamal staggered up from the table, staggered to his feet. I glimpsed him from the corner of my eyes, heard his raw, hoarse orders amidst the noise.

"Get her out of here! Get the gun!" he was rasping. "Get her out. The gun. Under the stove."

The thug beside me immediately rolled over on his stomach and jammed his hand under the stove, feeling for the gun. I jumped on him, grabbed him by the collar, pulled him back. The other thug grabbed me and the three of us went to the floor again, grappling, tearing, punching, gouging at one another.

Something almost like quiet descended on the room then. The alarm went on whistling its warning and Jamal rasped orders. Serena let out strangled sobs and gasps as she fought to get free. On the floor, we were grunting and panting in our struggle. But most of the shouting was over now, and it seemed uncannily still. It was eerie; frightening. As if all this turmoil were going on unheard, unseen, unknown, in the midst of a vacuum, or in the one lighted

place at the center of a vast surrounding darkness. It felt to me as
if my mother's kitchen were floating in emptiness and space, and
that, scrabbling and clutching and scratching on its fake brick
linoleum floors, I was, in fact, battling for every piece of living
territory left in all the world.

And I was losing the battle. The two men overpowered me now.
They forced themselves on top of me. They held me down. I fought
with one, our arms tangling and flailing. The other, meanwhile,
reared up on his knees and shoved his hand into his sweatpants
pocket, dug for something, came out with it: a folding knife. He
worked to open the blade so he could sink it into me. At the same
time, Jamal was trying to get around us to the stove.

"Hold him," he was saying. "Hold him!"—and his hoarse
voice was very clear in the grunting, whistling silence. "I'll get
the gun."

Over by the sink, meanwhile, the man who had Serena began
to drag her out of the room. Her feet kicked out and she twisted in
his grip as he pulled her backward across the threshold. I heard
her shrieking through clenched teeth, the sound muffled deep in
her throat. Then she must've realized it was hopeless. She cried
out—wailed—in her rage and despair:

"No! Jason! Daddy!"

I threw the two thugs off me. It was easy. It really was. I don't
know whether anyone will believe me or not. Even I look back at
it and think my memory must be false or overblown. But the way
it comes back to me: I heard Serena cry out, and all at once I
was rising off the floor and the thugs were flying across the room
to the left and right of me as if I were some kind of comic-book
superhero and they my merely human foes.

In an instant, I was on my feet. I could see Serena already disappearing into the shadows of the living room. The man who was
dragging her was already just a cowled phantom in the darkness

behind her. I tried to go after them, but the two thugs I had thrown aside lunged at me again. I grabbed one by the throat and drove him down onto the kitchen table. The other came with me as I moved and I turned and drove back again, shouldering him hard into the counter by the stove.

I heard Serena wail my name one more time. I gave a guttural snarl in my desperation to reach her.

Then the alarm went off and every other sound was swept away.

Oh, it was a wild and clamorous cry—a hellacious clarion. It filled the kitchen. It filled the brain. The shattering din of it flooded the house and became the medium through which we moved. The very first blast of it was so overwhelming that it seemed to me everything froze—we all froze—and then went on only thickly, slowly, slogging through the noise like fugitives in a dream.

Once again, I tried to charge after Serena but once again the thugs jumped on me, dragged me back. I thought I saw the flash of the knife blade. But now Jamal was coming at us, too. The thought-pulverizing volume of the alarm must've panicked him. He'd abandoned his search for the gun. He was waving his hand urgently. His eyes were big and white beneath his hood. His shouts were lost beneath the siren, but I could see his mouth forming the words "Go! Go! Go!"

The two thugs tore away from the fight—so suddenly I staggered back a step. They rushed out the door, into the dark, into the living room after Serena. Jamal was right behind them. I tried to throw him aside or climb over him—anything to get by. But Jamal turned and harried me with punches, knocking me back against the sink. I grabbed his throat as he tried to get away, and he grabbed mine. For an instant—it could only have been an instant—we twirled around the room locked together like that, the siren screaming and screaming. Our faces were close together. The hatred in his expression was startling, shocking—as if a beast of fire had leapt out of nowhere into life.

And yet, I felt no hatred for him in return. I remember that clearly. Clutching his throat, spinning around the room in his clutches, I had no feeling about him in particular at all. The philosophy he stood for, the murder he may have done, the beating he had given Serena, even the mass slaughter he was planning—it was as if these were just sad facts of the world to me, symptoms of its soul's disease, like a leper's ugly sores or his contagion. I didn't hate the man for them at all. I simply wanted to destroy him— crush him, kill him, whatever it took—just do the job that had to be done and finish him so I could get free and rescue Serena.

Then we broke apart, flew apart as if hurled from each other's hands by a force outside ourselves. My fingers slipped off his neck as I slammed backward into the refrigerator. He stumbled fast away until he caught himself against the stove. He coiled there with his cowled face twisted, and I thought he would leap at me again. But the next moment, he darted out of the room, darted into the same shadows in which Serena had disappeared.

I shoved off the fridge and went after him. Out of the light of the kitchen and into the dark living room. Through the dim shape of the living-room archway into the den at the back of the house. The siren kept howling, howling and howling, through the rooms, through my skull. I reached the den's threshold just as Jamal banged out through the backdoor screen. I ran after him. Caught the screen as it swung shut. Knocked it open again and tumbled out into the backyard.

The night smelled of autumn and of rain. The air was cool and misty and serene. I saw Jamal's shadow flitting from the glow that fell out of the kitchen window and sinking into the black of the cloudy night. I ran after him across the grass, slipping—nearly falling—on the damp leaves. The siren went on caterwauling behind me, insanely loud still, but softer out here, almost bearable.

I could hardly see at all, but I knew my way. The pachysandra patch was to my left. When I was a boy, it almost seemed a living beast to me the way it devoured our tennis balls and whiffle balls and never gave them back. The long-trunked sycamore was to my right—the Counting Tree, we called it, because it was the official spot to stand and lay your arm across its ridged bark and hide your face in the crook of your elbow while you counted off the time in hide-and-seek. And straight ahead maybe thirty yards was the old post fence on which, when we were ten years old, I once sat with Susan Patterson and asked permission to kiss her freckled cheek. There was a hedge on the other side of the fence and a gate in the fence where the hedge broke. It led out to Chatham Road around the corner from my house. I heard the gate squeal as it opened and heard it fall shut with a click and a thud—sounds I could have identified in my sleep. Jamal was younger and faster than I was. He had already crossed the yard and caught up to his companions.

I put on an extra burst of speed, raced after him even faster. In my acceleration, I slipped again, the slick leaves sending my feet shooting out from under me. This time I did fall, went down on my shoulder, the jolt of the impact aching in my bones. I slid several feet through the grass and dirt and leaves—then leapt up again without stopping. Even so, as I regained my feet, I could see they'd reached their car. I could see the interior light of it go on through the hedge's leaves. I could hear the engine revving to life.

I made the gate as quickly as I could, but I knew I'd lost her. I yanked the gate open, strangling on helplessness and suspense and rage. Everything in me wanted to get to her, to help her, to stop them from taking her away.

I worked the gate open without thinking. I dashed through onto the sidewalk.

Headlights snapped on and blinded me. The great green Cadillac roared and screeched and sped away, already passing me as I stepped off the curb into the street. I ran—ran after its red taillights, my arms flailing, my hands clawing at the air. I ran until I couldn't breathe and the big car was pulling farther and farther away from me.

Finally I floundered to a stop, bent over with my hands braced against my knees. I panted and gasped for breath. I could still hear the alarm wailing from my mother's house. And there were new sirens now, police cars, approaching fast. And there was the engine of the Caddy, too, gunning, shifting gears—fading rapidly as the car sped away through the streets of the town I knew by heart.

FRIDAY

28 · The Last Day Begins

I told the police detective everything. It sounded crazy, even to me. Murder in the swamp; an evil university professor; kidnapping; a terrorist attack in the making; and, oh yes, Patrick Piersall—that was the kicker.

"The admiral of the *Universal?*" the detective mused. "What was his name again?"

"Kane . . ."

"Augustus Kane, right. That was a hell of a show. I used to love that show."

The detective seemed a patient and jovial civil servant but I thought I sensed a rigidly precise system of moral accountancy at work in him. I suspected he had the Official Catholic Church Graph drawn inside his mind on which he could chart the right and wrong of every thought and action. Maybe it was just his name that gave me that idea—Detective Fitzgerald. But I thought I saw it in his steely blue gaze as well, and in the pattern of ridges dug into the pasty flesh of his rather enormous face. The smile lines around his mouth subtly became squint lines around his eyes, as if he could sit there and laugh with you while sending a narrow look into your soul at the same time.

Anyway, I knew myself the whole story sounded nuts. I told him I knew. I sat there next to his gunmetal desk in the remarkably spacious and spotless detective bureau in the Nassau County Police headquarters and I said, "Look, I know how this sounds. I really do." I said it several times. It didn't seem to help. Fitzgerald tilted back in his swivel chair and played with a pencil in his two hands. He considered me closely from under his bushy red eyebrows in a way that made me feel like a very suspicious character indeed.

The detective was neatly, even nattily, dressed in a white shirt with blue stripes and a jolly but professional orange tie. His red brown hair was close-cropped. His jacket was carefully draped over the back of his chair. I couldn't help but feel conscious of my own appearance under his gaze. My face was all banged and bruised, my right eye half closed, my lip split and bulging. My slacks and shirt were stained with dirt and grass. There were scratches and mud stains on my arms, mud caked under my fingernails. I'd refused to go to the hospital, but I had gone into the station bathroom when we'd first arrived to try to clean up. I got a good look at myself in the mirror there. So I knew I not only sounded crazy, I looked— worse than crazy—*disreputable*. Like some guy who'd been hauled in after a drunken, violent set-to with his wife.

I also knew—though I did my best to sound calm—that there was a fever of urgency in my eyes, signs of incipient panic in my fidgeting hands. Somewhere, Jamal and his cronies had Serena. Only his feelings for her had kept them from killing her after they'd cut Diggs's throat. Would that be enough to stop them now? And what about the attack they were planning? It was already two in the morning—a minute or so after. It was Friday, the eve of Yom Kippur and Ramadan. This was the day Casey Diggs had predicted they would strike.

You know, you have this idea in your head—I had this idea in my head, anyway—that once you go to the police, the machinery of law enforcement kicks into high gear. I had this idea there would be fast action: terse questions and quick answers followed by even quicker action, phone calls, racing to crime scenes, arrests. In fact, what happened was exactly the opposite. It felt like that, anyway. Once the police arrived, it felt as if everything just stopped. It was a matter of perspective, I guess. With the police on the scene, my frantic efforts to rescue Serena screeched to a halt. The active role in the drama passed over to them. All I could do now was describe the events of the week and then . . . well, then nothing. There was essentially nothing else for me to do. I sat there with Fitzgerald. We talked sometimes. Sometimes he made a phone call. Sometimes he wandered off and chatted with other detectives. Sometimes he tapped at his computer. And all the while, I just sat there. The clock ticked on the wall.

"Shame about what happened to the guy," he said now.

"To . . . ?"

"Piersall. Patrick Piersall."

"Oh."

"That scene down at City Hall the other day. Made a fine mess of himself over the years, it looks like. I guess a guy like that—he kind of has his moment in the sun. Then it's over and"—he made a drinking gesture, lifting and tilting his hand as if there were a glass in it—"I guess that's showbiz for you, huh."

I tried to smile as if I were not hysterical with anxiety. "Well, he's definitely a drunk, no question. That's why I didn't listen to him at first. But if they did murder this kid in the swamp . . ."

"Oh yeah, yeah, yeah, I follow you," he said, playing with his pencil, observing me, seemingly unconcerned. "Makes sense. I'm just saying."

He lapsed into silence. I watched the pencil moving in his hand. My eyes went to the clock on the wall.

"We should hear something soon," Fitzgerald said at once. He was watching me, reading my thoughts. "We got our guys all over it. NYPD, too. They have the mother in now. They're talking to her. That should help."

I nodded, but the fact they were talking to Lauren didn't exactly inspire confidence in me. I could just imagine her shrugging off Serena's story, shrugging off her danger. *I did much worse when I was her age.*

The detective waggled the pencil at me thoughtfully. "Gimme this again, though—about why you didn't come to us before. Or NYPD or someone. After Serena tells you about the Diggs kid in the swamp, you just . . ."

He let that hang there, waiting for me to fill in the rest. I rubbed my eyes wearily. "I was bringing her to them—to the NYPD. I was bringing her back to her mother's house and then we were going to go to the police. That was the whole idea. Then when she jumped out of the car like that and ran away with these guys, I guess I thought—"

"You're talking about the same young gentlemen she went off with tonight."

"Only she didn't go off with them tonight. Tonight they came after her."

"Right, right, I mean, the ones that came after her. These are the same ones she went off with before."

"Yeah."

"Okay," he said. "So I'm just trying to picture this. You were bringing her to the police and then she ran off with these clowns in the Cadillac and so you figured the whole thing was just a cock-and-bull story. About the kid and the swamp and so forth."

"Right. I figured: If they'd really killed him, why would she run off with them like that? It didn't make sense. That's why I didn't come to the police myself."

"And if they did kill him, going to the police might put her in danger—there's that to consider."

"Right."

"Then you just happened to see Piersall's show about the Diggs kid on TV," said Fitzgerald. "Just total coincidence."

"Exactly."

"So you knew there might be something to it now. To Serena's story."

"Well . . ."

"But you still didn't call the police."

"The whole thing just seemed too crazy, I just—"

At this point, the phone on his desk rang. Fitzgerald tipped his hand at it as if to say, *See? Here we go. Everything is being taken care of.* My heart seized on this in hope: Maybe they had found her. Even if they hadn't, I was glad of the interruption, glad of the chance to stop babbling, trying to explain myself.

"Fitzgerald," the detective said into the phone. He listened. "Yeah. Absolutely. Absolutely." He listened and frowned judiciously at me and held up a finger as if to say, *Wait. This is it. All things are being made clear.* But I couldn't shake the feeling that he had passed his rigid papal judgment on me and I had been found sadly lacking. I couldn't shake the feeling that his friendly, helpful demeanor was just a ploy to string me along until he could get at the truth—some other truth, I mean, besides the one I was telling him.

He hung up the phone. "Well, there we go," he said. That was all he said.

"Is there anything . . . ?"

"Yeah, they're all over it. It's covered. The mother's given them some good leads, and they're following up on your story too so it's . . . it looks like it's pretty much gonna be in their bailiwick now." *Your story,* I thought faintly. *They're following up on your story.* I forced this inner voice into silence almost before I heard it. "Whoever these gentlemen were she went off with, it's pretty sure they're based in the city," Fitzgerald went on. *These gentle-men she went off with.* "Thing for you to do at this point is for one of my people to take you home so you can get some rest. NYPD'll probably want to talk to you in the morning."

"In the morning?" This is what I mean: Everything inside me screamed to take up the hunt at full throttle. The bad guys had Serena. She was in danger. They were getting away. If the police needed to talk to me in the city, shouldn't I get on the phone with them? Shouldn't the Long Island cops be racing me to Manhattan in a screaming squad car? The idea of going home, of just sitting there . . . "Maybe I should just go into town tonight—" I began.

"Ah, no, no, no. You'd just be sitting there like you're sitting here. There's nothing else you can do tonight. They've got enough to go on. And you need your rest, too, I mean, look at you. With luck, you'll wake up and it'll all be over."

Fitzgerald was already rising to his feet to show me out.

A uniformed officer drove me back to my mother's house. I suppose I had some idea that a crime scene unit would still be there, searching for clues, dusting for fingerprints and so on. But if they'd ever done any of that, they were finished now. They were gone. They'd recovered the gun, of course. One guy had fished it out from under the oven, dumped it into a plastic bag, and carried it away. Another guy had taken some photographs of the place. Other than that, there was no evidence they'd examined or dusted or probed much of anything. The kitchen looked exactly as it had when I left.

I stood still in the silence of the room. In every corner, on every piece of furniture, on the appliances, on the floor, there seemed to be an imprint of the battle I'd fought for my life and for Serena not two hours before. Whenever I turned my gaze on something, the image would flash into view: Serena struggling by the sink; Jamal gagging and rasping orders from the table in the breakfast nook;

the thug reaching under the oven for the gun like a kid who'd lost a marble; me on the floor. It was as if those sixty seconds of fear and violence had burned themselves into the fabric of the place.

There were other images, too. Worse images. Images of things that hadn't happened, but might have. I'd been sure from the moment those bastards broke in that their plan had been not just to take Serena, but to execute me once they'd gotten her out of the room. I still believed that was their plan. I could see it in my mind. I could feel it. I could feel my face pressed into the linoleum, my heart beating against the fake bricks, my mind racing uselessly, looking for a way out and finding none so that I just lay waiting passively like a mouse in the jaws of a cat. I could see it as if I were someone else, someone else watching me. And I could feel the barrel of the gun against my skull. I could even see my body jerking as Jamal pulled the trigger.

Daddy!

The images made me shudder violently. I closed my eyes and shook my head, like a dog throwing off water. I tried to tell myself the police were "all over this," as Fitzgerald said, that they were following leads, pounding on doors, peppering suspects and witnesses with questions. But other things Fitzgerald said—those things I had forced out of my mind—kept coming back to me: *These gentlemen she went off with . . . They're following up on your story too . . . Went off with. Your story.* As if he didn't believe Serena's kidnapping had happened the way I said it had. As if there were my story on the one hand, and the truth on the other.

I stood in my mother's empty kitchen, trying to get the image of my own execution to stop replaying in my mind, trying to get the images of the fight to stop, the feeling of the bodies swarming over me, the hands grabbing at me, the sound of Serena's hopeless cry—*Daddy!*—to stop—stop. I felt sick with failure and frustration, helpless, alone.

My suitcase was in the television room, packed but unzipped, ready for my trip home. I got out some fresh clothes. Jeans, a black sweatshirt, and so on. I carried them into the bathroom. I took a shower. I worked the mud and dirt off myself. Put some antiseptic gunk on my cuts and bruises. Brushed my teeth to get the taste of blood and flesh out of my mouth. My face, though . . . I couldn't do much about that. It was still purple and swollen and misshapen.

When I finished cleaning up, I got dressed. I figured I might as well. I didn't think I'd be able to sleep. I didn't want to sleep. I just wanted morning to come so I could drive into the city, get to the NYPD, track down whoever was running the case, and find out what was going on.

I went back into the television room. The images of the fight kept running in my mind. The images of my execution. Serena's scream. I turned on the set to drown it all out. I put on a local news station for a while to see if they had the story on. They didn't. There was just some nonsense about celebrities flocking to Manhattan for the big premiere. Not just movie stars but dignitaries, too, said the breathless newswoman. The secretary of state, the governor, the mayor. All getting ready to join three thousand people at the New Coliseum for the first movie ever in Real 3-D: *The End of Civilization as We Know It.* As if nothing were wrong. As if nothing had happened here tonight.

I turned to one of the cable news networks. They were doing the wars in the Middle East. There was a spectacular video of a truck bomb exploding. An Islamo-fascist suicide killer had murdered a dozen Muslim civilians plus an American GI. The bomb sent up a fiery blast that could've come out of a Hollywood action movie. There were the usual frantic handheld shots of bleeding, weeping people wandering dazed through the debris.

I lay down on the sofa, my head propped against the arm. Not to sleep—I didn't think I could sleep—I didn't want to sleep. I thought I would get up in a minute or two and call the airline to cancel my flight home. I would write an e-mail to my wife, tell her I'd been delayed, tell her what was happening. Maybe I'd even call her, wake her up, tell her myself so she wouldn't worry too much. I blinked slowly at the TV screen. There was the usual mother on her knees, the usual body of a child on the ground in front of her, the mother's hands and her screaming face uplifted to heaven . . .

Then suddenly it was morning—just like that. Late morning, too, by the feel of it. I sat up quickly, surprised, fuzzy with sleep. Something was going on. There was noise. Banging. Someone was banging on the front door, banging so hard I could hear them even in here. On the TV, the news was still playing, the morning report now. I reached for the remote to turn it off. But then I didn't. The pounding at the door went on, but I sat another moment, watching the TV.

Men were standing at a podium—there, I mean, on the gigantic screen that took up the far wall. Men were standing at a podium and cameras were clicking and flashing.

". . . recovered over a thousand pounds of explosives," one of the men was saying.

There was a red banner at the bottom of the screen, a caption: TERRORIST ATTACK ON WALL ST. FOILED.

Now my cell phone started buzzing, its readout lighting up: BLOCKED CALLER ID.

"Two of them were enrolled as university students," the same man at the podium said in answer to a question called from offscreen.

They got them, I thought, as I came fully awake. Then I thought: *What about Serena?*

I was holding my breath, afraid to hear the news that she was missing or dead. I could imagine that whoever was pounding at the door was here to deliver the word, whoever was calling my phone . . .

Pictures flashed on the screen, black-and-white photographs of the five men, five terrorist suspects, who'd been arrested. There were two rows of pictures, two faces on the top row, three on the bottom. My eyes went over them quickly, searching for Jamal, searching for Rashid. Neither was there. I didn't recognize any of the men except . . . Except there was one, the man in the middle of the bottom row. He looked like—yes, I was almost certain he was—the young man who had followed me that day I went to the campus to listen to Rashid's lecture. Yes, of course he was: the young man with hooded eyes and a turned-down mouth who had been watching me as I said good-bye to Anne after the class. He was one of the conspirators.

This was it, then: the attack Diggs had predicted; the Friday terrorist strike orchestrated by Rashid. It was all true, and the FBI had stopped it in time. But where was Rashid? Where was Jamal? Where was Serena?

The knocking at my door had stopped for a moment but now it started again. My cell phone went on buzzing. Excited, I turned the TV off. On my way through the garage to the main part of the house, I answered the phone. It was Fitzgerald.

"Where the heck are you?" he said. "I'm outside your front door."

So he was, big as life, in a gray twill suit with the shirt striped red this time and the tie blue. There was a squad car waiting at the curb behind him.

"Did you find her?" I said at once—said before he could say anything.

"Nah, not yet. But NYPD says they want to talk to you right away. I guess they need some more information." He waggled his thumb over his shoulder at the squad car. "We'll bring you there."

I could see now for myself where the ridges on his big Irish face had come from. Because his mouth was smiling easily, but not his eyes. His eyes were watchful and steely as he smiled. I thought he looked like a hunter who was trying to coax a wild beast into a cage without a fight.

Later, I would remember that thought.

29 · The Allegory of the Interrogation Room

That last day, the sky was gray and roiling. The rain had stopped for now, but there seemed a great, surging turbulence in the thick, low clouds. Watching them from the squad-car window, I had the feeling a storm was being prepared behind them, like some spectacular effect being readied behind the curtains of a stage. The sight called forth a physical response from me: a churning in my belly; a sense of portent and foreboding. I was just worried about Serena—that's what I told myself.

But it was more than that, though I wouldn't let myself see it. And when I did see it, I wouldn't let myself acknowledge what I saw. That nausea, that foreboding: It was my brain picking up hints and details faster than my mind could interpret them. It was sitting in the backseat of the squad car like that and looking at the backs of the two heads up in front of me, the head of the young uniformed cop who was driving and the head of Fitzgerald, where he was riding shotgun. It was their terse answers to my questions and their subtle glances at each other and the tense irony in the eyes of the uniform when I caught a look at them in the rearview mirror and when they stole a look at me. I had no reason to see anything ominous or wrong in any of this, but I did see it—I saw it and I convinced myself I didn't.

"So you haven't heard anything at all about Serena?" I asked for maybe the third time.

"Nope," said Fitzgerald, in the tone of a man long comfortable with casual lying. "I guess we'll find out more when we get there."

"They didn't say why they wanted to talk to me?"

"Just, you know, follow-up. Pretty routine in a case like this."

"Those terrorists—I saw on TV they arrested some terrorists who wanted to blow up Wall Street. You think that's part of this?"

"You'll have to ask the guys in New York. Like I said, I'm sure they'll bring us up to date."

I turned away from the backs of those two heads and looked out the window, up at the roiling, ominous clouds.

It was almost eleven as we crossed into Queens. There was plenty of traffic, but the cop car, being a cop car, cut through it quickly, keeping to the left lane while other cars ducked out of its path like saloon dwellers in a cowboy movie dodging out of the way of Black Bart. Since Fitzgerald wasn't saying much, I used the travel time to make some phone calls. I canceled my flight home. I checked in at the office. I called my wife. I got Cathy's voice mail, both at home and on the cell. I remembered today was her day to play lunch lady at our daughter's school so she had probably shut her phone off. To tell the truth, I was glad of it. I had no idea how I was going to explain to her what was happening here. I left a message:

"Listen. I'm all right, but I've run into a problem. I can't come home yet. I'm with the police. I'm fine, but some men broke into the house last night and took Serena. Don't be worried or anything, all right? I didn't get hurt and it's gonna be okay. I'll call you when I can."

As I pressed DISCONNECT, I caught Fitzgerald and the uniform exchange another glance across the front seat.

I managed to ignore that or to ignore the fact that it fed into my suspicion that something was wrong, that there was some catastrophe impending. And I managed to ignore it when the squad car left the expressway for the parkway, too, and when it crossed the bridge into uptown Manhattan and when it crossed Manhattan to the West Side. Up until then, I'd just assumed we were heading for police headquarters downtown.

"Where are we going?" I asked the back of Fitzgerald's head. "Are we going up to the university?"

"They're working this out of the twenty-sixth," he answered. Whatever the hell that was supposed to mean.

We passed along several streets of aging brownstones, and finally turned onto a street crowded with cop cars. The cars were parked in slanted spaces outside a cookie-cutter New York precinct house of concrete and yellow brick. Our driver slid his county squad car in with the others.

They were waiting for us inside. That much seemed clear. Fitzgerald only had to flash his Nassau County shield at the officer behind the reception desk and a locked door buzzed open. We passed through it into the precinct's inner halls.

A man met us in a cinder-block corridor. He was about forty, youthful-looking, black or half-black—with tan skin, anyway. He was short and trim, with a round, hard, handsome face, a serious face under clipped, serious black hair. He was in shirtsleeves, a buttoned-up white shirt with a blue tie, the pants of a charcoal suit. Everything about him seemed serious and efficient.

I didn't like him. To put it bluntly, he frightened me. The second I saw him, I sensed he was a man of little feeling and dour expectations, the kind of person who waits for you to reveal the nature of your depravity, who doesn't wonder whether you committed a crime but only which crime you committed. The world to him was like a child's frame puzzle where there are empty spaces and a piece to fit the shape of every space—except that every space was a kind of sin and the pieces that fit them were human beings. Frankly, I thought that attitude probably made him a pretty good detective, but that didn't make me like him any better. Anyway, that was what I sensed about him in that first moment, and nothing I saw later made me change my mind.

He had a manila folder in his right hand. He didn't put it down or move it to his left hand, so naturally I didn't offer to shake hands with him. I had a feeling that was the whole point of the folder.

"Mr. Harrow, thanks for coming in. I'm Detective Curtis."

Fitzgerald hadn't introduced me, hadn't spoken at all. Curtis just knew who I was. Now his eyes shifted toward the Long Island detective. At once, Fitzgerald turned around and walked away, just like that, without a word to either of us. I'd been handed off—like a case file or a report—something that needed working on.

"What's going on?" I said. "Is there any news about Serena?"

Curtis gestured to a doorway with the folder in his hand. "Would you come this way, Mr. Harrow?" He didn't smile. He looked at me with interest, but without feeling as if I were . . . well, as if I were a puzzle piece.

He led me down the cinder-block hall to a door, through the door into a cramped, unpleasant room.

"Sorry for the accommodations." His voice had no more feeling than his eyes. "We're kind of short on space. I'll be with you in a couple of minutes. You want anything meanwhile? A cup of coffee or . . ."

"Yeah," I said. "A cup of coffee would be great."

"How do you take it?"

"Black."

He left me there, the door hissing shut behind him.

I turned to look at the room. It was cramped, as I say. There was a small wooden table in the center and three cloth-and-wood chairs. The furniture nearly filled the gray floor so there wasn't much space to move around in. The walls were cinderblock, painted an institutional pale green. The rough, naked, heavy look of them gave me the feeling of being bricked in. There were dingy white soundproofing tiles in the ceiling, and a single ancient air vent, and a single long fluorescent light that made my eyes ache. There was the door—a heavy wooden door—on one wall and on the wall to the right of it there was a mirror: one-way glass.

About ten minutes went by. Then a uniformed officer—a short, chesty black woman—brought me my coffee in a paper cup. She held the door ajar with one hand and gave me the coffee with the other.

I was already getting antsy, waiting. "Do you know when Detective Curtis will be back?" I asked her.

"He'll be with you as soon as he can, sir," she said in a flat singsong, the voice of an uncaring nurse speaking to a querulous patient. Then she drew back and the door hissed shut again.

After that, I waited some more. I waited a long time. As the minutes passed, the room began to have a strange effect on me. It began to seem as if the place had some kind of meaning, as if it were a metaphor for something, as if my being there were some sort of allegory, though I'm not sure even now what the allegory was all about.

I drank my coffee. I checked my watch. I checked my phone. There was no reception here, no way to call in or out. I sat in one of the chairs. I stood up and paced. The room was so small and crowded with furniture, I had to go to the edges of the floor to do it. I could take five paces along the width of the place and six paces along the length. Pretty soon, I sat down again. I drummed my fingers on the table. I got up and paced some more.

I eyed the door. The door was part of the allegory. The door was unlocked the whole time. I checked. I could've opened it. I could've stepped out into the corridor. I could've left the precinct house altogether, if I wanted to. But I didn't do any of those things. I never so much as poked my head into the hall to ask someone where the hell Curtis had gone off to. I thought about it. I argued with myself. I thought, yes, damn it, I should find out what's taking so long. But minute by minute, I put it off. I was afraid if I seemed too impatient, it would make me look bad somehow. It would make me look uncooperative or guilty. That was the effect the room had on me. Four men had broken into my house, nearly killed me, kidnapped a teenaged girl—and *I* was the one who was afraid of looking guilty. I even began to think of things I had done wrong. Not just recently, but in the past, too. I began to imagine Detective Curtis questioning me.

Why didn't you call the police after you heard about the murder in the Great Swamp? Why did you go to see Lauren without telling your wife? Why did you go to see Anne Smith? Tell me about That Night in Bedford.

I was interrogating myself in the interrogation room. Explaining myself to Curtis or whoever was secretly watching me.

Which brings me to the mirror, the one-way glass. That was part of the allegory, too. I could see myself in it, my face still badly bruised, painfully disfigured, purple and yellow all along one side. I looked into my own eyes, and I felt sure there were cops on the other side of the image, on the other side of the glass, watching me. I paced close to it and stole glances at it, trying to make someone out back there. But I didn't want to seem nervous about it so I didn't stop and stare or look too close. I wanted my behavior to convey that I was a good guy, that I was here to cooperate. That was part of the reason I never left the room, too, never complained about how long I'd been kept waiting. I was acting innocent, see— acting innocent for whoever was watching behind the glass. I was playing a role for them: the role of an innocent man. I watched my performance in my mind's eye. I imagined I was on the other side of the mirror looking in. It made me wonder: Why would a person have to pretend to be innocent unless he were actually guilty of something? I began to become suspicious of myself.

Why didn't you call the police, Mr. Harrow? Why did you go to see Lauren? Why did you go to see Anne Smith? What were you thinking when you went to see her? You didn't mention her to your wife, either, did you? What about That Night in Bedford?

I was in the interrogation room nearly an hour. Finally I began to get angry. I was sitting at the table again, drumming my fingers on the surface again. I thought: *This is ridiculous. I'm going to find Curtis right now. Right now.*

Maybe I would have. But I'll never know. Because just then, the allegory ended, whatever the allegory was. The door opened.

I looked up eagerly—and then my eagerness turned to surprise. Startled, I got to my feet quickly.

Lauren had stepped into the room.

30 · Lauren under Glass

The door swung shut behind her. The last time I'd seen her, she'd been screaming obscenities at me. *Fuck you, you coward. You hypocrite. You shit.* But of course all that was beside the point now—all our little dramas were beside the point now that Serena was in real trouble.

She gave a loud, weary sigh. Leaned against the wall, her arms crossed under her breasts. She shook her head at me.

"Can you believe this shit?" she said.

It struck a jarring note with me. She didn't seem as distraught as she should've been, not even as distraught as I was. Her daughter was missing—kidnapped at gunpoint—and she seemed merely annoyed, merely put out. The look of her bothered me, too. She was wearing loose black jeans and a baggy purple sweater, artfully arranged to smooth over the bulges of her slovenly body. And she'd put on heavy makeup, much heavier than when I'd seen her before. It covered over her rough complexion. It made her eyes look larger and softer than they had. I wouldn't've thought a woman in her situation would spend so much time in front of a mirror. I tried to tell myself that, well, she had cleaned herself up overnight, the same as I had. Still, it didn't seem right.

"Is there any news about Serena?" I asked her.

"No, no. They're looking for this Jamal character of hers. I got tired of sitting around waiting for something to happen. They told

me you were in here. I figured we could at least pass the time.
Fight with each other or something."

I nodded and looked away and let out a long breath, frustrated.

"What the hell happened last night, Jason?" she asked me. "I
mean, they just broke in, just out of the blue like that?"

"Yeah. Why? What do you mean?"

"I don't know. I mean, it just seems . . . bizarre, doesn't it?
They just—come to your house, they just take her . . . With guns?
I mean, it sounds like something out of a TV show or something."

I didn't like her saying that. It made me uncomfortable. I
glanced nervously at the one-way mirror. I didn't want the people
behind the glass to get the idea that my story sounded fictional.

"Well . . . I don't know how much the police told you . . ."

"Oh, they told me. You know how they are: They told me
what they told me. I want to hear it from you, though. You were
there."

"Well, I just . . . Look, I think Serena's gotten herself mixed
up in something pretty bad. I mean, she doesn't seem to have
understood what she was doing, but these guys she's with—Jamal
and the others—I think they're in league with this radical professor who may have been part of this attack they were planning on
Wall Street." I stammered through it. I couldn't just come out and
say it. It sounded ridiculously melodramatic, even to me. Like
something out of a TV show, yes.

That was how Lauren reacted to it, rolling her eyes with disbelief. "Come on, Jason. You think my daughter's a terrorist?"

I glanced at the mirror again. "I didn't say she was a
terrorist."

"Yes, you did. You said—"

"I said she's gotten mixed up with these guys, and I think
they're terrorists. I think they're connected to those guys who were
arrested today."

This time when she rolled her eyes, she snorted, too.

"Why do you react like that?" I said.

"Like what?"

"Like you don't believe me. You think I'm making this up?"

"I didn't say that."

"You're acting like it."

"Well . . ."

"Well, what?"

"Well, Jason!" she said, as if my name were an argument in itself.

"Jason what? You think I broke into my own house and beat the crap out of myself? Look at me!"

This was not what I wanted, not the way I wanted to behave. Squabbling with her. Right there in front of the one-way mirror. As if we were an angry divorced couple fighting over their kid. I could just imagine the sardonic cops exchanging sardonic cop glances on the other side of the glass.

"Look, I don't know what happened . . ." Lauren said.

I told myself not to respond to that—not to take the bait—but I couldn't help it. "What do you mean you don't know? I just told you."

"Yeah, well."

"Yeah, well what, Lauren?"

"Serena's sixteen years old, Jason. She's this little . . . fucked-up sixteen-year-old adolescent like every other fucked-up adolescent in the world. I mean, okay, you want to tell me she does drugs. You want to tell me she's doing unprotected sex or whatever. But she's not a terrorist, for Christ's sake! She doesn't even watch the news. What's she gonna be a terrorist about? 'Give me more pink camis or I'll blow up The Gap?' Can I ask you something?" Her tone changed instantly, became instantly casual. That *Can I ask you something*—it sounded as if she were about to ask

me where I'd bought my shoes. "Did you two, like . . . get into
something together?"

"What?" It came out of me like a chicken's squawk.

She leaned in toward me confidentially. "Well . . . you know."

I stared at her. "No, I don't know. What are you talking
about?"

"You know, Jason," she said out of one sly corner of her mouth.
"I don't mean you and her were, like, doing anything together,
obviously. But . . . well, I mean, I know you, Jason. I mean, you
have to admit: You can get up to some shenanigans yourself when
you're in the mood."

I opened my mouth to answer her, but I didn't answer, and I
shut my mouth again.

We were close together in that small room, face to face. I could
see the eyeliner around her eyes and the eyes themselves, the true
feelings in them. I could see the micro-expressions at the corners
of her lips, the little giveaways. It was all there, I just hadn't noticed it before. I had been too busy thinking about the cops watching me behind the mirror. I had been too worried that I might seem
guilty to them, that I might somehow reveal to them my private
sins and peccadilloes. I had been so fearful that they might come
to suspect me of some wrongdoing in Serena's disappearance that
the whole, awful truth of the situation hadn't really struck me. But
now I saw it. Now I thought: *Of course.* This was what had been
bothering me all morning, what had caused that sense of foreboding in me when I looked through the cruiser window at the roiling
clouds.

The truth was: The police suspected me already. It was just as
I imagined it, just as I worried, exactly as I feared. They already
knew my private sins and failings—whatever Lauren could tell
them, and no doubt she'd told them all with relish and malicious
glee. And then she had come in here. They had sent her in here,

to catch me off guard, to get me talking, to get me to confess to . . . what? To what? What the hell could they suspect me of?

I didn't know—I had no idea—and I was afraid. I felt cold sweat gathering on the back of my neck. I felt the fear show itself plainly in my expression, in my eyes. Lauren saw it. I could tell she did. I could tell she liked it, too. She had to fight down a smile.

"Something," she said with a horrible knowingness. "You got up to something, didn't you, Jason?"

I turned my back on her.

"What was it?" she said.

I stepped to the mirror. I glowered into my own frightened eyes, at my own battered face. Lauren's leering image was at my shoulder.

"What was it, Jason?" she said behind me.

"Get the hell in here," I said to the mirror. "This game is over."

I'd hardly finished speaking—I was still looking at the mirror—when the door to the interrogation room opened and Detective Curtis came in. He held the door ajar with his shoulder while he worked the sleeve of his jacket over his other arm. There were no apologies from him, no pretenses.

"Mr. Harrow" was all he said, slipping his jacket on. "Would you come with me, please?"

Of course, it wasn't really a question at all.

Detective Curtis walked rapidly down the cinder-block hallway. I
had to hurry to keep up with him.

"What the hell's going on?" I said.

He didn't answer me—didn't say a word—just walked on,
straightening the sleeves of his jacket, shooting his cuffs as he
went.

"Excuse me," I said a little more sharply.

"I'll explain on the way," he said. And he just walked on. I
followed, irritated—and sick with fear.

We came into another room. It was bigger than the interrogation room, but still small. There was a gunmetal desk in each of
the four corners, all of them chaotic with papers and coffee cups
and files. Three of the desks were unoccupied, as if their resi-
dents had been overwhelmed and fled. At another, a harried man
sat bent almost double in his chair, leaning urgently into a cell
phone as if he were talking a possible suicide off a bridge. There
were lots of cheaply printed flyers papering the walls, cheerful
pastel pages, some covering the messages on others. DO YOU HAVE
INFORMATION ABOUT . . . PROTECT YOUR CHILD . . . PATROL YOUR NEIGH-
BORHOOD . . . Somewhere the city was paying someone to print up
more flyers to cover over even these. On one wall, an open door led
into a connecting office. A dapper, silver-haired man was sitting
at the desk in there, signing papers with a mournful expression

on his face. He looked as if he'd been signing papers forever, and would go on signing them, always with the conviction that they were no more useful than the unreadable flyers on the wall.

The place had a strange embattled atmosphere. I couldn't quite pinpoint it at first, but after a while it occurred to me: It felt like an imperial outpost in some rebellious tribal backwater.

Curtis crossed to one of the empty desks. He snapped a clipboard from the mess on it. Handed the clipboard to me.

"Read that and sign it."

I stared at the page on the clipboard.

"It's your rights," he went on in a monotone. "You can remain silent. You can have a lawyer. It's all there."

I looked up from the page into his pale, passionless eyes. "Do you suspect me of something?"

"We have to inform you of your rights," he said. "It's routine." He didn't even try to sound convincing.

There was a pen wedged in the clip. I pulled it out and signed the paper. It didn't even occur to me to demand an attorney. Why should I? I hadn't done anything wrong.

I handed the clipboard back to him. He tossed it down onto the desktop as if it held no more interest for him. Then he grabbed a set of keys off a hook on the wall and walked out, leaving me to hurry after him again.

There was an unmarked car parked among the squad cars out front, a dark blue Dodge. We drove downtown in that. I sat in the front seat next to Curtis. The Dodge merged with a thick current of cabs and delivery trucks, moving slowly along the edge of the university campus. The campus and the street formed a corridor running to the low, churning gray-black sky ahead: classical buildings to the left of us, amidst lawns and pathways; scarred brownstones and ragged awnings to the right. Curtis kept his hard face forward as he drove, his hard eyes on the windshield. He still wasn't saying anything. I got the feeling he wouldn't say anything unless I badgered it out of him.

"Where are we going?" I asked. Angry as I was, worried as I was, I was still gauging my tone, gauging my words, just as I had when he was watching me through the one-way glass. I was trying to sound forceful now, but without sounding hostile. I thought I deserved some information but I still wanted to come across as one of the good guys, ready to cooperate in every way.

It was a long time before Curtis answered me. We drove another block in the stuttering flow. When he did finally speak, it was in a slow, reluctant drawl, as if he were doing me a favor. "Downtown. There's something I think you should see."

"Is this about Serena?"

"That's what I'm trying to find out."

"Look, could you tell me what's going on, please?"

"We're investigating your daughter's disappearance."

My daughter. That had to have come from Lauren. I was about to tell him Serena wasn't my daughter, but I didn't. What if she was? Would he think I had lied?

Instead I said, "You sent Lauren into that room to question me, didn't you?"

I thought I saw the faintest hint of a smile play at the corner of the detective's thin lips. "There wouldn't be any point to that. You hadn't been Mirandized. We wouldn't have been able to use any of your answers in court." He rolled his tongue around his cheek. "We just asked her if she wanted to see you—that's all."

It took a moment but then I got the joke. I managed a short, bitter laugh. I could picture that scene, all right. I could just imagine Lauren in the detectives' office, that chaotic little outpost of the empire with the four gunmetal desks. I could see her with a tall mocha latte the cops would've brought her from Starbucks.

Slouched in a chair beside Curtis's desk, laughing off my ideas about some sort of—get this!—terrorist conspiracy involving Serena. The other detectives would've tilted back in their own chairs with their hands behind their heads, listening, laughing along. I could see that, too. And I could hear Lauren describing me as if I were some sort of puritan evangelist, some sort of pinched, intolerant hypocrite, raining fire and brimstone down on her because she was a poor single mom doing the best she could. As the chuckling cops encouraged her, she would've grown more expansive, favoring them with detailed descriptions of our sex lives more than a decade and a half ago. That Night in Bedford—that never-ending night. *He could get up to some shenanigans, that Jason, when he was in the mood.* Then, when they thought she was really primed, the cops would've brought her into the observation room, the room on the other side of the one-way glass. They would've stood around her, snickering with her, as she watched me pace and drum my fingers and stew. *Hey, y'know, you're welcome to go in and talk to him if you want—for old times' sake or whatever.* They wouldn't have had to spell it out. She'd have known what they wanted her to do. She would have jumped at the chance to get me to confess. . . .

But to what? Confess to what?

"Look," I said to Curtis, "why don't you just ask me whatever you want to know? I haven't got anything to hide." That only got me more silence. So I said: "What is it exactly you suspect me of?"

He turned those cold eyes on me again. He wasn't smiling anymore. "I don't recall saying I suspected you of anything."

I felt my stomach curdle as if he'd caught me out at something, some revealing error. "Come on," I said. "You leave me waiting around for an hour. You send Lauren in to weasel information out of me. You read me my rights. What am I supposed to think?"

"I'm just trying to find your daughter, Mr. Harrow. That's all."

"You sure seem to be taking your time about it."

"We're doing what we can."

He had turned back to the windshield. His hard gaze seemed to stare right over the red brake lights ahead of him and the taxis' yellow rooftops, straight into the distance, at the liquid steel of the sky.

"Do you understand that the people she's with may be terrorists?" I asked him. "They may be part of that Wall Street attack they were planning today—you know that, right?"

He gave a slight, almost-imperceptible shake of his head.

"What?" I said. "You don't believe me?"

"According to our information, it seems unlikely."

"You don't think these guys murdered Casey Diggs, then, the way Serena said?"

"We're checking that story out."

I couldn't tell whether he meant he was checking Serena's story or checking my story about Serena's story or what. I was afraid to ask. In fact, every time he spoke, I felt that clammy chill again on the back of my neck, that sour bubbling in my stomach. It was not that there was anything accusatory or suspicious in his tone. There was only that mild, disdainful curiosity as to exactly what kind of scumbag I was going to turn out to be.

We turned east after a while and headed across the park. I brooded out the window on the clustered autumn trees, their red and yellow leaves. The sight made me ache for the suburban woods of home. It occurred to me that if I checked my phone right now, there'd probably be a message on it from my wife. She probably called me back while I was in the interrogation room where there was no reception. I didn't check the phone. I didn't think I could bear to hear her voice.

We came out of the park onto Fifth Avenue. The Metropolitan Museum of Art lorded it over the boulevard with its majestic columned front, like some palace in an imaginary Rome. The cars were moving faster, and the blue Dodge sped along beneath a line of yellowing sycamores. Wherever we were going, we were getting there faster now—which made me grow even tighter with suspense. The anxiety was making me jittery—jittery and increasingly pissed off. This bastard—his silences—I couldn't tolerate them anymore.

I turned on him. "Do you know about Diggs, about Casey Diggs?" He didn't answer. "You know about his theory about Professor Rashid?" Detective Curtis chewed the inside of his lip. "If the guys who took Serena killed Diggs, they were probably protecting Rashid, weren't they? Which means they were probably in on the Wall Street attack." Again, I caught that nearly imperceptible shake of the head. "You keep shaking your head. Why don't you believe me?" No answer. "What about the fact that one of the terrorists they arrested today was one of Rashid's students? What do you make of that?"

Finally, I got something out of him. We had stopped at a light at Grand Army Plaza. The buildings were low here and the boiling sky was big. The massive, mingled, steely clouds rolled and raced over the mansard roof of the hotel, over the statue of General Sherman on horseback, over the narrow side streets leading to the river. Curtis turned to look at me. What a look—I could almost feel him rifling my soul. I could see him going over the contents of my conscience with his dour cop intelligence. What must it take, I thought, to turn a man into a man like this? A whole lot of hours bearing witness to the blood toll of human malice and folly, I had no doubt. It must've taken a lot of dead bodies on a lot of floors to make Curtis Curtis.

He turned away. And the light turned green and we started moving again. Whatever it was he was searching for in me, I got the feeling he hadn't quite found it yet. I waited for him to say something. He didn't.

"All right, well, you got me—I'm baffled," I said, throwing up my hands. "Diggs says Rashid is a terrorist and then Diggs disappears. You bust a bunch of terrorists planning to blow up Wall Street, and at least one of them is Rashid's student. Why the hell aren't you investigating Rashid himself . . . ?" I was about to go on, but the words died in my mouth. I never finished the sentence. Instead, I guess I sat there like an idiot for a few seconds, staring at the detective's expressionless profile, mouthing thoughts I didn't speak, as an idea took shape in my mind. I wasn't sure I should say it aloud but finally, still unsure, I did. "You're not investigating Rashid," I said, "because Rashid is working for you." No reaction from him. "That's it, isn't it? He's working for you or for the FBI or for someone. That's why you ignored Diggs. And Patrick Piersall, too. That's why you shut them both down, publicly dismissed their ideas. You were protecting Rashid because he was your inside man. Diggs got it right, didn't he? There was a conspiracy centered around Rashid—a conspiracy to bomb Wall Street. Only what he didn't understand was that Rashid was an informer the whole time. Rashid turned them all in to you guys. That's how you got them. Right?"

One more time—the last time—I thought I saw that little smile play at the corner of his thin lips. I knew I had guessed the truth. I had gotten it exactly.

"But then . . ." I said—or started to say. I started to say: *But then where was Serena? Why did they take her? Why did they kill Diggs? I mean, if Jamal and the others weren't terrorists, who the hell were they?*

There was no point in asking. Those were obviously the exact questions he was wrestling with himself. And he thought something—something "downtown" that he was taking me to see— might help him find the answers.

So we went downtown—downtown and east to the river—to Bellevue Hospital. We had to go around, up from the south, to reach it on the one-way avenue. I only caught a glimpse of it: a sullen brick fortress over a century old set amidst the greater medical center of modern towers all white stone and glass. Then Curtis turned the Dodge into the parking lot of a side building. It was a low, grimy tiled box wedged in a corner of the vast complex. What was this place? I'd never seen it before. It was set beside a long, large garage or warehouse with several loading bays. Some trucks and ambulances were parked out front.

I tried to take a look around, but Curtis was on the move again. He snapped off the car's engine and leapt out almost in a single movement. Again, I had to hurry to keep up. I didn't reach his side until he was standing at the entrance to the grimy little structure. He flashed his badge at a security camera. The door unlocked with a buzz. It was only then—just as I was about to step inside—that I spotted a small plaque on the wall next to me: CITY MORGUE.

"Not Serena," I said softly, following Curtis down a faceless hallway of tiles and glass and metal doors.

He shook his head. We turned a corner. He pushed through another door. I went after him.

I found myself crowded with him now into a small, sterile green room. There was a folding panel stretched across the middle of the floor, dividing the space in half. There was nothing else there except, on a metal table to my right, a small closed-circuit television set. There was a picture on the set, black and white. It was a picture of a corpse on a gurney. The corpse was covered by a sheet, head to toe. I gazed at the image on the TV—gazed stupidly, confounded out of any feeling whatsoever, even a feeling of expectation. I couldn't imagine who it could be, lying there—who it could be, I mean, who might have anything to do with me.

Then Curtis stepped forward. He slid the folding panel aside. To my shock, the corpse—the corpse shown on the TV screen—was right there—lying right there in front of me. I caught my breath at the presence of it, at the fact of it, so near and real, so still and hidden and dead.

Without hesitation, before I could think, Curtis reached for the covering sheet. I had to fight down the urge to raise my arm in front of my eyes. I stood there, watching helplessly.

He pulled the sheet down quickly. I think he wanted to hit me with it fast, really rock me with the suddenness of the revelation. It worked. The breath came out of me in a slow, deflating groan.

I was staring down at the body of Anne Smith.

32 · The Corpse Factory

Horrible. Horrible, horrible. The color of her skin—a stony green—
the color of inanimate matter, not of flesh . . . The black bullet
hole in her sweet-featured oval face—in the forehead, left of center, on the side near me . . . The ragged edges of the hole—as if
she were just material that could be punctured and torn—that
pretty face that had smiled at me across the bar—that had leaned
in close to kiss me—just material, punctured, torn . . . And the
ladybug tattoo . . . Still there on her bare shoulder . . .

I like your ladybug.

Thank you. It speaks highly of you, too.

I remembered her kiss and could almost feel her lips on mine
and the tickling touch of her hair and now . . .

. . . that ragged hole torn in the stuff that had been her
forehead . . . Horrible.

I turned away.

"You know her?" asked Curtis.

"Yes, yes. Cover her up."

"Can you identify her for me, please?"

I met his eyes. He stood there stolidly, holding the sheet up
off her.

"Anne Smith," I said. "She was one of Rashid's students. And
she worked as a bartender at a club called The Den."

He stood as he was another defiant second, Anne's dead face
obscenely uncovered. His pale brown gaze searched mine. Then,

slowly, he set the sheet down over her again. I felt myself breathe as if for the first time in many minutes.

"All right," I said. "You've shown me. I'm shocked. You got the effect you wanted. Can we get out of here now?"

"When was the last time you saw her?"

"Can we talk about this somewhere else?"

He didn't budge. His gaze challenged me. I could see he was amused by my discomfort.

To hell with him. I walked out of the room.

I kept walking, heading down the hallway quickly. I wanted to get out of the building altogether. I felt the weight of the morgue bearing in on me, the fact of the morgue, the fact of Anne and all the dead pressing against the faceless walls. I hurried back to the entrance, pulled it open. Strode out into the parking lot. I didn't stop until I reached the blue Dodge. I stood by the side of it, my hands on my hips, my head lowered. I studied my sneakers on the asphalt. I inhaled the damp chill of the gray day.

After a moment, I became aware of the rush and rumble of the traffic on the avenue behind me. I became aware that I was sick to my stomach and that my forehead was damp with sweat. I went on standing there with my head down, my deep breaths trembling.

Now I knew. What Curtis suspected me of. What Lauren was trying to get me to confess to. Anne.

"She was shot with the gun we found in your kitchen."

I hadn't heard Curtis approaching. When I raised my head, he was there next to me, relaxed, hands in his pockets. He gazed coolly off at the street, chewing his lip, surveying the passing cars.

"Of course she was," I said hoarsely. "She was killed with the same gun because she was killed by the same people who took Serena."

He shifted his gaze to me. He did another of those mind in-ventories of his: I could feel him pawing through my thoughts and feelings one by one. Again, I got the sense he was searching for something he couldn't quite find. "When was the last time you saw her, Mr. Harrow?"

"I don't know." I tried to think. "Wednesday. I went to Rashid's lecture. I walked her to her next class."

Curtis tilted his head slightly. I thought of a dog picking up a scent or a sound, a hound on the hunt. "We have a witness who saw you going up to her apartment yesterday, right about the time she was killed."

"A witness," I said stupidly. Then I remembered. The skinny blonde on the stairs. The girl in the apartment I'd buzzed by mistake.

Curtis waited for me to speak again, watching me with that disdainful curiosity of his. I was still so shaken—by the sight of Anne—by the realization I was a murder suspect—that my thoughts were tumbling, disordered. But there was one thought— one thought I seized hold of: *Tell the truth. People always lie in these situations and that's what trips them up. Tell the truth. You're innocent. The truth will set you free.*

"Yes, that's right," I said. "I did go to visit her. But I never got to her apartment. I never saw her. I turned around and left."

"You were seen running away from the scene."

I swallowed something bitter. I tried to remember. "That's right. I *did* run," I said. "I ran. Yes."

"Why? What happened that made you run?"

"Nothing happened, exactly. . . ."

"You get in an argument with her or something?"

"I told you: I never even saw her. I never reached the apartment."

"You just went up the stairs, turned around, and ran away?"

"Yes."

"Why would you do that?"

I licked my dry lips, hesitated. *Tell the truth,* I thought again. But I could see now why people lied in these situations. The truth was so humiliating—so small, so sleazy—that the temptation to lie was almost overwhelming. Even as I opened my mouth, I wasn't sure I would be able to force the words out. But I did. I told him: "I went there because I was attracted to her. I wanted to see her, flirt with her, maybe even sleep with her, I don't know. But at the last minute, I thought better of it and I left."

"You left."

"Yes."

"Running."

"Yes."

He paused. He seemed to change tack. "How'd you know where she lived?"

"She gave me her address and phone number," I said. "She liked me. She told me to call."

He gave a short laugh. "She liked you. She told you to call her."

"Yes."

"So you went there—but then you ran away."

"It was stupid. I just wanted to get out of there without anyone seeing me."

"Because . . . ?"

"Because I'm married and I love my wife very much and it would hurt her very badly if I cheated on her and it would hurt my kids."

He gave me a conspiratorial grimace. Trying to form a bond with me, I guess, gain my trust. "Women, right?" he said.

I only shook my head in answer. It seemed an inopportune moment to tell him to go fuck himself.

Just then, a guttural grinding noise started up nearby. I glanced in the direction of the sound. I saw the door of one of the garage bays grinding upward, opening slowly.

"So let me get this straight," said Curtis. And as he spoke, there was another noise to go with the rumble of the rising door: a high, piercing tone repeating rhythmically. It was a truck—a small panel truck. It was backing toward the opening bay. The repeated blast of its warning signal stabbed into my brain like a baby's cry. Curtis had to raise his voice to speak over it. "You happened to show up at Anne Smith's apartment right around the time she was murdered. You went upstairs to bang her, but your conscience or whatever bothered you, and you ran away without even seeing her."

"My conscience or whatever—that's right," I nearly shouted back.

"That's what you're telling me: your story."

"That's right, that's what happened."

The truck stopped. Its signal stopped. The bay door came fully open and its throaty rumble stopped. The roar and rush of traffic on the avenue seemed like a whispering quiet after that.

"Or maybe you saw something," Curtis suggested helpfully. "Maybe you got there and you saw she was already dead. You saw her body and got scared and ran away. I could understand that."

He could understand that. The old confessor's ploy. Get it off your chest, son. I can understand. Oh, and by the way: You're under arrest for murder.

"That didn't happen," I said firmly. "I never reached her apartment. I just left."

"I don't know, man," Curtis said dryly. "You must have a lot of willpower. To come all that way for some action, then just go back down the stairs. You must have a lot of strength of character."

"Not enough, obviously, or I wouldn't have been there in the first place."

He shrugged. "Ah. Pretty girl. Guy on his own . . . These things happen."

His voice was sympathetic, but his stare was relentless and mocking. I turned away from it. I saw the truck backed up to the garage bay. A pair of men in white overalls were bringing a wooden box out of the garage. They carried it between them toward the rear of the truck. The truck driver was climbing out of the cab. He came back to open the truck's rear door so the men could put the box inside. The box was a coffin. It was a cheap wooden coffin made of naked pine boards sloppily nailed together. I could see more boxes piled up in stacks of three waiting just within the bay.

I turned back to Curtis. He went on in his sympathetic man-of-the-world voice. Making a face as much as to say: *Hey, we're both guys here, it's the modern world, no one's passing judgment on anyone.* "What I understand, this girl was into some very interesting stuff, sexually speaking."

"I wouldn't know." The lie came out automatically before I could stop it. I had to force myself to go back, to say: "No. That's not true. I did know. The last time I saw her, she was wearing an O-ring. I noticed it."

"An O-ring. What's that?"

My eyes locked on his, met the mocking humor in them. "I expect you know what it is," I said.

"No, no, go ahead. Enlighten me."

"It's a piece of jewelry people wear to show they're into sexual submission."

"Really? I'll be damned. An O-ring, huh? Funny you knowing

something like that. A straight-arrow family man like you. I guess you must be into some interesting sexual stuff yourself."

"I was," I said flatly. "It was a long time ago."

His jaw worked. He studied me. I think he understood what I was doing now. I think he understood that I was forcing myself to tell the truth, no matter how unpleasant. I think he thought it was a good strategy: You know, telling one truth to hide another. Being honest about everything except the one thing, the murder. I think he admired the cleverness of it.

I glanced at the garage. The two men in white overalls walked back from the truck to the bay, chatting between themselves, laughing. They lifted another coffin and carried it out.

"You know, in my experience," Curtis said after a moment, "people don't really change that much in this area. When you're into something you're into it, that's pretty much it. Nothing wrong with it, as long as no one gets hurt. I'm just saying—"

"Who are those dead?" I asked him.

"What?" He glanced over his shoulder, following my gaze.

The men in overalls put the next coffin into the truck, then went back into the garage for yet another. This time, one of the men came out alone. The coffin in his hands was so small, he could carry it himself. A child's coffin.

"They're John Does," Curtis said. "They're taking them out to Hart Island, to Potter's Field."

"Hup," said the man in the white overalls as he hoisted the little coffin easily onto the stack in the truck.

For the love of Christ, I thought. What a horrible place this was.

"So how about it, Mr. Harrow?" Curtis said.

Just then, an idea began to take shape in my mind. Something about the coffins being loaded on the truck, and the fractals I'd seen earlier on the computer screen. And Patrick Piersall. I thought of

Patrick Piersall—the ruin of Augustus Kane—hunkered over his beer and shot in the old Ale House downtown. Something he had said to me . . .

"Mr. Harrow?" said Curtis.

I faced him. Whatever the idea was, it flitted away, out of reach. "What? I'm sorry—what were you saying?"

"I'm saying I don't think people really change what they want sexually—not really, not where it counts." He tapped the side of his forehead with an index finger, right at the spot where Anne had that ragged hole. "In their fantasy life, you know. That stays pretty much the same."

This, I thought, was the sort of thing he lived for. He loved to find the squirrelly little man inside the man before him, to shine a light on the low humpbacked creature of the sewer-mind who a man pretends is not himself. I don't think it excited him to expose that scuttling Igor in me. I don't think it made him feel justified or superior or anything like that. I think he was long past that sort of motivation. It just entertained him, that's all. It amused him, satisfied that curiosity of his about the particular nature of each person's corruption.

I may have actually sneered at him then. "You want to know about my fantasy life?" I said. "In my fantasy life, I think of balling two teenaged girls at once. I think of doing my neighbor's wife from behind while my wife watches. I think of raping one of the local cheerleaders at gunpoint. And yeah, I still get into a little S&M from time to time. I also have one fantasy where I rescue the Queen of England from a burning building, and she makes me a knight of the realm. But I don't know: Somehow I don't think that's gonna happen, do you?"

The mockery died in his eyes. His gaze went hard and angry. His lips went thin. "I'm just saying, Mr. Harrow. It doesn't make sense to me. The kind of guy you are, the kind of twisted shit you're into. Pretty young girl comes along who's into the same shit. Gives you her number, her address, says 'Call me.' It doesn't make sense to me you go over there, then just run away like that without even seeing her."

"That doesn't make sense to you?"

"No. No, it doesn't. Scenario that would be more logical to me: The girl invites you to drop by. You're on your own, away from home. You go up there to see her—that's natural. The two of you start going at it. Maybe you get into a little of the rough stuff you like and it's feeling real good. Then—what?—maybe it gets out of hand. That can happen. Or maybe suddenly she's all, like: *I don't want it. Forget the whole thing.* Look, I mean, let's face it. Something like that: That's not your fault. Girl's a cocktease, gets you worked up, then suddenly she pulls a Virgin Mary on you, going no, no, no. Lot of women, they don't understand what that does to a guy—'specially if maybe it's something he's wanted real bad for a real long time, something maybe his wife won't do for him. And now this young girl says come and get it, gets him all turned on, and then, last minute, pulls the rug out from under him. Hey, there's not a guy in the world wouldn't lose it after something like that."

I stared at him. It was a strange moment, almost bizarre—almost unreal, somehow. There I was, telling the truth—forcing myself to tell the truth no matter how embarrassing—and it meant nothing to him. He didn't believe me. He was practically accusing me of murder. And I was so shocked, so confused, my thoughts all tumbling and jumbled, that I could hardly take the whole thing in. It was as if someone had pressed the MUTE button on the remote control and I could see the detective's mouth moving and I had the sense of what he was talking about but I couldn't actually hear him. Instead, a million other ideas and images were crowding into my brain, jarring and disjointed, like arguing voices. There

were the men in white overalls over there carrying out the coffins of the unknown dead, one after another after another of them
as if this place were some kind of factory producing corpses of
the dispossessed. Unbidden, the lives of the bodies in the boxes
came to me, too, their hopes and miseries swirling in my mind.
They had been children once, learning the names of things, and
now they were nameless and unclaimed, and there were so many,
swirling around me like phantoms. I don't know why I thought of
that then, but I did. And I don't know why, but then I thought of
the fractals again—the designs on my computer screen. Equations
like thoughts in the mind of God endlessly repeated to make the
patterns of the world. The million nameless dead and the million-
times-repeated equations and the raveling fractals and—God
knows why—God knows the chain of thought—but it all brought
me back to Patrick Piersall, to that old sorry has-been slumped
over his drinks, the forthright features of the *Universal* admiral
still pathetically visible beneath his fat, flushed face. Something
he said to me about Casey Diggs, about Rashid . . .

"It's not about sex," I heard myself say softly then. The idea
was coming to me as I spoke, all the swirling notions and images
in my head coming together into one idea as I spoke. "This whole
thing—you've got it wrong—it's not about sex. It's about God."

"Excuse me?" said Curtis.

"It's not about money, either. The Wall Street bombing. That's
what Casey Diggs was trying to tell everyone."

"You lost me now. This is the Smith girl we're talking about."

"Don't you see? Diggs predicted this. He said Rashid was
going to create a diversion. That's what Piersall told me in the
Ale House. Rashid was going to get the authorities to put their
resources into protecting military bases or economic centers or
political institutions. Wall Street, for example. Then he was going
to pull off the *real* attack somewhere else. On some cultural cen-

ter or something. Because he wanted to attack—what did Piersall say? The American imagination. That's his target. It's *always* been his target. Because that's where we live. That's where God lives."

"Look, I told you, the Rashid angle isn't gonna work . . ."

"Right," I said. "It doesn't work because he's your informer. He turned in the conspirators who were planning to blow up Wall Street, so you think he's working for you. That's the diversion. Rashid never cared about Wall Street. He just knew that if he was your agent, it would explain away all the evidence against him. The guys you arrested today? They were never meant to succeed. They were just there to throw you off the track, to make you think you stopped the conspiracy with Rashid's help. They were martyrs, sacrificing themselves for the cause: their god. I mean, why not? They're willing to blow themselves up to destroy us—you think they won't go to jail to accomplish the same thing?"

Curtis squinted. "I must be dense because I don't have a fucking clue what you're talking about now."

It sounded like babbling nonsense even to me. But the idea was still forming in my mind as I was speaking. And as the idea formed, the fear began to form, too, the fear that it was all real, all true, all happening—and that only I could see it. I babbled on: "It was Diggs—crazy little Diggs—who had it right all along. That's why Rashid's people killed him. And they killed Anne because she could link them to Diggs on the night of the murder. She knew Jamal. She probably knew a lot more than she realized. And once they saw her talking to me, they knew she and I might start to put the whole thing together. Maybe they were following me yesterday—who knows? Maybe they saw me going to talk to her again. So they killed her to shut her up. You see? Because they don't want anyone to stumble onto the other attack they're planning. Not the Wall Street attack—the real one."

"All right" was all Curtis said when I'd finished. He took a step toward me. He put his hand on my elbow. "All right, Mr. Harrow. We're not getting anywhere here. I think you better come back uptown with me."

I heard a clunking thud. Startled, I glanced over my shoulder. The coffins were all loaded. The men in overalls had shut the truck door.

At the same moment, with his free hand, Curtis opened the passenger door to the car. He began to guide me into it.

Panic hollowed my stomach, closed my throat. He kept his grip on my elbow. He kept tugging me toward the car. He was going to take me back to the precinct, back to the interrogation room. More hours of waiting, more questioning, more accusations. Hours and hours and meanwhile . . . Serena . . . Rashid's men . . . The plan going forward. The attack on the city. It was all real, all true, all happening somewhere, sometime today, the design of it unfolding like the fractals on the computer screen, moving down the assembly line in the factory of life and of the dead.

And I realized—it struck me like a blow: There was only me now. . . . It was ridiculous. It was insane. But it was true—there was only me who knew, only me who saw, only me who could stop it, who might be able to hurl myself into the machinery and bring it to a halt before it churned out more coffins, more and more.

I was almost at the car. There seemed no way to stop the detective from putting me inside. For a moment, I had the fantasy of punching him, knocking him down, running for it like some innocent fugitive trying to clear his name in a television show.

But in the end, it wasn't like that, not big and dynamic like that at all. It was the smallest thing, in fact; the smallest flutter. A little decision—yes or no—moving through me almost imperceptibly like the wind from a butterfly's wings.

I drew back just slightly in the detective's grip, resisted him just slightly. "Are you arresting me?" I asked.

He put more pressure on my elbow, drew me toward the car more firmly. "I think we need to talk some more uptown."

I pulled back, pressing the heels of my sneakers into the asphalt. "But are you arresting me? Am I under arrest?"

"I'm taking you in for questioning."

"No," I said.

"What do you mean, no?"

"I mean I won't come. I won't come with you."

He stopped pulling at me. For the last time, our eyes met and he looked right into me, searching, searching. He had his decision to make, too.

"Mr. Harrow," he said slowly, carefully enunciating every word. "That would be the biggest mistake of your life."

I started to speak, but I didn't speak. Maybe he was right. Maybe I was just making more trouble for myself. He seized on my hesitation. He started to move me to the car again. I took a half step toward it. Then I pulled back.

"I didn't kill that girl."

He kept up the pressure on my arm. "Well, we can clear that all up at the precinct."

I wouldn't move. All his soothing phrases. All his lies, not even meant to be believed, just meant to tranquilize me so he could take me away, take me back to the interrogation room.

"No," I said. "I won't go."

I thought I heard the faintest tone of anger in his level voice. "Mr. Harrow. I'm telling you: For your own sake, do not do this."

"I didn't kill her. You know I didn't."

"You walk away from me, and I can't help you anymore."

"You searched my mind. I saw you do it. You saw that I was innocent."

"What the hell are you talking about?"

"You know it's true."

"I'm telling you: You walk away, you're done. No one will be able to help you."

"You'd've arrested me by now if you thought I was guilty."

"We can talk about it as we drive."

"No. I'm not going."

"I'm telling you—"

"Arrest me, Detective. Arrest me or let me go."

We stood there, stood there, a moment like forever, his hand on my elbow, his eyes on mine. I could feel us balanced on a vanishing edge—him and me and Serena and the city—balanced there motionless while the gears of the corpse factory turned, the great equation of its limitless design working itself out with nothing to skew the end result—nothing except that butterfly flutter in both our breasts.

Then Curtis's hand opened. He released his hold on me. I went on standing there, staring at him.

"You are making a very big mistake," he said.

But at the same time, his arm lowered to his side. And still I went on—went on standing there. I couldn't believe what was happening. I couldn't believe he was setting me free.

"I have to do this," I said. I sounded unsure. I sounded as if I were waiting for him to talk me out of it.

"You try to leave town," he said, "and I'll bust you on the spot."

I took a slow, hesitant step backward.

"Mr. Harrow," he said, "you ought to reconsider—"

I took another step back. Another. Detective Curtis stood where he was, stood by the car, holding the passenger door open as if inviting me to change my mind, as if expecting me to change my mind.

I stopped backing away. I stood again, looking at him. Then I blinked. Then I turned around. I started walking out of the parking lot, walking away. I felt distant from myself, as if I were float-ing above my body, watching it go. I didn't know yet where I was headed. I just knew I was alone. That there was only me. Only me who understood. Only me who knew. Only me who could stop it.

The clouds darkened and billowed over the avenue. I hurried away from the morgue.

I was thinking, *God help me. God help me.*

33 · The Patriot Acts

When Rashid's secretary left for home that evening, I walked into the professor's office and hit him with a hammer. I would not have thought I could do such a thing, but in the end it was easy.

I'd been sitting in the park before that. Sitting on a bench in Central Park for hours, trying to figure out what to do. There was no one I could call, no one I could ask. My wife would tell me to act sensibly, go back to the police, straighten things out. The police, the FBI: They thought I was a killer; they thought Piersall and Diggs were cranks; they thought Rashid was innocent. The time was draining away, sand through an hourglass. And I was the only one who knew.

I watched the people pass, watched them walking by under the plane trees, by the statues, against the backdrop of the Great Lawn. I watched their faces. New York is a good city for faces. There are so many, all so different from each other, about as many different kinds as there can be. Overwrought as I was, I grew quite sentimental about it. You know: watching the black and the white and the yellow faces, different religions and no religion, straight-arrow and all the variations on the theme of strange. All of them going wherever they were going, doing whatever they were going to do. Making machines or businesses or works of art, debasing themselves for gain or praying for salvation, slavering after celebrities or caring for their children or mindlessly murdering time. The endless repetition of the human equation, of the original thought in the mind of God, free to work itself out each alone and all together into the pattern of history, our history. Yes, I grew quite sentimental. I thought: What a wonderful idea for a country this is. What a wonderful place for those men to have imagined for us, those men from the old days, those dead white European men. "A republic," they said, "if you can keep it." What a wonderful idea.

After a while, I got off the bench and went to buy a hammer.

I walked as if I were in a trance. My head felt as if it were full of cotton. My thinking was slow and muddy. My body seemed like a burden I was dragging behind me, a sack of wet sand. I knew now what I had to do, and yet there were still so many doubts, so many questions. Was Casey Diggs really the boy Serena had seen murdered in the swamp? Had she really seen it? Had it really happened? And the things Piersall said about Diggs—and the things Diggs said about Rashid—were any of them true? What was real and what wasn't?

The questions nagged me, bothered me, haunted me as I crossed the park. I couldn't answer them and I couldn't make them stop. At one point, I even began to wonder: Was it possible that Curtis was right? Had I killed Anne Smith and somehow repressed the memory? I mean, I could remember going up the stairs to her apartment well enough. I could remember running away. Was it possible I had blacked out what happened in between?

And yet, still—still—I knew what I had to do. And at the same time these questions played and replayed in my brain, I found myself going about the terrible business at hand. Hunting down a hardware store on Columbus Avenue, picking out the hammer, duct tape, a box cutter, a small sanding sponge that I could stuff into Rashid's mouth. Because they had Serena. Because they were going to attack the city—the country—my country and all its faces. Because I was the only one who could stop it. And Rashid was the only one who knew the plan.

When I look back now, the whole thing seems lunatic, impossible. But at the time, it seemed inevitable, a matter of destiny. I knew what I had to do.

I rode up to the university on the subway, sitting on the molded seat with my plastic shopping bag from the hardware store on my lap. Under the rattle of the train, the questions in my brain faded to a dim distance. I stared into space, my head stuffy, my thoughts dull. I jounced passively with the train's rattling rhythm.

When I reached my stop, I trudged wearily up the station stairs. My bag hung heavy in my hands. I was glad to step up onto the sidewalk and feel the cool wind blowing. There was moisture in the air now—not raindrops, just a refreshing dampness. That revived me a little as I trudged across the street to the campus.

The administration building was another of these grand, massive Roman places. It looked like the Pantheon with an expansive dome up top and a bold colonnade in front. Just the sight of the long sweep of stone stairs leading up to the entranceway made me feel tired. I actually had to stop to rest halfway through the climb. I thought: *I really am not feeling very well.* Then I started walking again. I really seemed to be in an altered state of mind at that point, feverish and detached. But I knew . . .

There was a pleasant lady with dyed blonde hair at an information counter just inside the door. I asked her where Rashid's office was, and she gave me directions in a friendly tone of voice. It was that easy. It reinforced my sense that this was inevitable, that it was meant to be.

Off I trudged again, out between the columns and back down the long, long sweep of stairs.

The office was not far. It was in a large, impressive building of brick and stone. The building was set in a peaceful corner of the campus. There were yellow plane trees on the path outside and a spreading black maple tree, its leaves a brilliant red. There was a bronze cast of Rodin's *The Thinker* under one of the trees. As I approached, a few students went walking past it, laughing, chatting, carrying their books in their arms or in packs on their backs. How stately and peaceful and academic it all looked. I continued along the path toward the building, carrying my plastic bag with its hammer and duct tape and box cutter and the sponge I would stuff in Rashid's mouth.

Somewhere during the afternoon, I had lost track of time, but I suppose it was already after four o'clock at this point. I went into the building and plodded laboriously up two flights of stairs to the third floor. There was a long green hall with many wooden doors. The hall was empty and quiet, though I could hear voices murmuring behind the doors. Rashid's office was at the end, the door open. I walked to it and looked in. There was a secretary sitting at a desk inside. That surprised me. I didn't think professors had secretaries. But I guess Rashid was very famous and important because his theories got so much attention in the newspaper and that book of his had sold so many copies. The secretary glanced up at me inquiringly. I made a show of studying the number on the pebbled glass of the open door, my lips moving as I read the name. Then, with an embarrassed smile at the secretary, I gave her a wave of apology—you know, as if I had come to the wrong place. I went back down the hall to the stairs.

I went outside again. I stood under the yellow trees, beside *The Thinker*. I leaned my elbow against the statue's base and waited. I remembered I had seen *The Thinker* in Paris once, a smaller version perched atop a sculpture of *The Gates of Hell*. In Paris, he brooded over churning scenes of the damned in their torments. Here in America, he just stared down at the ground, as if he were trying to decide whether to send out for pizza or head across the street for some Chinese.

Somewhere close by, a clock was chiming the quarter hour.

Somewhere a choir began rehearsing the *St. Matthew Passion.*
"Oh, pain!" they sang. "Here trembles the tormented heart." They
went over it several times, perfecting the harmonies. The students
came and went along the paths, their sneakers kicking the leaves.
White and black and yellow faces, laughing together. What a
beautiful place, I thought dreamily, distantly. What a beautiful
country. The choir sang far away. The clock chimed again. *The
Thinker* pondered the earth.

When I next glanced at my watch, it was two minutes after
five. I looked up and saw Rashid's secretary coming out of the
building.

I passed her as I went in, carrying my bag from the hardware
store.

What was I thinking then? I remember telling myself that it
wasn't my fault. I had racked my brains for another way, but there
was none, none. It wasn't my fault that Rashid had fooled the
police. It wasn't my fault that he had fooled everyone, that he was
protected from suspicion by his respectability and fame. It wasn't
my fault that no one would listen to me, that I was alone and could
think of nothing else to do.

I pushed into the building again. The hammer in the plastic
bag tapped against my leg as I walked. When I returned to the
third floor, I found the green hallway empty again, quiet again—
even quieter than before, as if the people I'd heard murmuring
behind their doors had all gone home. In my feverish mind, this
was further evidence that it was inevitable, that it had to be, that
it was not my fault. It was all so easy, you see.

Rashid's door at the end of the hall was closed now, but it
didn't even occur to me that he might not be in his office or that
I wouldn't be able to get in. I simply shuffled down the corridor
with my thoughts foggy and my bag in my hand. I simply grasped

the cool brass doorknob, simply turned it. It turned easily. I simply pulled the door open.

I stepped into the secretary's office. It was empty now. The lights were off. A computer sat quiet on the desk. A phone sat dark. I closed the door behind me. It clapped shut, the latch clicking loudly. At once, there came a voice from the inner office.

"Patricia?"

I recognized Rashid's voice. The light precision of his Oxbridge accent flavored with a touch of the Middle East. A voice reminiscent of literature and tea.

I reached into my bag and brought out the hammer. As I walked around the secretary's desk to reach the inner office door, I held the hammer low against my thigh with my right hand. I held the plastic bag in my left. I also used my left hand to take hold of the doorknob. But just as I did, the doorknob turned. Rashid pulled the door open from inside.

I followed the door in, stepping across the threshold so that the professor and I confronted each other just inside his office. That gave me a clear shot at him. There was no desk or chair or anything in my way. I had plenty of room for a good swing of the hammer. Again, it seemed perfect; inevitable; meant to be.

The office was small and close. There was a wooden desk cluttered with books and papers. There was a window behind it, with a view of autumn leaves close to the glass. Every open space of wall had a bookshelf on it, and every shelf was chockablock with books, upright volumes and volumes stacked on their sides and some stuffed into the spaces above the ones that were upright.

Rashid, I saw, was dressed casually but elegantly. He was wearing khaki slacks and had on a heavy black woolen cardigan over an open-collared shirt. With his thick, coiffed black hair and those classic features, with the background of the books and the cluttered desk and the autumn leaves, I thought he looked like a photo spread in a magazine: The Famous Professor at Work.

When he saw it was me instead of Patricia, a friendly, inquiring smile began to take shape on his lips.

Then I lifted the hammer above my head.

Rashid's eyes widened with shock and surprise. He had just enough time to throw his hands up in front of his face. But I swung low, whipping the tool around in a scything arc so that it struck him with full force on the side of his left thigh.

Rashid let out a strangled syllable of pain. He stumbled to his right, his body twisting. Then he crashed down to the floor on his side.

I fell on top of him, clutching the back of his neck in my left hand, driving his face into the edge of a braided rug, pinning his arms under my knees.

I leaned down close to his ear. "Scream and I'll bash your brains out," I said softly.

I believe I would have done it, too—although now, suddenly, beneath the dull fever in my mind, beneath the dull muttering mantra—it's not my fault—there was another voice speaking, muffled and distant. It was a high, wild, panicky voice screaming at me from far, far away, screaming that this was madness, that in the name of humanity I had to stop, that in the name of sanity I had to let him go. I had to run. I had to get the hell out of here.

"Who are you?" said Rashid, his smooth voice strained with pain. "What do you want?"

I didn't bother to answer. I knew there was no time. I knew I had to act quickly before he could think, act, fight back. I had already set the hammer on the floor and as he spoke, I was already reaching into the bag again. Now I had the sponge. I shifted my grip off the professor's neck and grabbed his coiffed black hair. I pulled his head back violently. I wanted it to be violent. I wanted him to be afraid, too afraid to try anything. I wanted to terrorize him into silence. As his head came off the floor, his mouth opened. I stuffed the sponge in. I was strangely aware that my face was contorted and twisted and terrible as I did this. I could see his eyes catch sight of me, and I could see that the sight frightened him. *It's not my fault,* I thought.

After that, I went to work with the duct tape. I did it with shocking speed, the speed of a madman. I taped his mouth shut so he couldn't spit out the sponge. I taped his wrists together behind his back. I taped his ankles together. Winding the tape around him with movements that were blurred, frenzied and yet utterly precise. Slashing through the tape with the box cutter and moving on. Like a madman jacked on adrenaline, desperate not to slow down, not to think, not to hear the screaming voice in my mind: *In the name of humanity . . .* Going quick, quick, quick before that voice broke through the dull, fevered refrain: *It's not my fault.*

Water dripped on my hands as I worked. I thought it was sweat, but when I went to wipe my forehead, the skin there was hot and dry. I heard a strange, choked, high-pitched sob and was startled a moment later to realize it had come from me. Then I understood. I touched my cheek with the back of my hand. There were tears there. I quickly wiped them away.

I roughed the bound professor of literature onto his back with his taped hands trapped under him. I knelt over him, straddling him, bracing my left hand against his chest, holding the hammer in my right hand, holding it up where he could see. His eyes were white orbs in that olive skin. There was fear in them—a lot of fear—but there was ferocity and defiance, too. I could see he meant to resist me and with nauseating certainty I realized I was going to have to go through with this all the way.

"Listen—" I started to say.

But just then, there was a burst of laughter right outside the door. There was a man's voice in conversation, loud, close: ". . . that would mean the department actually had to spend some money."

I froze, openmouthed. I held my breath. Rashid's white glance shifted to the door, hopeful, watching for salvation. Another man spoke out there and the first man spoke again, but I could hear now they were moving away down the hall. I waited, kneeling there, showing Rashid the hammer until the voices faded entirely as the two talking men went down the stairs together.

I breathed again, a trembling breath. "Listen," I said in a harsh whisper. "I know everything. All right? I know the Wall Street thing was bullshit. I know you're planning another attack today somewhere else. This is what I'm going to do. I'm going to ask you when and where that attack is going to take place. I'm going to ask you where Serena is. I'm going"—I caught my breath—"I'm going to ask you once and give you a chance to answer. If you don't answer, I'm going to shatter your left kneecap with this hammer. Then I'm going to ask you again, and if you don't answer, I'll shatter your right kneecap." Was this me speaking? I couldn't believe it. I wanted to laugh. I wanted to ask the professor: *Who is this guy? What is he, crazy?* "Then I'll ask you again," I said. "If you don't answer that time, I'm going to smash your testicles, one, then the other." I watched his eyes. He was thinking now, reading my face, gauging my sanity, my seriousness. "In the end, you're going to tell me what I want to know. So tell me now. Tell me now and I swear to God I will not hurt you. I swear to God." I took a couple of deep, heaving breaths, fighting down my nausea. It was hard, talking like this, but I knew that worse—much worse—was still to come. I knew he would resist me. I knew I was going to have to go through with it. "Do you understand me?" I said.

Rashid stared up at me. For a moment, he didn't react at all.

He just stared like that, reading my face, as if I hadn't spoken. Then he shook his head once: No.

No? What the hell did that mean? No, he didn't understand me? No, don't hurt me? What?

"Shit!" I said.

I realized I had to take the gag off him. I guess I hadn't thought things through all that well.

I peeled the duct tape away from his lips. I fished the sponge out of his mouth, my fingers growing wet with his saliva. I knew he might shout for help, and I knew without a doubt that if he shouted for help I would splatter his brains all over the braided rug.

He must've known it, too. He didn't shout. He spoke in a fierce, rapid whisper—as if we were children having an argument we didn't want our parents to hear.

"Listen to me," he said. "So help me, I don't know what you're talking about. I don't know anything about any attack. I'm not a terrorist. I'm a college professor. A professor, an intellectual. I have theories, that's all. Just theories, so help me . . ."

"Listen to me . . ."

"I write. I talk. That's all, I swear . . ."

"No. I was in your class."

"My class?"

"I heard what you said . . ."

"It's just talking, lectures . . ."

"I saw what you are."

"It's speech. Free speech. You believe in free speech, don't you?"

"I saw. I'm telling you . . ."

"You believe in rights, don't you? I have rights. I have—"

I stuffed the sponge back into his mouth. I clutched him by the throat. I saw the blood coming into his cheeks. *It's not my fault,* I thought again. But it was no good anymore, telling myself that. In the wild energy of the moment, in the surge of adrenaline, my head had cleared. The veil of fever had become a pane of glass. I could see: It was my fault. Of course it was. Maybe not all of it. Maybe not the fact that he was who he was and had chosen to do what he was doing. Maybe not the fact that I was alone and the police wouldn't listen to me and I had somehow wound up the only man in America who could stop him. Even this—this terrible thing I was about to do—maybe even this was not my fault because what else was there, what options did I have?

But the thrill of it . . . Yes, that. The coursing rush of excitement, the old dark, mesmerizing sadistic joy—that belonged to me. Even at that moment, I could feel it flowing into my brain, into my belly and my groin. I could feel the old smoky sickness of lust and pleasure spreading all through me. I had been saved from this once. I had been given the strength to walk away into a new life, a better life. And I knew with cold, bright clarity that if I chose to do this thing, if I brought this hammer down, if I unleashed this flood of feeling in myself again, there would be no second chance. I would be damned to this—damned from within—forever.

"This is the first time," I told Rashid hoarsely. I swallowed hard. "This is the first time I'm asking you. If you don't answer me, I shatter your left knee. You hear? Where is Serena? Where is the attack gonna be? When is it? Where and when? Tell me."

I let go of his throat. He worked the sponge out between his lips. I helped him with it, pulled it free. The fierce, rapid whisper streamed out of him again. "Listen, listen. For the love of God, please, listen, please. I'm not a terrorist. I'm a professor. Ask the police, the FBI. They know me. I helped them!"

"That was a trick, a diversion."

"No, no, no. Do you think they haven't checked me out? Do you think you know something they don't? Think about it! That doesn't make sense. I'm sorry if you don't like my ideas, but that's all they are, they—"

"It's not all. It's not all."

"Just stop. Stop and consider. I'm begging you. You're not thinking clearly. People sit in their rooms, they think things, they watch things on television and come up with all these crazy ideas."

"The TV lies. It's all lies."

"That's right, that's what I'm saying!" Rashid whispered up at me urgently. "Look, there's still time. You haven't hurt anyone yet. You can stop this. You can get help. I swear to you: There is no attack. Not from me. I swear—"

I jammed the sponge back into his mouth. I taped his mouth shut again. He struggled to speak around the gag, but there were only strangled mutterings.

I grabbed his shirtfront. My heart was banging in my chest so hard I thought it would explode or break through. I couldn't catch my breath. The fear, the moral agony, the thrill—it was nearly enough to make me faint. I felt as if I were spinning into the spout of a funnel, everything closing in, everything sinking, swirling down to a single impossible point.

I reached for Rashid's throat again, but instead my fingers touched his cheek. My fingers played against his cheek almost tenderly.

"Please," I said to him. "Please tell me."

He was shaking his head now frantically. He went on shaking his head: *No, no, no!* Trying to say the words behind his gag.

I climbed off him. I grabbed him by the ankle to steady his leg. He kicked and struggled wildly, shaking his head wildly: *No, no, no!* The shriek was jammed back into his throat by the sponge in his mouth.

I lifted the hammer in a trembling hand. I stared down at the twisting, struggling man on the floor. My mind flashed back to *The Thinker*—*The Thinker* in Paris staring down at the twisting, struggling figures in *The Gates of Hell,* the twisting, struggling figures of the damned churning in the vortical force of their passion and misery and self-destruction. I knew I would be one of those damned figures if I did this thing.

I forced the thought away. I forced myself to think about Serena. I thought of her face as she was dragged out of my mother's house, as she shouted for me: "Daddy!" I thought of all the faces in the park and in the city and on TV and I loved them and I loved my country. And I thought: What right have you in the end to hold on to your decency when the life of the nation is at stake? What is your sanity compared to that or even your salvation? You can't let thousands of people die simply to preserve your own righteousness.

I held the hammer high another moment. Rashid fought wildly in my grip, shaking his head, *No, no, no.*

All right, then, I thought, *I'll go to Hell.*

And I brought the hammer down on him.

34 · The New Coliseum

The lights outside the theater swept the night. I saw them criss-
crossing over the towers and billboards of Times Square when I
was still several blocks north. It was dark now, but whatever stars
there were were dazzled to nothing by the radiance of Broadway.
Spotlit images of half-naked women several stories high, soaring
electrified soda cans and golden arches, twinkling ads for shoes
and video cameras, gigantic heads talking on TV screens the size
of houses: They washed the sky black; they washed the faces on
the street below to a corpselike pallor. Thousands of faces, mobs of
faces, hustling, pushing, flowing under the lights, chalk-skinned
and dead-eyed. I shouldered through the crush of them as quickly
as I could.

I had called 911 from the cab. I must've sounded crazy to
the operator. I must've sounded almost as crazy as I felt. But I
didn't care. I babbled it all out in response to her bored, drawling
questions. A massive amount of explosives, I said. The New Coliseum, I said. *The End of Civilization as We Know It,* I said. There
would be over three thousand people there. The secretary of state,
the governor, the mayor. Not to mention the crowds in the street
turning out to watch the celebrities. My voice was strained with
exhaustion as I explained it. The olive-skinned driver in the seat
in front of me watched me warily in his rearview mirror. I went
on to tell the 911 operator what I had done to Rashid, how I had
left him broken and unconscious on the floor of his office. I stared

out the window. I thought: *I must be completely out of my mind.* I thought: *My life is over.*

The operator kept trying to pacify me. She kept telling me security on the scene was airtight. No one could get through, she said. No one could get explosives inside. I tried to explain that the explosives were already inside. Maintenance and security had all been compromised, infiltrated. It was a long-term plan. They had blueprints, C4, detonation cord to cut through steel, engineers with the skill to plant the stuff for maximum demolition. The operator kept changing the subject. She kept asking me about Rashid. She didn't seem all that interested in the rest of it. She didn't believe me.

The traffic grew steadily thicker as the cab neared Columbus Circle. By the time we were centrifuged out of the big rotary and fired off down Broadway, the flow of cars was congealing. A few blocks more and we had become one more irregular shape in a motionless patchwork of multicolored metal and taillights, stalled blue buses, shadowy heads behind panes of thick gray glass. The traffic lights strung above us went from green to red and back to green again, but nothing moved forward.

"You have to clear out the theater!" I croaked urgently into the phone.

The cabbie watched me anxiously in his mirror.

"What is your location right now, sir?" drawled the 911 woman.

Exasperated, I finally killed the connection. I slipped the phone into my pocket.

"There is an event up ahead," said the cabbie in what I think was a Turkish accent. "I can't go any farther." He wanted me out of his cab.

I took out my wallet. "I'll walk from here," I said.

He didn't try to disguise his relief.

I got out of the car and started jogging south along the sidewalk. There were couples all along the way, men and women arm in arm, dressed up for a night on the town. I dodged this way and that between them. The air was cold and damp on my cheeks, but there was still no mist, no rain. I could no longer see the roiling clouds in that blacked-out sky. Soon I was out of breath. I fell into a quick, striding walk. The crowd on the street grew thicker. I had to use my hands to get through like a man wading through the high reeds in a swamp. All the same, I was still traveling faster than the cars. Most of the cars had stopped dead. Only a few were jerking forward here and there, looking for half a foot's advantage. Horns blared. Exhaust gathered. The air was suffocating, rank.

Now the Broadway lights grew brighter up ahead. They rose higher and the sky was a deeper black. The crowd on the street swelled. As I twisted and wedged my way though the tide of bodies, I looked up—and it was then I saw Times Square, the boulevards intersecting and dividing, the great billboards lining them, and the towering lights—and I saw the kliegs of the New Coliseum, five of them, spearing the night and sweeping back and forth over the surface of it, crossing and uncrossing. I fought my way toward them through the crowd.

It seemed I would never reach the place. The square was packed with people, a heaving sludge of them making its slow way north and south. I edged into the southbound flow, but I couldn't break through it or get ahead of its inching, muddy pace. I felt trapped and smothered and small at the bottom of a canyon of lights, a canyon of enormous billboard bodies and enormous talking heads on their house-sized TVs. The nearness and solidity of all those other humans and the nearness and the stares and the corpselike pallor of so many faces pressing in around me and the crushing radiance of all the soaring, flashing, overhanging signs and screens made me claustrophobic and nauseous—or maybe it was the flashbacks that came into my mind now—now that I couldn't distract myself, couldn't run or shove or shout into a phone: images of Rashid rigid in agony, the sound his knee made when the hammer struck it, the sound of his frantic shrieks behind the gag—and me hanging over him with the hammer raised, and with the small, dark, secret hope hunkered in my consciousness like some bright-eyed gnome—the hope that the terrorist son of a bitch would refuse to answer me again . . .

Sick, I made my way in the human sludge, beneath the oppressive, towering Broadway lights.

The theater was off the center of the square, just west of the intersecting boulevards. I pushed into the side street and saw it. It rose spotlit above a dark mass of people crushed against the police barricades. It was elegant and vast, a swirl of pilasters and arched windows rising like a great stone wedding cake five stories high. The windows were bathed in golden light from the chandeliers above the lobby. You could see the guests rising on the spiraling marble stairways within: women of gliding elegance in sequined dresses and twinkling jewels, men of substance, confidence and wealth in suits as straight and black against the white steps as the sharp keys on a grand piano. And children—I was surprised to see so many children—the boys in ties and jackets, flumping about and clowning self-consciously, the girls in dresses, staring goggle-eyed and openmouthed, as if trying to remember everything forever. All in all, watching the glittering people on the spiral stairs through the window was like viewing a scene in a diorama or a snow globe, some faraway vision of yearning charm.

Out in front of the theater, off to one side between the theater and the crowd, the five big klieg lights swiveled on a couple of flat-bed trailers, sending their beams into the night. Next to the trailers, there was an area all aglow with spectacular silver radiance. I couldn't see it over the massed people, but I guessed that that was where the red carpet was, where the movie stars and dignitaries were arriving in their limousines and sweeping their glorious way past the cameras and microphones of the gawkers and reporters to join those already on the spiral stairs inside.

I approached the edges of the crowd. Jammed and throbbing with humanity as it was, the scene was more-or-less orderly. The police had closed the street to all traffic except the limousines coming from the west, and were allowing pedestrians to enter only from the east. As a result, the onlookers swarmed steadily in from Broadway while police calmly directed the limos swinging in off Eighth Avenue. I caught glimpses of the big cars approaching one after another, vanishing behind the throng to where, judging by the shouts and camera flashes, the celebrities disembarked. It was all very well organized. The sabotaged theater was filling up quickly.

I wedged my way into the crowd and started pushing toward the front. "Excuse me. Excuse me," I grunted again and again. There were so many people. Thousands inside, thousands more out here. They were packed together so densely, they formed a nearly solid mass. I had to shoulder and elbow and shove my way through—"Excuse me. Excuse me."—nauseated by the smothering flesh all around me, squeezing past body after body toward the barricades.

At last, clammy with sweat, I broke through to the front of the crowd and emerged into the magnificent silver light around the red carpet. It was a wonderful light, like none I'd ever seen. It turned the world the color of the moon. Emanating from a series of standing lamps arrayed around the edges of the mob, it poured down on the carpet and splashed up over the New Coliseum's pristine white facade. The black limos pulling up into the glow seemed to take on a startling added dimension. You know those books for kids, those pop-up books where 3-D objects leap up off the page

at you? That's how the cars seemed suddenly to leap out of reality
as they entered the light. One was arriving even as I reached the
barricade. I staggered, blinking, out of the darkness of the multi-
tude, and there it was. A doorman in a blinding livery of scarlet
and gold opened the back door. Out, then, into that extra fullness
of existence stepped a man I recognized from movie posters, one
of the popular comedians of the last few years, and with him, his
starlet wife.

There followed several swift, disorienting moments of ma-
chinelike efficiency, a human clockwork engineered to allow the
glamorous couple an assigned interval of the crowd's admiration
before they were ushered toward a fifteen-second interview under
the theater awning, and finally swept inside as the next limousine pulled up behind them. Through all this they were accom-
panied by a chittering, insectile swarm of paparazzi nibbling at
the edges of their silver space and by graceful television cameras
that swooped around them, dancing attendance in the outer shadows. It was a strange thing to see. It had a strange effect on me.
I found myself frozen there, staring, fascinated, my desperation
almost forgotten, as if I'd suddenly been rendered nothing more
here than an observer, as if I were at home, in fact, watching the
whole thing on TV. The passage of the arriving stars from limo
to interviewer to theater became everything, a sequence distinct
from its surroundings. The chaos around me, the terror inside me,
seemed to become dim and peripheral. The police working to keep
the crowd at bay, the sound equipment on its trucks, the klieg
lights, the photographers, and the chaotic depths of the mob itself,
became a blurred frame to the central progression, a border of living irrelevance to the fullness of the comedian's celebrated life.
All the force of reality seemed to me to be not with myself but with
the couple on the red carpet, with the white teeth in the comic's
tanned face, the sparkling sequins on his wife's black dress. The

truth of their being, the being of their being, the dimness of my own somehow-lesser presence on the border of the great glow, seemed to grow more intense with every precisely organized second until the sheer force of their actuality climaxed as they stepped up to the interviewer at the theater entrance and I recognized her— her blonde curls, her avid eyes, her bee-stung lips—it was Sally Sterling—and the shock of her familiar appearance rendered the scene on the red carpet so entirely *there* somehow that I felt, in contrast, I had all but vanished.

It was, as I say, strange; disorienting: the quickness of it, and the brightness of it and my own unimportance on the edges of it practically paralyzed me at first, paralyzed my mind. I just stood there—just stood there, staring. And even when I started to think again, I couldn't think clearly, I couldn't think of anything to do. How could I get closer to the theater? How could I get inside? How could I warn the people—so many people—that they were all about to die?

There were uniformed police patrolling the barricades at every point. There were many more plainclothes security people standing guard watchfully within the protected circle. I thought of grabbing one of them, screaming at him, warning them all of the danger. But they would've arrested me on the spot. I knew they would have. They would have called headquarters and found out who I was: a murder suspect trying to distract an investigation with unfounded terrorist scares. They would have carted me away and it all would've gone on without me. I could already see it in my mind's eye—the chaos—the rubble—the death.

So I stood there—that's all—stood there and stared, watching the scene with a swiftly growing sense of panic and helplessness and confusion. Another limousine pulled up and—great God— there was the secretary of state, tall and sleek in a shiny tuxedo. He stepped smoothly from the car. Took his moment in the moony glow, smiling, waving. And I stood there, watching him, fairly panting in my powerlessness, and thinking, *Him, too. They will kill him, too.* And looking at the crowds, the thousands all around, and thinking: *They will kill everyone for their unforgiving god.*

The thought brought me back to myself, back to my senses. As the secretary of state was swept along to his moment before Sally's microphone, I began to take stock. My eyes started moving, searching the scene here and there, looking for anything, any weakness in the defenses, any possible point of entry.

I found one.

The theater stretched over much of the block. On this side of it, near the corner, there was a kind of narrow courtyard, formed by the theater's wall and the rear of a massive hotel on Times Square. A short way into the courtyard, I could make out a door—a stage door or maybe an entrance for technicians—I couldn't tell which from where I was. The entrance to the courtyard was roped off. There were two patrolmen guarding the rope. Two more patrolmen stood on the other side of the courtyard, facing away toward the next street over. I thought: If I could create a diversion, if I could draw the attention of these two cops at the rope, maybe I could rush past them, down the courtyard to the door. Of course the door might be locked. And the two cops at the far end might spot me. And if I did get in, there'd be sure to be more cops inside. But it was the only thing I could think of, the only chance I had.

I began to try to think of ways to create the diversion I needed. Nothing came to me. My thoughts spun like tires in the mud. If I started shouting—"Fire!"—"Bomb!"—the cops would come right for me. I'd be the first one they carried off. Even if I managed to start a panic, I'd be trampled in the rush.

I stood there—stood there—the time passing, my heart beating, my thoughts going round and round.

Then—what happened next—well, it was simply unbelievable.

No one ever reported it—not in context, anyway—not as a
relevant part of the events of that night. The TV news never mentioned it. Neither did any of the major papers. I think it was just
as Patrick Piersall said, just as he had told me in the Ale House.
What happened next didn't fit the story. It was too ridiculous, too
undignified, completely out of keeping with the general tone of the
terror and tragedy that followed.

But it's the truth. So I tell it here.

The theater was now nearly full, the show about ready to begin. There were only two more limousines yet to arrive. These—
the most important limousines of all—had been saved for last.

As I stood there—racking my brains, helpless, fearful, expecting the explosion at every minute—the first of the cars pulled into
the heightened silver reality at the head of the red carpet in front
of me. The gold-and-scarlet doorman plucked open the back door.
Out into the light stepped Juliette Lovesey.

She leapt instantly into vital relief, radiating presence and
charisma. Even I—even at that desperate moment—started and
stared at her, struck to have her appear in person right there in
front of me like that. She was much smaller than she looked on
screen, just a little slip of a thing, really, but as perfectly proportioned as a doll. The swell of her breasts, the line of her short
white dress, the liquid curves of her tan legs all had the added
charm of a thing in miniature. So, too, the aching fragility and
vulnerability of her face, framed in the cascades of shining brown
hair, were all the more powerful when you could see for yourself
what a tiny and delicate creature in fact she was.

As she stepped gracefully out of the car onto the carpet, there
was a collective surging sigh from the crowd. It was an amazing

sound, deep, heartfelt, passionate beyond anything I could describe: a collective moan of admiration and affection and sympathy. They loved her. You could feel it in the very air: They loved
her as if she were their own.

I understood the phenomenon at once. They had all seen the
interview. That interview Juliette had done with Sally last night.
The announcement she had made: that she was carrying Todd
Bingham's baby, that she was going to keep the child even though
Bingham had left her for Angelica Eden. Everyone here had seen
it, just as I had. In the moment that one tear had fallen from
Juliette's lashes onto her cheek, she had changed in the public
mind. She had gone from being a spoiled, wealthy, irresponsible
narcissist to a wronged woman, ill used and left behind. She had
become, that is to say, something the women in the crowd could
understand, could identify with, something the men could sympa-
thize with and yearn to protect. She had become a sparkling version of themselves. And with that, she had won them over. They
loved her. Loved her.

Juliette felt this. I could see she did. She seemed to grow in
stature where she stood, transported into a golden awareness of
her own nobility. She responded to the people with a shy, sweet
wave, a gesture both patient and courageous. Then she walked
with modestly mincing steps down the carpeted path to where
Sally waited to receive her.

There followed a quick coda to their TV interview. Sally
wore the same girlfriend expression of tender concern. "How are
you feeling, Juliette?" she asked. The words were freighted with
meaning.

Juliette smiled brightly, bravely. "I'm doing great, Sally. It's
great to be here and I'm really looking forward to enjoying this
great . . . great moment in the history of movies."

The volcanic roar erupted from the heart of the crowd. They

cheered. They whooped and applauded. They loved her: her courage; her dignity. She was perfect. She waved to them again. Sally reached out and gave the actress's hand a gentle, encouraging squeeze: Never surrender. Then an usher guided Juliette to the theater doors—and she was gone, the crowd still applauding.

I stood watching after her, frantic, wanting to cry out, wanting to warn her, warn everyone, trying to think, think, think of what I could do to stop the coming massacre.

Then the last limousine drew into the glow around the red carpet.

It was Angelica, of course—Angelica Eden with her new lover, Todd Bingham. I read later in one of the celebrity blogs that the two of them had been watching Juliette's arrival on a TV in the car. They had seen what had happened, the outpouring of love and support from the audience. According to the blog—and I guess they'd interviewed the limo's driver—Angelica let out a snarling blue streak of curses. "That bitch! That fucking bitch! That fucking shit-faced bitch!" Because, of course, if the crowd loved Juliette, if they sympathized with her as the wronged woman, they were going to hate Angelica as the vixen who'd stolen her man, who'd left her child fatherless and caused that crystal tear to go spilling down her cheek on TV last night. There was no telling how many charity appearances Angelica would have to make, how many African orphans she'd have to adopt to win back the sympathy of the moviegoing audience. According to the blog, Angelica started hissing at Todd as if she were a snake. She said she would *obliterate* Juliette from the people's minds. She would *eradicate* the news coverage of her triumphant arrival.

"What are you doing? What are you doing?" Todd is said to have squealed at her.

"If nothing else," Angelica Eden announced to him, "I'm not gonna let that fucking bitch upstage me!"

The car pulled to a stop before the carpet. The liveried door-man opened the door. Todd fairly leapt out into the silver incan-descence—eager, maybe, to get away from his lover's tantrum. Like Juliette, he was also smaller in real life than he looked on television, even more delicate and insubstantial, though his blond, handsome head was large, almost weirdly oversized, which appar-ently made it look good on film. He smoothed down the front of his jacket with one hand, waved to the crowd with the other.

Then Angelica began to emerge from within the limousine—and the scene around me became a riot, descending almost in-stantly into a kind of mass madness.

The door handle in his hand, the doorman was standing off to one side to allow Angelica to exit. The car was wide open to the dozens of crouching paparazzi who lapped like surf just below its threshold. Angelica was wearing a very short dress, a dress as black as Juliette's dress was white. She had to turn her lower body forward to slide over the seat toward the door as the pho-tographers snapped their pictures and the TV cameras moved in behind them to take video over their heads. Then Angelica had to step down from the car onto the carpet in front of them and then rise up off the limousine's low seat. As hard as she may have tried, it would've been very difficult for her to keep her knees together throughout the entire process. In any case, she didn't manage it.

And suddenly, the photographers' eagerness was transformed into a mindless, rabid, eye-rolling frenzy.

There were gasps from the crowd. Grunts and little cries. I heard a woman say in a strangled voice, "No panties! No pant-ies!" I heard a man growl through his teeth like an animal, "Up-skirt!" Everybody—onlookers, reporters, technicians, security men, police—everyone within view of Angelica's suddenly ex-posed pudendum—even those only within earshot of the rumors of its exposure—swung in its direction with questing eyes, a single heaving movement like the ocean reaching for the moon.

As I say, it never made the news. And yes, it wasn't a very dignified or serious moment. It was ridiculous and completely out of keeping with the tone of what finally happened, with what was about to happen to those thousands of people, all those people. But it's the truth. And for myself, thinking back on it—I don't know—maybe it was apt, even emblematic in some way. I mean, if *God Creating Adam* on the ceiling of the Sistine Chapel represents our culture at its beginning, maybe a paparazzi upskirt of a starlet's quim is the central image of that culture now.

In any case, it gave me—so to speak—the opening I needed.

The incident lasted a second—one second. During that second, the rapid-fire buzz and snap of the cameras melded into a single chittering hum. A chorus of shocked murmurs rose to a cacophony of ecstatic shouts and cries. All eyes turned in one direction. My eyes turned. And, as they turned, they passed over the police officers who had been guarding the rope at the entrance to the narrow courtyard.

I saw them in motion. I saw them each take a step—then another—away from their posts—toward the red carpet, toward the black car, each extending his neck, each poking out his head, each seeking to steal a look between Angelica Eden's legs.

For one instant, the rope behind them stood unguarded, the path into the courtyard, the path to the theater's back door, was unmanned.

Some part of my brain was still pulling my eyes toward the limo, toward Angelica, but I fought against it. I knew I had only an instant. I started moving. I squirmed between two barricades. As the policemen craned their necks to get a look through the limousine door, I strode boldly, quickly behind them. I ducked under the rope. I ducked out of the wonderful silver light and entered the shadows of the narrow courtyard. I stood straight and started running hell-for-leather toward the door.

Three seconds. Three seconds of pulse and motion, every moment exposed. The cops at the courtyard's far end had their backs turned, but could glance over their shoulders and spot me at any time. The cops behind me were sure to return to their posts in the next instant. And wouldn't one of the people in the crowd have seen me break out? Wouldn't one of them point his finger and alert the law? Three seconds, my feet slapping the bricks, my breath in my ears, my heart hammering. Then my hand was on the cold door handle, my thumb was on the latch, my heart was turning to ice as I thought: *Don't let it be locked, don't let it be locked!*

It was not locked. I pressed the latch and pushed. There was a snap—I felt it jolting through me. I felt the latch give beneath my thumb. The door swung open. I tumbled through it.

I was inside the New Coliseum.

35 · Darkness Visible

I crouched there motionless. I was stunned. My mind was blank. Everything had changed so fast, so unexpectedly. One moment, the thing was impossible, the next it was done. I was completely taken by surprise. I could not believe I was actually in the building.

For another second, I hunkered, breathless, gaping at the wall as the door to the outside slowly swung shut behind me. I was in a long, dark, unadorned corridor. There were men in workclothes on either side of me. An efficient-looking young woman in jeans and a sweatshirt was carrying a clipboard somewhere. A security guard in a blue uniform scanned the area, a two-way microphone clipped to his shoulder. There was also a plainclothes security man at the far end of the hall.

For that one instant, as I crouched near the door, in a daze, all of them were occupied. None of them was looking my way. Even in my startled state, I realized I must have no more than a finger-snap's worth of time before one of them noticed me and raised the alarm.

I had to get going. I had to get out of sight.

My eyes shifted quickly, this way, that. I saw another door, about two long steps to my left. I had no choice. Another moment, I'd be caught. I stood up and moved to the door. I pulled it open. I went in.

I was just in time. Even as I drew the door closed again, I heard a low, crackling voice come over the uniformed guard's two-way.

"One-oh-one, you report any intruders at that location?"

I heard the guard answer out in the corridor, probably not more than ten yards away from me, "No, everything's clear here."

The crackling radio voice: "Okay, we had a civilian sixty-three report."

"Nope, it's four, it's good."

"Roger."

I heard the guard's footsteps stroll past, just on the other side of the door from me. I heard him push the door open—the door to the courtyard outside. I guess he wanted to make sure no one was lurking out there. I stood where I was, breathing, listening, waiting—wondering if he might check behind this door next. I turned around to get a better look at where I was, where I might hide.

That's when I saw I was trapped.

I was in a closet, a long storage closet. There was all sorts of junk in here: brooms, mops, buckets, ladders, coats and jackets hanging from a rod, a shelf full of paper towels and toilet paper, another shelf with boxes of stationery and markers, and so on. A bright light shone down on all of it from the high ceiling. There were no shadows to sink into. There was only the one door, the one way in and out.

I held my breath. I leaned my ear toward the door. I listened over the beating of my heart. But the guard didn't try to come in. I heard his footsteps moving on now. I heard his voice speaking again farther along the corridor—speaking to another security guy.

"NYPD outside had a citizen's report of someone in the courtyard. You see anything?"

"Nah. I been right here. I'd've noticed anyone come in."

"Me, too."

I let out a long sigh of relief.

Then the closet doorknob turned and the door came open.

I was standing so close to it, trying so hard to hear through it, that it nearly smacked me in the side of the face. But it opened only a crack. Then it stopped—a centimeter from my jaw.

A woman's voice called from the corridor. "House is full, Maryanne. Five minutes to lights out."

"Okay." Maryanne's voice came from the other side of the door, inches from me. "I'll be right there. I just gotta get something."

The door came open the rest of the way. But by then, I was already gone. I'd taken two gigantic, panicked strides down the length of the closet and slipped behind the last coat hanging on the rods. It was a long trenchcoat. It covered me to my knees. Still, it wasn't much of a hiding place. You only had to look down to see me from my shins to my shoes. And if you came close enough, I'd be visible plain as day, my back pressed into the corner, my face rigid with fear.

Maryanne stepped into the closet and shut the door behind her. Peeking through the coat hangers, I could see her. She was a typical backstage worker, slovenly, rad, short-chopped black hair and crystal blue eyes in a pudgy, pixie face, an enormous shapeless sweatshirt and ridiculous striped tights ending around her calves. The kind of glamourless girl the glamour-puss actresses like to have around because they don't steal the limelight. Just a misfit from the Midwest, you know, calling her divorced mom back home every other day to tell her about her cool job in the big city.

I wondered if I was going to have to knock her out.

I couldn't think of what else to do if she saw me. I wasn't expert enough to deck her with a punch, but I could probably choke her until she lost consciousness. Find something to tie her up with. Gag her so I'd have time to get away.

I huddled behind the trench coat. I closed my eyes. I prayed she would leave the closet before I was forced to hurt her. Rashid

flashed into my mind again. Rashid writhing and sobbing behind
his gag after I'd shattered his second kneecap. Thank God he'd
started talking then. Thank God he'd confessed the whole thing—
the whole plan, years in the making, devised way back during the
New Coliseum's construction, run with the help and permission of
terror masters in the Middle East. Thank God he'd sobbed out the
whole story before I had to start crushing his balls.

But it was enough. Enough to show me to myself. *Enough,* I
said to God. *Don't make me hurt the girl, too.*

My fingers curled at my side as if they were already around her
throat. Images flashed unbidden in my mind, images from long ago
of other women in my harsh hands. I shook them away. My heart
strained up to Heaven, praying I would not have to do this thing.

I opened my eyes, peeked through the hangers. Maryanne was
coming forward, coming right toward me. Now she was two feet
away, standing beside the coats dangling in front of the trench
coat from the same wooden rod. She was so close, I could smell
her perfume, tart and coy. I could see strands of her black hair
shining in the closet light. Sweat coursed down my forehead, over
my cheeks.

She began sorting through the coats. She was searching for one
in particular. Each one she pushed aside brought her closer to me,
closer and closer. I could hear her breathing. I could feel the heat
of her skin.

Father in Heaven, I prayed. *No more. No more.*

Maryanne pushed another coat aside. Now she was only two
coats away. Her perfume surrounded me. Looking through the
hangers, I could see a crescent of the white skin of her cheek.
Another moment, another coat, and we would be face to face and
I would have to do it.

But now she paused. I felt a coat moving as she handled it.
She must have stuck her hand into a pocket because I felt the

cloth-softened shape of her fingers graze my hip. I heard a rattling noise. Pills in a bottle. She was taking a pill bottle out of a coat pocket.

At that moment, the lights went out. Startled, I stiffened, held my breath. Then they came on again—then went out and came on. It was a warning signal. The show was about to start.

Maryanne pulled back from the coats and for a moment her full profile was clear to me, inches from my nose. I could've leaned forward and kissed her cheek with no effort at all. But she was already turning away, turning to the door. I heard the pill bottle rattle again as she carried it off. I heard her footsteps. The scent of her perfume grew fainter around me.

Thank you, I thought.

The lights started blinking again. The closet door opened and shut. Maryanne was gone. I brought my palm to my face and swabbed away the sweat.

Thank you.

I stumbled out from behind the coats. I felt empty. Disgusted. Weak and dead. I stood in the center of the closet, hunched, panting, pouring sweat. I stared grimly at the base of the door. In the line of light at the bottom, I saw shadows passing: the workers, the guards out there. I was still trapped. In minutes, the theater would be ready, the show would begin. Rashid's gang of killers would be ready, too. I had to find them. I had to find Serena. I had to clear out the theater. And I couldn't even think of a way to get out of here.

Once more, the lights began to blink, and now there was a rhythmic chime as well, a warning tone, telling the audience to take their seats. I looked around me, searching for an idea. I noticed the shelves holding stationery and pens and the like—metal shelves with gray cardboard boxes on them. Some of the boxes had lids; some were open to show pads, envelopes, and forms of

various types inside. I stepped over to them. I saw a smaller box
with a blue fabric lanyard snaking out of it. I looked in and saw
a tangle of lanyards attached to the sort of plastic envelopes you
use for ID cards. Quickly, I untangled one lanyard from the rest,
tugging until its plastic envelope came free of the others.

I glanced down at the line of light beneath the door. The shadows had stopped moving there. The people, I guess, had taken
their places. The show was about to begin.

I grabbed a piece of paper off one of the pads. Tore off a square.
The light in the high ceiling above me dimmed and dimmed and
went out. Darkness settled over me. Feeling my way, I worked the
blank square of paper into the plastic envelope. I pulled the lanyard
over my neck. In the dark, maybe it would pass for an ID card.

I could see nothing now but the light at the bottom of the door.
It had changed from a bright line to a smoky red glow. That would
be the glow of the sign above the emergency exit, I figured. Aside
from that, it must be dark now in the corridor, too. If I had any
chance of getting out of here unseen, this was it. Empty as I was,
weary as I was, weak as I was, it was time to move.

I took a breath. I went to the closet door. For a second, I
thought about cracking it open, peeking out to see if the way was
clear. But I decided that now, in the dark, it was best to act boldly,
as if I belonged here. So, with tension like a fist in my throat, I
pulled the door open quickly and stepped out into the hall.

I entered the dim red glow of the exit sign. At the edge of
the glow, I could see other figures: those workers and guards. I
could sense more people farther off along the hall as well. I could
feel them there, standing still and quiet as the show began in the
auditorium.

Music started. Brass and strings, slow, solemn, and yet somehow triumphant: the grand opening theme of the first Real 3-D
movie ever, *The End of Civilization as We Know It*. The music was

muffled by the corridor walls, but still loud. It still surrounded me. As I started striding along the corridor, my footsteps fell naturally into sync with the majestic beat of the sound track.

Soon I could make out the plainclothes security man posted at the far corner. He stood with his hands behind his back, scanning the shadows. As I came near him, the gleam of his eyes, the outline of his features, the coiled wire running up his jaw to his ear, all became visible in the red light. I offered him a quick businesslike smile. A wave of the hand to distract him from the blank ID card around my neck. He smiled back indulgently. I went past him, and continued around the corner.

There was more red light in the next hall, a sign about halfway down pointing back to the exit behind me, and a bare red bulb at the far end. The bulb illuminated a heavy metal door with a push-bar across it. Yet another guard was posted here, standing to one side of the door, a great black shape limned by the misty red light. Judging by his position, he was distracted at the moment. He was leaning off to one side, trying to catch a glimpse of the show. The music lifted and swelled as I went toward him.

As I came near, the guard noticed me. He straightened, looked me over. I smiled again, pointed at the metal door, and held up the bogus ID tag around my neck as if to let him read it. I covered it with my thumb, but it didn't really matter. He barely glanced at it. He went back to trying to see the movie.

I approached the door. I could make out a word stenciled onto it: STAIRS. That's what I wanted. Rashid had told me the blast would be most powerful in the cellar. He told me he thought Jamal would leave Serena there. Because he loved her and wanted to impress her, because he wanted her to witness his great achievement and to be a part of it.

I pushed the door open carefully to keep the noise to a mini-mum. At that moment, there was a loud gasp of delight from the theater. I hesitated—but it was just the audience—some three thousand people getting their first look at Real 3-D technology. There was an outbreak of applause.

I went into the stairwell. The applause faded behind me.

At first, there was dim white light in here. A small square fluorescent lamp was fastened to the wall just above my head. It spread a pale glow over the falling and rising flights of gray steps. I was glad it was there. It helped me find my way to the downward flight, helped me get a grip on the banister. But as I descended into the theater's cellar, the light grew fainter. The music grew fainter, too. I heard another burst of applause and a burst of laughter, but they sounded very far away.

Then, when I reached the cellar door and pushed through, I stepped into what seemed at first impenetrable blackness. I knew at once that this was strange; wrong. There should have been some light, some small light somewhere. But when the door slipped from my hand and clacked shut on the stairs behind me, I could see nothing, absolutely nothing out in front. There was silence, too. The air felt deep and thick with it, like a cushion pressing in on me.

I stood where I was, staring uselessly, afraid to move away from the exit, afraid to remain there and do nothing. That dark, that silence—they were so dense, so present, so palpable that, for the first time, I began to believe I was going to die here. For the first time, that possibility became real to me. With the dark so deep, so vast, with the silence so eerie and oppressive, I could not see how I would be able to do what I needed to do here; how I would ever find Serena, how I would locate the detonators and disable them. Even with Rashid's frantically precise directions, his complete knowledge about how and where the explosives were planted, it seemed an impossible task. I had a sure sense that time was running out, that it may have run out already. The show had already started. There was no more reason for them to wait. There was just me and the dark and the silence and the coming explosion.

So I began to believe I was going to die. At that point, the thought came almost as a relief. I was so sick of myself, so sick of the things I'd done that night. Sick at what I'd done to Rashid. Sick that I had crouched in that closet as if I were some kind of predatory monster, ready and willing to strangle that poor girl, Maryanne. How was I supposed to go home after that? Make love to my wife, play with my children? How was I supposed to go to church again and shake the hands of my neighbors there and wish them God's peace?

To be honest, if it had just been me, I think I would've sat down right then, right there, invisible in the darkness. I think I would've just laid my forehead on my knees and waited to be blown away.

But of course it wasn't just me. It never was. Serena was out in that blackness somewhere. And the people upstairs—all those thousands of faces, flickering in the movie-light—and the faces waiting on the street outside—and the faces all over the city and on the TV, too—the faces in the wars all around the world which somehow were one war and which somehow, insanely, I'd become a part of.

So I took a step forward, a slow, tentative step into that almost-visible dark. I began edging forward bit by bit, staring, listening. Unable to see—blind here—blind completely—I became aware of sounds first. It was not as silent in the cellar as I'd originally thought. There were still some muffled noises from the theater above. Voices—music—dim—impossible to make out. And there were other sounds, too: a steady hum of machinery, an electric buzz, a soft click or two, the hollow whisper that a furnace makes. My foot touched a wall, but when I reached out my hand to the right, I felt a space beside it, an opening, maybe, into another room, another hall. I couldn't tell. I went through. I went slowly on, feeling my way. I could sense death near me, like a figure walking beside me in the dark.

Soon I became aware of something else. A smell. It was faint but definite. Sour, stinging, organic. It was the smell of sweat and urine, the smell of fear: a human smell. I tried to follow it.

The scent grew thicker, harsher, step by step. My heart beat harder. I paused to sniff the air, to test it, trying to figure out the way to the source. Then I started moving again, reaching out with my hands to feel the way.

I don't know how long I went on like that. I remember I banged my shin at one point. At another point, I stumbled over something hard and staggered into nothingness a few terrifying steps before I regained my balance. Mostly, though, I just moved, slowly, blindly, my hands out in front of me, until the progression became dream-like, until it seemed it would simply continue and continue and never end.

Then at last—at last, I began to see. Not much at first. Small lights here and there, lights I guess the killers couldn't disable. There was a green indicator on a machine of some sort and a red indicator not far from it. And there was another of those soft white fluorescents glowing somewhere around a corner out of sight. My eyes fed on these and began to pick out shapes. Large, looming structures all around me. There was nothing I could make sense of. The trace of grillework here, a clawing metallic arm arching overhead, a large clockwork of some sort with pendulums and pistons moving quietly but powerfully. I felt I had stepped into the heart of some great and terrible machine.

I stopped moving. I peered around me, disheartened, bewildered. Where the hell was I? What was I supposed to do now?

How would I ever find the detonator in this dark? How would I ever find Serena?

The smell was dense here, dense as dense. My nostrils stung with it. My eyes teared. And the noises: guttural hums, periodic soughs, steady whirs of movement—they were louder, closer. I felt as if black mills and engines were hovering over me in the darkness, hovering almost hungrily, like living creatures, ravenous beasts. For a moment or two, in my tension and confusion, the sounds of them, their huge presence, that smell—it all nearly overwhelmed my senses.

And so, for a moment or two, I didn't hear those other, softer sounds nearby: the sound of something moving on the floor, the sound of a soft, struggling, breathless human voice.

Then I did hear it. I turned quickly, searching for it. I stepped blindly toward it. My foot touched something heavy and soft. I dropped to my knees, reaching out with my hands. I felt her. Yes, and I could see her now, too. I could make out the dim shadow of her. Struggling, tied. I put my hands on her arm.

"Serena!" I said, my voice breaking. "Serena. It's me. It's Jason."

She struggled harder, went on trying to speak even more urgently than before. I felt my way to her shoulder, to her face. I felt for the gag across her mouth. It was the same sort of duct-tape gag I'd used on Rashid. My heart was wild as I tried to get a purchase on it. I was wild with surprise and joy—and surging terror, too, because she was alive—which meant there was a chance I might save her—which meant there was a chance I might fail to save her, a chance she'd die under my hands.

My fingers found the edge of the duct tape. I worked it off her. I felt for the rag in her mouth. She was already trying to spit it out. I got the tip of it, worked it between her lips and pulled it free.

Serena gasped and coughed. She gulped air. I held her close to me, my eyes swimming. I felt her press her face against my neck. Then she pulled back. She looked up at me. I saw her eyes gleaming out of the dark.

"I knew it, I knew it, I knew it," she whispered fiercely. "I knew you'd come for me."

36 · A Lost Chance of Escape

I tried to free her. I picked at the duct tape that bound her wrists behind her back.

"Don't," she croaked. "There's no time. Jamal already went upstairs. He has the button."

"Damn it!" I said. I couldn't get the tape off her. I couldn't find the end of it.

"Stop," she whined. "We have to go."

"Okay." I looked around at the vague and monstrous shadows. "We have to find the detonators."

"That's no good. They're all over. They go off if you touch them. There's a timer, too. It goes off no matter what. We have to get out."

I nodded once. She was right. I worked my hands under her. I took her into my arms and stood. She was small and light, nothing to carry. And I guess the adrenaline must've been pumping through me, too. I barely felt the weight of her.

As seconds passed, I stood there, holding her, looking around, disoriented. The looming, grinding machines—whatever they were—seemed to hem me in and bear down on me on every side. I couldn't see a way through them. I wasn't even sure which way I'd come.

"Go that way. That light," Serena said, lifting her chin toward it.

I found it. That pale fluorescent light around the corner, the one I'd noticed before. I moved toward it, maneuvering through the gothic silhouettes. Now I could make out the doorway. I maneuvered her through it. I came into a corridor. I saw the light. It hung above a door.

"Hurry," she said.

I carried her down the hall. The smell of her surrounded me. I could smell her fruity little-girl perfume and the cotton of her sweatshirt, clean and soft as a baby's pajamas. I could smell the urine where she'd wet herself and her sweat which carried the scent of her sex in it and the scent of her fear which was stronger than all the rest. In the pale light, I could see her frightened features, scrunched and shuddering. She was crying with terror. I felt an almost-crushing tenderness for her, something like what I'd felt for my children when they were babies in their cribs.

"We're gonna be all right," I told her.

"We're not," she whimpered. "He's already there. It'll happen any second. We're not gonna get out in time."

I set her down, one arm around her, so I could get a hand on the doorknob, open the door. I lifted her into my arms again and carried her into the stairwell.

I went up the stairs quickly, taking them two at a time, rising toward the brighter light above. I could feel now how unnaturally strong I was, how quickly my mind was working, outstripping time. I thought about what I would do when I got upstairs. Would I be able to save Serena and come back to try to clear the theater? No. I knew there was no time to do both. I had to choose. I either had to get her out or try to get everyone out. As I took that single flight to the upstairs door, whole worlds of tragedy flashed through my mind. There was the world in which I rescued the girl but all the others in the auditorium died; the world in which I tried to save everyone, but Serena was killed for my useless heroics; the world in which I got some people out, but not Serena . . .

I crested the flight, reached the landing, the door. This time, I managed to turn the knob without putting Serena down. I pushed the door open with my foot and held it open with her body. I stepped out into a dark corridor.

At once, there was a loud blast, a huge explosion. Serena cried out. The floor rattled under my feet.

I froze, eyes wide, mouth open. I felt Serena's body seize and stiffen in my arms.

But nothing happened. No gust of wind and flame, no destruction. Music rose. A patter of small arms fire sounded.

"Shit!" Serena said. "The movie."

I gave a quick, silent laugh.

The exciting music soared. I took one quick look around, this way and that.

There it was: the red light of an exit sign to my right, a guard standing underneath it. It was our chance of escape. I could get out that way. I could save Serena's life and my own.

To my left, I saw the swinging doors into the auditorium. There was a uniformed usherette standing there—a tiny old woman with black and silver hair.

I looked toward the red light. I looked back to the swinging doors. I made my choice. I barreled down the hall toward the auditorium. I had to try to clear the place. Even if it killed us both, I had to try.

I reached the doors. I turned my back to them. Serena's feet swung around and the ancient usherette had to leap out of their way.

The usherette began to say something. It sounded like "Ut—"

Then I hit the doors with my back. I carried Serena through, into *The End of Civilization as We Know It*.

37 · The End of Civilization as We Know It

The music surrounded us, brash and loud. We were bathed in strobic light and shadows. I charged through the flicker, up an inclined aisle, gathering my breath, gathering my courage.

I started shouting even before I reached the auditorium, my voice nearly drowned by the music.

"Bomb! There's a bomb in the building! Get out! There's a bomb!"

I plunged into the center of the movie.

It felt like that. It felt as if I'd crashed through the surface of the show and become a part of it. I had broken out of the aisle onto the stage of a vast amphitheater. Tiers and tiers of seats rose into the glimmering darkness all around me. Eyes gleamed up there, gazing down at me. Hundreds of faces came halfway into view then vanished as the shifting light from the scene below played over them and passed by.

I was in that scene. I was lost in that light: light and color and shapes and figures ringed round by the tiers of gazing eyes. There were the pyramids of Giza rising toward the sky; and there the sphinx of living rock standing its ancient guard. Trucks were rumbling past in the distance. Men in khaki uniforms ran here and there. Other men in flowing white Arab robes strode past. On every side of me the lone and level sands stretched far away.

Apparently, the way the new 3-D technology worked, no matter where you were in the seats above, the images seemed clear and life-sized and bizarrely real. But down where I was, the picture was distorted. The buildings were slanted, some huge, some too small. The people were stretched and blurred and of different sizes. Vehicles and running men became elongated as they went past, then suddenly vanished. Images became more and more transparent the closer they came. The effect was swirling, dazzling, phantasmagorical—yet even for me, at moments, it was completely three-dimensional, thoroughly alive.

I was dazzled by it all. Confused. I had stepped in an instant from present-day New York into ruins and sand. The scene surrounding me was at once utterly unreal and utterly present. The scene above me was all faces—faces rising into infinity—flickering in the flickering light—climbing tiers of eyes staring down at me. It was more than I could take in. It stopped my thinking cold, shut down my mind. All I could manage to do was turn from place to place, holding Serena in my arms, and shouting wildly:

"Bomb! Bomb! There's a bomb in the theater!"

A man stepped right up to me. Startled and afraid, I spun to him. I recognized him at once: It was the actor, Todd Bingham. For a second, he seemed enormous and elongated like pulled taffy. The next second, he snapped into his proper shape but became transparent. It was the phantom of Todd, his character in the movie.

"I've had enough of being afraid," he said to me.

Other people were shouting around me, running past me, soldiers and natives and sheikhs.

"There's a bomb!" I screamed at Todd.

A woman behind me spoke, her voice very loud. I swung around to her, Serena's tear-streaked features going bright and dim as they slashed through the center of a nomad's skirt. There was Angelica Eden on the other side of me, solid and vital. She looked cool and witty in khaki slacks and a purple blouse open on her famous cleavage. She laughed around her cigarette. She said, "You can never have enough fear, Jason. Fear is how America rules the world. If we can make them fear these Muslims, all their oil will be ours!"

I blinked, confused. She'd used my name. Was she real? Was she speaking to me? No, dimly, even in my confusion, I realized she was part of the scene. I realized, too, that the scene—its music, its dialogue, the rumble of its stretching, moving, vanishing trucks—was swallowing my shouts, was encompassing my presence altogether.

This, I later learned, was the part of the film in which Todd, playing a hard-boiled CIA agent, first begins to realize that the terrorist explosions bringing chaos to the Middle East are in fact being engineered by American political and business interests who are then putting the blame on innocent Muslims in order to start a war and take over their oil fields.

"There's a bomb in the theater!" I screamed, my voice cracking.

"Wait! Jason, wait!"

Again, disoriented by the sound of my own name, I turned to see a woman striding toward me—striding toward me and shrinking from a monstrous taffy string into the transparent image of Juliette Lovesey. She looked strong now, clear-eyed, dynamic; not the fragile creature I'd seen on the red carpet outside. "Before you make up your mind, there's someone I think you need to talk to."

Suddenly another man was standing beside me. He seemed to have appeared out of nowhere. He was an Arab man about sixty years old with a black beard and a black turban. His face was lined but kindly. His eyes twinkled with wisdom.

"This is Muammar al-Qadi," said Juliette.

"Of Hezbollah?" Todd said in terse surprise.

"Listen to me!" I shouted up at the flickering faces in the surrounding dark.

"You must listen to him," said Juliette.

"They don't know we're real!" Serena cried to me.

"I should've killed you when I had the chance," said the evil Angelica to the Arab man. Her father, it would turn out, owned a controlling interest in an oil company.

Now, yet another man rushed beneath the base of the gazing sphinx and stumbled toward Todd with flying footsteps. He was all in black, black jeans and a black hoodie. The outfit seemed almost to make a human-shaped hole in the surrounding scene. His face, though—his face was preternaturally bright. It was like a sunburst, burning with prophecy, ecstatic, insane.

Dazed and squinting through the dazzling light, I didn't recognize him at first. Then Serena let out a short, sharp scream and I realized it was Jamal.

"Sometimes," said the old, kindly Arab man, his wise eyes twinkling, "sometimes we must turn to the beautiful wisdom and imagery of the Koran for guidance."

"*Allahu akbar!* God is great!" Jamal shouted.

Now the music swelled romantically to underscore Muammar al-Qadi's wisdom. The bearded old man lifted his hand. There was a venerable leather-bound book in it. Jamal lifted his hand almost simultaneously. There was a detonator in it. I could see the red button under his thumb.

"*Allahu akbar!*" Jamal shrieked.

I had one last moment to look around me, to turn and cast my gaze over the shifting phantoms on the dazzling stage. There was Todd with the tough-guy stubble on his chin and Juliette looking bold and adventurous and Angelica looking wicked but strong. I saw the kindly old Arab with his turban and black beard and

Patrick Piersall in sweatpants and an orange pullover of some kind . . .

And the last thing I remember thinking before the blast was: *Patrick Piersall? Is he in this, too?*

Apparently he was. He had entered from the direction of a passing truck. He was standing in the yellow sand right there beside me. Even here in the movie, he appeared pudgy and yellow-eyed and dissolute. Yet in this role at least, he managed to put on a heroic demeanor. He was planted firmly with his legs apart and wore a look on his face so stalwart and grim, he might still have been piloting his spaceship through the galaxy as in days of yore. I saw Todd stride manfully past him to Juliette. He put his hands on her shoulders and drew her to him and said, "Where the hell have you been?"

"God is great!" shouted Jamal, holding up the detonator.

"Eat shit and die!" said Patrick Piersall.

He lifted his hand, too. He was holding a gun in it. It was that 9mm automatic he had shown me in the Ale House.

The music was blossoming around us like a sudden garden with a scent redolent of courage and romance. Then came the blast—a shocking blast. It wasn't loud—not as loud as the explosions in the movie—but it was real and vibrant, sucking the air into itself and blowing it out again so that I felt it like a punch to the cheek.

Piersall had pulled the trigger of his weapon. And now he pulled it again and again. There was another blast and another. And another as he pulled the trigger again.

I turned and turned in confusion and terror, Serena screaming in my arms. I saw Todd drawing Juliette to him. I saw Juliette lifting her lips for a kiss. I saw Angelica looking on in fury and frustration and the old Arab man looking wise and kind.

And I saw Jamal. His eyes were wide. His arms were flung

out on either side of him. The front of his shirt was being torn to
bloody shreds in front of my eyes as Piersall's bullets pounded into
his chest. The detonator fell from his hands as he reeled backward
a step, his arms pinwheeling. He tumbled right through Todd and
Juliette and dropped down into a pool of light that swirled over the
stage floor like sand.

A girl shrieked. I looked toward the sound. No, it wasn't a girl.
It was a skinny little man jumping to his feet in the first ring of
seats above me, his hands clutching the sides of his head. It was
Todd—the real Todd, up in his seat, watching the movie. His face
was quivering with realization and fear. His hands flew from his
head to grip the tier rail in front of him. He let out another high-
pitched shriek.

"That's not in the movie!" he screamed. "That scene's not in
the movie. Those people are real!"

"There's still a timer," Serena said to me. "It'll still explode!"

"There's a bomb!" I shouted. "It *is* real! There's a bomb in the
theater!"

For one more moment—one more and then one more—all
those faces flickering in the seats rising higher and higher around
me remained as they were. Coiffed and bejeweled and beautiful
and distracted. It struck me as an almost wistful tableau, like a
daguerreotype of a vanished and well-loved past. For one more
moment, all those rich, lovely, comfortable cosmopolitans gazed
down at the movie, their minds trying to convince themselves that
whatever was not the movie must just be some kind of joke or
mistake.

Then at last—at last—the truth dawned on them: They were
under attack.

As if on cue, there were more explosions. It nearly stopped
my heart as a medallion of fire and debris leapt out of the air
at my feet. A moment later, I realized this, too, was only part of

the movie, another scene in the movie in which bombs went off. But even as I realized that, I became aware of another noise, a deeper noise: a low rumble as of a great beast stirring. I listened to it through the blasts and the music. On every side of me, there were murmurs—murmurs becoming voices, voices spiraling up into cries—a rising grumble of movement as people stood up out of their seats, a growing thunder rolling down from tier to tier and over the stage to tremble above me, beneath me, around me.

An explosion went off beneath the sphinx, hurling bodies and flame and sand: still the movie. I lifted my eyes in the blazing, flickering light and saw the faces above me starting to flow and migrate into the aisles. I heard more voices, more screams.

"It is real! There's a bomb!"

"Someone's been shot!"

"Oh my God! Oh my God!"

I saw a man in a tuxedo tumble frantically over a low railing to get down to the stage. Another followed. Then more men and women started to spill over and others above them were pushing out of their rows of seats, fighting their ways to the aisles. Every moment, there were more of them moving, a thick flow of them moving faster and faster.

"It's real! It's real!"

"Is there a bomb?"

"Someone said there's a bomb in the theater!"

"There's a bomb, a bomb!"

Suddenly I saw Todd racing toward me—wispy little Todd in his tuxedo—racing across the bright stage with his arms and legs churning, running for his life with all the intensity and dedication of a cartoon mouse. I stood and watched fascinated as he rushed right into the gruff three-dimensional image of himself—Todd with a day's growth of beard and a gun in his hand. For an instant, they seemed to be a double image of one man. And then the real Todd burst out of the phantom Todd and dashed up an aisle and vanished into the shadows.

I turned—turned with Serena in my arms—turned past the phantom of Angelica Eden as she laughed wickedly at the destruction around her. I turned to Patrick Piersall. He stood where he was, staring down at the sprawled, bloody body of Jamal on the floor. Piersall's arm was still extended in front of him, the gun still in his hand.

As I watched him, he seemed hardly to notice the commotion growing around him. He lifted his eyes slowly. Vaguely, he looked up at the tiers of seats. He seemed barely to know where he was.

The music thrummed dangerously now. Phantoms fired phantom rifles in our direction. Phantom explosions went off at our feet and in the sand and around the pyramids.

"Piersall!" I shouted.

The old actor blinked. He looked at me vaguely.

"It's done," I said to him. "Let's get the hell out of here."

There were others running across the stage now—real people, I mean—more and more of them. Men in tuxedos and women in evening gowns legging it through the desert sands beneath the sphinx's impassive gaze. The rumble above me was growing louder, stronger as more and more people began to panic and flee. The atmosphere quivered with their movement. The shouts and the footsteps were merging into a single quaking thunder.

"Let's go!" I shouted.

I broke for the aisle behind me. Carrying Serena in my arms, plunging through the phantasmagoria, out of the light, back into the flickering shadows of the aisle. I raced down the short slope, charging at the swinging doors.

I made it out into the corridor, headed down the corridor toward the red exit light, part of a swiftly moving stream of black dinner jackets and glittering gowns. The whole building seemed to be shaking now with footsteps and motion. The walls seemed almost to be rocking. The ceiling seemed to jump as if the roof would fly off. My stream of people crashed into another coming from the opposite direction. We converged and meshed and became one greater stream under the red light.

The door under the light was open by the time I reached it. Serena and I went through it with the rapid wash of rhinestones and bow ties flashing past on either side of us. I stepped out into the cold, damp air and took a great, welcome breath of it. But there was no time to feel relief. I was in an alleyway—a different one from before. I had to keep running or be knocked over. We all kept running, trying to reach the alley exit, trying to reach the street and put some distance between us and the doomed theater. Even here—even outdoors like this—we could hear the thunder in the theater continue to grow. It sounded as if some enormous tsunami were ripping itself out of the ocean bed and hoisting itself up to the surface of the sea.

I was halfway down the alley when the tidal wave caught up with us. Every theater door flew open. The people burst from them in the full flight of panic and swept over me in a flood. I clutched Serena to my chest with all the strength I had. I heard her scream, then heard her screams lost in the thousands of screams all around me. Wild faces were everywhere and the solid softness of bodies engulfed us. The tide pushed us and stopped and spurted forward suddenly in a broken rhythm impossible to outguess. I fought frantically to stay on my feet, clutching Serena, shoving to left and right to make a way for us. I felt myself lifted up and carried and hurled down to the pavement so hard I thought I would fall. But the crush lifted me up and bore me on, my toes scraping over the alley floor. I had lost all control. I was being carried along at the mercy of the billowing surge of the mob. I was conscious of my racing heart and a flow of some chemical energy through me that I suppose might have been called fear. But I was detached from it. It was something happening inside my body, not to me. In me, there was only an intensity of experience and force all funneled into my effort to keep my feet, to hold on to Serena, to go on, and to survive.

Now, as if gushing from a culvert, we broke out of the narrow alley and spread out into the street. We were broadsided, jostled, and then joined by the greater crowd swarming out of the front doors. As if we were one enormous force, we carried the barricades away, knocked them down and trampled them. We caught up the thousands of spectators waiting outside and engulfed them and bore them on. Finally we began to spread out over the streets and the sidewalks, flowing in both directions toward the avenues, away from the theater. With every step, the mob's first explosive energy diminished. It began to flow and eddy. I gained my feet again in the midst of it. I began to move by my own will. I began to think again. I felt the rhythms of my body beginning to slow and calm.

By the time Serena and I reached Broadway, I was able to stop, to turn and look back at the New Coliseum. Its gorgeous white facade stood imperturbable and grand. The spiraling sweep of arched, column-framed windows were bathed in the spotlights and the kliegs sweeping back and forth majestically in front of it. The last of the people inside were just now spilling out of the various doors, the flow of black tuxes and brightly colored gowns filling the street and spreading toward the avenues. As the people began to disperse and calm, their rush of movement slowed. Like the surf breaking into pools on the shore, the mob broke into groups and couples and individuals again. Some continued running toward the avenues in their anxiety, but most were content to slow down and walk away or stop at the corner or even just outside the theater's doors. People began to look at the theater over their shoulders or to turn around and watch it expectantly.

Nothing happened. The movement of the crowd slowed even more. More and more people came to a standstill. Some began to curse. Some began to shake their heads and laugh.

I was at the corner of Broadway. The lights of Times Square soared into the night behind me. The spotlit grandeur of the New Coliseum rose above the milling people on the street before. After the thundering panic, the honking horns of the jammed traffic and the shouts and talk and footsteps and music of New York everywhere seemed almost harmonious and sweet.

I set Serena down on the ground, holding her up on her bound feet with my arm around her shoulders. With my free hand, I worked the duct tape off her wrists. Then I held her under the arm while she bent over and worked the tape off her ankles. I looked out, meanwhile, at the gowns and tuxes pooling in the street. I heard more laughter—cursing, too. My eyes passed over smiling faces and puzzled faces and angry faces. I saw people who had fallen or simply collapsed in the gutter and were lying there with others kneeling beside them. Finally my gaze came to rest on one man standing in the street about twenty yards from me—twenty yards, I mean, closer to the theater. It was Patrick Piersall. He was panting, out of breath as I was, exhausted. He looked old, deteriorated, squat and paunchy in his black sweatpants and orange pullover. He was still gripping his gun, holding it down by his side now. He was staring up at the swirling rise of the theater facade with a sort of dazed, stupid fascination.

Serena straightened beside me, unbound. She looked at the theater, too. We all looked at it, waiting for something to happen. Nothing did.

"What the hell was *that* all about?" I heard someone say.

I wondered myself. I felt a fresh anxiety slowly growing up inside me. In my spent, empty mind, bits of information were beginning to assemble themselves like pieces of matter coming together in space. An entire alternative story told itself to me in an instant. In this story, I had inherited my mother's disease, had begun to see connections and patterns and logical progressions that had no bearing on reality. I had found a teenaged girl in a bad situation and connected it to a professor whose philosophy I didn't like. In my madness, I had tortured the poor professor into inventing some sort of conspiracy against American culture, an attack on the New Coliseum. Maybe I was even suffering hallucinations, and my life had become like one of those French theories in which reality could not be distinguished from the images thrown up by society . . .

"My God—" I began to whisper.

Then the New Coliseum exploded.

I could not take in the vastness of the catastrophe. I could only stand and stare.

There was a hugely loud yet strangely echoless thump. There was a great heaving movement in the street. There was a punching blast of air and heat that knocked me back on my heels. I felt a jolt of terror and a kind of awe as every one of the big arched windows that spiraled up the front and side of the building flashed with fire then went suddenly black. Glass flew—enormous slanting shards and little confetti fragments of it flew out everywhere—fanned out into the night with what almost seemed an air of frantic gaiety. The glass caught the white of the spotlights. It caught the colored lights of Broadway. It glittered and sparkled gaily, shattering and tinkling and raining down over the ducked heads and raised arms of the crowd in the street. The whole theater seemed to expand for a moment and then, remarkably, settle back into itself as if it were unharmed.

After that, there was a second of uncanny stillness.

After that, the theater crumbled.

Before our eyes, the fabulous structure turned to jagged stones and dust and, with a long, dying roar, spilled down out of itself and over the pavement. Once again, the people began screaming. They ran and stumbled over each other, trying to get away from the white onslaught of debris and the thick spindrift of dust. I saw people caught by the tide of stone and knocked over. Some were buried under it. Some were carried away.

The rubble that had been the theater rolled clear across the street. It splashed and crashed against the walls of the brick buildings opposite. More windows shattered. Blood splattered against the stone. The debris seemed to rise up high into the night and hurl itself down again, leaving a thick mist of motes choking the air. At some point, the spotlights were knocked over. There was a brittle crash of glass and metal and that beautiful silver light around the red carpets was snuffed out. The kliegs fell, their beams toppling out of the night sky like towers. Where the bright theater stood, there was all at once a black hole, a ruin of girders and cement caught in places by sweeping brightness and then released again into shadow as a single klieg—swept off its truck bed but still somehow standing on the street—swung back and forth, its shaft crossing back and forth beneath the bellies of the roiling clouds above.

The panicking people poured past me, jostling me where I stood. Covered with dust and glass, catching, like the glass, the Broadway lights, they looked like strange rhinestone ghosts with dark O's where their mouths should have been. I kept my left arm around Serena's shoulders and pulled her to me to hold her upright, to keep her from being swept off as the people knocked into us and flowed past on either side.

I sought out Patrick Piersall again and found him. He was not far from where he'd been before. It was as if the collapsing theater had simply passed over him, as if the running, panicked crowd had passed over him, and all of it left him untouched. He was dusty—his pullover white, his face gray and white—but otherwise unmoved and unharmed.

And he was still just standing there, just staring up at the theater—or at the ruin that had been the theater, the emptiness of slanting girder and jagged stone. Then, the next moment, he was laughing—laughing hard, with his debauched wreck of a face thrown back and his shoulders going up and down and his round belly quivering. His laugh broke high once, then settled into a long baritone guffaw. I could hear him clearly over the shouts and screams and honking horns and traffic.

He began to look around, as if searching for someone he could share the joke with. He found me. Our eyes met.

Through the floating mist of ruin, as the people ran screaming for their lives, Patrick Piersall sent me a flamboyant salute. Laughing like a madman, he braced the tips of all five fingers of his left hand against his forehead and then flung the hand toward me, opening it in my direction. It was a grandiose, flyaway gesture, a gesture of pure, alcoholic derangement, both exalted and absurd. I returned it in a more restrained fashion, a finger to my eyebrow, then pointed at him. Piersall went on laughing. Even I couldn't help but smile.

Because the fact was—when the dust and insanity settled— the fact was we had saved them. Oh, there were terrible tragedies that night, terrible injuries that would never be healed. Children lost limbs. Women's faces were slashed and ravaged. A couple of men were paralyzed. A couple had heart attacks. A few were buried under the rubble for hours. There were hundreds hurt, some in ways almost unimaginable, ways too disturbing to describe. Still . . .

Still in all, not one person died as a result of the terrorist blast in the New Coliseum Theater. Todd, Juliette, Angelica, the secretary of state, all the others in the audience and all the people who'd been standing and watching on the street outside—miraculously, every single one of them—every single one of them survived.

So Patrick Piersall laughed and I managed a small smile and we saluted each other, standing on the corner of Times Square. Because we saved them, he and I—and Casey Diggs, too. We saved them—that was the truth of it. A paranoid wannabe journalist barred from his profession for telling the truth. A drunken has-been Hollywood actor who once pretended to be the admiral of a spaceship. And me. Not much in the way of heroes, I know, but all the heroes we could muster in a desperate hour.

And it was enough. Just barely enough.

Because we saved them all.

EPILOGUE

On a clear fall afternoon not long after the explosion, I came home to the Hill. As I stepped out of my car into the driveway, my wife and children rushed the door of the house so fast they got jammed up in it together. Then they broke out one at a time and came hurtling toward me. Chad and Nathan were racing in the lead with little Terry running behind. As I stepped out of the driveway onto the front walk, they flung themselves at me. In a moment, I had a boy in each arm and the girl wrapped around my leg, and Cathy, smiling and crying at once, moving in among them with a kiss.

I wanted to weep when I saw them. I wanted to fall to my knees and press my forehead to the flagstone and sob enormous racking sobs until I heaved up some portion of the thick, strangling mass of my self-revulsion. I wanted to slobber over the goodness of those children's heads and wallow in the sweetness of my wife's bosom and grovel on the earth in front of them. I wanted to rip open my shirt and bare the ugliness of myself to heaven and beg their forgiveness for what I was inside.

But no. I was Cathy's husband, the children's father, and they were all of them in my care. If I wept, they would weep. If I showed them my misery, they would be miserable, too. I had no business bringing my moral nausea to their happy occasion. I settled instead for many misty-eyed kisses and embraces all around. Then, with what I hoped was insouciant Dad gallantry, I said, "So—

what's for dinner?" They all laughed and we headed together into the house.

It was the beginning of a very hard winter. A black depression soon settled over me. My old joy of life seemed to seep through my fingers as I desperately tried to hold it fast. At last, it bled out of my life entirely. I walked through the days hollow-hearted and soul-dead. Day by day, hour by hour, I used all the strength of will I had to hide my emptiness from the children. I went through the motions of driving them to school and playing with them in the snow and taking them to movies, but that's what it was: just going through the motions. Joking with them, wrestling with them, setting rules for them, hearing them out. None of it seemed real to me. My life did not seem real.

I told my wife how I felt, but I tried not to show it to her too much. I tried to describe it to her without complaining or moping or carrying on. One night, I confessed to her what I did to Arthur Rashid, forcing myself to remain dry-eyed as I described pulverizing his kneecaps with the hammer. Cathy reached across the table and took my hand.

"That's awful. What an awful experience," she said.

But I could see the doubt and horror in her eyes. I could see her hold back the question: "Wasn't there anything else you could have done?"

I couldn't bring myself to tell her the rest, to describe the pulsing excitement that went through me as I brought the hammer down, or about how I hid in the theater closet, ready to lay hands on Maryanne.

I tried to pray about these things, but I couldn't somehow. I tried to ask God to forgive me for what I'd done and what I'd felt, but I couldn't. The truth was: I was too angry at him to pray. I felt he had asked too much of me. It wasn't that he had asked me to sacrifice my decency or my complacency or even my joy of living.

Those were his to give and his to take away; I understood that. But before he would allow me to save those thousands and thousands of innocent lives—his damn lives, his creations—God had demanded that I know myself, and for that I could not forgive him. I could not forgive him and so I could not ask him to forgive me.

So what else was there? I tried going to a psychiatrist. He listened to me talk for fifteen minutes, then wrote me a prescription for pills—some of those anti-depression pills I'd seen advertised on TV. I was so dejected at that point I actually filled the prescription. But I never took them. Listen, to each his own. For all I know, you could pop a couple of those suckers and spend the rest of your days dancing in the sun. But the way I saw it, my problem wasn't chemical, it was spiritual. The spirit has to have its journey, has to go through its stations, you know; that's how it's shaped finally into a soul. I took the pills down to the lake and hurled them in.

Now I guess you may say to me: Well, that's all very well and good, but what if you can't make it through the stations of the spirit, what if the journey's too much for you? What if you get so depressed you go out and buy a rope and hang yourself? And I guess I would answer you: Them's the breaks, pal. There's no freedom without the possibility of failure. And I'm not afraid to die.

I thought about it a lot, in fact: killing myself, I mean. I took long drives to deserted country lanes, parked in the grass by the roadside, and thought about ways to do it. After months of considering various methods, I settled on a gun as the surest and quickest. I even began shopping around for a gun and had my eye on an elegant little Beretta 9mm. With that, I figured, if I decided to live, I would still have something for home protection.

So it went, through Christmas, into January, February, March. And all in spite of the fact that most of my worst fears of what would happen in the aftermath of *The End of Civilization* never actually materialized. For instance, I had worried quite a lot early

on that I might have to go to jail for what I did to Rashid or at least
stand trial for it. I had worried that I might even still be a suspect
in Anne Smith's death. For weeks I had bouts of paranoia during
which I imagined that all the details of my sordid earlier life would
somehow become news and so become known to my children
and my neighbors on the Hill. Even the idea that my children and
neighbors would hear about Rashid—how I had taped him up and
gagged him and shattered his knees with a hammer to make him
talk—haunted and sickened me and kept me awake at night.

But none of the things I worried about happened. What happened instead was this:

I was questioned for nearly a week after the explosion. Police
officers, FBI agents, spies, lawyers, people who for all I know
were just dropping by to deliver Chinese food—everyone seemed
to want to hear my story. As I had with Detective Curtis, I stuck
to the truth with all of them no matter how awful or embarrassing
it was. I told the tale day after day, again and again and again.

Then, after I don't know how long, Detective Curtis himself
showed up. I was relaxing between interrogations in a pleasant
room on one of the upper floors of One Police Plaza. It was a
conference room, with a long table and a wall of windows looking
out at the big white clouds over the Brooklyn Bridge. I was sitting at the head of the table, swiveling in a chair, reading about
the explosion in the *Times*. There were the usual angry and fretful stories asking the usual angry and fretful questions that arise
after such an incident: How had the terrorists infiltrated security?
Where had they gotten the C4? Which conservative politician was
to blame? Which American policy had driven the murderers to
act? And how could anyone call Christianity a tolerant religion
after the Crusades? And so on. There was even a piece demanding to know how Patrick Piersall had gotten into the building with
a gun. I knew the answer to that one: celebrity. He'd wangled a

ticket to the show from his manager, then found a die-hard *Universal* fan among the guards, one of those guys who attends *Universal* conventions dressed up as a Borgon in his spare time. He'd convinced the guard to let him in early so he could tour the theater, and made sure the idiot neglected to put him through the metal detector. Piersall was clever, I'll say that for him. It was a good thing he was on our side.

I was still paging my way through the stories when the door opened and in came Curtis.

His tough brown face went wide with a shockingly friendly smile. It didn't suit him. It looked foreign to his features. Even as I stood up to meet him, even as he swung his hand to me for a friendly shake, I could see in his eyes that he was the same, that he discounted any illusion of decency in me or in anyone. I was just another squirrelly felon who hadn't been caught out yet, that's all. He knew a lot about people, Curtis did, but all of it was bad.

He gestured me back into my chair and sat in a chair beside me. He laid a manila folder on the table between us, but he never opened it. He just liked them, I guess, those folders. He always seemed to have one around.

He pointed casually to the *Times* open on the table in front of me. "So? What do you think of the coverage?"

I shrugged. "Seems like you haven't told them much yet."

"Not too much. They just get it wrong anyway."

"I notice, for instance, you haven't told them about Rashid." That was foremost in my mind. I figured once the press found out he was involved, the whole incident would become public start to finish.

"Well, we will," Curtis said. "We're going to tell them today."

"All right."

"We're going to tell them Rashid is gone."

My reaction must have looked comical, a comical imitation of surprise. I bolted straight up in my chair, opened my mouth wide, blinked my eyes. "Gone? What do you mean?"

"I mean gone," said Curtis, smiling again beneath those suspicious eyes. "We've searched his office, his apartment, his weekend place: no sign of him."

"But he was *in* his office. That's impossible. How could he get away? He couldn't walk."

Curtis seemed to consider it. "I don't know. Maybe he had some help. Maybe you didn't hurt him as badly as you thought you did."

I added a few moments of comical sputtering to my ridiculous facial expression. "I . . . I . . ."

"Anyway . . ." Curtis slid the folder off the tabletop into his hand and rose from his chair. I was too flummoxed to stand up myself. I just sat there, staring up at him. "We're gonna tell the media we suspect he may have been smuggled out of the country by his masters and possibly executed for betraying the Wall Street operation. That's it. Anything else you want to tell them is up to you. It's a free country."

He was at the door before I managed to say, "Is that really what you think happened? You think someone smuggled him out of the country?"

Curtis snorted. It was quite a sound. It was hard and mirthless, and yet it registered a deep, genuine amusement of a kind I don't really like to think about. It made my balls tighten and go cold. For a moment, after the door shut behind him, I just sat where I was, swiveling slightly, trying to think. I thought: *I'm free then. They're not going to prosecute me. I'm free.* But I didn't feel free or, if I did, I didn't feel much joy about it. I just kept thinking about that sound, Curtis's short, snorting laugh. A deep feeling of pity welled up in me—pity for Rashid—and maybe a sense of awe and terror, too. I did not think he had left the country. And I did not think his life was going to be very pleasant from now on, or that it would be pleasant ever again until its end.

So the rest of the story—the story of how I tortured a university professor on what was essentially a hunch—never came out—not until now, at least; not until I told it here. In fact, after that week or so of questioning, the law was more-or-less done with me.

The media, on the other hand—they were a different story altogether.

At first, they treated me as a hero—a second-string hero maybe, next to the celebrity, next to Patrick Piersall, but a hero still. The newspaper writers and TV and radio commentators compared me to characters in movies, guys who hunt down the truth when the authorities suspect them or won't believe them, who stop the killers in the nick of time, and so on. Some of the praise started to sound pretty overheated, even to me.

Then one day, Piersall and I were interviewed on a television show together. It was one of those morning news programs with a sort of domestic feeling—you know, some perky female and some housebroken male acting almost like husband and wife as they chat with newsmakers and celebrities.

Anyway, it was the perky female interviewing Piersall and me. And she was basically asking the same sorts of questions all the other journalists I'd spoken to had asked. "Were you scared?" and "How did you feel?" and "What was the first moment you realized this was really happening?" Even with the bright lights and with the cameras swirling around me and with the perky female's face uncannily sharp and distinct in front of me because of her makeup and celebrity, I grew bored with the whole thing and my mind began to wander. I began to think about the television room in my mother's house. About the fact that I'd programmed the TiVo there to record every show that had Patrick Piersall in it. I wondered if my old friend the enormous TV was recording me right now.

Then, unexpectedly, the perky female interviewer put on her Serious and Thoughtful Face. She leaned toward me over her crossed knees and asked, "When you look at a situation like this, do you have any thoughts about what the root causes of our current troubles in the world might be? Do you think America might share some of the responsibility?"

She was giving me a chance, you see. A chance to show I was deep and nuanced like herself and could understand that some-times the victim of an attack is really the perpetrator and vice versa. Unfortunately, the question caught me off guard. I had no prepared response. I just began speaking and I said, "You know, Perky (or whatever her name was), I saw one of these fundamen-talist imams on TV recently. And he said that when the Soviet Union fell, the forces of faith had triumphed over the forces of atheism. And he said that now, we had to fight a holy war to decide which faith would rule. The more I think about that, the more I think maybe he got it exactly right. Maybe in some sense, this is a holy war . . ."

Now, I was about to go on to say that, with atheism a discred-ited force in the world, there were basically two different ways in which you could believe in God. You could believe in a God who had spoken one time and then demanded submission ever after to his Word. Or you could believe in a God who was still speaking, still unfolding his creation to us in the strange equation of every soul and in the unfathomable design thrown up by all our souls together. That God—that second God—requires not submission but liberty, so that every soul can speak, even the errant and fool-ish ones. Ultimately, I was going to say, one of those two versions of God has to triumph over the other. They obviously can't live side by side.

But before I could go on, before I could say any of that, the perky female interviewer interrupted me. Her startlingly present features were suddenly far less perky, far more dark and fierce.

"So what are you saying? Are you saying this is something like *Smackdown: Jehovah Versus Allah*? Either believe in our Judeo-Christian God or we kill you?"

"Oh, no," I said, horrified. "No, not at all, what I meant—"

"You believe this is some kind of New Crusade—because many in the Muslim world are afraid of exactly that."

"No, that's not what I'm saying, what I'm saying is—"

"Are you a Christian?" she asked me accusingly.

"Well, yes—yes I am, but—"

"So you believe your religion is the right one and other religions are false?"

"Well, yes, I suppose in some sense I do, but—"

Too late. The perky female interviewer rested her case. She swiveled her crossed knees away from me decisively and re-pointed them at Patrick Piersall, where he sat fat and kingly in the chair beside me.

"Patrick, do you agree with that?" she said—and I thought there was a clear tone of warning in her voice.

But Piersall knew the ropes of these things far better than I. "No, no, no, no, no," he said in deep, mellow, almost Santa Clausian tones. I noticed he had carefully tucked the tail of his sports jacket under his buttocks so it wouldn't ride up to his shoulders when he leaned forward. And I noticed he leaned forward whenever he talked. This, I learned later, gave him a more animated, active appearance onscreen. He leaned forward and began to cut the air with his hands in that Patrick Piersall way of his, speaking in those patented Patrick Piersall syncopations. "With respect to my friend—if anything—I think what happened this past week shows"—and his expression here became almost mystic, his hand trembling like a trapped bird in the air in front of him—"It shows the—the *need* for greater—sensitivity—understanding—among peoples of the world. Because war—war is—not the answer."

The perky female interviewer turned from him to look directly into the camera. "We'll be right back," she said.

The bright lights dimmed and we sank into a duller shade of existence.

Patrick Piersall turned his bloated face toward me and winked broadly. "Kid," he said. "I don't think you're quite ready for TV."

Well, that didn't say the half of it. After that interview—that's when the attacks started. The endless op-eds and editorials in the *Times*. The subtle but unmistakable shift in the tone of coverage on the networks. The honk of that jerk on cable news, the one with a voice like a traffic jam, going on and on about me. Before the interview with the perky female, I was a "hero," a "heartland entrepreneur," an "unprepossessing everyman." Now I was suddenly a "racist," a "rabid right-winger," a "fundamentalist theocrat, as bad as the terrorists themselves." And those were only the opinions. In the news reports, I went from being "handsome with an ironic smile" to "short" and "bland" with "a receding hairline." I went from having no political or religious affiliation to speak of to where journalists seemed unable to mention my name without pointing out that I was a conservative or a Republican or a Christian. Juliette Lovesey, Todd Bingham, and Angelica Eden all condemned me publicly. "It was exactly to change bigoted attitudes like Mr. Harrow's that we made our movie," Juliette said, her eyes growing damp. "This makes me feel the entire project was in vain." For a while, a group called Arab-American Rights got big headlines by demanding an apology from me, and calling for anti-hate-speech legislation to prevent "such dangerous incidents from occurring in the future." Fortunately, the group's leader was soon after indicted for having ties to Palestinian terrorists—whereupon the story vanished from the news altogether.

Conversely, the "true hero of the New Coliseum" (*Times*), "beloved TV star Patrick Piersall" (CBS Evening News), was soon signed to "light up the airwaves once again" (CNN) with a featured role as "a former sixties revolutionary now turned heroic defense attorney on the surefire hit *False Convictions*" (Sally Sterling). Hey, I was happy for him. He had not spent half a lifetime trying to claw his way back into the limelight for nothing.

The media attacks went on forever, but I hardly minded. My attention was taken up by my other nagging anxiety, which was, of course, Serena. I did not see how she could avoid going to prison. I was fearful that her role in the murder of Casey Diggs would get her a long sentence, possibly even life. She was in custody much of the winter as her case dragged on. When I wasn't lying awake at night thinking about suicide, I was lying awake at night worrying about her. I had a half-acknowledged sense that prison was what she deserved, but I was certain it would be the ruin of her.

In the end, again, the outcome was nowhere near as bad as I feared. I helped Lauren pay for a good lawyer, and I spoke to anyone and everyone I could on her behalf. Serena's youth, her role in alerting me to the plot at the theater and a convincing argument that she had been used by Jamal and never fully understood his plans won her some sympathy from both the authorities and the media. She had valuable testimony to trade, too, and some good intelligence she had overheard while in Jamal's company. The feds wound up giving her a suspended sentence on a conspiracy charge and the state finally made a deal that got her one and a half to three years in a juvenile facility in Dutchess County, with time served and a strong possibility of parole after only six months. It was a hell of a break for her, far better than I'd dared to hope for.

And, in the end, as it was Serena who had gotten me into all this in the first place, so it was Serena who began to bring me out.

It happened early in May, early on a Sunday morning after a particularly bad night. With the coming of better weather back east, my mother's house had finally sold the day before for a decent price. I had approved the deal in the afternoon and barely thought about it for the rest of the evening. Then, shortly after midnight, I awakened with a crushing sense of grief and loss. I felt as if that week I had spent in my mother's house had been the last real thing that had happened to me. Here in my own house, I felt I was living in a kind of delirium, a kind of running fever dream. With my mother's house gone, I could never escape from here, never go back to that reality again. It felt like a great weight was sitting on top of me. I felt very sad, very heavy, very terrible.

Somewhere around 3:00 A.M., in this agony of sadness, I reached a decision that, yes, I would buy the gun I had chosen. The decision gave me a sense of certainty and direction and it offered the promise of an end to this depression that had drained the joy out of me since my return. I felt energized and excited by the finality of it and I couldn't get back to sleep.

Finally, as dawn began to lighten the windows, I slipped out of bed. I pulled on a pair of jeans and a sweatshirt and went downstairs. As an act of—I don't know—nostalgia, maybe, I turned on the television in the living room. I sat slumped in an armchair with the remote control held slack in my hand, my chin on my chest, my eyes peering up at the screen from under my eyebrows.

There was a news program on. One of those Sunday talk shows where a moderator sits at a table and interviews a newsmaker or a pundit face to face. As a lead-in, they were showing video of the wars in the Middle East, quick cuts of American soldiers braving bullets flying out of gutted houses; car-bomb blasts and the bleeding injured wandering dazed among the ruins; an Arab woman fallen to her knees before the corpse of her child, her hands up-lifted to the sky as she keened for the dead.

When the video ended, the show returned to the moderator and his guest at the table. The moderator was a rather dapper middle-aged man, and his guest was a solemn but still-dynamic fellow of sixty or so with silver hair atop a pug-nosed and rather mischie-vous face. He had been a senator once, but had been thrown out in the last election. Ever since then, he'd been making the rounds of talk shows, having a good old time saying whatever came into his head.

"These wars in the Middle East—they're like treating a dis-ease with too short a dose of antibiotics," he was saying now. "The disease comes back stronger and adapts to the medicine. You have to snuff it out completely before you're cured."

"Which means . . . ?" said the moderator.

"Well, it means in this case," said the former senator, "that we have to conquer these people, literally take over their countries and run them until they can run them themselves, if ever. Look, the attack on the New Coliseum—an attack in which no one was killed only through the sheerest, blindest good luck—that attack should stand as a warning that they're going to strike at us again and again and again until we stop them or they destroy us."

The dapper moderator sat back in his chair and smiled mildly with lofty patrician disbelief. "But aren't you getting dangerously close to talking about a kind of . . . imperialism?"

"I *am* talking about imperialism," said the former senator with the cavalier self-assurance of a man who has no job left to lose. "Empire is a phase in the life of great nations. It's like adulthood. You can either embrace it or die. The question is whether this particular generation, that hasn't even been able to grow up on an individual level, is going to accept the responsibility of growing up on a national level."

The commercials came on. In the middle of an ad for tomato soup, I narrowed my eyes. Wait a minute, I thought. Had I actually just heard that? *Empire is a phase in the life of great nations.* Wasn't that one of the things my mother had scrawled in one of her Spiral Notebooks? I was no longer sure. I could no longer remember. Maybe I had it wrong, or maybe I had just fallen asleep in my chair and dreamed the man on TV had said it. I couldn't tell.

After a time—a long time—I became aware that the rest of the house had awakened around me. The boys were on the floor in their pajamas, playing with a computer game of some kind. Cathy was in the kitchen, banging the coffeepot around.

Now my daughter Terry climbed into the armchair beside me. She worked her way under my arm to snuggle warmly against me.

"Daddy," she said, "can we watch cartoons?"

I hugged her to me and pressed the buttons of the remote control. I found a lot of cartoon ponies with feathery wings. Terry seemed to like that.

I sat with her there and stared at the television set, lost within myself. When I finally heard Nathan speaking to me, I had the feeling he'd been trying to get my attention for some time.

"Dad? Dad?"

I shuddered out of my reverie and turned to him. He was on his feet now, looking out the big window at the backyard. In a voice hushed with mysterium, he said, "There's somebody on our swing set."

"Who?" cried my daughter. Affronted that any stranger might be on a swing set that was largely hers, she wriggled out from under my arm, and jumped off the armchair to have a look for herself.

I rose heavily from the chair and joined the children at the window. The morning light was spreading over a sweet blue spring day. Small white clouds were sailing past the sun and over the pale green of the budding treetops and over low bushes white with flowers. I could see their reflections moving stately across the lake beyond.

Through the last faint trailing remnants of mist off the water, I saw Serena. She was down there at the bottom of the grassy slope. She was sitting on one of our swings, one hand slack in her lap, the other loosely holding the chain. Small and forlorn, her eyes turned down to the ground, she rocked herself gently back and forth, pushing off the sand with the tips of her tennis shoes. There was a canvas bag on the lawn by the side of the swing set.

"Who is it, Daddy?" Terry asked me.

"Cathy!" I called. "Could you come here a second, please?"

My wife came in from the kitchen, looking fresh and cheerful in her opalescent quilted bathrobe. She saw us all standing there—because Chad, curious, had come up off the floor to get a look out the window as well.

"Oh, boy, what are we watching?" she laughed. She moved to stand with us, looking out over Terry's head.

"Serena," I told her.

She took a long breath. "Did you know she was getting out?"

I shook my head. "She didn't say so in her last letter. She never does say much."

"How on earth did she get here?" my wife wondered.

One corner of my mouth lifted. I gazed out the window at the girl on the gently moving swing. "She walked," I said quietly, after a while. "She's a good walker."

There was silence between us another second or two. Then, "The poor thing," Cathy said. "She must be hungry. Go bring her in. I'll start breakfast."

I nodded as she headed back for the kitchen. I stood another long while at the window, watching Serena rock herself. Finally I let out a sigh between pursed lips.

Nathan caught that. He caught my mood as a ten-year-old will. He imitated my quirked mouth, my expression of knowing cynicism.

"Well," he said up at me, "this can only mean trouble."

I laughed. "All my children are trouble," I said. "Go turn off the TV and get ready for church."

I pushed out the back door and walked down the hill toward her. What a beautiful morning it was, I remember. The mist kept the air cool, but there was a sweet scent of blossoms and the breeze off the lake smelled of trees thick and green with full summer foliage. I breathed in deeply as I crossed the grass.

Serena didn't see me. At least, she didn't look up as I approached. She just went on swinging gently back and forth, studying the tips of her pink sneakers as they pushed off the sand. She had a cheap blue windbreaker on, but it was unzipped. I could see the dull gray sweatshirt underneath it and the brand-new jeans. Her hair was a little longer than it had been the last time I saw her, pulled back and tied up in a ponytail. Even from a distance, her face seemed very pale, very thin. I don't think she was wearing any makeup.

Finally, when I was standing directly in front of her, she lifted her eyes to me. It hurt me to see how gaunt her face was. Her skin had gotten bad, too. Her cheeks were patched with acne. Her eyes seemed dull as if a film lay over them. Her mouth was set in a tense, grim line. She gave off a sickbed air. Prison had done this to her. Prison had worn her down.

I didn't say anything but I smiled at her. She got up out of the swing. We stood facing each other. I reached out and put my hand tenderly on her shoulder.

At that, Serena's chin bunched, her lips trembled, and she dissolved into tears. I pulled her to me and held her. Her crying grew more violent. She pressed her face into my shoulder and her whole body bucked and shivered as she sobbed. The sobs were very loud, raw, and hoarse. I kept my arms around her and rubbed her back and kissed her hair.

I looked out over her head to the sky and the water. Strangely, after my long, miserable night, I had a sense for the first time then—just an intimation really—that it was going to be all right. You know? That *I* was going to be all right, that I was not going to shoot myself with any damned gun, that I was going to damn well live—I was going to live a good long time and meet my grand-children. I had a faint but sure and certain sense that this sadness was going to lift finally and that there was a kind of peace waiting for me beyond it, not as far off as all that, a bearable distance, a journey I had the strength to make.

My daughter sobbed against my shoulder and shivered in my arms and I held her. And I felt something that had been closed in my mind open again like a child's cupped hands. I felt something fly up out of me and I don't know why but I felt it was my spirit and I was almost visionary. For just a second—just a second or two—I could imagine myself moving above the Earth as it was, above everything, I mean, the mothers and the murderers, the idiots and empires, the spinning patterns and fractals of history developing endlessly out of the few simple equations of the human heart. I imagined myself sailing above and beyond the whole of it until I reached a blazing presence at the source of it all. I felt my spirit yearn toward that unfathomable blaze until it was thrown back at me like a fiery reflection, so that I thought I saw one approaching in the sky like a Son of Man, his arms outstretched over the tear-stained, bloodstained world beneath him as he declared,

Behold: the Kingdom of Heaven, which is Love;
Love—in all its majesty and madness.

Acknowledgments

My deep thanks to my excellent researcher Carolyn Chriss; to Professor Alan J. Fridlund, U.C. Santa Barbara, who helped me create Mrs. Harrow's illness; to the Army's Lieutenant Colonel Paul Sinor for information on explosives; to my wonderful agent, Robert Gottlieb, at Trident Media Group; to my editor, Otto Penzler, and all the great people at Harcourt; and to my wife, Ellen, who also helped with research and whom I love more than words can say.